"I HAVE SO LONGED TO HOLD YOU," JULIAN WHISPERED HOARSELY.

Tasharyana froze. She couldn't allow him to go any further, yet she didn't want him to stop holding her. She turned in his embrace and backed against the railing.

His eyes smoldering and serious, Julian took her elbows in his hands and gazed at her with a searching expression. He bent down to her and she raised her chin, drawn to the kiss that they had known was inevitable from the moment they had recognized each other in the opera house.

She felt herself opening to him, her soul reaching upward to meet his. Without thinking, she raised her arms and wrapped them around Julian's neck. Gently, she pressed the back of his head to keep his mouth joined to hers as he was meant to be joined, and then she kissed him with a fire born of unquestioning, unwavering love.

Books by Patricia Simpson

The Lost Goddess
The Night Orchid
Raven in Amber
The Legacy
Whisper of Midnight

Purrfect Love
(with Debbie Macomber and Linda Lael Miller)

Available from HarperPaperbacks

The Lost Goddess

PATRICIA SIMPSON

HarperPaperbacks
A Division of HarperCollins*Publishers*

This is a work of fiction. The characters, incidents, and dialogues are products of the author's imagination and are not to be construed as real. Any resemblance to actual events or persons, living or dead, is entirely coincidental.

HarperPaperbacks *A Division of* HarperCollins*Publishers*
10 East 53rd Street, New York, N.Y. 10022

Cover illustration by Jeff Barson

First printing: April 1995

Printed in the United States of America

❖ 10 9 8 7 6 5 4 3 2 1

Many thanks to "The Creeps,"
NB, SK, TD, and the mysterious BB,
and to my daughter, Jessica, for her excellent input

Author's Note

We just might have to recall all the history books that mention the Sphinx. In my research for this story I came across an article in the *Chicago Tribune* (February 24, 1992) in which new evidence proposed that the Great Sphinx at Giza might be a lot older than Egyptologists previously believed. Vertical crevices etched in the wall of bedrock limestone surrounding the Sphinx are exactly like those produced by rain over a long period of time. Yet the monument stands in a region that gets a mere inch of rainfall a year. For centuries, the Sphinx was covered by drifting sand which protected it even further from water erosion. Given the area's lack of rain, plus the limited time the Sphinx was fully exposed to the weather, a construction date of 2550 B.C. doesn't allow enough time for the vertical crevices to have appeared. A more likely date would be somewhere between 7000 and 5000 B.C. During that era, the Sahara wasn't yet fully formed and Egypt enjoyed a more abundant rainfall.

For the Sphinx to have been built during this earlier period, a civilization much, much older than that of the pharaohs must have flourished in Egypt. Yet no evidence of these people has been discovered. We can only guess who built the Sphinx. Perhaps there existed an ancient line of priestesses whose power was absolute, whose secret rites included the levitation of huge stones through the use of sound, thus explaining the construction of the pyramids. Perhaps the Sphinx was not simply a guardian of other monuments, but was itself an important temple, whose yet to be excavated underground chambers were used for purposes we know nothing about. Could the enigmatic Sphinx be even more mysterious than we first supposed? Some scholars say it's time for the Egyptologists to get out their shovels and start digging a little deeper.

Prologue

Johns Hopkins Hospital—Baltimore

The room was as quiet as a tomb. Troubled, Asheris watched his wife walk to the window and stare at the city below as she waited for the physicians to return. He wondered if she really took notice of anything outside the window, for she had been preoccupied since the moment they arrived in Baltimore. But he wouldn't ask. They rarely spoke to each other anymore. His gaze ran the length of her, from her jet black hair pulled into a shining chignon, down her delicate neck and slender figure, to her long, shapely legs. She wore the jade green suit that she often took when she traveled, and which she accented with gold and jade jewelry handmade by an artist friend of hers in Paris. As the Americans would say, she looked like a million bucks, and he felt the old stirring shifting inside him. How long had it been since he held her in his arms? Weeks? Or was it months? How could their marriage have come to this?

It was his fault, really. If he had confided in her from the very beginning, all the little things that had grown into full-fledged conflicts would simply have been minor misunderstandings. But each misunderstanding had built upon the previous one, and before he realized what was happening, a wall had risen between them. At first he tried to explain it away by saying she was always gone during their first years of marriage, always traveling from one show to another, which required readjustment each time she returned to their home in Egypt. But he couldn't fool himself any longer. Her career as a sculptor wasn't the reason for their failing marriage. It was his own reluctance to cooperate with her ideas of child-rearing that was at the root of the problem. Yet how could he be sure her modern practices were any better than the ancient ways? What made her think that she knew all the answers when it came to raising their precocious daughter, Julia?

Asheris rose, compelled to speak to her despite the barriers that had sprung up between them. "Karissa?"

She turned and a shaft of spring sunlight slanted across the side of her face. Asheris was struck anew by her beauty, which had become haunted and ethereal since they drifted apart. Her large dark brown eyes leveled upon his. They were full of troubled lights shaded with resentment or sadness, he wasn't certain which.

"Yes?" she replied, her voice husky.

As if timed to thwart him, the door opened behind him. Asheris scowled and looked over his shoulder as Dr. Edward Thompkins and the consulting otolaryngologist, Dr. Wally Duncan, filed into the room.

Asheris quickly masked his countenance before his beautiful little two-year-old daughter entered the room after them, for he did not wish to worry her. His child was acutely perceptive, uncannily attuned to the nuances of emotion, especially his. But Julia did not appear.

Alarmed not to see her, Asheris looked across the massive wooden desk as Dr. Thompkins took his seat and then glanced back at the door. "Where is Julia?" he demanded.

"She's with a nurse so that we may talk privately for a few minutes."

"What nurse is this?" Asheris stepped toward the desk.

"My associate, Janet Burns," replied Dr. Thompkins, somewhat defensively. "A pediatric nurse practitioner who is highly reliable."

Karissa shot Asheris one of her looks that made him feel his protective instincts were wholly unjustified. Still, he worried. When it came to Julia's safety and well-being, he trusted no one, especially here in the United States.

"Your daughter is fine, Mr. Asher," Dr. Wally Duncan put in. "There's no need to worry. Please, sit down."

"This will only take a minute," Dr. Thompkins added.

Unconvinced and edgy, Asheris sighed and sat in his chair. But he couldn't relax. Karissa, sleek and graceful, slipped into the chair beside him, careful not to come in contact with his legs or feet. Was it his imagination, or was she leaning to the side so that her shoulder remained separate from his? How he ached for the warmth of her.

Adjusting his black-framed glasses, Dr. Thompkins

opened the file folder on his desk blotter and looked down. His head shone beneath the strands of hair he had combed over his balding scalp. For a moment he seemed to be perusing the data in the folder, as if looking for answers. Behind him Dr. Duncan crossed his arms over his chest and tapped his fingers on his upper arm. Asheris felt a heavy cloud of unease descend upon him.

Then Dr. Thompkins shook his head, weaved his fingers together on top of the file, and looked up. "To begin with, I have never seen anything like it."

Karissa leaned forward. "What do you mean?"

"I mean that in my forty years of practice, I have never seen a patient with your daughter's developmental characteristics, nor have I ever read or heard about such a patient in any medical journal." He took off his glasses and rubbed the bridge of his nose while Asheris burned with curiosity.

Dr. Thompkins put his glasses back on. "At first I suspected progeria."

"Progeria?" Asheris repeated, unfamiliar with the term.

"It's a rare disease that produces accelerated aging. But Julia has none of the classic symptoms of progeria—hair loss, wizened features, and limited mobility. She seems to have accelerated development in selected areas, such as her neurological system, her speech, and her skeletal system. We also discovered that her vocal chords are unusual. That's why I brought in Dr. Duncan, an ear, nose, and throat specialist."

The red-haired doctor nodded to Asheris and Karissa. Asheris surveyed the young doctor, wondering if they should put much stock in the findings of a man whose dry thatch of red hair hung in wisps over his pale, acne-scarred forehead. He didn't seem much older than George, their thirteen-year-old houseboy back in Luxor.

Dr. Thompkins continued. "Between my tests and those of Dr. Duncan, we have found nothing to explain her accelerated development. When did you say she got all her baby teeth?"

"When she was two. Four months ago." Karissa leaned back in her chair. "That was when she had the fever I told you about."

"When she was delirious," Dr. Duncan put in. "And the toys appeared to move around in her room on their own."

"Yes."

Asheris shifted uncomfortably in his seat. Why had his wife told everything to the doctors? Why did they have to know the details of his daughter's powers? He had tried to tell Karissa that no American physician would be able to explain such a phenomenon. And yet she had insisted upon tests and analyses, as if modern science could answer all their questions.

"I must say," Dr. Thompkins shook his head, "that I am at a total loss to explain the movement of the toys."

Asheris remained silent, well aware that Karissa did not need to hear him say, I told you so.

"However, Dr. Duncan did some tests on her that proved interesting, if not puzzling."

"And I came up with a theory about the toys," put in Dr. Duncan, his tone much lighter and happier than the sonorous tone of his colleague. He opened a file folder, pulled out a piece of paper, and handed it to Asheris. He stepped closer in order to point to the graphs printed on the sheet.

"This is the result of one of the tests I ran on Julia yesterday—a Fourier analysis." He pointed to the top grid crossed by curved waves in a uniform pattern.

"Fourier?" Karissa asked. "What's that?"

"It's a method of mathematically resolving a wave form into a series of its simpler composite sine waves. To illustrate, take a look at the top graph. It's a diagram of the sound wave produced by a high quality tuning fork. See all those curving lines running parallel to each other?"

"Yes," Asheris replied, intently staring at the paper but wondering all the while how any of the lines pertained to his daughter.

"Those are all the component sine waves associated with the tuning fork, from the waves vibrating at the tip of the fork to the ones emanating from the base. They all look alike, and while they are parallel, they are not completely in synch with one another."

Asheris nodded. Karissa leaned closer to his shoulder to study the graph, and he felt a tingling sensation on his skin where she nearly came in contact with him.

"Now this," Dr. Duncan pointed to the second graph, "is a diagram of the sound produced by Julia's voice when I asked her to mimic the sound of the tuning fork."

Asheris looked at the wave, whose pattern was similar in height to the sine curve of the tuning fork wave, but with many more zig zags crossing the axis back and forth, tightly bunched together.

"Why is there only one wave?" he asked.

"Good question!" Duncan glanced at Asheris and his blue eyes gleamed in appreciation of his quick observation. "I wondered that, too. In fact I did three separate Fourier analyses, suspecting my equipment was faulty because the results were produced so quickly. I thought it wasn't getting the correct amount of data."

Karissa looked up at the doctor, her brown eyes intent. "And?"

"Well, to be short and sweet, your daughter's voice is so pure it has only one component. One. And that, folks, is highly unusual."

Karissa exchanged a quick glance with Asheris, the first open expression he had seen on her face for months. He almost reached out for her hand but stopped when she returned her attention to the doctors.

"Plus, and this might not mean much to you," Duncan explained, pointing to the second graph again, "but when I see a wave like this, I'm usually looking at a sound of very high frequency, one that can't be heard—kind of like a dog whistle."

Asheris doubted that lines on a paper could explain the mystery of his daughter, but he remained silent.

"What are you getting at?" Karissa asked.

"That your daughter has a unique voice. Not only is it unusually pure, it produces a sound of extremely high frequency that can still be heard within the range of sound normal to the human ear. I've never come across this before. So I took X rays of her larynx and found an interesting thing."

"What was it that you found?" Asheris inquired.

"Julia has two openings in her vocal chords instead of one. In addition, her vocal cords are thinner than usual, which may account for the extraordinary vibration she can achieve."

Asheris frowned. He didn't like the idea that his daughter was being discussed by two scientists as if she were some curiosity, some freak of nature. He opened his mouth to demand his daughter be brought to him immediately so they could leave, but Karissa interrupted him.

"But what does all this have to do with toys floating in her room?" she asked, leaning forward.

"A lot," Duncan answered, without waiting for his colleague. He sat on the side of the desk. "Recent research has shown that sound can actually suspend objects in space. Sound waves can create pockets of opposing energy, so to speak, that can trap small objects in between the peaks of the waves." He crossed his arms again. "So far in the laboratory, we have done this only with very small articles such as Styrofoam beads. But it can be done. Sound can suspend objects."

Asheris lowered the paper to his thigh. "You are saying that my daughter suspended the toys with her voice?"

"Perhaps." Duncan leaned forward, his eyes alight. "I believe that during her delirium, Julia moaned or cried or did something on a continual basis that could have caused a lightweight object to vibrate enough to lift it in the air."

"She did moan quite a bit during her fever," Karissa put in. "I didn't connect the two."

"Who would?" Dr. Duncan replied. "It's quite phenomenal!"

"Enough!" Asheris said, jumping to his feet. "It is but conjecture. Theory."

"Right now, yes." Duncan rose as well. "But with some testing, I could prove it, I am sure. All I need is your permission to work with Julia for a few months."

"Months?" Asheris boomed. "A child needs to be in her home, Dr. Duncan, where she is safe and secure, not in some laboratory being studied like a creature in a cage."

"It wouldn't be like that, Mr. Asher—"

"She is too young to be subjected to tests. I won't have it!"

Dr. Thompkins stood up. "Please, Mr. Asher. Reconsider, won't you? We could learn so much from Julia!"

"Learn from one of your apes," Asheris countered. "Julia is but a child!"

"In body only. Her comprehension levels test out many times greater than the average two-year-old. She's not your normal toddler. That's why we want to know more about her."

"Julia will not be made a subject of study!" Asheris rarely lost his temper or raised his voice but felt himself getting dangerously close to the edge of his control the more these modern scientists pressed him. He clamped his jaw tight, suppressing his anger. "I have said all that I am going to say. Now bring Julia to us at once."

"Of course." Dr. Thompkins frowned slightly and picked up his phone. He gave a quick call to his nurse and then glanced up at Asheris. "I am sorry you feel this way, Mr. Asher. We mean no harm to Julia."

Asheris did not comment, and his eyes felt as hard as shards of topaz.

"Well, if you ever change your minds," Duncan put in. "I would be happy to run tests on her free of charge. She's a medical anomaly, something we doctors don't get to see all that often."

Before anyone could make a reply, Asheris heard the door open. He turned to see his daughter standing on the threshold. For an instant Julia paused in the doorway, appearing more like a tiny version of an adult than a two-year old child, with her shoulder-length raven hair, golden skin, and slender figure. Then her face lit up when she caught sight of her parents.

"Mommy, Daddy!" she exclaimed in delight, and raced to Karissa.

"Hello, *azeez,*" Karissa said, using the Arabic word for "beloved," as her daughter flung her arms around her knees. Karissa reached down and lifted Julia onto her hip. "Did you have fun with Dr. Duncan?"

"Oh, yes! He has lots of machines in his lab. He even let me color in some of the pictures of my throat! Dr. Wally has many colored markers! Seventy-two—isn't that right, Dr. Wally?"

Wally smiled and nodded, and Asheris felt himself relax to a degree now that his child had come into the room. He glanced from the freckled countenance of the red-haired doctor to his daughter's pretty face with its flawless skin and intelligent eyes. Between the doctor and the girl flowed a current of camaraderie and good humor that he couldn't deny.

"Dr. Wally has lots of music, too. He let me listen to some songs and then I picked out my favorite to sing into his tape recorder."

"And which did you select, Julia?" Asheris asked, touching her hair.

"'Unforgettable.'"

"The Nat King Cole song?" Karissa asked, as if surprised Wally hadn't presented her with more appropriate songs, like nursery ditties.

"Yes." Wally grinned. "And you know, old Julie McWulie here memorized that song after hearing it only once."

"He calls me Julie McWulie," Julia giggled. "Isn't that a funny name?"

"It is not your name." Asheris's curt tone wiped the smiles from everyone's faces, including Julia's. "It doesn't become you, Julia."

Karissa glared at him. He glanced back at her and then at Wally, feeling an odd mixture of shame and outrage at her reprimand. Why would she reprove him for correcting the doctor? Didn't she have a sense of proper respect for a member of their family? In the ancient days, people lost their lives for simply sneaking a glance at the royal family. Since his marriage to Karissa he had allowed a lot of modern customs to replace the old ways, but he wouldn't stand for improper address, especially when it concerned his daughter.

Modern society had stripped him of many things—limitless wealth, absolute power, and a sense of continuity in life, religion, and government. But modern man would never strip him of his honor. Asheris supposed Karissa's broad acceptance of casual address stemmed from her American sense of equality—a trait he found both highly fascinating and maddening. She hadn't even taken his name when they married, no matter how royal it was. But now was not the time to explore her philosophy of equality.

"Come, Karissa," he demanded.

Wally straightened. "I meant no offense, Mr. Asher."

"May I remind you that Julia comes from a long and noble line, Dr. Duncan. She is to be treated with respect in all ways."

"I was just kidding around."

"It is not your place to 'kid around' with my daughter."

"I'm sorry." Wally flushed and glanced at Karissa, as if to ask for help in dealing with her husband.

"No offense taken, Dr. Duncan," she said. "And thank you for your help. Say good-bye to the doctors, Julia."

"Good-bye, Dr. Thompkins," Julia said. Then she turned to the younger red-haired man and grinned. "See you later, alligator."

Wally tried to hide his smile. "Good-bye, Julia," he replied, holding out his hand and formally shaking hers. "I'm glad to have met you."

"Come, Julia." Asheris took his daughter in his arms and stepped toward the door. There he turned. "Good day to you, gentlemen." He bowed his head slightly and glanced expectantly at Karissa. She picked up her purse to follow him but was stopped by Dr. Duncan.

"Just one more thing, if you don't mind, Ms. Spencer."

"Yes?"

"I just happened to see in the medical records that you grew up in Baltimore. You aren't by any chance related to Julian Spencer, are you?"

"Why, yes. I'm his daughter."

"Really?" Wally's face lit up. "I can't believe it! I'm a big fan of your father's work."

"His Egyptian studies?"

"No, his work in sound. I know he was better known for his historical discoveries, but his treatise on sound and vibration was the stepping off point for my own research."

"Really?" Karissa's eyes widened in surprise. "I wasn't aware my father had studied that branch of science."

"You've never read his theories on sound and movement?"

"No. His interests lay in archaeology."

"Not entirely. Your father was a universal man, Ms. Spencer, that's why I admired him so much. He was the type of man who could grasp the most widely ranging concepts with ease and use them in brand new ways."

Asheris saw Karissa flush with pride upon hearing

praise of her father. He was well aware that over the years she had heard only recriminations and criticism of him by her mother and grandmother.

"You wouldn't know then, if he had any unpublished research lying around. I'd be happy to help get it published for you. The scientific community should be informed about anything he's done."

"I've never seen his research, Dr. Duncan."

"No private library? No old files?"

"No. I was young when he died. I don't know what was done with his papers."

"That's a shame. He was way ahead of his time, you know." Wally slid his hand in the chest pocket of his lab coat and pulled out a card. "Well, here's where I can be reached if you change your mind about Julia."

Karissa took the card and glanced at the Baltimore address.

"It was nice meeting you," he said, holding out his hand and grinning. "Julian Spencer's daughter, I can't believe it!"

Asheris saw the happiness in Karissa's face, wrought by the praise of her father, and wished he had been the one responsible for the smile. Though Julian Spencer was long since dead, his last days were still shrouded in mystery and still part of the trouble between him and Karissa. In fact, no one really knew much about the last years of J. B. Spencer's life. What other secrets had died with him in the lost sphinx so many years ago? And which of them would come back to haunt Asheris's beautiful little girl?

Four Years Later—Luxor, Egypt

"May we open the crate now, Mother?" Julia inquired, walking across the tiled floor to the door of the garden.

Karissa glanced up from her sculpture and across her studio to the lithe form of her six-year-old daughter, who possessed such grace that wherever she went her feet seemed barely to touch the ground. Sometimes when Karissa looked at Julia, she was amazed at her own child—as if seeing her for the first time—and was struck by the girl's adult demeanor.

"Please, may we, Mother?"

"I told you I must work until seven and then we can stop."

Julia glanced at the dainty watch on her delicate wrist. "It *is* seven, Mother. Five past, as a matter of fact."

"Oh, all right then. Come and help me clean up these tools and we'll see what's in the crate."

She was rewarded with one of Julia's blinding smiles, so like her father's, it tugged at Karissa's heart. How long had it been since she saw Asheris smile like that? Much too long. Seven years ago when she had married her Egyptian love, her life had seemed poised on the edge of a romantic, exciting, and slightly dangerous adventure. She had been aware of the difficulties inherent in becoming the American wife of a man from another country and culture, but she had been certain her love for Asheris and his for her would smooth the rocky path of such a union. Now, however, she wasn't quite as confident. Had she been blind to reality? Had she believed too much in true love and its ability to conquer all? Her storybook romance had altogether ceased to be the happily-ever-after scenario that she assumed would continue forever.

Karissa had done everything she knew to recapture the spark between them, but Asheris had grown more silent and removed with each attempt to draw him closer. He rarely spoke to her and barely took notice of her, no matter how she fussed with her clothes and hair or how many small things she did for him. Sometimes she doubted he would notice her if she walloped him over the head with one of her sculpting mallets. Had she grown so ordinary to him that he wasn't attracted to her? The thought devastated her, for she loved her husband as much if not more than she did the day they married and was still powerfully affected by the sight of him. He was as lean and elegant as the day they had met. His glossy black hair was still as thick and lustrous. He provided her with everything she could possibly desire—a lavish home in Luxor, the finest clothes, and plenty of household help. Yet her deepest need, that of Asheris's sharing of himself, was no longer fulfilled, and the loss robbed her heart of happiness.

Sighing and putting her exasperating husband out of her mind, she wiped her hands on a towel and surveyed the clay sculpture before her, the first human body she had ever sculpted. It was a nude figure of a woman singing, her arms stretched out on either side of her body, palms upward in a gesture of glorious ecstasy, her eyes closed, her face raised to heaven. For a first try, it wasn't bad. Not bad at all.

Perhaps her panther-sculpting days were over and a new phase in her life had begun. God knows her marriage could use a new phase. And though she tried to ignore the darkness in that part of her world by filling the hours with her work and her daughter, she could not deny that her heart suffered greatly because of the trouble with Asheris. She had always guarded against a man consuming her life and overshadowing her career, but the early years with her husband had been months of unparalleled sweetness and intimacy into which she had willingly immersed herself. Her greatest concern—that of losing her independence to her marriage—had been swept away ten times over by Asheris's love and understanding. She longed for those days to return and craved the closeness she had once known with her handsome husband. But their closeness had faded with the birth of Julia and had dimmed even further when the medical specialists pronounced Julia to be much more than "daddy's little girl" four years ago.

"I've washed your tools, Mother. Now may we get on with the scheduled events?"

Karissa smiled at Julia's choice of words. She certainly wasn't a typical six-year-old, especially in the vocabulary department. Julia's English was flawless, for Asheris insisted everyone speak English in his home, including the servants. "All right." She tucked a piece of plastic over the clay, to retain as much moisture as possible in the arid Luxor air, and then followed her daughter to the entryway at the front of the house where the crate had sat since late afternoon. Though Karissa was curious as to what lay in the box, she had kept to her work schedule, not only to teach her daughter a lesson in diligence, but also to put off facing the contents of the crate. She had seen the return address: Frances Petrie, 33 Brindlewood Lane, Baltimore, Maryland, U.S.A., the address of her cold and spiteful—and now deceased—grandmother. What could Grandmother Petrie have arranged to send to her? Why would she have bothered sending anything to a granddaughter of whom she had never approved?

George, the houseboy and nephew of Eisha, the housekeeper, hurried up as Karissa reached for the rough rope handle at the end of the crate.

"*Sayyidah,*" he said. "The crate is heavy. Let me help you!" He bent down and grasped the other handle.

"Thank you, George," Karissa replied, hoisting the crate a few inches off the ground. No matter how many times she told him to call her by her first name, he insisted on referring to her as madame. The title made her feel old and somewhat removed from ordinary people, much like Grandmother Petrie. Yet George clung to his manners as if they were beyond reproach. "Let's take the crate out to the garden. It's cooler out there."

"Yes, *sayyidah.*"

They passed through the shadows of the April evening, which slanted across the tile and up the plaster walls of the entryway. The dark shapes reminded Karissa of the times she had ventured into subterranean burial chambers of Egyptian noblemen, with her flashlight beam following the muted murals on the walls and drowning in the gloom ahead. She remembered well the hush inside the tombs, as if it would be sacrilegious to disturb the dead with harsh noises—at least she had always felt that way—and even as a child had respected the dead with her careful silence.

Julia held open the door to the garden and then hurried after them to the edge of the pond where the palms and vines ringing the water provided an oasis of cool foliage after a long hot day. They set down the crate with a slight noise, which disturbed a flock of sparrows in the date palms. With a flutter of wings, they dispersed into the dusk. The sound reminded Karissa of bats flapping their way out of a cave, and she shuddered even though the night was still warm. Throwing a glance over her shoulder, she caught sight of the crescent moon just beginning to crest the mud brick wall that bordered the southeastern side of the garden. In the daylight, the garden was a glorious jungle and a welcome respite from the harsh desert just outside the walls of the compound. But in the night, the garden took on an eerie and haunted character. Or perhaps she was simply in a strange mood, a result of the arrival of the crate.

"Looks like we'll need a crowbar," George said, bringing her back to the task at hand. "Shall I get one, *sayyidah?*"

"Please. And turn on the garden lights, will you?" She smiled at the reed-thin seventeen-year-old boy, who teetered between adolescence and maturity.

"Certainly." George turned on his heel and rushed

out of the garden, apparently as anxious as Julia to see what was in the box. Karissa crossed her arms and stared at the crate.

"I met Great-Grandmother Petrie once, didn't I?" Julia asked.

"Yes, you did. When you were two and we took you to Baltimore. So you remember her?"

"She was the forbidding old dowager-type who stared at me all the time, wasn't she?"

"Yes." Karissa tried to hide her smile at her daughter's description. She shouldn't encourage her child to make disparaging remarks, but in this case, the remarks were accurate and went unchallenged.

"She didn't like me. I could feel it," Julia continued, "even though I didn't do anything to make her angry, did I?"

"You are always well-behaved, my *azeez.*" She reached out and stroked the glossy black hair of her daughter. "Grandmother Petrie was that way with everyone, not just you."

"Why do you suppose she was so grouchy?"

"Because I think she felt angry inside. At what, I'm not certain. She didn't lack for anything."

"I have a theory about people like Great-Grandmother Petrie," Julie mused. "I believe people like that are very lonely because nobody really talks to them much, and they don't think people like them. So they get more lonely and angry all the time. It has to do with communication."

Surprised, Karissa stopped stroking Julia's hair and looked at her face. "Where did you ever come up with that philosophy?"

"From watching Hamid."

"The gardener?"

"Yes. Everyone thinks he's surly and mean. At first

I did, too. But recently I changed my mind because I figured out why he's gruff and quiet."

"And why is that?"

"Because he has that limp from polio. And he thinks people make fun of him behind his back. But I have never made fun of him and he's come to realize that I don't even notice his limp. And now I am his friend."

Karissa gazed at her daughter, amazed at the depth of understanding she possessed. Julia's comprehension and compassion went far beyond the normal range of a child, and most adults for that matter—another trait passed down from her father but sadly no longer evident in his marriage. She was about to ask Julia what she and Hamid talked about, when the lights blinked on, startling her, and George rushed back to the garden.

"Here is the crowbar, *sayyidah*," he declared, holding it out.

"Thank you." She never thought twice about wielding the crowbar and bending to the task of prying the lid off the crate. In her profession of sculpting, she was accustomed to the weight of a heavy tool in her hand and took pride in the strength of her arms and hands. Asheris had remarked on more than one occasion that a massage given by her strong hands was one of the most pleasurable experiences imaginable. She flushed at the memory of Asheris in bed with her—an event that had become a thing of the past—and quickly blinked the vision away. It made her body ache with longing to recall their nights of lovemaking, and she knew better than to torture herself with such memories.

The screeching noise from prying loose the nails split the calm of the garden and rattled her out of her thoughts. A flock of teals suddenly flapped across the reflecting pond and glided to safety among the clumps of papyrus on the other side, leaving silver traces lit by the moon on the surface of the water. Karissa glanced at them, thinking she was as far from Asheris's heart as the birds were from the nearby shore.

Beads of perspiration popped out on Karissa's forehead with the effort of pulling off the lid. Even though the sun had gone down hours ago, the heat from the desert would remain a while longer before the evening chill descended. She and George struggled to pull the lid off, and then set it against the garden table, careful to keep the side with the nails facing away from them.

Julia craned her head around them to glance into the box. "My goodness!" she exclaimed, almost losing her adult vocabulary in her excitement. "What a jumble of oddities!"

Karissa peered into the box and stepped aside to allow light from the garden lamp to illuminate the contents. In the crate was a carefully arranged stack of leather-bound books, a strange metal disk that looked like a serving dish, old clothes and toys that must have been her father's when he was a boy, and a cardboard box taped shut. A veil of foreboding settled on her at the sight of her father's belongings. Why had this crate come to her twenty-three years after her father's death? When J. B. Spencer was crushed in a booby-trapped tomb, all his possessions had been reviewed by his wife and sent back to the States. But where had this particular crate been for twenty-three years?

"Are these Great-Grandmother Petrie's things?" Julia asked.

"I don't think so. By all appearances, these items belonged to my father."

"The one who got squished in the sphinx?" George asked, unaware of the insensitive bluntness of his question.

"Yes." Karissa was grateful for the darkness, which hid her pained expression. To distract herself, she feigned interest in an envelope taped to the top of the stack of books. "Perhaps this note will explain why this crate was sent to us." Carefully she opened the envelope and drew out a piece of her grandmother's expensive linen stationery. "It says here," Karissa stated, scanning the typed note, "that Grandmother's house is being sold. Her sister found this box in the attic and thought I might want the keepsakes of my father."

"So they do belong to Grandfather Spencer," Julia said.

"Yes." Karissa tucked the note back inside the envelope. "I'm glad Great-Aunt Helena cared enough to ship them. It must have cost a fortune, though." Easily paid for by the Petrie millions, she added to herself. She not only didn't expect to get a dime of Grandmother Petrie's money, she didn't want an inheritance from her spiteful relative and hoped this crate was the last she'd hear of the woman. Karissa reached for the book to which the envelope had been taped as George sidled closer and peeked into the box, displaying admirable restraint for a teenager.

Karissa held the heavy volume up to the light and read the embossed lettering on the front.

"Journal," she stated. She looked down at the name stamped on the bottom of the cover. "J. B. Spencer." A thrill coursed down her spine. Her father had kept journals? No one had ever mentioned it. A wealth of information about her mysterious father lay bound in these books, waiting for her to discover the real man behind the sullied reputation, an inheritance far more valuable to her than money.

"Julian Bedrani Spencer," Julia put in proudly. "The grandfather after whom I was named."

"Yes." Karissa smiled sadly and glanced at her daughter. "I wish he could have known you, Julia. He would have liked you very, very much."

"I would have liked him, too." She reached into the crate for the cardboard box. "May I open this, Mother?"

"Of course. But be careful. Some of these things are old, you know, and might break easily." Karissa opened the journal, wondering why she had admonished Julia. Unlike most children, Julia was unusually careful with everything around her and had never gone through a clumsy stage where she tripped over her own feet or broke things.

While Julia fussed with the tape on the box, Karissa sank into the garden chair and flipped through the thick yellowing pages of her father's journal, her heart beating wildly. Most of the entries were done in fountain pen, something she rarely saw anymore. It was odd to see the small handwriting of her father, its small capital letters spanning the pages in neat orderly lines. The handwriting reminded her of the last letter she had received from him, the fateful letter that had brought her back to Luxor when she was twelve years old. For a moment she closed her eyes and remembered the letter written on nearly transparent blue onionskin paper.

"Dear Karissa," it had begun.

Now that you are a young woman and grown up enough to know just how very much I love you, I want you to learn more about the Spencer family, and much more about your mother. I am sure there are questions in your mind about my many trips to Egypt and about your future as well. These are things I want to tell you myself, so I have arranged for you to spend your Christmas holidays with me here in Luxor. Enclosed you will find your airplane tickets from Baltimore to Cairo, and where in the Cairo airport I will be waiting for you. I am looking forward to showing you my favorite spots in Egypt, including a wonderful rose garden.

With her eyes still shut, Karissa remembered how thrilled she had been at the news of spending time with her father in the far-off land of Egypt. She never seemed to get enough real time with her father, not without her mother and grandmother butting in and ruining their special moments together. But Karissa's excitement had been short-lived. Not only had her grandmother refused to let her go on the trip by herself, she had insisted that her mother, Christine, accompany her to make certain that J. B. was made to understand in no uncertain terms just what an insensitive cad he was for splitting up the family during Christmas. It was bad enough that he spent every spare moment digging in the sands of the Sahara, looking for God knows what. But to tear his daughter away from friends and family during the holidays was simply unspeakable. Besides that, no twelve-year-old girl would be content to spend countless hours with a preoccupied man, even if he was her father.

Karissa sighed in frustration, though many years had passed. She had longed to spend time with her father. No one understood how she loved any time they spent together—not even him. He was often gone from the house, with his university work or his archaeological expeditions. From a child's viewpoint Karissa had believed he was just a busy man. Now seeing the situation from an adult perspective, she suspected that he hadn't spent much time at home because he was avoiding both his wife and his mother-in-law's never-ending criticism of his career move from promising young lawyer to reclusive Egyptologist. Perhaps J. B. had never considered the fact he was abandoning his daughter to the very world he could not abide. If he had lived longer he might have come to recognize his own spirit in Karissa and might have saved her from her lonely adolescence living with her grandmother. But his violent and untimely death in a booby-trapped tomb had robbed her of the only person with whom she had ever felt a true kinship. And having been a witness of his grisly death had made the loss even harder to bear.

Then sixteen years after the death of her father, she had met Asheris, a man whose soul she had felt connected to on a very deep level. Yet when their relationship became strained after the birth of Julia, she had slipped back to her old ways of silence and stifled anger, worried about Asheris and heartbroken at the way he had left her bed. But she was reluctant to question him about it and too full of pride to let him know how she wept at night at having been abandoned once more by a man she loved with all her heart and soul.

How had it happened? They had been so happy with each other, so right for each other. When they fell in love, she had been able to tell Asheris everything. She told him things she hadn't shared with another living soul—her dreams, her feelings, and her fantasies. He had been her friend, her lover, her father, her brother, and her confessor all rolled into one. Through Asheris's understanding and encouragement she had come to realize that she hadn't been responsible for the death of her father. Asheris had released her from years of guilt—the greatest gift she had ever received.

How could they have lost the ability to talk and to share? Was it because Asheris no longer encouraged her to speak to him? Was it because he had closed himself off for some reason and now spent many hours away from the house? Did all men act this way once the honeymoon was over? Was this the direction most marriages took? She had no one to ask and no trusted female friends with whom to compare marriages and husbands.

"Mother, did you hear what I said?" Julia inquired with a slight frown creasing the brow between her large, dark brown eyes.

"I'm sorry, *azeez*," Karissa replied. "I was thinking about something else. What did you say?"

"I was requesting that you look at this strange box."

Karissa glanced at the sandalwood box carved in the shape of a cat with its paws out in front and its tail tucked close to its hindquarters, very much the reflection of a sphinx. She had never seen the box. Karissa slowly stood up.

"It's beautiful," she whispered, oddly drawn by the wise eyes of the cat. Whoever had carved the animal was a master artist, far superior to herself. In respect and awe, she ran her hand down the slope of the cat's neck and across its back. Yet when she did so, her sensitive fingertips felt a score of tiny lines that shouldn't have marred the surface of the wooden box. She leaned closer as did George and Julia. "Isn't this curious," she said. "The box appears to have been extensively repaired."

"Maybe Grandfather Julian dropped it," Julia mused. "And it fractured."

"Into a hundred pieces?" George retorted, slanting a contemptuous look her way since she was a girl and much younger than he. "There are cracks all over the box."

"Someone has glued it together," Karissa observed. "Painstakingly so."

George pursed his lips. "Why wouldn't someone just throw it away instead of wasting all that time gluing it together?"

"Perhaps it was too valuable to throw away," Julia replied, undaunted by George's attempt at superiority. "Perhaps it was not simply a wooden box, but a possession of the heart to my grandfather."

"Hmph," he said, without taking his gaze off the cat.

Karissa smiled to herself at the interplay between her daughter and George and hoped her daughter would never cease to value her own opinion. Karissa knew that Julia was much stronger than she had been at this age, and she did everything she knew to nurture her daughter's self-esteem.

"Let's open it," Karissa said. "And see what's inside."

Carefully, she pulled upward, sliding the top of the cat from the base, which released the sharp musky scent of sandalwood that had been trapped in the cavity of the box. It wafted upward, filling the night air.

"Look," said Julia. "There are crystals inside!"

"Crystals?" George repeated in disbelief.

"No, they're not crystals." Karissa picked up one of the objects in question, a metallic rod about six inches long. "These are small obelisks—you know, Julia, like Cleopatra's Needle." She held it up so the others could see the angled sides that formed a pyramid shape at the top. Everyone stared at the obelisk as Karissa slowly turned it in the air.

"What is it made of?" George asked. "Gold?"

"No. It's not yellow enough to be gold. It looks like electrum—a mixture of gold and silver."

"These must be very valuable," Julia said. "How old do you suppose they are?"

"I don't know. My father never mentioned this box."

George reached into the cavity of the cat and pulled out a folded paper. "Look, *sayyidah*, here's a note. Maybe it is from your father."

Intrigued, Karissa took the folded paper from the boy and slowly opened it. The creases were deep and the edges well worn, as if the paper had been handled hundreds of times and then refolded. When she pulled back the bottom half, five dried rose petals fluttered to the ground.

"Oh, dear!" she exclaimed, upset at losing any small piece of her father's memorabilia.

"I'll get them, Mother." Julia knelt down and gently rescued the fragile petals, cupping them in her hand as she stood up.

"Thank you, sweetheart." She glanced at the handwriting and immediately recognized her father's distinctive printing.

"Tasharyana," he wrote.

Robert Burns has said how love is like a red, red rose that's newly sprung in June, how love is like a melody that's sweetly played in tune. May this flower and this music box always remind you of my enduring love. When we are apart and loneliness comes upon you, listen to this music, sweet Tasha, and think of me as I will be thinking of you. Upon my heart I promise we will be together soon and together always.

My love forever, J. B. S.

Karissa swallowed, thankful the shocking words had struck her mute and kept her from reading the note aloud. Who in the world was this Tasharyana? One of her father's lovers? Her mother had claimed that J. B. was an incurable womanizer and had suspected his many forays to Egypt were thinly veiled trysts with a long succession of women. With Asheris's help, Karissa had come to learn that Julian Spencer was not a womanizer, but a highly dedicated amateur Egyptologist, consumed with discovering secrets of the past. She had gradually come to share Asheris's faith in her father and had learned to suspect her own mother's narrow-minded motives for accusing J. B. of despicable behavior. But how did this letter fit in? Whom could he possibly have vowed to love forever? And when?

"Mother?" Julia touched her arm. "What does the note say?"

"Nothing. Nothing about the obelisks." Karissa marshaled her whirling thoughts and breathed in, hoping to regain her composure before Julia questioned her further. "It does mention that the cat is a music box."

"It is?" Julia picked up the base and held it toward the light, inspecting it.

"There," George exclaimed. "On the bottom."

Julia tilted the box and found a small metal key recessed into the base.

"Wind it up," George urged.

Julia shot him a dark look as if to chastise him for his impatience. Then she turned the key, winding and winding it, until she could turn it no farther.

A few notes tinkled out of the base of the box and then stopped.

"It's broken!" Julia cried, disappointed.

Then, as though the pleading tone in her voice had some effect on the mechanism, the music box started up again and cycled through a haunting melody again and again, holding the three of them in a pleasant trance until the notes grew slower and slower and died away in the darkness.

Julia sighed. "That was exquisite, simply exquisite. Do you know what song it was, Mother?"

Karissa shook herself out of the trance of the music and the shock of the love letter. "The title?"

"Yes."

She thought a moment while she hummed a portion. "I think it's from a classical piece—Dvořák. His *New World* symphony."

"Are there words to it?"

"Well, someone made a popular piece of it years ago. Let me see." Karissa closed her eyes and recalled the poignant words of the main theme of the music. "River road, river road, winding to the sea. River road, I'll come back, where I long to be."

"River road. Is that the Nile?"

"Not in Dvořák's case, I don't think," Karissa replied, holding out her hand for the old rose petals. Julia gently let them slip into her mother's hand. "But perhaps in this case, yes."

"Grandfather Spencer liked the Nile a lot, didn't he?"

"Yes, he did. He loved Egypt. He grew up here."

She let the petals fall onto the heartfelt words written to an unknown woman. Perhaps he had loved the Nile and a woman of the Nile more than anyone had ever known. Karissa struggled valiantly to keep the pain and confusion this new discovery caused her from showing in her face. What about her mother? Had J. B. ever truly loved Christine Petrie? If so, had something gone terribly wrong between them, just as something unspeakable and undefinable had come between Asheris and herself?

Who *was* Tasharyana?

Distracted and troubled, Karissa rooted through the rest of the items in the chest while Julia wandered off to the edge of the pond, taking the music box with her. Karissa was vaguely aware of Julia's beautiful humming as the child repeated the haunting tune of Dvořák's melody, sending it drifting through the hush of the garden. Julia often spent many hours by herself and hummed constantly, as if her spirit needed a connection to the world through her uncommonly pure voice. Sometimes Karissa noticed small objects vibrating near her daughter when she hummed—teacups, cut flowers, pens, and other lightweight items. But she never made mention of the phenomenon and Julia seemed blissfully unaware of the effect her voice had on the world around her, usually because the child was concentrating on a task while she hummed, just as she was concentrating now on the small obelisk she held in her hand. She was intently staring at the metallic shape, rotating it in the moonlight as she hummed.

Karissa smiled and turned back to the crate. Near the bottom of the box was notebook after notebook of experiments and test results, just the sort of research work Dr. Duncan had asked her about four years ago. Karissa flipped through the pages, hardly able to make out her father's tiny writing, and barely able to follow the scientific language of the text and detailed diagrams. Whatever her father had been investigating was something far beyond her realm of understanding. Perhaps she would contact Dr. Duncan and allow him to peruse J. B.'s papers. She smiled at the prospect. It would be wonderful to be involved in a positive way with her father's work and to read his journals. This crate was a second chance to get to know her father, and she was anxious to begin. As soon as she put Julia to bed for the evening, she would curl up with the first of J. B.'s journals and read until she fell asleep. She might as well, for Asheris spent nearly every night working late at the university.

"Mother!" Julia cried, startling Karissa out of her thoughts.

Karissa glanced at her daughter, alarmed by the sound of urgency in Julia's voice.

"Mother, look!" Julia stood near the edge of the pond, pointing at the water, her entire body rigid with alarm.

"What is it?" she asked.

Julia didn't even turn around. She kept staring at the water, as if too shocked to speak. Julia never lacked for words. That in itself worried Karissa, and she dashed across the tiled path to her daughter's side.

"Look there!" Julia whispered.

"What?" Karissa glanced at the surface of the water, expecting to see something unusual, such as a deformed carp or a dead animal of some kind. But she saw nothing—only the reflection of the moon.

"Don't you see?" Julia gasped.

"See what?"

"Her!" Julia pointed again, imperious in her excitement. "There!"

"Who?"

"The lady!" Julia leaned closer, peering into the water.

"I don't see anything, *azeez.*"

"Oh, no!"

"What?" Karissa stared at the water and then at Julia, concerned at her daughter's strange behavior. "What is it, Julia?"

"Oh, no! She's gone! She disappeared!"

"Who?"

"The lady in the water." Julia tilted her head, peering into the pond. Then she paced the bank, staring at the surface from many angles, as if the moon's reflection blinded her from seeing what she was trying to locate. Yet the moon couldn't have been at fault because it was blocked from view by the fronds of a date palm.

Karissa watched her, frightened by her peculiar agitation. "Julia, please, stop for a moment and tell me what this is all about!"

Julia glanced at her, her eyes wide, and then she turned back to the pond. "I saw her, right there, as plain as day, Mother, and then she just vanished!"

"Whom did you see?"

"A lady. She was quite beautiful. She had long black hair and large sad eyes. And she said her name was Tasharyana."

A cold feeling uncurled in the pit of Karissa's stomach at the sound of the name, the same name from the note in the music box. "Who did she say she was?"

"Tasharyana. An odd name, yes?"

"Very odd." Karissa heard her own voice speaking, but her words seemed to be coming from far away. "You say you saw her in the water?"

"Not exactly in the water. On the water."

"Standing?"

"No, she was on the surface, like in a mirror. And she was moving and speaking, like she was on television."

"What did she say?"

"She spoke of herself, her name, and then started to tell about her life, as if she wanted someone to know what had happened to her."

"And then she disappeared?"

"Yes." Julia frowned. "As quickly as she had appeared. Oh, Mother, it was unlike anything I have ever seen!"

Karissa put a hand on Julia's shoulder. "I wish I could have seen her."

"I wish you could have, too." She sighed. "I am not fabricating this, Mother."

"I never said you were."

"But you must admit it seems quite odd."

"Yes."

At that moment, the music box lurched into the last strains of its song. Karissa glanced down at the sandalwood cat as Julia knelt to pick it up. She noticed the lid had been removed and one of the obelisks was sticking out of the interior of the box.

"What's this?" she asked, pointing at the upright obelisk.

"I discovered there were symbols on the obelisks," Julia explained as she reached in to take the metallic rod out of the box. "See at the base, there's a little hieroglyph."

"The ankh, sign of life."

"Yes. And then I noticed the holes inside the box." Julia tipped the base toward her mother. "See there? The holes have glyphs, too."

Karissa leaned down to inspect the box. "So you put the obelisk with the ankh hieroglyph into the hole marked by the ankh symbol."

"Yes. I assumed they matched in some way. And when I did that, I heard a voice and I looked up to see the lady on the water."

"Strange," Karissa declared in a low voice.

"Mother, I believe this box is very special. Perhaps that was why someone glued it after it had been broken."

Karissa glanced at the grave face of her six-year-old child. She almost had to smile at Julia's gravity, and yet a smile would have insulted her.

"I believe you're right, *azeez*. But it's bedtime. We'll investigate this further tomorrow, all right?"

"But Mother—"

"Tomorrow." Karissa made certain her voice was firm and her expression full of determination.

"Oh," Julia sighed, "all right."

Karissa reached for the box, anxious to get it out of her daughter's possession, suddenly fearful that Julia's strange powers were connected to this sandalwood cat in some way. Slowly, Julia relinquished the box into her mother's hands. Karissa arranged the obelisks so that she could replace the lid, and then carried the box with her into the house.

Julia insisted upon hearing the song of the music box before she went to sleep. Karissa granted her request, content to let the song fill up her daughter's bedchamber. Julia lay back, her eyes closed, her thick black lashes sweeping her cheeks, while she listened with a half smile on her lips. When the song ended, Karissa realized she had been sitting on the edge of the bed in a daze, thinking about the Nile and the desert. What was it about the song that induced a trancelike state? Disturbed, she shook off the feeling and rose.

"Good night, sweet *azeez,*" she said softly, leaning over to kiss her daughter's brow.

Julia was fast asleep.

After closing the door of Julia's room, Karissa hurried to the garden, anxious to get back to her father's crate. She took the box with her, intending to put it back in its protective cardboard carton, but when she got to the garden and saw the moon once again hanging above the pond, she decided to try what Julia had done, just to see what might happen. As she stepped upon the sandy bank, the crickets and frogs ceased their chatter, leaving the garden ominously still. Karissa put the box on the ground and knelt in the sand beside it, remembering to hum as she removed the lid. Carefully she found the obelisk with the ankh sign and slipped it into the corresponding hole. A moment later she heard a soft female voice speak behind her.

Karissa jumped to her feet and peered at the water. Sure enough, there upon the surface of the pond was the form of a woman with long black hair much like her own. In fact, the woman's eyes were the shape and color of her own as well. Yet her face was pale and drawn, and Karissa could tell that beneath the beautifully embroidered galabia the woman wore, she was nothing but skin and bones. The woman was speaking and gesturing with her long graceful hands.

Karissa heard her name, Tasharyana, and then listened in complete fascination as the woman continued to speak.

"I have set down this tale," the woman declared, her dark eyes glowing against her pale skin, "so that those with the special gift will know my story and know that I am not mad, I am not histrionic. I have never been histrionic, though Madame Hepera, my voice teacher and manager, did her utmost to discredit both my character and my sensibilities. Be it known that I have made choices of the heart and of the soul, choices that led to my disgrace and downfall, but were I given the opportunity to make them again, I would do so without a moment's hesitation.

"I am using Madame Hepera's own sorcery to record this visual journal in hopes that my secret shall remain inviolate until a Special One, perhaps my own child or one of our line, shall use her voice and the light of the moon to unlock the story within. The story will be told from visions taken from my heart and mind, so that everything I experienced will be shared as if the viewer is seeing it with my eyes. The tale is told in the language of the heart. Therefore, it is not necessary to translate into a familiar tongue, for what is more familiar than the words of the human soul?

"It is now 1966, but my tale begins in the year 1958, when I was sixteen years old and still living in Luxor."

A riot of goose pimples flew across the surface of Karissa's skin. Had her voice been the key to unlocking the story? Did she as well as Julia possess the power to activate the obelisks through humming? Before she could consider anything more, she returned her attention to Tasharyana, curious to know who the woman was and unwilling to miss a single word she uttered. The vision of the woman shimmered on the surface of the pond for a moment longer and then faded. In her place, as clear as an image on television, appeared a scene in vivid color of a younger, healthier Tasharyana, dressed in the uniform of a young woman enrolled in a language school.

Tasharyana's Tale—Outside Luxor, Egypt, 1958

Tasharyana heard a twig snap behind her and whirled, worried that she might have been followed by one of her boarding school classmates. Or, worse yet, trailed by one of the instructors who seemed bent on hounding her every minute. Yet the path behind her appeared empty. Sighing with relief, Tasharyana relaxed and let her gaze wander over the sweep of the mimosa trees and the lush river grasses swaying in the breeze, growing so green and high that their blades nearly reached the branches of the trees. Birds of every sort hopped among the vegetation, adding flashes of brilliant blue, crimson, and yellow to the green backdrop. Ants marched around her sensible oxfords and across the track, and countless winged insects buzzed in the warm air of late summer. Tasharyana drank it all in, for she didn't often leave the compound of the school or the rigors of the classroom. This small taste of freedom was quite heady to a sixteen-year-old girl who rarely saw the outside world, and even more rarely experienced anything outside the company of other girls or teachers.

She wouldn't have chanced sneaking off the school grounds had it not been for a note smuggled to her by the cook, who was related to the housekeeper of the Spencer family. The note had been from Julian

Spencer, her childhood friend, asking her to meet him on the riverbank. He had something important to tell her. Tasharyana rubbed her bare arms as a nervous thrill passed over her. What could J. B. possibly want? Had he come for her at last? He had promised to rescue her from the school as soon as he was able to direct his own life. He was eighteen now. Was he coming to take her away? She had often thought about the possibility, and prayed that J. B. would soon take her from the Luxor Conservatory for Young Women, where she had lived for the past six years.

She was just about ready to search for a place to sit and wait when a movement near the river caught her eye. Tasharyana turned and spied a young man getting out of a small boat. He dragged the craft up the sandy bank as she stepped closer, her heart pounding in her chest. Could the young man be Julian? He seemed so tall, so broad shouldered—not the slender youth she remembered from years ago. What would she do if he were a complete stranger, and not the old friend for whom she had been waiting?

Quickly she concealed herself behind a small palm, hoping her navy and gray uniform wouldn't betray her hiding place. From behind a lush frond, she watched the man walk up the bank, his dark head bobbing, until he reached the top of the trail and looked up.

Tasharyana's heart caught in her throat at the sight. Though she had stolen away to see J. B. once or twice in the past few years, she was still not accustomed to his altered appearance. During the past two years Julian had transformed from a raw youth to a handsome man. His sharp features had broadened, become more pronounced, but somehow they fit the more rugged contours of his face. His black hair, proof of his half-Egyptian heritage, was cut short in the fashion of the day, but a stubborn lock fell upon his forehead. In an impatient gesture, so familiar and dear to her, he brushed the hair away as he looked around the clearing. Had he been completely transformed by adulthood, Tasharyana would have recognized him by that one impatient gesture. She stood up behind the palm and smiled.

Catching sight of the movement, Julian turned, and for a moment they simply stared at each other.

At eighteen, he was tall and well formed for his age, with powerful-looking shoulders beneath his khaki shirt and the shadow of a beard on his jaw. His slenderness had hardened into masculine leanness, his forearms had acquired sinew and strength, and his eyes flashed with a jaunty confidence that made her feel every inch an unworldly schoolgirl. What must he think of her in her pleated uniform skirt and white blouse, her anklets and oxfords? What a child she must appear! He had been out in the world, learning and growing, while she had been a prisoner of a boarding school, all but cut off from modern society.

"Julian?" she called, hesitantly stepping away from the palm.

"Tasha!" He rushed forward.

Before she knew it, he had swept her into his arms. He had never embraced her before and the sensation of being crushed against his hard frame was both alarming and wonderful. Over the years he had taken her arm or held her hand, but he had never hugged her. She had always thought of him as her brother, her playmate, her friend—not as a boyfriend. At least not until this very moment when her breasts were pressed against him and a strange thrill flared through her. Not until that instant had Tasharyana thought of herself as a woman and J. B. as a man, and what that might mean between them now. Tasharyana didn't know how to react, where to put her hands, or what to say, she was so overwhelmed by the unexpected physical impact of his embrace.

Before she could speak, he stepped back and his hands slid down to cup her elbows. "Look at you!" he exclaimed.

She stared at him, realizing from his beaming expression that he was pleased by what he beheld. Julian shot a glance down her figure and quickly looked back at her face.

"You're all grown up!"

"So are you!" she replied, grinning.

"You're beautiful!"

She blushed.

"I mean to say that you were always pretty, Tasha, but damn—you're beautiful now!"

"Julian!" she protested, pulling away in embarrassment. She took a few steps toward the center of the clearing and he followed her, staring at her the whole time. She could tell by the burning sensation she felt on her back. At the center of the glade she paused and faced him.

"How are you?" she asked. "How is your mother?"

"Fine. Excellent. Oh, Tasha, how good it is to see you again!" He grinned, his eyes dancing, looking every inch the boy she had once known as he walked toward her. "And you, how have you been?"

"All right."

"Just all right?"

"I have never liked the school, J. B. It is a lonely place for me."

His smile faltered and he reached for her arm. "I know, Tasha."

"I can't wait until I leave the school. I will never look back."

His expression darkened and Tasharyana felt a shadow of unease. If he had come to rescue her from the school, he would not have reacted in such a way. She blinked in uncertainty as her dream of freedom began to tatter.

"Julian," she stammered. "You–you are not here to take me away?"

"No, Tasha, not immediately. I—"

She turned away from him, cutting him off, unwilling to let him see the crestfallen expression on her face. She hadn't realized how much she was counting on him to help her escape from the school. Why else would he have sent her the urgent message? She hadn't considered any other possibility, fool that she was.

"Tasha!" he came up behind her and tried to take her shoulders, but she shook him off and scampered across the clearing toward the river. She couldn't let him see the depth of her disappointment. It would only hurt him and make him feel as if he had failed her. She wasn't J. B.'s responsibility, and she couldn't allow him to take on the role of her savior. Besides that, she had known for some time now that she would soon be grown up and on her own. To be rescued and taken care of by J. B. would plunge her right back into dependency, a position she had vowed to overcome as soon as possible.

"Tasha!" J. B. called, running to catch up with her.

She came to a halt where the shade of the foliage met the blazing afternoon sun of the riverbank and made a supreme effort to steel herself. Years of practice at choking back her wants and needs had made her a master of harnessing her emotions. By the time J. B.

came up beside her, she had masked her disappointment and stared across the water with a calm numbness she knew well and often compared to death.

"What's the matter?" J. B. demanded. "Are you all right?"

"Yes." Her voice was flat.

"Did you think I was coming to get you?" he asked, his voice breaking.

"Not at all. Why should you?"

"I promised you I would."

The last of her hopes plummeted at the constricted tone in his voice. She glanced sidelong at his face and saw that he was deeply troubled. Remorseful that she had ruined their meeting with her expectations of freedom, Tasharyana touched his sleeve. "J. B., you made that promise years ago. I'm not holding you to it."

He looked up, his eyes glinting with sadness. "I wish I could take you away, Tasha, but I can't."

"I know."

"And to tell the truth, now I'm a bit reluctant to admit why I *am* here."

"Don't be. It's all right." She gave him a brave but tentative smile. "Why have you come, Julian?"

He regarded her for a long moment. Then he spoke, his voice husky. "Tasha, I've come to say good-bye."

"What?" She thought her heart would stop beating, and she clutched the blouse at her throat.

"I've come to tell you that I've been accepted at Eton. I'm leaving for England in a week."

"England?" she gasped, unable quite to comprehend what he was saying, her ears were ringing so loudly.

"I'm going to university, Tasha. It's a great opportunity for me. I'll be able to make something of myself so that —"

"England?" she repeated, aghast. "You're going to England?"

"Just for a while. I'll be back during the holidays. I'll write to you constantly. Oh, Tasha, don't look at me like that! I thought you'd understand. I thought you'd be happy for me."

"I am. I just can't believe you'll be so far away!"

"You can pretend I'm still in Luxor. It's not as if I get to see you every day as it is, you know."

"But England!" She squeezed his fingers. "Think of it. You'll be so far away. We'll lose touch with each other."

"No, we won't, Tasha. Don't think such a thought!"

He searched her face and she did her best to choke back her despair. But though she struggled, hot tears welled in her eyes.

"Can't you see," he said, pulling her closer, "I have to do this. I will have a profession, a career, the means to make a good life."

"You will be leaving Egypt. You will be leaving me."

"Not forever, Tasha. Not forever."

Much to her chagrin, she felt tears sliding down her cheek as her heart broke into painful shards. Never in her wildest dreams had she ever envisioned a day when J. B. would be telling her that he was leaving Egypt. Once he left the land of the Nile he would forget all about his childhood friend, his childhood home, and his days along the river with her.

"I'll never lose touch with you," he said, wrapping his arms around her. "Tasha, I love you."

As his admission of love sank into her consciousness, she felt him gathering her into a strong embrace. Then he bent to her mouth and his warm lips opened upon hers. For an instant the touch of his mouth stunned her, and all she could do was stand there and let him kiss her. Then her love for him empowered her, and she slipped her arms around his neck and pressed into him, aching to be held, to be kissed, to be cherished. Her life had been bleak, and the past years had been bereft of love and human kindness. She had known only discipline, work, and vigorous voice lessons at the school, which had left her spirit crying out for sustenance. Julian gave it to her, with his arms, his lips, his hands, caressing her, nurturing her with the emotional manna a man gives a woman when he truly loves her.

"Oh, Julian!" she cried, clinging to him. His back was wider than she remembered, his muscles hard and demanding. She ran her palms over his shoulders, exploring him, reveling in the strength she felt beneath her fingertips.

A strange throb twisted inside her as his hands explored her as well. She closed her eyes and trembled as his hands swept down her back and went lower still, tentatively tracing the contours of her hips. At her sigh, he grew bolder and gently pulled her against him until she was pinned to him. With a rush of surprise and arousal, she felt the hard male part of him between them. As if by instinct, she arched upward slightly, rubbing her breasts against his chest. J. B. gasped and clutched her even closer, leaning down to kiss her again.

Their mouths were as hungry as their hands. They kissed each other, discovering a newer, more powerful dimension of a friendship they had enjoyed since they were children. But now they were man and woman, and they each knew what path their friendship was to take should they continue to writhe in each other's arms. The temptation to sink to the ground and join as one, to celebrate what had always been between them, was almost too powerful to resist. But Tasharyana knew J. B. was about to leave for England. She couldn't succumb to him, experience love with him, and then let him go forever. It would be torture to taste love with him and have to give it up for years afterward.

She drew away, breathing heavily. Her lips felt bruised, her breasts were swollen and aching with desire. But she pulled back and gazed up at him.

J. B.'s eyes glowed with fire and his cheeks were flushed as he returned her stare.

"Tasha," he blurted, trying to pull her back against him.

"We must stop," she declared. "Julian, we must."

"You're right." He licked his lower lip and stroked her hair as he fought to control himself. "I lost my head."

Reluctantly he released her. "I have something for you," he said at last. "Stay here for a moment."

He walked away, slowly, toward the boat in the sand. Then he bent over and pulled a bag out of the bow. Tasharyana watched him, her body singing and grieving at the same time for the man coming toward her.

J. B. held out the paper sack. "It's for you," he said. "A going-away present."

She took the sack and carefully opened it. Reaching inside, she pulled out a sandalwood box, carved in the shape of a cat.

"It's beautiful!" she exclaimed in delight. "Where did you ever find it?"

"At the bazaar. It's a music box. Wind it up."

Smiling through her tears, Tasharyana found the key on the bottom of the box and turned it. A poignant melody tinkled across the clearing. She looked at J. B.'s face, which was full of tenderness so sweet that it warmed her heart.

"Thank you, J. B.," she whispered, her voice choked by emotion.

"There's more inside," he replied. "But you can look at it after I am gone, all right?"

"All right." She gazed at him, her eyes filling with tears, and slowly stroked the side of his face. "Oh, Julian, I shall miss you!"

"And I'll miss you—like crazy!"

"I will think of you every day!"

He crushed her into his embrace, kissed away her tears, and held her tightly to his heart.

She returned his embrace and wondered how she would have the strength to let him go, to say the final good-bye, when she heard a shout at the far side of the clearing.

With a jerk, she pulled away and turned to see who had spoken.

"Miss Higazi!" hissed Madame Emide, the headmistress of the boarding school.

Backed by three of her female administrators and the watchman, the severely thin headmistress marched into the clearing, her eyes blazing and her face white with outrage. She pointed at Julian, her bony hand curled like the claw of a bird.

"Step away from that young man at once!"

Tasharyana had witnessed the wrath of Madame Emide many times, but she had never seen her as angry as she was now. Alarmed by the cruel glint in Madame Emide's eyes and the tight white grimness about her mouth, Tasharyana obeyed her orders to return to the school at once, knowing that to glance back at Julian would be to heap more punishment upon herself. Even so, she defiantly looked over her shoulder to see J. B. watching her leave, one hand rubbing the back of his neck as if tormented by indecision. The headmistress barked at her to quit gawking and turn around. Tasharyana took one last look at her childhood friend, and then clutching the music box to her breast, she followed the others down the trail, back to the boarding school and her sterile, rigid life. She was too distraught at J. B.'s news to care what might happen to her as a result of disobeying the rules.

After a few minutes they gained the school

grounds and entered through the gate. Down the walk filed the silent parade, up the steps to the main entrance and across the hall to the headmistress's office. Tasharyana trudged into the stuffy room where the walls were lined with racks upon racks of books and dark wood paneling that was original to the Victorian building. She turned in surprise when Madame Emide slammed the door behind her.

"You!" the headmistress spat out the word, barely in control of her rage. "I knew you were trouble from the moment you came here!"

Tasharyana stepped back against the wall of books, clutching her gift. Though she had done little wrong since arriving at the school, she had always been singled out by the headmistress and punished for crimes she did not commit. She knew better than to argue with the woman; arguing only made the punishment more severe. Yet sometimes her stubborn nature would not allow her to hang her head in shame, especially if she had done nothing to deserve a reprimand. This was such a time, for she was not ashamed of a single moment she had spent with J. B. Spencer.

"You have had traffic with a man!"

"No, I haven't!"

"Liar! You blatantly disobeyed the rules and consorted with a man!"

"He is an old friend who is leaving the country. Surely you don't begrudge—"

"Silence!" roared the headmistress. She stepped forward, grabbed the music box, and yanked it out of Tasharyana's grip.

"What is this, payment for your favors? Hmm? How many times have you met him before today? You little whore!"

Tasharyana felt the color drain from her cheeks.

She was not so sheltered she didn't know what the word *whore* meant. How could Madame Emide accuse her of such conduct?

"I am not a whore!"

"Silence! You will speak when I ask you a question and not a moment before!"

Tasharyana pressed her lips together, fighting down rage and hurt, well aware she was at the mercy of the headmistress. If she were turned out of the school, where her room and board were supplied as part of a government program for homeless children, she would have nowhere to go. Her parents were dead. She had no relatives. J. B. would soon be gone. There was no one else in the world she could go to for help.

"You will have no reward for your behavior, young lady," Madame Emide snapped. "In fact, there is only one punishment for you, one that will dissuade you from ever consorting with a man again."

Tasharyana blinked, confused by her words.

"And as for this," the headmistress continued, raising the music box above her head. "You will have no reminders of your shameful transgression."

Before Tasharyana could yell in protest, she saw Madame Emide hurl the music box to the marble floor of the office. The delicate sandalwood shattered, sending wood and metal flying across the floor. Among the debris, a green leaf and a stem peeked out from beneath the cracked lid. Had J. B. given her a flower?

"My box!" she wailed in despair. She bent down to recover what looked like a rose.

"Leave it! You have more important things to worry about than that trinket, believe you me." Madame Emide reached for her intercom and buzzed her assistant. "Call Dr. Shirazzi," she instructed. "Schedule a surgery for this evening at seven o'clock."

"At once, madame," came the scratchy voice at the other end.

Slowly the headmistress straightened up from her desk and leveled her cold eyes on Tasharyana.

"I shouldn't schedule surgery for you. You should be left uncut and shown for what you are—a whore—not a decent young woman."

Tasharyana blanched. She was going to undergo circumcision? Most girls her age had been cut long ago, as little children. But for some reason Tasharyana had never been circumcised, perhaps because she had lost her parents so early, perhaps because no one cared enough about her to ensure that she would be acceptable as a bride to an Egyptian man. Circumcision was usually something one's mother or aunt arranged for a girl, rather like the piercing of ears. One of the girls at school had helped her pierce her ears, but her unusual state of being uncircumcised had hitherto gone unchanged.

"I am to be circumcised?" Tasharyana inquired, nearly in a whisper.

"Yes. Perhaps if we cut out the sinful center of temptation, you will find no reason to sneak out of school to visit boys. And you just might find a husband, if you seek reconstruction and convince him that you are a virgin."

"I am!"

"There is no need to lie to me, Tasharyana Higazi. I know what kind of slut you are. You don't fool me." She lowered herself primly to her seat. "In the meantime, you will spend the remainder of the day in solitary confinement. I suggest you do a bit of praying, Miss Higazi, so that you might seek atonement for the sin of fornication."

"I did nothing!"

"As well as for prevarication."

"But I did not—"

"You will not speak for the rest of the day. Not a single word, Miss Higazi, or you will spend the entire month in the solitary cell."

Seething, Tasharyana bit back her words of protest, well aware the headmistress did not make idle threats. Though she wouldn't mind a day in solitary confinement, away from the other students and the teachers, she couldn't bear the thought of spending an entire month locked in a bare windowless room with nothing to do but sit on a hard cot and burn with hatred for the school and its headmistress.

Devastated, frustrated, and frightened, Tasharyana followed the headmistress out of the office, leaving behind J. B.'s shattered music box and the gifts inside that she would never see.

The door of the solitary room shut behind her and the heavy tumblers in the lock turned over, echoing in the large empty hall beyond. Tasharyana sank onto the cot and leaned her elbows on her knees. J. B. was leaving Egypt and she was to undergo evening surgery. Some girls never came back from evening surgery, but no one ever said why. The prospect of being cut frightened her, even though it was expected of Egyptian women to be circumcised. No man would want to marry a woman who, because she could achieve sexual pleasure, might stray from her marriage vows. The absence of sexual pleasure, most of the girls claimed, was a small price to pay for a lifetime of security. Yet Tasha wondered if any of them knew what they were talking about, because none of the girls at the school, as far as she knew, had ever been with a man.

Intact female sexual organs were the mark of a slut or a woman who dared defy convention, and those women had hard lives in Egypt. Still, she didn't think it was quite fair that men didn't have the same requirements for marriage. They retained full use of their sexual organs. They did not have to come to the marriage bed as virgins. Yet, life had been hard enough for Tasharyana already. She wasn't sure if she was the type of girl who possessed enough strength to defy convention. And what would J. B. think if he found out? Would he be pleased? Were English women circumcised? Were Americans? She didn't know. It wasn't something one asked strangers. She frowned, wondering if she would even survive the operation, while her young heart hardened even more with hatred for the Luxor Conservatory for Young Women.

Tasharyana woke up, alarmed to find herself in the infirmary and surprised that it was morning. Bright sunlight slanted through the high windows above her head. She struggled to sit up but was seized by nausea and a sharp pain between her legs. Slowly she sank back to the pillow, fighting off the urge to retch. When the nausea passed, she gingerly explored the dressing that had been crudely taped beneath her panties. She closed her eyes, suppressing her nausea, and thought she would turn inside out with despair.

She could remember snatches of the previous evening, and knew that she had protested when they came to get her for surgery. At the last minute, she had decided that, yes, she was the type of girl who would defy the rules if they didn't make sense. And circumcision made no sense to her. In fact, in her grief and anger, she had struck out as never before, kicking and screaming and vowing to run away. After a great deal of struggling, someone had poked a hypodermic needle in her arm. Only then had she had become too groggy to move or speak.

Left alone with the doctor in the infirmary, she had been vaguely aware of Dr. Shirazzi's bent shape, of the blurred sight of him sticking something in his own forearm, and sitting on the end of her bed for what had seemed like hours.

Even in her drugged state, she worried that the doctor had taken some type of narcotic and was going to perform the operation on her while in an altered condition himself. She also suspected he had misjudged the dosage of her anesthetic, because she should have been rendered completely unconscious. Instead, she had been left in a half-sentient state, floating in a nightmare world in which she could see and hear but could not move, waiting and waiting for the terrible surgery she was to undergo.

A noise in the hall seemed to have shaken Dr. Shirazzi to his senses. He scrambled to his feet and fumbled with his tools, when Madame Emide opened the door.

"Is she done?" the headmistress had inquired, her voice ringing through Tasharyana's blurred world.

"In a moment, madame. A moment."

The physician had bent over Tasharyana. She felt a slight pricking sensation in her crotch and saw Dr. Shirazzi reach for a pad of gauze.

"Is she giving you trouble?"

"Not at all. Not at all."

Tasharyana had heard the words of the doctor, slurred far beyond her distorted hearing. How could they let an addict perform surgery on helpless girls? No drug could blunt the rage she felt building inside as she watched him push a thick black thread through a curved suturing needle, his hands shaking.

Madame Emide swept across the floor of the infirmary toward them. Dr. Shirazzi's needle flew as if he were in a rush. By the time the headmistress approached the bed, he was already applying the dressing. Tasharyana quickly closed her eyes before Madame Emide noticed she was not fully anesthetized.

"I hope you didn't butcher Higazi like you did the last one."

"I didn't butcher the other girl. There were complications, infection."

"Be that as it may, Dr. Shirazzi, I can't explain too many fatalities in one year. The authorities will begin to question us, and you know what that could mean to your practice."

The doctor sighed. "You needn't remind me, *as-sayyidah.*"

Madame Emide sniffed. "This one will learn her lesson, anyway. After tonight she will never find pleasure with a man."

"A hard lesson, to be sure, but one they all learn eventually."

"It's the least we should do to hot-blooded little whores like her who will only breed more brats for the government to feed."

"Your foresight is admirable, *sayyidah.*"

"The shame of it, Dr. Shirazzi, is the behavior of our young people. This one is but sixteen years old and already she is spreading her legs for the first boy to come along."

"Shameful indeed."

For a long moment the headmistress had remained silent. Tasharyana had wondered what was happening. Then she heard a rustle of the headmistress's dress as she turned.

"Clean her up, for the love of Allah. There is blood everywhere! I hope she isn't a bleeder!"

"Of course, Madame Emide."

Tasharyana listened to Madame Emide's footfalls fading away while the doctor sponged the blood from her legs. The infirmary door closed.

"Bitch," Dr. Shirazzi had sworn under his breath as he threw the bloody gauze in the trash can near his foot. "We shall see who ruins whom. A simple slice and a drop of blood has fooled you, you heartless daughter of a dog."

Simple slice? What had the doctor done? How had he fooled Madame Emide? The questions swirled in Tasharyana's head until she finally succumbed to sleep late that night, and the same questions plagued her the moment she had awakened.

Now she lay in the recovery room, replaying the events of the previous night, getting angrier with Madame Emide with each pass through her memory. Tasharyana's wound might heal, but she would never recover from the burning inside her, the burn of helpless rage against the bitter cruelty of Madame Emide. Tasharyana let out a ragged sigh. The headmistress had beaten her again. But for the last time. As soon as the opportunity presented itself, Tasharyana would run away. Even if she had to live on the streets, she would choose such a life over the one she had endured at the conservatory.

Two days went by. No other girls arrived in the infirmary, and she rarely saw the nurse, who refused to tell her anything about the surgery. That was for the headmistress to discuss. Tasharyana forced herself to eat, though she had no appetite. She knew she had to have all her strength when the time for escape arrived.

On the third morning she heard a commotion out in the hall, and a voice she didn't recognize—a rich, powerful female voice. Whom did it belong to? No one ever came to the government-funded school. All the students were orphans or children of parents who couldn't care for them any longer. Visitors were unheard of. New instructors were unheard of. The only person who arrived and departed on a regular basis was Dr. Shirazzi. Tasharyana heard the clipped tones of the headmistress and then the deep reply of the stranger. The door to the infirmary opened and Tasharyana stood up near her bed, lightheaded but determined to keep to her feet.

Through the door sailed an immense woman. Everything about her was blocky, from her square face to her heavy body and sturdy black pumps. She wore a black dress pinned with a rhinestone brooch above a huge bosom that seemed to direct the woman's progress across the room, as if she were a huge ship bearing down upon the hospital beds. Tasharyana had a great urge to step backward, out of the way of the large woman, but she held her ground, refusing to give in to anyone anymore, no matter what punishment she received for her independence.

The woman drew up in front of Tasharyana. Her black hair, streaked with white from a widow's peak, and her unusual triangular-shaped eyebrows lent her a sinister appearance. The woman's eyes flashed with intelligence, however, and her mouth did not have the tight-lipped lines of cruelty evident in the face of the headmistress.

"Leave us," boomed the large woman with the volume and precise enunciation of someone accustomed to addressing large crowds.

Madame Emide opened her mouth to protest.

"I said leave us!" repeated the stranger evenly.

The headmistress snapped her jaw shut and turned on her heel, marching to the door in her stiff-backed, rigid manner. The door clicked shut behind her and Tasharyana breathed a small sigh of relief.

The stranger smiled and gestured toward the bed with an eloquent sweep of her plump hand, which was encrusted with rings. "Sit down, Miss Higazi."

The command was imperious but couched in a warm tone that Tasharyana didn't even consider disregarding.

She lowered herself to the edge of the bed.

"I was told you underwent surgery recently. You should not tire yourself."

Tasharyana made no reply since she was unwilling to discuss her intimate surgery with a complete stranger.

"Turn so that I may see the back of your head."

Puzzled by the strange request, Tasharyana glanced up.

"Turn, Miss Higazi!"

Tasharyana presented her back to the woman and felt her braid being lifted. The woman lightly touched the base of her skull with the tip of her finger.

"Hmm," the woman murmured and then released her braid.

Tasharyana wondered what the stranger had seen on her neck but didn't ask, certain she wouldn't receive an answer anyway.

"All right, girl, you can turn back around. I've seen all I need to see."

Tasharyana straightened her shoulders and looked away, more distrustful than ever of the behavior of adults.

"My name is Madame Hepera," the woman offered,

bowing her head slightly. "I have been following the progress of your voice lessons for quite some time."

Tasharyana glanced up at her in surprise.

"In the past few years, you have made considerable improvement, Miss Higazi, so much in fact, that I have decided to take you on as one of my students."

Tasharyana stared at her, not knowing whether to be suspicious or happy. The only facet of her life she enjoyed was her music. If she escaped from the school and never completed her education, not only would she face a life of hardship and poverty, she would be giving up her music as well. Yet who was this Madame Hepera? And what connection did she have with the school?

"Your voice is uncommonly pure, Miss Higazi, but not fully trained. I can teach you how to use your voice to its fullest potential, as well as instruct you in the areas of interpretation and dramatics."

Tasharyana said nothing. Over the years she had learned to stifle all anticipation, all hope, and replace it with guarded reserve.

"Did you hear me, young lady?"

"Yes." Tasharyana glanced at the woman's face in search of a hint of kindness in the dark eyes, a sign the woman could possibly be trusted. So many adults could not be trusted. But the woman's eyes were hard and probing, not in the least gentle or kind. Had she been cut from the same cloth as the headmistress?

"You do not smile, Miss Higazi. You do not thank me."

"I have no reason to thank you, madame. I know nothing of you, or into what situation I will be thrust as your student."

Madame Hepera regarded her for a moment, as if deciding whether to be pleased or offended by the remark. Then she clasped her hands together beneath the swell of her large breasts. "The situation, as you call it, Miss Higazi, will be your removal from this institution, your establishment in my private residence in Cairo, and the onset of your training in opera."

"Opera?"

"Yes."

"My departure from this school?"

"Yes." Madame Hepera lifted the corners of her brightly painted lips. "Do I detect the faintest hint of approval of this situation, Miss Higazi?"

"It would give me great pleasure to leave this place, madame."

"And to study opera?"

"My heart's desire."

"Well, then, my girl, I will instruct the headmistress to have your things packed. You leave for Cairo immediately."

Madame Hepera turned to leave. "Remain here until someone comes for you."

"Yes, madame."

Tasharyana watched the woman flow to the door of the infirmary, and marveled that a person of her size could possess such graceful carriage. Was she an opera diva? Madame Hepera seemed too old to portray young women onstage, but she certainly had the presence of a star. Tasharyana didn't recognize the woman's name. Yet, she was so cut off from most of the world, she wouldn't know one famous prima donna from another. Tasharyana smoothed back her hair, doing her best not to let her hopes build. Madame Hepera seemed far less harsh than the headmistress of the school, and might be much easier to get along with. But one could never count on first impressions. There were many forms of cruelty and unkindness and many types of people in whom cruelty dwelled. Until Madame Hepera proved herself otherwise, Tasharyana would not allow herself to harbor the slightest expectation about the future.

A few minutes later the door opened and the janitor, Jabar, shuffled in carrying a suitcase. He was a middle-aged man with an unhurried limp and a dull look in his eye, seemingly content with his position at the school and not one to bother the girls. He performed most of the heavy work around the school and all the cleaning. In return, he was given a room in the basement near the boiler, and half an afternoon off on holy days. Of all the adults at the conservatory, Jabar had been the least unkind to her. In fact, she had often seen him lingering in the doorway with his broom while she practiced her singing with the voice teacher, and she wondered if he might love music as much as she did.

"Your bag, miss," he mumbled, placing the suitcase at the end of the bed.

"Thank you, Jabar."

"You are leaving the school, then?"

"Yes. I'm going to Cairo to study opera."

"Ah, miss! This is wonderful news!" He smiled, displaying a chipped and discolored upper tooth. Just as suddenly his expression changed, drawing down his thick eyebrows and mustache. "But my ears will miss your singing and all those beautiful melodies. You have the voice of an angel, Miss Higazi, truly the voice of an angel."

Tasharyana blushed. "Thank you."

He blushed, too, as if not accustomed to speaking such words. The color spread from the tips of his ears down his neck to the collar of his cotton shirt. Then he fumbled with something he was holding behind his back and presented a crumpled paper sack. "Here, this is for you. I saved it."

She accepted the sack, wondering what it could be, and opened it. The smell of sandalwood drifted up and her heart skipped a beat.

"I was outside the window, pruning the hedge, when I saw what the mistress did to your pretty music box, Miss Higazi. I saw how heartbroken you were."

"Jabar!"

"She's a mean woman, that Madame Emide. She'd no right to ruin your box. So after she left, I swept up the pieces, every little splinter and put them in a bag. And I took them to my workshop and glued them all together. The box is almost as good as new, Miss Higazi. There is a note, too, and a poor little rose. But it has dried up the past few days, I'm sorry to say."

Tasharyana looked up at him, struck by the man's sentimental gesture. "Jabar, you don't know what this means to me!"

"It was from your sweetheart, wasn't it, Miss Higazi?" He grinned and blushed again. "I had a sweetheart once, before I got the fever and got all twisted up."

"Jabar, thank you!" She hugged the bag and fought back tears of joy. "How can I ever repay you!"

"It's all right, Miss Higazi. It was just a little repair job." He limped to the end of the bed. "But you better hide that bag in your suitcase, before Madame Emide comes in and sees it. She's a nosy old witch who likes to see people as miserable as she is."

"You're right. I should hide it." Tasharyana flipped the clasps of the cheap suitcase and carefully concealed the bag beneath the layers of clothing. Then she closed the case and set it on the floor.

"Thank you, Jabar. Oh, thank you so much!"

"Good luck to you, Miss Higazi." He smiled shyly. "And may Allah protect you."

Hours later, Tasharyana sat in a private coach on a northbound train, which slowly crawled between the cliffs and the Nile on its way to Cairo. Madame Hepera sat across from her, reading a copy of the daily newspaper, *Al Ahram,* and drinking chilled white wine, an unusual beverage for an Egyptian woman, since most Islamic people eschewed alcohol. Was Madame Emide not a follower of Allah? Tasharyana nursed a glass of iced tea especially prepared for her by Madame Hepera while her thoughts raced ahead to Cairo and what life might lay ahead for her, and then back again to the school and what had been done to her. She had looked at her wound as best she could, but with the stitches still intact, it had been difficult to tell just what was done to her. Would the scarred flesh make her more desirable to a man? It didn't seem logical. Yet thousands of Egyptian women had been disfigured and they had found mates. What would J. B. think of her should she ever find herself in intimate circumstances with him? She felt herself grow pale at the thought and quickly took another sip of the tea. The beverage had a strange calming effect on her that did a marvelous job of muting her sudden attack of anxiety.

Luxor, Present Day

Asheris slipped through the back garden gate, hoping he wouldn't arouse the servants. He had nothing to hide in regard to his late-night comings and goings, for most of his evenings were spent in his office at the university, but still he didn't wish to inconvenience any of his staff with his habit of keeping odd hours. They should not be made to suffer because of his personal demons.

At first, staying away during the evening hours had been the only solution he could find for easing the tension between Karissa and himself. Now, working late had become a habit and a sure defense against his increasing insomnia. As of tonight, however, he had decided to surmount the problems between his wife and himself. Life was too short to squander on such misery.

He walked along the garden path, drawing a sense of serenity from the placid scene of the pond and acacia grove. The night was clear and crisp, the cold black sky strewn with stars. He felt clean spirited and strong, and only hoped he could hang on to the feeling long enough to approach Karissa in the morning and settle their differences at last.

For a moment he had a flash of memory—of prowling through the night like this, but not as a man. In his memory, he prowled on all fours, as dark as night, as cold and black as the sky above, his feet padding soundlessly upon the tile, his muscles far more powerful than those of a mortal man, his hearing infinitely more acute. Asheris drew to a halt beneath a palm. Never before had he so clearly recalled the time he spent as a man trapped inside the body of a panther, the centuries he had endured as part of a spell cast upon him by ancient priestesses over three thousand years ago. He had thought his life was to be relatively normal now and that the panther would never be a part of him again. Yet here he was, experiencing the sensation of being a big cat.

The memory fled as quickly as it had appeared. He sighed, wishing he could remember more. In the old days he had been more powerful, or so it had seemed. He had been confident of protecting his own then. Or had he just been fooling himself? For centuries he had faithfully guarded the tomb of his long lost love, Lady Senefret—lying in a sarcophagus as a man by day and prowling the desert as a panther by night, cursed to remain mummified alive for eternity. Then Karissa Spencer, connected by blood to Senefret, had released him from his curse with her admission of love. From that day forward, he had ceased to transform into a cat. But from that day forward, he had begun to doubt his mortal abilities. If the priestesses were to rise again and hunt him down or—worse yet—threaten his family, would he be capable of protecting them? No ordinary means would vanquish the followers of the temple of Sekhmet. And now, unfortunately, he was just an ordinary man.

Deep in thought Asheris walked toward the house, skirting the western edge of the pond. It was then he saw the body lying on the sand at the edge of the water. A woman?

His heart thudded in his chest. He knew the slope of that hip, the sheen of that jet black hair, and the long slender length of those legs. Isis! Had the priestesses already taken their revenge?

Panic flooded him.

"Karissa!" he shouted. He got no response. "Karissa!"

He dashed toward the pond.

"Karissa!" Asheris gasped, finding his wife unconscious on the sand. Gently he rolled her onto her back so he could see her face. In the dim light he gave her a quick physical assessment checking for head injuries and listening to her heart. She was breathing steadily and didn't seem to be in any distress, but why was she lying on the ground?

Asheris glanced around for evidence of what might have happened to his wife and saw the open box with the obelisk sitting on the sand near her head. He had never seen anything like the tiny metallic obelisk and the strange cat-shaped box. The moment he spied the feline figure, he felt a chill run across his scalp. In the ancient days, the priestesses of Sekhmet, keepers of the temple of the lion goddess, had been recognized by their cat symbols. Had the box come from them? If so, it would confirm his worst fears—that of the priestesses' existence in modern-day Egypt and their knowledge of his family, especially his daughter.

Julia, sweet beautiful Julia, had the strange strawberry birthmark on her scalp at the base of her skull that would have branded her as one destined for the priesthood at the temple of Sekhmet. Karissa bore the birthmark in her hairline, too, at the back of her head. Both his wife and his daughter, the two people who meant everything in the world to him, were connected to the temple, but for what purpose he didn't know. He had hoped that the powerful priestesses, who had been more sorceresses than religious practitioners, were long dead and the worship of Sekhmet long since abandoned. He had hoped to spend a lengthy and uneventful life with Karissa and Julia. But lately his hope of escaping the priestesses had begun to fade. And now his wife lay unconscious in his arms.

"Karissa!" He stroked her cheek and then lifted one hand and squeezed it gently. "Karissa, wake up."

Her eyelids fluttered.

"Karissa!" he repeated, stroking her glossy hair while she opened her eyes and stared at him as if he were a complete stranger. He touched her cheek. "It is Asheris."

"Asheris?" Her voice was vague, dreamy. He didn't like the sound of it.

"What are you doing out here?" he demanded. "What happened?"

She struggled to sit up and he assisted her, all the while waiting impatiently for an explanation. But Karissa seemed disoriented, as if awakened from a powerful dream and still partially in the fantasy. Slowly she rose to her feet. Asheris stood up and watched her, deeply concerned by her behavior. She blinked and stared down at the box and then craned her neck to peer at the pond.

"What is it?" Asheris asked. "What?"

"I saw—"

She broke off and ran her hand from her chin down her long slender throat to her chest in a gesture of complete bewilderment.

"What did you see?"

"I'm not certain." She glanced back toward the box. "I must have been dreaming."

"Here in the garden? You fell asleep on the ground? That isn't like you." He reached down and picked up the box. "And what is this?"

"A music box."

"Where did you get it?"

"From—from my father." She snatched the box out of his hands as though his touch would defile it in some way. Her eyes glinted a cold warning that the box was none of his business.

Asheris stepped back. His solicitous questions had been misinterpreted as judgmental interrogation. Why? Had the box come not from her father but from someone else? Could Karissa have an admirer? A lover? He couldn't conceive of such a thing. Yet why had she taken a defensive stance? Instead of turning to him for comfort and safety, Karissa stood before him now with distrust and alarm in her eyes, her body poised for flight. Her distrust cut him to the core. Even so he was unwilling to see her leave the garden just yet, especially when the distance between them had suddenly grown colder and wider, exactly the opposite of what he wanted to have happen.

"A music box?" He had a difficult time keeping the strain out of his voice. "A curious music box, wouldn't you say?"

"Somewhat." She slipped the obelisk out of its hole and laid it alongside the others in the bottom of the box.

"And what are the little metal rods?" he inquired.

"I don't know. Part of a puzzle perhaps." She reached down for the lid and carefully put it on the base.

Asheris watched her, suspecting that she knew more about the box than she was telling him. Had she lost all desire to confide in him? What could he do to scale the wall that had come between them? He knew he would have to take small steps and plumb the depths of his sensitivity to recapture the special bond that had once held them fast. He would do anything to have his wife return to his life and to his bed where she belonged.

"Are you all right, then?" he asked.

"Yes. Yes of course. I must have fallen asleep out here."

He slipped his hands into the pockets of his slacks. "Well, since we are both awake, would you care to join me for a drink?"

She glanced at him in surprise.

"There's some excellent French brandy in the study, or if you'd care for something cooler—"

"Not tonight, Asheris." She walked up the bank to the path. "I need to put this away and tidy up a few things. But thanks anyway."

"Very well." He tried to conceal the disappointment he felt at being turned down. Perhaps she had experienced the same letdown when he refused her invitations for candle-lit dinners, using pressing business as his excuse to avoid intimacy with her. How it stung to have the refusals thrown back in his face. Even so, he lingered, unwilling to leave her. "You really shouldn't be out here by yourself, you know, not at night."

"I'm fine. Don't worry about it."

"You may not be safe."

"Why not?"

He sighed, still unwilling to bring up the subject of the priestesses before he knew the extent of their presence. "There is danger, that is all."

"What danger?" Her eyes flashed at him. "You are always talking about danger, always worrying about threatening strangers lurking around the house—and some mysterious plot to snatch Julia and me away. You don't know how oppressive it is to live every single day with your big ugly cloud hanging over us."

Stunned by her harsh words, Asheris felt the right corner of his mouth twitch. "Big ugly cloud?"

"Yes! Big ugly cloud!" She pushed a tendril of her hair back in an impatient sweep of her hand. "It's always there, always throwing a pall over our lives. How can you expect Julia to have a normal life when you're constantly bringing up these threats?"

"Julia is not a normal child. She will never have a normal life."

"She could if you'd back off!"

Back off? Asheris drew up to his full height. *Back off?* He felt as if she had slugged him with all her strength. Never in his wildest dreams would he have expected Karissa to tell him to do such a thing. Didn't she realize his worry stemmed from his deep love for both her and Julia? He could feel the color draining from his face, both in hurt and outrage. He knew if he spoke he would either shout at her in a torrent of anger and say things he would regret later or he would break down in tears and reveal his fears and insecurities. He would not allow himself to indulge in either outburst. Without saying another word he turned on his heel and strode toward the back of the house.

"Asheris!" she called after him in an exasperated tone.

He didn't answer. He just kept walking, well aware it would be an even greater task now to reconcile with his wife.

In the morning, Karissa waited impatiently for Asheris to rise. In the old days, when he had spent the dark hours in the form of a panther, he had prowled all night and slept until noon. Though he no longer took the shape of a cat, he continued to keep the same hours. He still went to bed just before dawn and rose shortly before the midday meal. She often wondered if his strange sleeping habits were the root of their relationship problems.

Karissa paced the morning room, waiting for her husband to appear. She had sent Julia out to the garden with George, in hopes that she would have a few minutes of privacy with Asheris while he took his morning coffee. Anger still flared within her from their exchange last night, and she held on to the anger to sustain her through the upcoming trial, that of convincing Asheris to agree to let Julia attend school.

Just to be sure she had all the paperwork and brochures, Karissa checked the file folder in her hand and then placed it on the table. A movement caught her eye and she turned to see Asheris standing in the doorway. He still moved with the grace and stealth of a big cat, another carryover from his previous life. His silent entrances into rooms sometimes startled her, such as now, when she turned to find him standing behind her.

To hide her surprise, she raised her chin. "Good morning."

"Good morning." He returned her frosty stare, his brown eyes smoldering, his hands in the pockets of his loose-fitting linen slacks. Karissa was struck anew by his dark good looks, stamped with the unparalleled pedigree of aristocratic blood mingled with keen intelligence. He wore his hair shorter than when they had first met—just above his ears—which accentuated the sweep of his black brows and the sharply sculpted lines of his lean face. His highly expressive mouth, wide with a generous lower lip, was set in a grim line.

"I wish to speak with you on an important matter," Karissa began.

"Oh?" Asheris moved toward the sideboard where a coffee service had been placed by Eisha, the housekeeper, a few minutes before. "What matter?"

"Julia's schooling."

Asheris poured two cups of coffee with slow, deliberate movements, as if he wished to delay facing her. He carried them to the table and put one in front of Karissa.

"Thanks," Karissa said, taking a seat.

"You're welcome." Asheris pulled out a chair and sat down.

Karissa looked across the table at him, trying to read his expression, but he had pulled an impassive mask across his features. No matter. She had to disregard Asheris's feelings in this case and press on. She slid the file folder in front of her and opened it.

"As you know, I have home-schooled Julia for years. And she has come a long way. But I believe that it is important for her to learn people skills as well as academics. So, I have been investigating various schools."

"Schools?"

"Yes. Julia will soon surpass my knowledge anyway. She needs skilled teachers who can offer her more than I can."

"We will hire private tutors then. We can afford the best."

"Asheris, she needs to be around other children and learn what it's like to be out in the world."

"The world is a cruel place. She doesn't need to discover that fact."

"Yes, she does. The sooner, the better." Karissa leaned forward. "You can't shelter her forever, Asheris. And it isn't fair of you to do so. You will be doing her a disservice in the end. Can't you see that?"

"Not at all."

"She will grow up without having developed coping skills or knowing what people are really like. What she doesn't learn now will have to be learned later, when it might present far greater problems to her. She might be theoretically brilliant, but she will be at a disadvantage compared to those who have been out in the real world."

"The real world." Asheris sighed as she took a sip of the strong coffee, fragrant with cinnamon. "For Julia the real world is far too dangerous."

"What do you mean?" she put down her cup with a clatter. "What danger?"

"Danger that is more real, more lasting than anything you can imagine."

"What are you talking about?"

Asheris looked into her eyes, as if he were trying to decide whether or not to disclose a secret. Then he sighed and stared down at his long, slender hands. Karissa gazed at his hands, too, knowing that centuries ago he had been commander-in-chief of the army of the pharaoh, a brilliant strategist and fearless soldier. It was hard to picture his elegant hands gripping a sword and shield, and it was harder still to believe her husband was afraid of anything.

Silently Asheris raised his coffee cup and took a long drink, still deep in thought. Then in his quiet way, he placed the porcelain cup back into the saucer, without the barest rattle of china.

Karissa watched him, aching to reach out to him, to wrap her arms around him and assure him that all would be well. But she was reluctant to make the first move because of the many times Asheris had turned away from her, as if he no longer needed her comfort. Nevertheless, she couldn't resist touching him.

"Can't you tell me what's bothering you?" she asked gently, laying her fingertips upon his wrist. He slipped his arm away, not abruptly, but quickly enough to offend her.

"I do not wish to worry you."

"Worry me?" She felt patches of heat on her cheekbones at his disregard of her feelings, and sat back in her chair, ramrod straight. "When did we start keeping secrets from each other, Asheris? When did we stop working as a team?"

"There are some things better left to men."

"Better left to men?" She jumped up and the chair scraped loudly across the tile behind her. "What are you saying? That I'm not capable of understanding? That I'm not capable of helping?"

"No." Asheris rose to his feet. "It is not a case of capability. It is a case of keeping you safe."

"Oh, good! So one day something awful might happen to you and you'll just disappear and I'll have no idea what's going on?" She crossed her arms. "That's an excellent plan!"

"Better I should disappear than get you involved in something that could endanger both you and Julia."

"Oh, really?" She could hardly contain her anger. "I think there's more to this than simple protection."

"Such as?"

"Such as I just might be too independent for you, Asheris. You're afraid that I'll teach Julia to be independent and self-reliant, too, aren't you? And you're afraid that she'll soon see through the limits men have placed upon women since time began and refuse to play the game."

"This is no game, Karissa. I assure you."

"Then what is it? Tell me!"

"It has to do with the past and with the future. And until I feel it is safe to talk about it, I shall speak of it no more." His voice was low and controlled, a voice Karissa recognized as being a sign of barely suppressed anger. He continued to speak in the quiet tone. "You must understand that my silence is born of love and not of senseless limitations. You know me better than that, Karissa. I know you do."

"No." She glared at him. "No, I don't believe I do know you anymore, Asheris. I wonder if I ever did."

"Can you say that with honesty? From your heart?" He leveled his golden brown eyes upon her and she felt the old magnetism that once could hypnotize her and induce her to tell him everything. But Karissa wasn't about to succumb this time. Before she fell under the spell of his gaze, she turned away and changed the subject.

"Just so you know, I am going to enroll Julia in the Luxor Language School. It has an intensive music program that will be good for her."

Asheris was silent behind her.

"She'll love it. Julia is a sociable little girl. She will love having friends and outside activities to keep her busy. I have a brochure on it, in case you're interested."

She heard Asheris push in his chair. "I am not interested in any school."

Frustrated, she turned. "I am meeting with the headmistress this afternoon."

"If you are seeking my blessing, Karissa, you seek in vain." He threw her a hard glance and, without saying another word, quickly left the room.

Karissa watched him go, wondering why every discussion between them had to end with one of them stomping away in anger. Still full of resentment, she hurried out to the garden, determined to bury her frustration. The best way she could find at the moment was to immerse herself in her father's journals. She would spend the morning reading about his past, drive out to the school in the afternoon to enroll Julia, and investigate the visions of the music box later that night. She was anxious to see if the story of Tasharyana would continue if she stuck a different obelisk into the base of the box.

When she got to the crate, she saw Julia on a bench near the pond, drawing in her sketchbook with the music box tinkling beside her. The Dvořák melody drifted toward Karissa, comforting her, as she reached into the crate for the journal with the earliest date written on the inside cover. Karissa sank into a garden chair and read a few pages. It seemed her father's journals started at the same time Tasharyana's story began, the time at which the two young lovers were separated.

J. B.'s Journal Entry—August 30, 1958

Well, here I am in England, settling in as best as I can. I'm to share a room with an American from Baltimore, a Charles Petrie. I haven't met him yet since he won't be arriving for a few more weeks. I suppose I should enjoy the solitude while it lasts, for some roommates can be troublesome, or so I've heard. I've met a few decent guys here and we've played some soccer on the field behind the dormitory. I sign up for undergraduate classes tomorrow. Mother wants me to go into law like my father did. I'd much rather take history and physics. Perhaps I can squeeze all three into my schedule. All in all, I think I may like it here at Eton.

J. B.'s Journal Entry—September 3, 1958

It's raining again though it's still summer. I can't bear the rain. It makes me long for Egypt and the balmy cloudless days along the Nile. It also makes me think of Tasha. How I hated to leave her like that at the river's edge with the awful headmistress yelling at her and thinking the worst. Yet nothing I could have said would have convinced the old bat that we were perfectly innocent. My greatest disappointment was in being robbed of saying good-bye to Tasha in the way that I wanted. I never got the chance to tell her how I really feel about her. I hope she is well and reasonably happy, although I know she hates the school. If I were older and had more money I would take her away from it. But then what would we do? I am still dependent on my mother and the scholarship I won here at Eton. I won't be financially independent for quite some time. I only hope that Tasha understands and will be patient. I miss her so much. I can't wait for the Christmas holidays when I can go back and see her.

* * *

Karissa kept reading through the volume, fascinated by her father's account of his first year at the university—his worries about doing well in his classes, his exploits with the other young men, his burgeoning interest in science, and his ongoing thoughts of love for the Egyptian girl, Tasharyana Higazi. Karissa stopped reading when Eisha served lunch, and tried to keep up a conversation with Julia, who chattered away in her usual fashion. But Karissa found herself distracted, pulled back into the past by her father's journals. How long would he remain true to Tasharyana? How long would their love endure before time and distance blunted their feelings for each other? And when would he meet Christine Petrie, his future wife and her mother?

That evening, after having visited the school and being pleased by the order and by the educational theories enployed there, Karissa tucked Julia into bed early so she would be well rested to start classes the next morning. Then Karissa returned to the garden. The moon was just rising over the garden wall. She opened the sandalwood box and inspected the obelisks, wondering which one to choose. If the obelisks were storage units like a videotape, each one might contain a different vision. But how could she be certain she would see them in the right order?

Carefully Karissa lined up the metal rods upon the table in the garden. There were five of them. She turned them so the symbols stamped near their bases faced her. Upon doing so, she noticed that each one bore a different amount of symbols. The one she had viewed the previous night had only the ankh sign on it. The others had marks of two to five symbols.

Karissa smiled to herself. She would place the obelisk with two symbols in the base of the cat and see if the vision portrayed was in chronological order.

Her heart pounded as she carried the music box to the edge of the pond. She hadn't realized until that moment how anxious she was to learn the rest of Tasharyana's story. What if the box didn't work? What if last night had been a fluke she couldn't repeat? She hoped her theories about the obelisks were correct and that there was enough moonlight to produce the vision in the pond. And she hoped this time she wouldn't lose consciousness to the vision.

With shaking hands she wound the music box and hummed along with the tune, closing her eyes to the sweetness of the melody and saying a silent prayer that Tasharyana would appear once again. As the music faded to a close, she heard the soft voice of the vision speaking in the darkness. Karissa opened her eyes and was thrilled to behold the sight of the beautiful woman in the ornate galabia rippling gently on the surface of the water.

"This is the second installment of my story," Tasharyana explained, much to Karissa's gratification. "It begins in the winter of 1959 when I am seventeen and living outside of Cairo with Madame Hepera. Then it will jump seven years into the future, when I make my American debut."

Karissa stared at the vision, mesmerized, as Tasharyana shimmered and disappeared and was replaced by a new scene, that of a brightly lit room dominated by a grand piano and a jungle of potted plants. Tasharyana, dressed in a modest navy skirt and white blouse, stood near the piano, appearing much more grown up in her fashionable flats and nylons than in the image of a few months ago, when she had worn ankle socks and oxfords. A dark blue headband held back her long black hair, accentuating her high cheekbones and large black eyes. She held a sheet of music and practiced a few measures over and over again, perfecting the musical phrase. But she broke off abruptly when Madame Hepera made a dramatic entry into the room.

Tasharyana's Tale, 1959

Tasharyana saw the letter on the tray Madame Hepera carried and her heart caught in her throat. Could she have possibly received a letter from J. B.? During the summer and fall she had written to him, wondering why she hadn't heard from him. J. B.'s silence worried her. Had he forgotten her as soon as he left the country? If not, he should have written by now. Why hadn't she heard from him? For all he knew, Tasharyana was still in Luxor. But surely Madame Emide would have forwarded any letters J. B. sent to the school. She had even tried writing to his mother, Menmet Bedrani Spencer, only to have her notes returned, stamped that the addressee had moved. It was as if the Spencers had dropped off the face of the earth.

"Were you practicing the aria?" Madame Hepera smiled, her mouth perfectly painted with deep red lipstick.

"Yes." Tasharyana watched her teacher approach. She found some facets of Madame Hepera to be ungenuine, such as her ingratiating smile, her mincingly delicate table manners, and her soothing voice over the phone. She could see into Madame's flat dark eyes and knew the person inside was unhappy, cold, and driven—all traits she tried to disguise by affecting a friendly personable nature. But Tasharyana was not fooled by the mask. In fact, once when she was sick and walked through the dark house to the kitchen in search of a headache remedy, she had come upon Madame Hepera standing by the table in the center of the room. The older woman was gorging on all kinds of meat, from leftover roast to chicken wings, making no effort to disguise her animal grunts and smacking lips. Upon hearing a step in the doorway, Madame Hepera looked up in shock, a bone with a chunk of lamb at her lips, appearing more like a ravenous beast than a human. The sight had disgusted and alarmed Tasharyana. Without a word, Tasharyana had turned and fled, and neither one of them had ever spoken of the incident.

Since then, however, Tasharyana was more aware of her teacher shouting at the servants, her voice cracking with rage. Worse, she had seen the woman come upon a starving dog sniffing through the garbage in the alley, and before Tasharyana could act, Madame Hepera strangled the dog with her own hands. Afterward, she threw the carcass into the garbage can, seemingly with no remorse. Tasharyana had also followed Madame Hepera into the private chambers below the house, where her teacher performed strange ceremonies. At first Tasharyana thought Madame Hepera retired there to practice a dramatic part for an upcoming opera. But she soon deduced that Madame Hepera went to the subterranean chamber to perform religious rituals often involving smoking braziers and statues of lions.

Tasharyana turned her thoughts from the odd character of her teacher and focused her attention on the envelope lying near the cup of tea. Madame Hepera brought her tea every day without fail, claiming her special blend was the secret of a great singing voice and produced a calming effect in young ladies. It was true. Often after finishing her tea, Tasharyana felt a sense of relief, and all tenseness in her throat vanished, making it possible to achieve the highest notes in her range. Then after singing, Madame Hepera would fix her milk with drops of iodine to soothe the tissues of her throat, always taking care of her protégée to ensure the best quality in her voice.

"Is there mail for me today?" Tasharyana ventured, praying the letter was from J. B.

"Not directly, my dear. But it is mail that concerns you." Madame Hepera waved the letter. "This is an invitation for you to sing at the Cairo Opera House, as part of a program for young people."

"Oh." Tasharyana's hopes plummeted.

"I thought you'd be happy, Tasharyana. This will be good experience for you."

"I was hoping to hear from Julian Spencer at long last."

Madame Hepera tilted her head. "Are you sure your friend is attending Eton?"

"Quite sure."

"Something must have happened. Perhaps his plans changed and he was accepted somewhere else."

"No, he said Eton." Tasharyana bit her lip to keep it from trembling in disappointment. Just like that, J. B. had dropped out of her life. She had thought they would be together someday. Lately she had even wondered what it would be like to be his wife and live with him in a house of their very own. She hadn't lived in a house since she was ten years old and was weary of boarding with strangers. But she should have known better than to entertain such fantasies about J. B. Judging by what she knew of life already, her way was never going to be smooth, easy, or blissful. And whatever path her life took, the road was going to have to be of her own choosing and carved by her own hand.

"You are distressed." Madame Hepera lifted the cup of tea off the tray. "Drink this and it will settle your nerves."

"Thank you." Without thinking twice, Tasharyana accepted the tea and sipped it while Madame Hepera put the tray on a nearby table. She could feel the immediate effect of the brew as it passed through her, helping her relax.

Madame Hepera swept to the piano and lowered herself to the wide bench, arranging her dress to prevent undue wrinkling. "Do you know what I think you ought to do, Tasharyana?"

"What?" Tasharyana glanced at her.

"I think you ought to forget the boy."

"How can you say that? You don't know Julian."

"But I know men. They aren't worth the trouble women go through. They forget much more easily than we do, especially when they are away from us, such as that boy of yours." She turned the music score to the first page. "They get distracted, they get lazy, and sometimes they get influenced by the wrong people, especially by other women."

Tasharyana flushed at the thought of J. B. finding another girl. Yet what other explanation could there be for his silence? She could feel tears pricking her eyelids but refused to break down in front of Madame Hepera. During her schooldays with Madame Emide, she had vowed never to let anyone see her cry, and she had clung to that vow with stubborn determination ever since.

The older woman rubbed her hands together, trying to stimulate the circulation in her pudgy fingers. "This is the first time for you, isn't it, such heartbreak?"

"Yes."

"Do you wish to live a life in which you often feel heartbreak?"

"No."

"Then don't take men seriously. Let them amuse you. Let them shower you with adoration and gifts. But don't give your heart to them, or you will suffer."

"But J. B. was my best friend, Madame Hepera."

"Friendships change just like everything else, my dear." She sighed and smiled, almost gently. "There is one good aspect in your disappointment, however."

"What could that be?"

"You have learned the sensation of sorrow. This knowledge can be put to good use by incorporating it into your singing. When you sing *Carmen*, you will be able to translate true emotion into the role. Someone who has led a happy, well-adjusted life will never possess soulfulness, which sets the true prima donna apart from a mere singer in the chorus. Someone who has never known heartbreak and disappointment cannot convey real passion onstage, because they are strangers to the poignant side of life."

Tasharyana considered the advice as she set her empty cup on the tray.

"Use this boy to your advantage," Madame Hepera

continued. "Take him out of your heart and put him in your voice. You'll be much better for it. Much happier."

"I don't feel at all happy."

"Not now. But you will learn in time. If you remember to keep men in their proper perspective, you will discover a different kind of happiness, a kind of peace."

Still fighting back tears, Tasharyana looked up at her, wishing she had never heard of J. B. Spencer.

"Trust me, my dear." Madame Hepera smiled and then turned her attention to the music in front of her. "Now then, let's hear the aria you've been practicing."

Karissa watched as Tasharyana stepped up to the piano and sang the first few notes of the aria, and then the vision of the music room slowly faded to black. Seconds later a new scene appeared, in which twenty-four-year old Tasharyana, dressed in the black and red dress of the gypsy woman Carmen, waited in the wings of an opera house.

Tasharyana's Tale—Washington, D.C., 1966

Tonight was Tasharyana's televised American debut, her big moment, when she would show the world to what heights and depths she could bring the doomed character of Carmen. Many famous opera divas had made a career of the title role of Carmen, and had spent years singing the same themes over and over again. Tasharyana prayed that she would not only do her predecessors justice, but would surpass them with her voice and acting ability. Madame Hepera had told her time and time again that she possessed the qualities of a star—in voice, in dramatics, and in beauty—and once the world heard her sing, she would be on her way to fame and fortune.

Since losing her ties with J. B., Tasharyana had thrown herself wholeheartedly into her singing career and had concentrated all her energies on perfecting her technique. For the past seven years she had studied voice four hours a day, dance for two, and then had worked six hours more with private tutors who taught her everything from French to calculus. Madame Hepera had provided her with the best of everything in regard to education and living accommodations. But in the eight years she had lived in Cairo, Tasharyana had rarely known any freedom. Even when traveling, she couldn't visit a museum or buy a pair of earrings without the company of a chaperone or Madame Hepera herself, and had only managed to sneak out on a few occasions, only to be found and convinced to return. Sometimes she thought her guardian had convinced her to return against her will, as if she were being hypnotized or brainwashed. But she could never recall a single instance of being mesmerized.

Madame Hepera explained that all true artists made sacrifices for their art, especially those in opera. To achieve excellence, one had to concentrate all energy on self-improvement and the study of voice, on music theory, foreign languages, and history. What better way to do it than being sequestered in a luxurious estate outside Cairo where her genius could be nurtured without distraction from the outside world. According to Madame Hepera, Tasharyana should count herself extremely fortunate not to have to earn money for lessons and subsistence as some students did. There was no time for dallying and no room for deviance from work in Madame Hepera's ladder to success. Even their trips to foreign capitols centered around her stage performances. But of course Madame Hepera could all but guarantee fame to her diligent protégée.

Yes, fame would be nice. But to Tasharyana freedom would be heavenly. In the past few years, she could think of little else.

Tasharyana sucked in a deep breath and released it slowly, trying to relax her diaphragm. She was nervous, even too nervous to drink the tea Madame Hepera had nearly forced upon her, insisting that Tasharyana must relax. But Tasharyana had refused the tea, concerned that her stomach might become upset. As a result, she felt uncommonly clear-headed, perhaps because of the adrenaline rushing through her system, but perhaps because she had not drunk the soothing tea as well.

Her apprehension wasn't centered around her upcoming performance, however. She had far more at stake than her debut. Trembling, she slipped her hand into the pocket of her dress and checked the diamonds for the tenth time. The jewels were still there, cool and heavy in their velvet bag. She had spent years saving her meager earnings to purchase the gems and had kept them hidden from Madame Hepera. For years Tasharyana had plotted to escape to the United States once she got the chance. And the diamonds would fund her way to freedom.

She breathed in again and watched the soldier onstage pouring out his song. In moments she would turn off her worried thoughts, step into the hot bright lights, and sing with every shred of passion she could evoke. Then when the curtain came down and the rest of the company took their bows, she would slip out the side entrance of the opera hall with the diamonds in her pocket, and make a dash to freedom.

She wouldn't be destitute after she sold the gems.

She wouldn't be desperate for employment. She could audition for another opera company, as long as they could overlook her odd behavior during the curtain call of her American debut. If she failed to find a place in opera—and truly her heart lay with music and the stage—she would look at other careers. At twenty-four she had a first-rate education, college degrees in music and math, and plenty of experience traveling abroad. Madame Hepera had seen to her complete development, and for that she would be forever grateful. But she could no longer bear her lack of personal freedom. She also suspected Madame Hepera of having some secret agenda for her future that didn't include any more discretionary time than that granted in the past. The thought occurred to her that Madame Hepera might be expecting to cash in on her fame by acting as her manager, and pushing her into a rigorous schedule of performances, just as she had pushed her through years of intensive training.

Tasharyana, however, had been pushed too far. She needed time to herself, the opportunity to mold her own life, and the freedom to make her own decisions. She longed to be her own person, no matter what she owed her voice teacher. If her plan of escape was successful, she would get a job and little by little repay Madame Hepera for the eight years of instruction, room and board, and travel expenses. She imagined the sum would be astronomically large, but she would chip away at it. And one day, far in the future, she would be free at last, obligated to no one. The thought made her heady with anticipation. Just like Carmen, she intended to be truly free, though the cost would be high.

Then Tasharyana heard her cue, and she swept onto the stage.

Halfway through the performance, when Don José was revealing his love for Carmen and Tasharyana was standing silently at his side waiting for him to finish his song, she looked out at the audience. Most of the crowd was a glittering mass of black finery topped by light indistinct faces. But the people in the first few rows could be seen fairly well. She scanned their expressions, wondering how they were receiving the opera so far. And then she saw a familiar face.

For a moment her breathing seemed to stop and her legs felt as if the bones inside them were dissolving. There in the first row, sitting next to an attractive blond young woman, was J. B. Spencer. She knew it was Julian, though in his formal black attire he looked much more mature and refined than the memory of the young man she carried in her thoughts. There was no mistaking J. B.'s dark eyes and black hair—a strand of which fell rakishly over his forehead as if to offset his conservative dress—and his alert, proud carriage, the mark of a person physically and mentally fit. Even his mouth, with its jaunty lift to the right looked the same. He appeared confident and handsome, and still by far the most attractive man she had ever met.

She saw the familiar flare of his prominent jaw line above his white tie as he turned to the blond beside him and made a comment in her ear. Tasharyana felt her heart twist painfully at the sight of his lips in such close proximity to the woman's ear. Who was she? What relationship did she have to J. B.? Was she the woman who had been distracting him all these years?

Soon J. B. returned his attention to the stage and Don José's impassioned singing. Tasharyana watched J. B.'s regard range over the man beside her and then shift her way. For a tense, shattering instant that seemed to last forever, their gazes locked and held. A shaft of pure recognition and awareness shot between them, immobilizing her.

Then Tasharyana felt Don José squeeze her fingers, and she realized she had completely lost track of the performance. Shocked that she could let any man affect her so deeply, Tasharyana turned and picked up Don José's saber as she was supposed to do. In only seconds she would throw the saber behind the table, whirl to face Don José, and demand of him that if he loved her, he would give up his life for her and carry her off to the mountains. If he truly loved her, he would spend the rest of his life with her and turn his back on his country. But she wasn't certain she could utter a sound. A huge lump constricted her throat. How would she be able to fling her challenge to Don José when she longed to shout the very same questions at the black-haired man in the audience? If J. B. had truly loved her, why had he deserted her? If he had loved her, why had he allowed eight years of silence to come between them? Tasharyana gripped the saber with trembling hands. How would she ever be able to get through the love song, let alone begin it?

To fortify herself, she called to mind Madame Hepera's advice about keeping men in perspective. They weren't worth the anguish, her teacher had told her. Surely J. B. Spencer hadn't proved himself worthy of her anguish. Why let such an insensitive, uncaring man ruin her American debut and quite possibly the rest of her career? If her voice cracked even once or wobbled because of lack of control, she would be judged harshly by critics ready to pounce on a new talent.

With more force than necessary, Tasharyana threw the saber and scabbard behind the table, vowing then and there not to allow J. B.'s presence to have any more effect upon her. She had dedicated eight difficult years to this night of opera and she wasn't about to let a thoughtless man destroy her moment of glory.

Tasharyana promised herself to ignore the first row for the rest of the evening. In fact, she wouldn't focus on the audience again. She turned, centered her attention on Don José, and forced herself back into her role. She was playing Carmen, after all, one of the greatest parts ever written for opera. For the next hour she would become the tragic gypsy and forget the very existence of Tasharyana Higazi.

Her resolve produced astounding results. The rest of her performance was flawless and electrifying, and she could tell by the way the rest of the cast threw themselves into their parts that her fervor inspired them. Rehearsal had never gone so smoothly, so magically. By the final scene, when Don José plunged the knife in her breast, she knew she had achieved the musical heights to which she had aspired. As she collapsed on the street outside the bull ring, dying of her wound, she could feel the rapture of the audience, and then heard the thunderous applause as the curtain came down.

As soon as the velvet and fringe swept the floor of the stage, Tasharyana scrambled to her feet, her heart pounding in triumph and apprehension for the moments to come when she would make her escape. She took a bow with the American who played Don José, and then slipped offstage to allow the toreador, Escamillo, to take his bows. She had counted upon his vanity to give her time to slip away. True to form, the toreador basked in his applause and remained center front. Tasharyana slipped past her fellow performers, ignoring their gasps of surprise as she headed in the opposite direction of where she was supposed to go, back to the stage for another round of applause with her leading man. She pushed open the side door of the stage, ran up the incline of an empty corridor, and found another door, locked from the inside. She turned the knob, opened the door, and slipped out, discovering she was near the side hall of the opera house. To her right was the ladies' lounge, to her left a short flight of stairs. She fled up the stairs, knowing they eventually led to the front doors of the building. As she ran, she could hear the roar of the crowd, still clapping and cheering the performance, and felt a swell of pride at having done so well in her debut. She didn't need the words of a critic to tell her the performance had been exceptional, and not just in regard to her work, but that of her fellow artists as well.

Tasharyana heard a door slam behind her and the faint sound of footsteps as she raced down a thickly carpeted hall to another set of low stairs, nearly tripping on the long, heavily sequined costume she wore. She ran up the stairs and looked over her shoulder, worried that Madame Hepera had already figured out something was amiss with her protégée and had sent someone after her. She couldn't see anyone in pursuit yet, and turned around to the front, only to plow into a man running toward her.

Crying out in surprise, Tasharyana grabbed his jacket to keep from falling. For a moment her nose pressed into the man's white shirt, fragrant with the clean smell of soap and his light musky scent. Almost immediately, she recovered from the impact and pulled back, but the man clutched the tops of her arms, preventing her from running away.

"Tasha!" his familiar voice exclaimed. Only one person in the world called her Tasha.

She glanced up in shock to see J. B. Spencer.

"Let me go!" Tasharyana cried, trying to wrench free.

"Tasha!" he said again. "What's the matter? Why are you running?"

"I must get away. Let me go!"

"But you're running away from a standing ovation!"

"I have to!" She glanced behind her, frantic to be out of the opera house. She saw two stagehands pounding toward her, and behind them Madame Hepera and the producer. She turned back to J. B., her cheeks flushed and hot. "Now let me go!"

He stared at her for an instant with concern and bewilderment wrinkling his brow. Then he released her and she dashed around him, sweeping her velvet skirt up with her right hand and nearly colliding with J. B.'s blond companion and an older lady who had come out to the lobby. She careened to the side and headed for the foyer doors, but J. B.'s detaining hold on her had given her pursuers enough time to catch up with her. Ten feet away from the outside world, she was grabbed from behind and pulled roughly against the hard frame of the tall brown-haired stagehand.

Shattered, Tasharyana steeled herself to withstand the shafts of devastation that shot through her as she saw her dream of freedom dashed. Would J. B. Spencer always come between her dreams and her hopes? Would his intervention prevent her escape this time? She had come so close to freedom, so close! She bit back her tears and raised her chin to face Madame Hepera.

"Tasharyana," her voice teacher called, sweeping forward in her black satin gown with pearls and diamonds dripping from her ears and throat. "My dear, what has gotten into you?" Her tone was expertly modulated to convey concern for the benefit of the onlookers, but Tasharyana knew Madame Hepera's solicitous manner masked her terrible temper—and only just barely.

Tasharyana glared at her, not fooled for an instant, and made no answer.

With polished aplomb, Madame Hepera smiled and glanced at J. B. and the two women as they watched the stagehand drag Tasharyana away from the doors. No one seemed to recognize the seriousness of her predicament.

"I'm afraid Miss Higazi is a bit temperamental," Madame Hepera explained with a small light laugh. "Most artists of her caliber are uncommonly high-strung, you know."

"I am not high-strung!" Tasharyana countered, and knew as soon as the words flew out of her mouth that they only confirmed what she denied.

Madame Hepera stepped closer. "My dear, the pressure of your debut is understandable. But you mustn't let it overwhelm you."

"I am not overwhelmed!" Tasharyana retorted. "And if you don't tell this idiot to release me, I'll scream and then you'll really have a scandal!"

"My gracious!" the young blond woman gasped in surprise, as if unaccustomed to emotional outbursts of any kind. Tasharyana shot her an angry glance and wished the annoying trio hadn't gathered to witness her failed escape and ensuing embarrassment.

"You have no right to detain Tasharyana," J. B. put in. "Let her go."

"And just who are you?" Madame Hepera demanded.

"A friend. Now will you let her go, or must I call security?"

"No need." Madame Hepera gave a curt nod to the stagehand.

The instant Tasharyana felt the grip let up on her arms, she yanked free and took two steps away from the stagehand and Madame Hepera, which forced her to stand next to J. B. He looked down at her.

"Are you all right?" he asked.

"No, I'm not all right, thanks to you!"

"Me?" His arched dark eyebrows raised even higher in surprise.

"My dear," Madame Hepera said, interrupting, "I insist you return to the stage at once and take your final bow. Listen to them—they're cheering for you."

Everyone fell silent for a moment as the noise of the crowd thundered around them.

"I'm not going back!"

"You can't disappoint your audience," the producer added. "It could have disastrous results."

"I didn't disappoint them! My performance was everything they could have asked for and more."

"But they want to honor you."

"I can't indulge them at the moment."

"Can't indulge them?" Madame Hepera stepped toward her and pointed a fat finger at her. "You're cutting your own throat with behavior such as this!"

Tasharyana glared at the finger and then at the woman, refusing to submit to her teacher.

Madame Hepera's poise slipped a notch. "What in the world do you think you're doing, you ungrateful girl? If you turn your back on your audience, you turn your back on your career! This could ruin you!"

"And you as well?" Tasharyana taunted. She received a small amount of gratification when she saw slight blotches of anger bloom beneath the powder on Madame Hepera's face. Tasharyana turned to the producer. "And you?"

"I insist you return to your dressing room," Madame Hepera said, her eyes flashing with anger. "You must make yourself presentable for the dinner party with Senator Delman. We leave in an hour."

"I won't be joining you."

"What did you say?"

"I'm not going. I am sick to death of your schedules and your demands!"

Madame Hepera stared at her. And then she seemed to realize how she might appear to onlookers. Once again she pulled on the cloak of graciousness, and with a calm expression of understanding, she touched Tasharyana's arm.

"My dear," she began in a warm tone, "Obviously you aren't feeling well. I quite understand. Opening night can tax even those with years of experience. I know it has been a strain for you. But remember what

I told you about your art, my dear." She smiled and spoke a phrase in Arabic, certain that the Americans wouldn't understand the meaning of the words. Instead of delivering a philosophy on art, Madame Hepera threatened to make Tasharyana's life a living hell if she didn't return to her duties immediately. Madame Hepera, however, obviously wasn't aware that J. B. Spencer had lived eighteen years in Egypt and understood Arabic perfectly.

"Hold on," J. B. said, slipping his hand around Tasharyana's elbow. "Who do you think you are, threatening Tasha like that?"

Madame Hepera paled and glanced from Tasharyana to J. B. and back again. "Who is this man?" she demanded. "Do you know this person?"

"I'm asking the questions, madame," J. B. retorted coldly. "Miss Higazi is not a minor. A person of her age is under no one's guardianship. She is under no obligation to you or to anyone else, at least not in this country."

"She owes an obligation to her art, young man, to her career, and to our producer." Madame Hepera grabbed Tasharyana's forearm. "And I kindly ask you to mind your own business."

"I'm making this my business." J. B. raised his arm to slip it around Tasharyana's shoulders, but she lunged forward, shouting that she was no one's business, and dashed to the doors. By that time, a crowd had surrounded them as the audience left the theater. Tasharyana took advantage of the milling throng and pushed her way through the doors before the stagehands could follow her. She skittered across the foyer, burst through the second set of doors, and raced down the steps to the sidewalk, unmindful of the stares and gasps as the people recognized her. She ran into the street, frantically waving her arms for a taxi as she heard J. B. calling her name. The April night was chilly after the hot lights of the stage, and she shuddered as she waited for the taxi to approach.

A yellow cab pulled to the curb and she jumped in, slamming the door shut just as J. B. skidded to a stop beside the vehicle.

"Drive!" she cried.

Before the cabby could respond, J. B. yanked open the door and barreled in beside her, his broad shoulder pushing her aside.

"The Fairfax," he said. "And step on it!"

"How dare you!" she exclaimed.

"Drive on!" J. B. repeated to the driver.

The cabby glanced into his rearview mirror. "Is he with you, lady, or not?"

"Please, Tasha," J. B. grabbed her hand, "we must talk!"

Tasharyana searched his eyes and saw the depths of his concern. She had little patience for J. B. but decided in the interests of speed to allow him to stay in the cab. She jerked her hand from his grip and sat back with an exasperated sigh. "It's all right. He's with me."

The cab roared into traffic, leaving the producer and the stagehands staring after them, empty-handed at the foot of the steps. Tasharyana put her hand in her pocket, just to make sure the diamonds were still there.

Then she slid across the seat to the other side of the taxi so their bodies would make no physical contact. She stared straight ahead, at the back of the cab driver, while J. B. turned to face her, stretching his arm along the back of the seat and almost touching her with his hand. She was too conscious of the nearness of his fingers for her own peace of mind. "Two minutes, J. B.," she snapped.

"What do you mean, two minutes?"

"I mean that you can say your piece and then you're getting out."

"You can't mean that."

"Why can't I? I didn't ask you to run after me."

"But we haven't seen each other for eight years!"

"Exactly." She glanced at him sharply and then back at the cab driver's collar. "So I don't expect you to have too much to say to me."

"You're serious!"

"I am." She made a great show of looking at her watch. "You have one minute now, Julian."

"Damn the goddamn time! Look at me, Tasha!"

She refused. She felt hard and cold inside, the best defense against pain.

J. B. sighed. "Okay, then, don't look at me. Just tell me what's going on."

"Why should I? I see no reason to include you in my affairs."

"Oh, come now!" J. B. retorted. "You can't mean that, Tasha!"

"Yes, I can. I learned long ago not to include anyone in my affairs. It's better that way."

"The hell it is!"

She pressed her lips together at his outburst and refused to look at him.

"Tasha, listen to me. I don't know what happened in Luxor. We've got to talk about that. But right now, you need to trust me."

"Trust you?"

"So I can help you."

"I don't need your help. I am through accepting anything from anyone."

"But what are you going to do? Where are you planning to go? Are you leaving your friends back there for the evening or for the rest of your life?"

Tasharyana crossed her arms. "I haven't decided."

"You're going to give up your career, just like that?"

"If I have to."

"Why?"

Before Tasharyana could reply, the taxi pulled up to the curb of a hotel, its gilt doorways gleaming in the darkness and five flags of various countries waving in the breeze.

"The Fairfax," the driver announced as the doorman walked their way.

"Come inside for a moment, Tasha," J. B. said, gently taking her hand. "Let me buy you a drink and we can talk for a few minutes."

"I don't drink."

"Then let me get you a cup of coffee. Something. I need to talk to you."

"It is better that we part now, Julian."

The doorman opened the cab and discreetly waited for J. B. to get out of the taxi.

"Please, Tasha." J. B. raised her hand to his lips. "A few minutes. Then you can be on your way."

She watched him kiss her fingertips and a shiver of delight blossomed on the surface of her skin. How could she let him affect her so easily? What spell could J. B. throw over her, to make her set aside her resolve?

The cab driver glared over the soiled top of the front seat. "You staying or leaving, buddy?"

"Leaving."

"That'll be three seventy-five, if the lady's going with you."

At the mention of the fare, Tasharyana realized she'd have to be very careful with her money. What cash she carried must be spent on a train ticket to Philadelphia. It would be best for her to try to sell one of the diamonds or at least find a pawnshop, and preferably do so in the company of J. B.

"I'm going," she said at last, trying not to notice J. B.'s happy smile. He pulled out his wallet and withdrew a five-dollar bill. "Keep the change," he said as he guided Tasharyana to the curb.

"Thanks," the driver drawled.

"Good evening, ma'am, sir," the doorman greeted, closing the cab door. "How was the opera?"

"Wonderful, Rivers, thank you." J. B. guided Tasharyana through the heavy gilt-and-glass door that the doorman held open for them. "And if Miss Petrie happens by, will you tell her I'm in the lounge?" J. B. slipped him a bill.

"Certainly, sir." The doorman gave Tasharyana's ornate costume a brief perusal and then returned to his post. She realized that she should have worn something practical underneath, so that she could slip out of the gown and avoid the curious stares directed toward her unusual attire and her heavily applied stage makeup. She would never escape notice walking around Washington, D.C. in a red velvet gown encrusted with black and red sequins, and wearing a black mantilla pinned over her mass of ebony curls.

Unconcerned by the stares, J. B. ushered Tasharyana through the huge luxurious lobby, across a sea of plush dark maroon carpeting, and down a hall to the lounge. She walked next to him, wishing his hand at her elbow had no effect on her. But she couldn't deny the fact that his touch sent a warm thrill through her and made her heart race. She had dreamed of walking beside J. B. like this, and now he was here with her. Yet she knew it was foolish to let her fantasies loose in regard to him because J. B. couldn't be trusted and shouldn't be trusted. Besides that, she had other things to concentrate on, like how she was going to continue her escape.

An awkward silence fell between them as they found a table in the corner and sat in silence while the waiter approached. She wasn't accustomed to making small talk with men. In fact, she had never been alone with a man for eight years, not since the terrible day on the banks of the Nile, when J. B. had said goodbye.

"What would you like?" J. B. inquired, jarring her out of her thoughts.

"Milk."

"Milk?"

"I always drink milk after a performance. It soothes the throat. Madame Hepera puts ten drops of iodine in it as a remedy for abrasion, but I don't have any with me."

"You drink iodine?"

"Just tiny drops of it."

J. B. made a face and turned to the waiter. "A milk and a Scotch on the rocks."

The waiter put his hands behind his back and Tasharyana thought she detected a grin hiding at the corners of his mouth. "Will that be a small milk, miss, or a large?"

"Small, please."

She leveled a stare at him, daring him to make fun of her choice of beverage, for she felt no shame in her selection.

"Thank you." The waiter hid a smile and turned.

As soon as he was out of ear shot, J. B. gave in to a

hearty chuckle. "Did you see his expression?" He laughed quietly. "Smug bastard. He could hardly keep from smiling."

"I wouldn't have minded if he had."

"Yes, but that would have ruined his deportment. Can't have that, you know, not at the Fairfax!"

He grinned and gazed at her across the table, his dark eyes brimming with pleasure and friendliness. "I'll bet it's not every day he gets a milk-drinking Spanish gypsy in here." He laughed again. Tasharyana felt herself drawn to the warmth of J. B.'s personality but still tried to hold back.

His eyes sparkled at her. "You look—" He paused and let his gaze wander over her hair and face, the warm smile still playing on his lips and in his eyes, "—you look absolutely beautiful, Tasha."

A searing blush spread across her cheeks. Many men had told her she was beautiful. From the moment she had first sung in public, she had been pursued by admirers who sent her gifts, cards, and flowers. But none of their attention had made her blush because she hadn't cared what they thought of her. And she was trying her hardest not to care what J. B. thought either. Yet her blush betrayed her.

"Thank you," she replied, looking toward the bar and forcing herself to take on a casual air even though her heart pounded against the thick velvet of her bodice. Surely he could see the sequins twinkling at the movement.

"That costume looks great on you."

"Do I look like a gypsy?" she asked, tilting her head coquettishly.

"Every inch. But you don't fool me, miss."

"I don't?"

"No." He shook his head and his smile gradually

faded as he gazed at her. She gazed back, unable to break from the sudden serious look in his eyes. "Tasha," he said in a low voice, "I can't believe it's you. I can't believe you're here." He pushed the unruly shank of hair off his forehead. The familiar gesture made her heart ache for the old days, but she quickly turned off the feeling as J. B. continued to speak. "Two weeks ago I opened the paper and saw an advertisement for *Carmen*. And there was your name in big flowery letters. I couldn't believe my eyes! And I knew it had to be you, because there could only be one Tasharyana Higazi."

"I'm amazed you remember my name at all." Her remark had the calculated effect of dampening his enthusiasm. She knew if he weren't so warm, she would have less trouble resisting him.

"What do you mean?" He sat back and his glance turned cool. "How could I ever forget it?"

"Easily. For the past eight years you've put me out of your mind altogether."

He leaned forward to protest just as the waiter appeared at the table. Tasharyana watched the server's movements so she wouldn't have to look at the stormy expression in J. B.'s eyes. Unaware he had interrupted an important conversation, the waiter carefully put down coasters and then placed the drinks on top of them, precisely in the center, taking all the time in the world.

"Will that be all, sir?" he asked.

"Yes, for now, thank you." J. B. reached for his scotch.

Tasharyana lifted her glass of milk and took a sip, but she had suddenly lost her thirst and her enjoyment of J. B.'s presence. The sooner she excused herself and got on with her travel plans, the better.

J. B. put down his drink and shot her a hard look. "Pardon me, Tasha, but it was you who put me out of your mind. You were hurt that I didn't take you away from your school that day, weren't you? But what did you expect me to do?"

"Nothing. I didn't expect you to do anything. Not then and not now!"

"So you punished me."

"Punished you?" She rose to her feet, unmindful of the other patrons glancing her way.

"Just as you are punishing me now with this cold prima donna act."

"I beg your pardon, Julian Spencer, but this is no act." She pointed to her sequined chest. "This is what I am today, no more and no less. And with no thanks to you!"

She swept away from the table as J. B. fumbled for money to pay for the drinks. Furious, she hurried through the bar, fighting back tears of frustration, unmindful of what she would do or where she would go, only that she had to get away from J. B. During the last few minutes with him, she was being just as histrionic as Madame Hepera made her out to be, and she felt desperately out of control. If only she had some of Madame Hepera's quieting tea.

"Tasha!" J. B. called after her. She didn't look back and continued to walk briskly toward the front of the hotel. As she passed the bank of elevators, however, she caught sight of two women, the young blond and the older woman from the opera house, who were strolling toward her.

"Tasha!" J. B. caught up with her and grabbed her arm, unaware of his acquaintances approaching. "Don't walk away like this!"

"J. B.—"

"There must have been a misunderstanding!"

"I must go!" Tasharyana tried to extricate herself as the other two women came up from behind.

"Really, Julian!" the older woman remarked in a severe voice. "Does your little friend cause scenes wherever she goes?"

Shocked, J. B. jerked around.

"Julian, dear," the blond woman crooned, taking his arm, "we didn't know where you'd gone. Why did you run off like that?"

"Sorry, Christine." Julian frowned. "I had no time to explain."

"If I didn't know better, I'd have thought you abandoned us."

"Sorry."

"Lucky for us Mother had cab fare."

"Yes. But I'll have you know, Julian, that I don't appreciate being abandoned like that." The older woman sniffed. "Ladies shouldn't be hailing taxis in the middle of the night. There's no telling what kind of hoodlums might be out!"

"Oh, for goodness' sakes, Frances!" J. B. shook his head.

Tasharyana watched them, and for an instant felt sorry for J. B.

Christine looked at her dainty watch with the safety chain dangling. "If we hurry, we can still make our dinner reservation."

"I don't know if I can—" J. B. glanced at Tasharyana and then back to the blond woman.

"Why not?" Frances demanded. "Don't tell me you dragged us all the way down here to see that opera and now you won't take us to dinner?"

"I don't mean to be rude, Frances," J. B. said, his eyes stormy, "but something has come up."

"That something doesn't happen to be your little friend, does it?"

"My friend has a name, Frances—Tasharyana Higazi."

Frances smiled coldly and nodded her way in a stiff and unfriendly manner.

"Miss Higazi." Christine smiled, obviously struggling to make peace between her mother and J. B. "Why don't you join us for dinner? We would be honored."

"Thank you, but no."

"Please? J. B. says you're an old friend of his from Egypt. I'd like to hear about your childhood together."

"Really, no. I'm not dressed appropriately. And I must be going. Good-bye."

Without glancing back, Tasharyana turned toward the front lobby. Perhaps the concierge could help her sell a diamond, even at this late hour. Otherwise she wouldn't have enough funds to go very far. She headed for the front desk, hoping J. B. wouldn't follow.

Much to Tasharyana's dismay, she heard J. B. come up behind her just as she had caught the concierge's attention. The middle-aged man was balding and slightly overweight but his blue eyes sparkled with friendliness and intelligence.

"Yes?" he asked.

J. B. stepped up to the counter. "Would it be possible to have the women's dress shop opened, just for a few minutes? It's rather an emergency."

The concierge glanced at Tasharyana and then back to J. B. "For you, Mr. Spencer, of course. Just a moment, while I get the key."

As soon as the man disappeared into an inner office and was out of earshot, Tasharyana whirled to accost J. B. "What do you think you're doing?" she demanded.

"Allow me to buy you a dress so that you can have dinner with me."

"J. B., I don't have time to have dinner with you!"

"Why? What is so threatening about that Madame Hepera person?"

"Plenty." Tasharyana crossed her arms over her sequined dress, trying to control her anxiety and her anger with J. B. for not recognizing the danger she was in. "I have to get out of Washington, J. B. I can't be wasting time chatting over chateaubriand with you and your lady friends."

"Yes, you can, Tasha. Just look at it this way. If you were escaping, you'd head for the nearest airport or train station, wouldn't you?"

"Yes. And if not for you thwarting my plans, I'd be there right now!"

"Don't you think Madame Hepera would have sent someone to look for you at all those places? They're probably waiting for you to show up. Why not stay here and confuse them?"

Tasharyana stared at him, considering his logic, while the concierge returned to the front desk with an older woman.

He smiled and handed the keys to his companion, a graying woman in a smartly tailored suit. "Margaret will be happy to assist you in any way she can."

"Thank you," J. B. replied.

"Right this way, Mr. Spencer," Margaret said, motioning for Tasharyana to follow her. "Miss—?"

J. B. raised an eyebrow and looked down at Tasharyana, his mouth lifted into a provocative boyish smile.

She realized she wasn't going to get out of the shopping excursion. "Higazi," she replied in a flat tone.

"Well, Miss Higazi, let's see what we can do for you." The clerk swept down the hall with Tasharyana and J. B. in tow.

Tasharyana was determined to end this evening as soon as she could. She hoped the store was short on stock. If she weren't able to find a dress in her size or one that would match her black shoes, then she might get out of the hotel without too much delay or too much interference from J. B.

With a majestic sweep of her hand, the clerk pulled open the door, flipped on the lights, and ushered them inside.

She turned to Tasharyana. "Now, what is it you are looking for exactly, dear?"

"A cocktail dress," J. B. put in.

"Oh, we have some gorgeous cocktail dresses," Margaret replied, turning both palms outward as she looked around the shop. "What color are you looking for?"

"Black." Tasharyana glanced around the subtly lit room. Most of the dresses had about as many sequins as the dress she was already wearing. She looked back to find J. B. surveying her.

"And what size, dear?" Margaret continued distantly.

"Let's see," J. B. mused in a soft tone, meant only for Tasharyana. "I'd say you were about a size six."

She was surprised at his accurate guess. "Six or eight, depending upon the label," she declared to the clerk.

"Black, size six or eight. I'll see what we have." Margaret minced away, intent on her search.

"Something black," J. B. repeated, stepping close enough so the warmth of his words tickled the back of her ear. "Nothing flashy. Tasteful but not too conservative."

"No fringe," she put in drolly, her anger giving way to amusement at seeing J. B. so interested in buying the right outfit for her. Even more amazing was the fact that he seemed to know just what type of clothing appealed to her, though he hadn't seen her for years and only then in some type of uniform or costume not of her own choosing.

She flipped through a few dresses hanging on a rack near her elbow, finding it hard to concentrate when all she could think about was Madame Hepera's threat to make her life a living hell. Wasting precious hours in Washington would be a dangerous use of her time. Unmindful of Tasharyana's fear, J. B. strolled away, searching through the displays. She hoped he wouldn't find anything suitable, for she really didn't want him spending money on her for a dinner she would be leaving as soon as possible.

"How about this one?" Margaret asked, holding up a short little dress with fringe at the bustline. Obviously she hadn't heard Tasharyana's droll aside to J. B.

"I'm afraid not," Tasha answered. "Something plainer, perhaps?"

"All right." Margaret replaced the dress on the rack.

"How about these?" J. B. ambled over the plush mauve carpeting toward her, holding up three items.

Margaret looked up. "Very nice selections, Mr. Spencer." She held each of the dresses up for inspection. "You have excellent taste, I must say." Then she turned to Tasharyana. "Why don't you slip into a dressing room, dear, and try them on?"

"All right."

Margaret paraded the dresses to the fitting room, hung them on a hook in the spacious changing room, and left Tasharyana alone.

Quickly Tasharyana disrobed, hoping the Petries weren't growing too impatient with J. B.'s absence.

The first two dresses were the wrong size. But the third, a sleeveless style with a cowl neckline that draped gracefully from her shoulders, fit her as if she had been the model for the designer. The hem broke just above her knee and tucked with the exact amount of snugness around her slender waist.

"Well?" J. B. inquired, looking her way from the jewelry counter.

"This one isn't too bad," she replied, glancing at the mirror again.

"Let's see."

He ventured closer as she opened the louvered door and stepped outside. J. B. didn't say a word and she looked up at him, suddenly self-conscious, to find him gazing at her with an appreciative gleam in his eye.

"Turn around," he murmured.

Again he was silent as he inspected the dress.

"Well?" she said.

"You look like a million."

She flushed.

Margaret appeared at J. B.'s elbow. "Oh, yes, Miss Higazi. That's gorgeous on you! Simply gorgeous!"

"It needs something, don't you think? It's plain."

"Earrings." J. B. grabbed her hand and towed her toward the counter where the till sat guarding the costume jewelry. She let him pull her, infected by his enthusiasm. Margaret slipped behind the counter and turned on the display case light.

"How about those?" he exclaimed, pointing to a pair of glass earrings in a gold setting. They were large enough to set off the dress without being gaudy. "What do you think?"

"I like them," Tasharyana replied.

Margaret slid open the door at the back of the case. "Let's see what they look like with the dress."

She unfastened the earrings from their card and put them on the counter. Before Tasharyana could pick them up, J. B. scooped them into his hand. Then he leaned closer. Tasharyana stood before him and battled the effect his nearness had on her as he carefully slipped the post through her earlobe. Their mouths were much too close for comfort, and all she could think about was what it might feel like to kiss him. She lowered her eyes, hoping he wouldn't take long, yet wanting him to stand there forever, doting on her. The cuff of his jacket grazed her cheek as he put the back on the post and then reached for the other earring. When he was finished, he lightly brushed back the hair at her temples and framed her head with his hands.

"How do they look?" she asked, hardly able to meet his gaze.

"You're up to two million now, my dear. At least." His hands slipped away. "Take a look."

He stepped back to allow her to turn and glance in the oval mirror on the counter. But she was too conscious of the reflection of his face beside hers to take much notice of the brilliant earrings. How handsome and alive he looked with that happy smile dancing in his eyes and his glossy black hair glinting in the low light.

"Another excellent choice." Margaret beamed.

At that moment, Tasharyana was so unaware of the other woman, her voice seemed to come from miles away. All she was conscious of was J. B.

"We'll take them," his voice boomed behind her.

"How much will all this cost?" she asked.

"Don't worry about it." He stroked the tops of her arms and then stepped away. "Do you have something I can cut off the tags with, Margaret? Miss Higazi's going to wear the outfit out of the shop."

"Certainly, sir."

She handed him a pair of scissors from a shelf near the till. He cut off the price tag and pulled out the connecting loop of string. Tasharyana stood without moving a muscle, overcome by the intimacies they were sharing. Until this moment she never would have guessed how wonderful it felt to be taken care of by a man like this.

"Why don't you run back and get your things while we find a clutch to go with your dress?"

"J. B.—"

"You need one. Go on now."

Though she protested the purchase of a purse, she was grateful to have a safe place to put her diamonds, for the black sheath had no pockets.

After Margaret rang up the bill and J. B. paid for everything, he ushered Tasharyana out to the hall, her costume folded in a large bag with handles and her diamonds safely tucked inside the purse. Tasharyana excused herself, saying she'd like to go to the rest room to remove some of the stage makeup. J. B. took the bag with the costume and agreed to meet her near the elevators.

In the bathroom, Tasharyana couldn't help admiring herself in the mirror. Madame Hepera had never allowed her to buy a dress this fashionable or this revealing. Most of her dresses, though well-made and elegant, had been knee length or longer and covered her shoulders, in keeping with the modest fashions of Egyptian women. Though this dress was not at all suggestive, it was the loveliest, most stylish outfit she had ever worn.

Quickly, she dabbed at her makeup, taking most of the foundation off and removing the heavy black eyeliner. Her lips, though naturally ruby colored, would have looked better with a coat of lipstick, but she didn't have any. She rearranged her hair, using the combs from her costume to hold up most of her ebony tresses, and letting a few curls dangle at her hairline. Did she really look like a million to J. B.? She hoped so. She wanted to look her best for him, wanted him to be proud of being seen with her. Though many men had told her she was beautiful, her looks had never been important to her. Until now. She gave her reflection a final glance and then left the rest room.

J. B. watched her walk toward him, unabashedly staring at her as she approached. She should have felt nervous being watched like that, but she knew the dress fit her well, and by the look on J. B.'s face, he thought so, too, which gave her the confidence to smile and stare right back. The diminishing space between them crackled with the same magnetism that drew their eyes to each other.

"Ma'am," he greeted, offering his arm. "I am your slave."

"And I, sir," she replied, slipping her hand around his elbow, "am in your debt."

"Which you can repay by allowing me your company at dinner."

"Hardly a sensible transaction," she countered, laughing softly as they walked together, as easily and naturally as if they had walked arm in arm for years.

He headed for the restaurant in the east wing of the hotel. "You don't think it makes perfect sense for me to shower you with tokens of my affection?"

"Not from a financial standpoint. I already owe you far too much!"

"Finances have nothing to do with it. Some of the best things in life have no monetary value, my dear." He patted the back of her hand and grinned at her.

She felt his smile caress her. At his smile, their steps slowed and they stared at each other, their shoulders touching and their arms linked.

"Tasha," J. B. said in a low voice, "let's not go to the Dahlia Room. Let's go somewhere else, where we can talk."

"We can't do that."

"Why not? I'll just tell them I got waylaid."

"J. B., it wouldn't be right."

"But once we're with them, it won't be the same. I don't want to share you with them, not tonight."

"They're waiting for us."

"And once we get there, you'll find it won't matter if we're really there or not. You don't know Frances and Christine. They can talk all night about the most inconsequential things."

"But you promised to have dinner with them, didn't you?"

"Yes." He scowled. "I should learn better than to make promises I don't want to keep, shouldn't I?" Then his expression brightened. "But you must promise to have dinner with me alone—soon."

"Soon." She watched as a smile played at the corners of his mouth.

"I'm going to hold you to that promise, Tasha."

"It's one I would like to keep," she said, although she wondered when and if she and J. B. would find any time to spend together.

"Well, I guess there's no putting if off any longer." He grimaced dramatically. "Are you ready to face the dour dowager of Baltimore?"

"As in Frances Petrie?" She arched an eyebrow.

"None other." He offered his arm.

She slipped both hands around his elbow and leaned into his shoulder. "Compared to Madame

Hepera, dealing with your dour dowager will be a—how do you say it?—a piece of cake."

"I wouldn't count on it."

As J. B. pushed in her chair, Tasharyana looked up to find both Frances and Christine inspecting her. But as soon as Christine was caught staring, She looked away and reached for her drink, a frothy green concoction in a fancy glass.

Tasharyana had to admit that Christine Petrie was attractive in a general way, much like the platinum-haired actresses in American films of the fifties. Her face was symmetrical with no one feature too large or two small, which, while pretty, was not distinctive. She had fine blue eyes, but the black dress she wore turned the blue to gray, downplaying her best feature. And though Christine appeared even-tempered and kind, there was a certain lack of spirit in her speech. Perhaps her lack of spirit was the result of living with her censuring, critical mother. Regardless of the source of Christine's bland nature, Tasharyana knew she would not be able to put up with her blandness for very long, and wondered why J. B. had chosen such a companion.

Frances, however, had continued to stare at Tasharyana and J. B., her head thrown back at an imperious angle.

"There you are, Julian," Frances exclaimed. "We were about to send security to look for you."

"We were just down the hall, trying on dresses. Well, not me specifically," he added with a wink, as if hoping to diffuse Frances's anger. "Just Tasha."

Frances sniffed and raised her water glass to her pinched mouth.

"Your dress is lovely," Christine commented in a voice well modulated to show neither admiration nor condescension. Tasharyana wondered if Christine ever slipped and spoke a heartfelt word without first filtering it through her good breeding.

"Thank you," Tasharyana replied, deciding not to tell her who had made the selection.

J. B. sat down opposite Tasharyana, and Christine immediately reached out and draped her fingers over his wrist as if to mark him as her possession. The gesture was not lost on Tasharyana. She hoped she could cling to her good manners enough to disguise her jealousy.

Frances fingered her water glass. "I hope you don't intend to spend any more of your precious time on shopping sprees."

"What do you mean?" J. B. asked.

"You realize how busy the upcoming week will be for all of us, Julian, what with your engagement party scheduled for Friday evening."

Engagement party? J. B. was going to marry Christine? She should have guessed. Only serious couples traveled in the company of a future mother-in-law. Tasharyana hid her surprise by picking up her napkin and spreading it on her lap while a blush flooded her cheeks. She hoped the dim light would hide her reaction.

"Engagement party?" Tasharyana's head came up. J. B. repeated, surprised himself. "Now wait a minute—"

"We thought it best to announce your plans while Aunt Helena was still in the country. She'll be thrilled."

J. B. shot a glance at Christine. "This Friday?"

"Don't you remember, Julian? I told you all about it a few months ago."

"This Friday?" he repeated. "I don't remember anything about this Friday."

"Men!" Disgusted, Frances waved him off. "You always listen with one ear. Then you wonder why you never know what's going on. And I'm telling you, Julian Spencer, you're the worst at letting important plans go in one ear and out the other."

"There's more to life than cotillions and soirees, Frances."

"Well, there's nothing more important than an engagement party, I'll have you know, except for the wedding itself. And I would have thought you'd have the decency to recognize the significance of the date, Julian."

J. B. sat back and for an instant his stormy glance met Tasharyana's questioning one.

She wondered what he would do about the engagement party. Obviously he was surprised and upset about the plans for an announcement of his upcoming marriage. Was he not ready to commit to Christine? Tasharyana longed to know the answer to that question. Just then, however, the waiter arrived to take their order, temporarily halting the discussion.

Surely Frances Petrie wanted only the bluest-blooded man for her daughter. Was she aware of J. B.'s heritage? Tasharyana studied J. B. as he perused the menu. His blood was a mixture of Egyptian and English, bestowing upon him an unusually attractive combination of physical characteristics. His father had been an attorney turned foreign agent who was assigned to North Africa before and during World War II. It was there he met Menmet Bedrani, an Egyptian beauty, whom he had loved from the moment he saw her. They had only five years together before J. B.'s father was killed by Nazis during the desert campaigns. Menmet had never married again and had raised her son to be the image of his father in both appearance and character.

The mark of his Egyptian blood wasn't obvious. J. B. could pass for a black Irish with his dark glossy hair, not nearly as wavy as the hair of most Egyptians, and his lean, taller-than-average height. His English accent, picked up from tutors and his years abroad, belied his North African roots, and his education marked him as a man of the world, not the resident of any particular country. Perhaps Frances was less discriminating in the case of an attractive and successful man, and J. B. certainly belonged in that category.

While the waiter took their orders, Tasharyana let her gaze drop to the surface of the table where J. B.'s hand rested beneath Christine's graceful fingers. Whenever he moved slightly or changed positions, she made a point to reestablish physical contact with him. What Christine may have considered romantic closeness with J. B. seemed to Tasharyana like an unhealthy attachment, much like a child with a security blanket. Didn't J. B. feel the suffocating effects of such attachment or did he actually enjoy it? She couldn't imagine anyone wanting to be constantly clung to in that way.

"You aren't angry, are you, Julian?" Christine asked, her voice wavering.

"No," he answered immediately, but to Tasharyana's ears, his curt tone was at odds with his reply. "I just don't like surprises, that's all."

"You haven't even got a ring for Christine," Frances put in. "Have you?"

"No. I haven't."

Christine smiled tremulously. "We can get a ring tomorrow, Julian. In fact, Mother said she'd be happy to wait if you'd like to go to a few jewelers' tomorrow and pick something out. I have a few styles in mind already, so it shouldn't take more than a few hours."

"Really?" J. B. lifted the corners of his mouth, in what some people might have interpreted as a smile but Tasharyana recognized as a grimace. She remained silent, wishing as much as he obviously did that the engagement subject had not come up.

"Don't you rush finding a ring," Frances advised, dabbing her lips with her napkin. "You'll be wearing the ring your entire life. I can't tell you how important it is to make the right choice. A ring says so much about a person, so much."

Tasharyana looked down at her hands, which were bereft of rings, the result of being repulsed by the pudgy beringed hands of Madame Hepera. Tasharyana never wore rings and rarely donned any other jewelry, either. She wondered what bare fingers revealed about her character.

"I won't rush it, Mother. But I really like the one my friend Sue just received from Mark—that marquise cut, you know. I think that's what I'd like."

"Just don't rush on my account, Christine. And don't worry about me waiting around in the hotel. It's supposed to be a special time with your fiancé and I want you to enjoy it."

"Thanks, Mother." Christine smiled and squeezed J. B.'s forearm. He looked down at her, his mouth a flat terse line.

"I don't want to disappoint anyone here," he began, "or upset your plans, Christine, but I promised to help Tasha get settled tomorrow."

Tasharyana glanced up in surprise. He was using her as an excuse? For what purpose? Marriage to Christine seemed inevitable. He couldn't put off buying a ring forever.

"Didn't I, Tasha?"

All eyes turned to her. Tasharyana glanced at J. B.

and saw a dark look of angry frustration in his face. Even though he had got himself in this predicament and should extricate himself without telling fibs, she couldn't turn her back on him. He'd helped her. She'd return the favor by playing along. "Yes, J. B. graciously offered to help me get to Philadelphia."

"Philadelphia!" Frances retorted. "But Friday is only three days away, Julian."

"I am well aware of that, Frances."

"You simply can't be traipsing about between Philadelphia and Baltimore this week! There is too much to do!"

"You only need me to show up at the party, right?" he countered. "You always tell me I just get underfoot during these things."

"You never get underfoot, Julian," Christine put in. "You're always so busy with your experiments and things, I wish you *would* get underfoot sometimes, just so I know what it's like to have you around."

Frances leaned forward. "Helping your opera singer friend will only make you busier, Julian. And you really can't spare the time."

"How I choose to spend my time is my concern, Frances."

She ignored his reply. "Allow me to help. I have a secretary who can take care of everything Miss Higazi needs to have done. He's very efficient."

"Frances, your secretary is an idiot. I wouldn't trust him to find me a candy bar on Halloween."

"Julian!" Christine gasped, pulling her hand away.

Tasharyana hid a smile behind her napkin.

The waiter appeared again, setting fragrant plates of food before them. But soon after the waiter left the table, J. B. stood up.

"Excuse me. I regret that I've lost my appetite."

Christine stared up at him in alarm, holding her drink in midair. Frances narrowed her eyes and surveyed him, her back ramrod straight.

"I am sorry to have spoken harshly to you, Frances." He raised his chin. "I will see to the bill. Enjoy your dinner, Christine."

"Julian!" Christine blubbered, losing her poise. "You can't leave. Where are you going?"

"To get a room reservation for Tasha and then I'm turning in. I'll see you in the morning." He leaned down and gave her a perfunctory kiss on the forehead.

Tasharyana watched him, clutching her napkin. J. B. wouldn't dare leave her in the company of these two women, would he? Yet what if he walked away without a backward glance? How could she excuse herself and follow him and not make Christine insanely jealous?

"You're not angry, are you?" Christine inquired again, clutching his forearm.

"He's just suffering last-minute jitters," Frances put in, "aren't you, Julian?"

"Something like that." He straightened. "Tasha, when you finish your dinner, just ask the front desk about your room arrangement."

She rose, mustering a regal pose and glad for her stage training. "I'm not really hungry, either. There's been far too much excitement for me this evening."

Frances smiled archly. "Then take care, Miss Higazi. Being escorted to your room by a man like Julian might prove far too exciting for a girl of your delicate sensibilities."

"Mother!" Christine gasped anew.

Tasharyana refused to be intimidated by the stiff old woman and decided not to comment on Frances's remark. Carefully she set her napkin beside her plate. "Good night, ladies."

Grandly she swept away from the table, hoping Frances Petrie would choke on every suspicious thought she harbored regarding J. B. and herself. J. B. waited for her and they walked out of the restaurant.

As they passed into the hall, Tasharyana noticed a small thin man rise from his chair and walk out behind them. Ordinarily she wouldn't have paid any attention, but the man's rumpled tweed coat looked oddly out of place in the fine dining establishment. She was surprised they had let the man in since he wasn't wearing a tie.

J. B. took her elbow. "Nice dinner, eh?"

"I'll say."

"I warned you."

"But what about this engagement party. Didn't you know about it?"

"It was mentioned quite a while ago. And to tell you the truth, I'd put it out of my head. But let's not talk about that, if you don't mind. Let's get you settled instead."

"You don't have to help me," Tasharyana said. "I can take care of myself."

"I'm sure you can." He glanced down at her. "But we haven't had a chance to really talk yet."

"I thought you said you were tired."

"I am. But not enough to give up talking with you." He smiled and took a step toward the front desk. "Come on. We'll get the paperwork out of the way, and then maybe you'll let me buy you another glass of milk."

"J. B., wait." She pulled back. "I think we're being followed."

"Being followed? By whom?"

She lowered her voice. "See that man in the tweed coat? The one standing by the column behind us?"

"Yes."

"He got up when we left the restaurant. And now he's lingering there, watching us."

"Maybe he likes looking at beautiful women."

"J. B., I'm serious!"

He urged her forward. "It's probably just a coincidence. He's probably waiting for a cab or something."

"I don't know. I don't like it."

"You think he's working for your Madame Hepera?"

"He could be."

"How could she have found you so quickly?"

"Maybe someone followed us from the opera house."

"Old Madame Hepera isn't going to get you, not

while I'm around." He squeezed her elbow gently. "Come on, let's get your reservation made."

She paused. "There is one more thing."

"What?" J. B.'s hand slid away from her.

"I don't have enough money for a room in a hotel like this."

"I noticed you didn't have a purse."

"A purse would have aroused suspicion. But having one wouldn't do me much good anyway, because I rarely have cash."

"Spent your entire paycheck on red and black sequins, did you?"

"No, I never buy anything. I don't make much money."

"Don't they pay you?"

"A little. I try to save it."

"Haven't you been working steadily?"

"Yes, but I don't earn much salary because most of my needs are already provided for."

"What kind of arrangement is that?" He stared at her.

"A strange one, I'll admit, but it's the only one I've had for years. At first I was so young, I didn't have a choice. Then Madame Hepera offered to provide private tutors and my room and board, as long I kept up with my music. I couldn't pass up such an opportunity."

"But why would she do it?"

"I guess because of my voice."

"Your voice?" J. B. frowned in disbelief. "Don't get me wrong, Tasha, your voice is marvelous. But usually people don't make grand gestures for nothing. What does she want in return?"

"I don't know, J. B." Tasharyana shook her head, worried. "And that's what concerns me."

"Is she independently wealthy?"

"She appears to be. But she has prohibited my independence and my freedom. I can't make a move without her, literally."

"That's ridiculous, Tasha! You're twenty-four years old!"

"Why do you think I ran away from the theater tonight? I have no life to call my own. And this is all I had to take with me." She slipped her hand in the purse and drew out the black velvet bag. Carefully she eased the little packages containing the gems onto her palm so they wouldn't drop to the floor. "These diamonds."

"You don't happen to have a marquise cut in one of those bags, do you?" J. B. joked. "It might make my life a whole lot simpler."

Tasharyana grimaced at his dark humor and then observed him as he inspected the gems. She was highly aware of the golden tone of his hands, so similar in coloring to her own, and the close proximity of his body. She could smell the clean scent of his black hair and the fragrance of his after-shave, both a familiar heady perfume. She longed to hold him close and burrow her nose into his silky hair, to take in deep draughts of his scent and taste his skin and his lips again.

J. B. straightened. "These rocks should provide you with a decent nest egg. Where'd you get them?"

"I've saved everything I've earned for the last three years to buy them."

He glanced at her in approval. "Well, put them away for now. I'll help you get a good price for them later. As for tonight, we'll put your room on my bill."

"You've done too much for me already, J. B."

"It's no problem. Think of it as a loan. When you sell your diamonds, you can pay me back if you wish."

She looked into his eyes and saw they were full of sincerity.

"Okay, Tasharyana?" He tilted his head. "It's really no problem."

"All right. Thank you." Greatly relieved, she walked with him to the front desk and registered for a room near the Petries on the fourteenth floor. As they turned around to head for the lounge, Tasharyana stiffened.

"What is it?" J. B. inquired, still highly attuned to her body language, just as he had been when they were children.

"That man." Tasharyana nodded to a column where a small man had just turned around to walk the other way, in the direction of the elevators.

"The one in the tweed jacket?"

"Yes. See him?" She clutched J. B.'s arm. "He followed us to the front desk."

J. B. gave the man another glance as he ushered Tasharyana toward the lounge. "He isn't following us now."

"How do you know? He could just be pretending to wait for the elevator."

J. B. shrugged. "He's probably just staying here. And the restaurant is a popular one. It could be simple coincidence, Tasha."

"He doesn't look like the type of person to stay here," she mused, walking through the doorway of the crowded lounge. "I don't like it."

"I think it's highly unlikely someone would have tailed you from the opera house." He pulled out her chair.

She sat down, slightly put off by his incredulity. "You don't know Madame Hepera," she commented. "She might have had me followed the entire time I've been in the U.S."

Almost immediately after they sat down, a waiter appeared at their table.

J. B. looked up at him, a different server than before. "A small milk and a Scotch on the rocks, if you please."

"Thank you, sir."

The waiter turned and disappeared. Tasharyana glanced around the lounge, which was full of patrons laughing and talking. She was in a much calmer state of mind this time, having a room to go to, some food in her belly, and attired in a properly fashionable outfit.

J. B. unbuttoned his black suit jacket. "Promise me you won't run off this time, Tasha."

"I can make no promises, J. B."

"Well at least stay long enough to finish your milk."

"Then don't insult me this time."

"I'm sorry about calling you a cold prima donna. But you must admit that you've been acting pretty chilly to someone who's supposed to be an old friend."

"Old friends keep in touch, J. B."

"It isn't as if I didn't try."

"Really?" She swept a cool glance across his figure, certain that he had to be lying. He hadn't tried very hard at all. Maybe he had thought about writing and about her, but that wasn't enough to redeem him in her eyes. "I beg to differ."

"You were the one who couldn't be bothered to write to me."

"I wrote to you, J. B.!"

The waiter returned to the table and slid the drinks in front of them and J. B. paid him, anxious for the man to leave them alone.

"You wrote to me?" he repeated, incredulous.

"Yes! But since I didn't have the correct address, you must not have received them. I spent a whole year of writing disgusting heartsick letters to a boy who didn't care enough to respond."

"What do you mean, I didn't respond?" J. B. pushed back the strand of hair that had fallen over his forehead. "I wrote to you every week, sometimes twice a week."

She glared at him, still not believing him.

"My letters never came back to England," he went on, "so I assumed you had received them."

"No. I received nothing."

He sat back in his chair. "And I can see you are sitting there and not believing a single word I'm saying."

"I don't believe in anything anymore, J. B. Only in my music."

She gave him a frosty look to hide her broken heart and then stared down at her tumbler of milk, where the little beads of moisture that clung to the side of the glass reminded her of the tears she had kept inside for years upon end.

J. B. leaned forward. "Don't you think it's possible that Madame Emide kept my letters from you? Or if Madame Emide did forward my letters, then quite possibly Madame Hepera intercepted them?"

"Why would she do that?"

"Because she wanted to keep us apart."

Tasharyana slipped her fingers around the cold glass, but she was too upset to drink. "It didn't occur to me that she might withhold your letters."

"And after months of getting no response, Tasha, I quit writing. I thought you were angry with me for leaving you at that school and had decided to break it off with me."

"I would never retaliate in that way, not to you, J. B."

"How could I have known? When you didn't write back, what was I to think?"

"That something had gone wrong—something I couldn't fix?"

"But in any case, it had to have been my fault?"

She glanced up, confused.

"Did you give me the benefit of the doubt, Tasha?" He reached out and enclosed her wrist with his hand. "Did you ever once consider something had happened to my letters, something that had nothing to do with the way we felt about each other?"

"No." She stared at him as self-doubt of such intensity swept over her that she felt sick to her stomach. Could she have spent eight years resenting J. B. for circumstances over which he had no control?

"So all these years you believed I went off to England and never looked back, never even thought of you?"

"What else was I to believe?"

"You could have believed in me." He squeezed her hand and she looked down, nearly overwhelmed by tears at his gentle gesture. "As you still can."

She glanced up at him. "You never wrote. You never came back to see if I was still in Luxor."

"I had no money to travel. And my mother moved to London while I was at university."

"She did?"

"Yes, so we could be close to each other."

"Where is she now?"

"Back in Luxor." His words faded as he gazed at her, his warm hand still on her wrist. She gazed back, trying to work her way through the conflicting emotions caused by his revelation. It wasn't an easy task to regain her definition of J. B. Spencer and men in general, not after the years of blame, heartache, and recrimination.

"Tasha," he said softly, "did the words inside the music box mean nothing to you?"

"I wanted them to mean something."

"But they didn't?"

"After a few years of silence went by, I decided we had been too young and foolish to make promises to each other."

"Do you still feel that way?"

She blinked, wondering what he was asking and uncomfortable with speaking about her innermost feelings. She had spent most of her life concealing her thoughts from everyone and relying solely upon herself. Such habits were hard to break. Besides, revealing her old feelings for J. B. would do nothing but complicate their lives, since she had her career to worry about and he had Christine. And her feelings for J. B. were just that, old ones, memories of puppy love and childhood friendship—all better left in the past.

"Do you think we were too young to know what true love was?" J. B. repeated.

She leveled her gaze at him, commanding her eyes to remain dry and unwavering. "Yes. We were children."

"But seeing you now, talking to you, Tasha, it's as if we had never been apart, as if the years dividing us have fallen away."

His words echoed the feelings in her heart. It was true. She felt the same familiarity with J. B., the same easy manner with him that let her words pour out and her heart open to him, just as it had been so long ago. She had always thought they shared one mind, one heart, and one day would share one life. But that was long ago, and life had come between her childhood dreams and adult reality.

He squeezed her wrist again. "Don't you feel it, that sense of enduring friendship?"

"No," she said softly and slipped her hand from his

gentle grip. "I don't, J. B. It's been too long, too many years."

He retracted his hand and took a drink, obviously surprised by her answer. "Have I changed that much, Tasha?"

"We have both changed." She raised the glass of milk to her lips and took a sip to steady her nerves. "And our paths are no longer as simple or as easy to see as they once were."

He sighed, dissatisfied with her general answer. Then Tasharyana lost all thread of their conversation when she saw the man with the tweed jacket drift into the lounge. He carried a folded newspaper and sat down at a table a few feet behind her.

"There he is again," she said, leaning closer to J. B.

"Who?"

"The man in the jacket."

J. B. glanced behind her at the man, frowned slightly, and returned his attention to her face. "What hold does this Madame Hepera have on you that she has to have you followed?"

"I don't know. I've been closely watched for years. Since the school in Luxor."

"Since the time they found you with me that afternoon?"

Tasharyana stared at him and felt a blush creep up her neck to her face. "Yes."

"So they are protecting you from the males of the species?"

"Perhaps."

He smiled wryly. "And just what would Madame Hepera do to you if you were seen in the highly suspicious act of talking with me?"

Tasharyana looked down, nearly unable to speak. He had no idea how insensitive his sarcasm sounded to her. Years ago she had been punished for the mere act of speaking with him, and he was totally unaware of how severe the punishment had been.

"Tasha?"

"I must go." She pushed back her chair. "It grows late."

"Wait a minute!" He reached for her wrist again. "Did I offend you in some way?"

"Not at all."

"It wasn't my intention. Please, sit down, Tasha. Please."

She glanced at him, wanting more than anything to stay and talk but unwilling to submit to questions J. B. would assuredly ask about her past. It was difficult to hide her unease from him or her thoughts, for he had always possessed the uncanny ability to see into her heart.

"We may not have a chance to talk privately again," he added. "At least for a while. So please don't go yet."

"Then we must speak softly. I don't want to be overheard."

"All right." He smiled as she settled back in her seat. "But what we've discussed hasn't exactly been top secret information."

"Still, I don't want anyone to know of my plans, J. B., especially Madame Hepera."

"What are your plans precisely?" he inquired, setting down his empty glass. "What are you going to do?"

"Find another opera company I hope," she replied, relieved that the questions had veered from their relationship to her career. "Find an agent to represent me in America, and become an American citizen. I want to make a new life—far away from Madame Hepera."

"And away from Egypt?"

"It is the only way. I will miss Cairo and the Nile,

but I will never be free of Madame Hepera if I remain in my country."

"But what will you do? Go to New York?"

"Not right away. I have a friend in Philadelphia, a soprano whom I met when we did *Aïda* together in Cairo. One time when I had a few moments alone with her and told her of my intentions to escape, she offered the use of her apartment to me."

"You plan to go to Philadelphia?"

"Yes. Just until I get my bearings."

"Does your friend know you are here?"

"Not yet. I intend to telephone her."

"What if she isn't home? What if she's on tour?"

"I am praying that she is at home. If not, I will stay in a hotel."

"If not, Tasha, you must allow me to help you. I have a town house in Philadelphia that I hardly ever use."

"You reside somewhere else?"

"In Baltimore. I started a law practice there recently and haven't sold my Philadelphia property yet. You're welcome to use it. It's a great little place."

"That's very kind of you, J. B., but—"

"Don't say but. I want to help you. And besides, it would benefit me to have the house lived in for a while. It's asking for trouble to leave a place vacant for weeks on end."

He reached into his jacket pocket and slipped out a slender wallet from which he extracted a business card. "Here's where it is," he said, printing the address in small capital letters. "Right on Elfreth's Alley in the heart of the historic district. You'll love it. There's a key hidden in the pot by the front door."

She took the card and glanced at it. "So you are a lawyer?"

He nodded.

"A lawyer?" She raised one eyebrow. "I always thought you'd become an explorer or a jet pilot—something exciting and dangerous."

"Yes, well." J. B. glanced down. "My father's initial occupation was as a barrister, you know."

"I remember."

"My mother encouraged me to enter into my father's profession. I humored her, though I have never been fascinated with law, simply because the loss of my father was so difficult for her. It was the least I could do to honor his memory."

"You don't sound happy with your life's work."

He scowled. "To tell you the truth, Tasha, I'm not."

"Then why continue?"

"For one thing, because of the years I committed to my education. I can't start over now, not after all the time and money I spent on a law degree."

"You are still young, J. B. You have years ahead of you."

"I know. I've got plans to implement in a few years and a bunch of physics projects I work on in my spare time, which have kept me from seeing Christine on more than one occasion, just as she said."

"But for now you are going to keep up the law practice."

"Yes." He sighed. "I had to take over the late Mr. Petrie's firm when he died of a stroke three years ago."

"Why you?"

"Because." J. B. looked down at the tabletop in an unusual moment of hesitation, and his hand curled around the coaster. "You might say I owed him." Then, as if to drop the subject, he glanced up, a jaunty grin on his face. "And I must admit, there are plenty of opportunities for a young lawyer, especially around here. People seem to think my British accent is the sign of higher intelligence, fools that they are."

"In your case, I wouldn't think they were wrong."

He gazed at her, his eyes dancing again. "Why, thank you." He smiled. "Being introduced to the Petrie's circle of friends hasn't hurt my career either."

"They are well connected?"

"One of the oldest families in Baltimore. I wouldn't doubt but Frances Petrie was personally acquainted with the founding fathers of America."

Tasharyana laughed softly, and realized with a start that the sound seemed foreign to her. Had it been that long since she had chuckled out loud?

"And Christine?" she asked, to get the topic out in the open. She wanted to ask if he was in love with her, and if he envisioned a future with the blond woman, but she simply let the phrase hang on the air, hoping J. B. would provide the information without her putting a label on it.

"Christine is someone I've known for a long time."

"From Eton?"

"In a way. Her brother was my roommate."

"Oh."

"I've spent a lot of time with the Petrie family. They're good people. Frances is rather hard to take at times, but one gets accustomed to her after a while. And Christine, well, there's a lot more about the Petries that needs to be told."

J. B. looked away, as if preoccupied, and Tasharyana wondered in what direction his thoughts drifted—to Christine upstairs in her bed? She had closely held on to him and obviously cared for him. But how did J. B. feel about her? It wasn't her business to pry, however, and she wasn't certain if she wanted to be informed of J. B.'s depth of feeling for another woman. She didn't begrudge J. B. a happy and full life with a woman, but for some reason she couldn't see him with Christine Petrie.

After a long moment, he snapped out of his preoccupied look and glanced back to Tasharyana. "So will you be leaving for Philadelphia tomorrow?"

"Yes. As soon as possible."

"I'd be happy to help you. You'll need to get around the city."

"You don't have to, J. B. You have the Petries to consider."

"I can take them home and come back here in the morning. It's only forty miles or so up to Baltimore. I could be back by noon."

She gazed at him, warmed by his generosity. "All right. I accept your help, J. B. In fact, I don't know what I would have done without you tonight."

He rose. "Good. Let me walk you to your room then, and we'll talk in the morning at breakfast."

She got to her feet. "I don't want to impose on your time with the Petries."

"You mean with Christine and her ring expedition?"

"Well, yes."

"Don't worry about it."

"Besides, I don't have anything to wear to breakfast."

"That dress will do." He glanced down at the simple black sheath.

They walked through the doorway of the lounge and headed toward the elevators. A movement caught Tasharyana's eye, however, and she glanced covertly behind her. The man with the tweed jacket had risen from his seat and was ambling out of the lounge.

"He is following us!" Tasharyana said under her breath as J. B. punched the elevator button. "I'm certain of it now."

The doors opened and they passed into the elevator car. Tasharyana watched J. B. survey the man in the tweed jacket as the elevator doors closed in front of them. She stood against the flat wooden hand rail and was struck by a sudden attack of nerves at being in such close proximity again with J. B.

He turned to the side and slanted a gaze down at her. "Would you rather stay in another hotel?"

Tasharyana sighed. "No, I guess not. Not after all the trouble I've put you through."

"It was no trouble."

Tasharyana glanced at J. B. and suddenly found herself forgetting about the suspicious character already floors below them. All she could see was J. B.'s warm attractive face, the slight laugh lines at the corners of his intelligent eyes, and the tinge of a smile lifting the left side of his mouth. All she could think of was how alone they were in the elevator, and in how small a space they were confined. Her right elbow and hip were acutely aware of the nearness of his body, and when she shifted to face him, she felt an awakening tingle in her breasts, as if her body had suddenly recognized J. B. and longed for the way he had once crushed her to his hard frame.

"Tasha, are you all right? You look pale."

"I'm fine." She gave him a bright smile. "Just tired, that's all."

"It's been a big day for you. And you didn't get to finish your dinner, thanks to me." He leaned against the side wall of the elevator and drank in the sight of her, seemingly unconcerned that he might be considered rude for the way in which his warm gaze traveled slowly over her. She stared back, mostly studying his face with its proud strong features—his sharp straight nose, high cheekbones, and ebony black eyes. She would never tire of looking at him, and knew that no matter how many years passed, his appearance would never cease to please her.

The elevator car dipped to a stop and the doors slid open, breaking the potent silence. J. B. guided her into the corridor with a palm at the small of her back. Quietly they padded down the hall, past an intersecting hallway, and turned a corner.

J. B. reached into his pocket and retrieved the key attached to a metal tag. He opened the door, flipped on the lights, and ushered her inside.

The room was done in gold, with a gold-and-brown pattern on the bed and chairs. Tasharyana ambled into the entry, feeling odd without any belongings to unpack or arrange in the bathroom. For the past two years she and Madame Hepera had spent many nights in hotels much like this. She poked her head into the bathroom while J. B. checked the curtains at the window.

"Well!" he declared as he walked back to the center of the room. "You should be relieved. No men in cheap coats here."

Tasharyana returned his jaunty smile. "Thank you for checking, Inspector."

"My pleasure, ma'am." He gave her a mock salute. "I could stay and stand guard if you would feel safer."

Tasharyana flushed at the thought of spending the night in the company of J. B. "No thanks," she stammered. "I'll be fine." She hoped she didn't sound rude for refusing him.

"I'll be right across the hall if you need anything."

"All right. I appreciate it, J. B."

"I'm here to help, Tasha." He reached for her hands and she didn't resist him. "I like being useful, especially to you."

A shadow passed through his eyes, darkening the usual sparkle there, as he lifted her right hand to his mouth. Touched by his courtly manners, Tasharyana felt a shimmer of delight as he kissed three of her fingertips. She regarded the side of his face, savoring the way he closed his eyes and paused tenderly for a few moments over her hand.

Finally he straightened and his eyes smoldered at her as he stood in front of her, still holding her hands. She knew in that instant she could lift her face to him and he would kiss her. She could take the barest step toward him and he would enfold her in his comforting embrace—like the embrace emblazoned upon her memory when he had held her on the banks of the Nile. But she couldn't move. She couldn't allow herself to indulge in a reawakening of feelings for J. B. One glorious moment in his arms would lead to much more, and she would rather die than have the effects of her "evening surgery" discovered. Besides that, he was to be engaged to another woman in a matter of days. She had no right to kiss him or even think of kissing him. To be safe, she had to keep her distance from him in all ways, even though the slightest space between them felt harsh and wrong.

"Good night, J. B.," she said, her voice choked to a whisper.

He breathed in and gently lowered her hands as he sighed. Was he disappointed to have lost the sweet moment that had hung so tenuously between them? Was pulling back as difficult for him as it was for her?

"Good night." He squeezed her right hand and then quickly turned for the door. Once in the hall, he paused and looked back. "I'll see you in the morning, say around eight thirty?"

"Yes."

Exhausted, Tasharyana quickly undressed to get ready for bed. She splashed water on her face and hung up the beautiful dress. Then she pulled the bag of diamonds out of the purse and stood near the bathroom doorway, wondering where she could hide the gems. They were all she had in the world, and she had no intention of allowing a common thief to slip into her room while she slept and disenfranchise her. She had traveled enough to know not to let valuables lie about in a hotel room.

Where would a thief look for something to steal? Tasharyana bit her lip and scoured the room for a hiding place. Where would a thief not look or not want to look for valuables? The most distasteful place in the hotel room was the toilet. She walked over to the toilet and lifted the tank lid. Inside the tank was plenty enough room to hide the velvet bag. In fact, if she hung it on the inside mechanism of the handle, the diamonds would remain quite dry. To ensure their safety, she grabbed the plastic bag supplied by the hotel for a shoe shine cloth, slipped the velvet pouch inside, carefully draped it over the bar attached to the flushing mechanism, and then replaced the lid.

Satisfied, she padded to the bed and pulled down the covers.

Not long afterward, just as Tasharyana drifted off to sleep, she was jerked out of the gentle hands of slumber by a clicking noise at her door. Heart pounding, she sat up and yanked the sheet over her nakedness. The door swung open, allowing the light of the hall to pour into the room and illuminate the large outline of a familiar figure.

9

Tasharyana's pounding heart sank as Madame Hepera flowed into the room carrying a small satchel. The man in the tweed jacket followed her, stuffing a small case, which Tasharyana guessed held lock-picking tools, into the breast pocket of his sagging coat.

"Get up, young lady!" Madame Hepera ordered, flicking on the lights with a dramatic gesture. The raw glare blinded Tasharyana momentarily, and she blinked, struggling to readjust her vision. Madame Hepera glanced around the room, her chin at an imperious angle. "You are alone?"

"Yes."

"Oh?" Madame Hepera raised one triangular eyebrow. "I find that hard to believe."

"Believe what you like." Tasharyana clutched the sheet more tightly to her chest, aware that the man with the tweed jacket openly ogled her, more lascivious than J.B would ever dream of being. Unsavory characters such as the man in the tweed jacket were the ones she should be shielded from, not J. B.

Madame Hepera pursed her lips and held out a Styrofoam cup with a lid on top. "Here, my dear. I knew you'd be upset. I brought you some tea."

Tasharyana eyed the cup, wondering suddenly if the tea made her malleable and complacent—and easily controlled by Madame Hepera. Since the past few hours when she hadn't drunk any of the brew, she had found her thoughts clearer and her anger sharper. Had the tea blunted her thinking processes? If so, she would have no more of it.

"Come, Tasharyana. You know the tea will do you good."

"No, thank you."

"I'll leave it here in case you change your mind." Madame Hepera frowned slightly and set the cup on the dresser near the television. Then she deposited the bag on the end of the bed. "I have brought you some clothes, Tasharyana. You will dress immediately and return to the hotel at once."

"I am not going back."

"You cannot be serious."

"I've never been more serious in my life."

"How unlike you, Tasharyana, to lose your head. And for nothing. This man is far beneath you."

"He has nothing to do with my decision to leave."

"You don't know what you're saying." Madame Hepera clasped her hands under her huge bosom. "He has you so completely under his control that you have lost your power of reason."

"My reason is just now awakening, Madame Hepera."

The older woman sighed in exasperation and unzipped the satchel. She pulled out a carefully folded cotton shift and shook out the creases. "Mr. Gregg, please wait in the hall. We will be out in a moment."

With a smirk, the man nodded and ducked out of the room while Madame Hepera turned back to Tasharyana. "My dear, listen to me. I have taught you, cared for you, and have seen to your every need for the past eight years. In that time, was I ever cruel to you?"

"No."

"Did I ever mistreat you or lie to you?"

Tasharyana shook her head, well aware of the references Madame Hepera made to the perceived transgressions of Julian Spencer and the real ones of Madame Emide.

"And did I keep my promise to make of your voice all that it could be?"

Tasharyana swallowed, ignoring the fluttering wings of guilt in the back of her throat. "Yes, Madame Hepera."

"And yet once you set eyes upon this man, this nobody from your past, you decided to throw aside everything I have done for you, as if it meant nothing?"

"That isn't the reason!" Tasharyana tossed back her hair with an impatient gesture. "You have taken my life from me, Madame Hepera. My freedom! That's why I ran away."

"Your freedom?" Madame Hepera stepped closer, a huge wall that dominated even the queen-sized bed. "Child, nothing in life is free—least of all the best in life."

"The best?" Tasharyana retorted scornfully.

"Yes, the best." Madame Hepera's eyes blazed. "I have given you the chance to gain immortality, world fame, and a glorious life few will ever know. You have the chance to be a star, to live like a queen." The older woman shifted closer. "Without me you will be nothing—at best a laundress in some rich man's home, perhaps a factory worker or a shop girl. Is that what you want, Tasharyana? The freedom to slave away the years as a faceless clerk?"

"I need to live *my* life, Madame Hepera. I need to be on my own."

"You wouldn't survive. You are a hothouse flower, my girl. You are beautiful and cultured, but extremely fragile. You have known the world only through a veil of protection—my protection."

"I need to find out for myself what the world is like."

"The world out there will tear you down, break your heart, and eat you alive, Tasharyana. I didn't spend all these years molding you for a life in the common world."

"But you have no right to choose these things for me. And it is time I took charge of my own affairs!"

"You, take charge? All you know is opera, Tasharyana. What will you do here in America—sing for your supper on a street corner?"

"I shall find a part in an American production."

"Hah!" Madame Hepera threw the dress upon the coverlet. "I am warning you, my dear, if you do not return to the stage tonight and finish the tour, you will be blacklisted throughout this country—throughout the world, for that matter. You may have the voice of an angel, Tasharyana, but histrionic undependable prima donnas are not in demand these days. In fact, should you not return, I will make it my business to see that you never perform anywhere ever again!"

"It is not that I am ungrateful for all you have done for me, madame."

"Then show it. And consider more than yourself when you do, Tasharyana. Think of the millions of dollars depending upon you, upon the other members of the company. Finish *Carmen* and do the private engagement for the minister of antiquities in Cairo, and I promise you, you will be granted time off. Well-deserved time off. You may go anywhere you like—Paris, Rome, anywhere."

"By myself?"

"Yourself?" Madame Hepera stared at her. "Of course not. By that time you will be recognized everywhere you go. You will have a bodyguard for protection."

"What if I don't want a bodyguard? What if I would like to go alone?"

"Out of the question. Out of the question, my dear. It would be far, far too dangerous."

"Then it won't be the respite I need, Madame Hepera. I need to get away from everything, from everyone. Don't you understand?"

Madame Hepera's dark eyes narrowed beneath her prominent brows. "I understand more than you think. It is the man, Julian Spencer, who drives you to want your freedom. But let me warn you, Tasharyana, a man's hold on a woman is more constricting than you can imagine. With a man you will run blindly into a prison whose walls are thicker than the stones of the pyramids."

"I don't believe you."

"I have lived longer than you, Tasharyana. Far, far longer, and I know what I am talking about. Now please, get dressed. Forget about all this nonsense of running away. You were superb this evening.

Tomorrow night you will be even better. But you must get your rest. And you mustn't strain your voice with all this arguing."

"No."

"No?" Madame Hepera shook her finger at Tasharyana. "Listen, my girl, I won't have any more of this rebelliousness. Either you dress yourself within the next five minutes, or I will have Mr. Gregg pay a visit to your friend across the hall."

"You wouldn't dare hurt Julian!"

"Wouldn't I?" Madame Hepera replied, her eyes glinting. "Are you certain?"

Tasharyana paused, realizing Madame Hepera was fully capable of carrying out such a threat. The last thing she wanted to do was get Julian further embroiled in her affairs. She sighed and swung her legs off the bed.

"All right," she stated in a resigned tone. "I'll do what you ask."

"Good girl." Madame Hepera smiled and watched as Tasharyana wrapped the sheet around her naked body, picked up the shift, and walked to the bathroom. "I knew you'd see reason."

Tasharyana didn't make a comment, though she burned with resentment and rage at the botched escape from Madame Hepera. She should have run out of the opera house and continued to Philadelphia without delay. But she had lingered, wanting to see J. B. and talk with him, and in doing so, she had given the others time to find her.

"Don't languish in there," Madame Hepera advised from the other side of the bathroom door. "It's late."

Tasharyana frowned and reached into the satchel for the rest of her clothes. After dressing in the cotton shift, light jacket, and flats, Tasharyana pulled down her still damp bra and panties, which she had rinsed out, and dropped them in the satchel, along with the black high heels she had worn onstage as Carmen. Then, trying not to make a sound, she lifted the porcelain toilet tank lid and set it on the toilet seat. She picked up the plastic bag, slipped out the velvet pouch, and stuffed it in her jacket pocket, making sure it wouldn't be able to fall out unnoticed.

There had to be some way to escape from Madame Hepera and Mr. Gregg. She couldn't have come this far, only to be forced back into her old life.

Heart heavy and angry, Tasharyana zipped the satchel. Then she bent down to replace the tank lid. The rectangle of porcelain was heavy, heavy enough in fact, to hurt someone. What if she could hit Mr. Gregg over the head with it and knock him unconscious?

Still forming a plan of action, Tasharyana lifted the satchel. It was large enough to hold the tank lid.

"Are you finished in there, my dear?" Madame Hepera called from the other side of the door.

"Almost," Tasharyana replied, grimacing at the sweet inflection she forced into her voice. Over the years she had become a consummate actress, almost as accomplished as her teacher. She flushed the toilet to allow her more time.

Tasharyana unzipped the bag and removed the shoes. Then very carefully, so as not to make a sound, she lifted the heavy porcelain lid and laid it upon the lingerie on the bottom of the bag. On either side of the lid she placed one of the expensive Italian shoes to hold the lid upright, and then she closed the satchel. She lifted it, satisfied with the weight, and gently swung it around to test her theory that the bag could make an effective weapon, if not against a man's head, perhaps against his knees.

Madame Hepera she could outrun. Not so Mr. Gregg. But if she could incapacitate him with a powerful blow to his legs, she might cripple him momentarily to give herself enough time to dash to the stairs. She would run even if he had a gun, for she was certain Madame Hepera would not allow her rising star to be shot at, not only because it would endanger her career, but because the noise would wake up the patrons of the hotel and madame would be discovered trying to strong-arm Tasharyana out of the building.

Her plan depended upon timing, luck, and the courage to strike another human being. Tasharyana opened the bathroom door, praying she would be able to seize the moment if and when it occurred.

Madame Hepera gave a gracious smile, glad to see she had convinced the younger woman to return to her senses.

"What about your dress?" Madame inquired, pointing to the black sheath in the closet. "Don't you want to take it?"

"The dress?" Tasharyana had to think quickly. If she opened the satchel to tuck the dress inside, she would surely reveal the white toilet tank lid. Though she hated to leave the beautiful dress behind, she knew she must. "No, I'm leaving it. It didn't fit well."

"It is quite short, my dear. I'm surprised you chose to wear it."

"Yes. I thought it would be all right, but I felt uncomfortable in it."

Madame Hepera shook her head sagely, as her conservative opinion regarding clothing was affirmed by her student's newfound knowledge. She opened the entry door and held it for Tasharyana to pass through. At the sound, Mr. Gregg jerked up from his slouch against the wall and adjusted the front of his jacket.

"Ready to go?" he asked.

"Yes."

Silently the trio walked down the hall toward the elevators. On the way Tasharyana kept her eyes open for an Exit sign marking the stairs and spied one down the intersecting corridor. Mr. Gregg pressed the button for the elevator and they waited for the car to arrive. Tasharyana stood beside Madame Hepera, her heart thudding in her chest, as she waited for the right moment. When the elevator doors opened, Madame Hepera, accustomed to providing direction, flowed forward. Mr. Gregg hung back, waiting for Tasharyana to enter the car. She paused.

"After you." Mr. Gregg motioned with his hand.

"No!" Tasharyana twisted her torso, caught sight of Madame Hepera's shocked expression, and swung the satchel around the front of her body, throwing her weight behind the bag as it arced toward Mr. Gregg. She let it fly, and with a thump it hit his legs, knocking him to the floor. He cried out in pain as Madame Hepera angrily punched the button to keep the doors open.

Tasharyana dashed in the opposite direction, toward the stairwell and the bright green sign glowing in the dim light ahead.

"Get her!" Madame Hepera shrieked, losing the last shred of her composure. "Get that little Jezebel!"

Tasharyana didn't look back. She ran as fast as she could, pushed through the heavy door, and galloped down the stairs, flying around the corners by grabbing on to the metal handrail and pulling herself along. She went two flights and then sprinted across the hotel to the opposite bank of elevators, knowing that if she didn't get to the lobby before Mr. Gregg, he would block her exit and she would be made prisoner again.

Gasping for breath, she stabbed the elevator button and waited for what seemed like hours before the car arrived. She rushed inside and pressed the button for the lobby, hoping Mr. Gregg hadn't recovered enough to run after her.

In the elevator, she quickly ran her fingers through her tousled hair in an effort to make herself presentable and tried to command her labored breathing and pounding heart by taking three deep breaths. She had no desire to draw attention to herself, thus leaving a trail for Mr. Gregg or J. B. Spencer to follow her. She didn't want to endanger J. B. any further by involving him in her escape.

The elevator doors whisked open to the subdued ambiance of the marble and mahogany lobby. A quick scan showed no evidence of Mr. Gregg or Madame Hepera. She punched the buttons for every floor, knowing the elevator would have to stop on each level, which would delay Mr. Gregg should he be waiting above to use the car. Then she stepped out, walked briskly across the lobby to the main doors, exited to the temperate night air without waiting for the assistance of Rivers, the liveried doorman, and waved her hand for a taxi. A yellow cab pulled up alongside the curb and Tasharyana yanked the door open. She slid onto the cracked leather seat and looked back in time to see Mr. Gregg limping toward the revolving door. She slammed the door.

"The train station, please," Tasharyana gasped. "And take an indirect route. A man is trying to follow me and I must get away from him."

"Are you in trouble with the police, miss?"

"No. It's a personal matter. And if you get me to the station without him catching me, I'll give you twenty dollars."

"You got a deal, lady."

The taxi pulled away from the curb, just as Mr. Gregg stumbled out to the sidewalk. Tasharyana sank back against the worn seat, trying hard to relax. But she wouldn't feel safe until she was on board the train to Philadelphia with no tweed jackets in sight. She shut her eyes and the sight of J. B.'s face loomed up. What would he think when he found her gone? Would he worry? She hoped not. She didn't want to cause him undue alarm. And though she hated to leave without saying good-bye, it was better this way, to break it off suddenly. The longer she stayed and the more she saw of J. B., the harder it would be to leave him. And in her heart she knew that leaving was inevitable.

Luxor, Egypt, Present Day

"Mother, Mother!"

Feeling drugged and disoriented, Karissa slowly raised her head and looked around for Julia, her thoughts sluggish and her limbs stiff. She was surprised to find herself sprawled on the sand by the pond, just as Asheris had found her the previous evening. Did scrying put her in some kind of enervating trance, robbing her of her senses and inducing her to fall asleep? Was it dangerous to succumb to the visions in the water? Tasharyana had mentioned using the sorcery of Madame Hepera to record her visions in the obelisks. Could the witchcraft affect modern-day viewers by robbing them of consciousness?

Karissa caught sight of Julia standing near her feet, and she rose to a sitting position on the sand.

"Mother, are you all right?"

"Yes, *azeez*. I must have fallen asleep."

Julia glanced from the cat-shaped music box to the placid water of the pond. "Did you see her—the lady in the water?"

"Yes. She's set down her life story in a visual diary, so that others can see what happened during her life."

"I'd like to see it. May I, Mother?"

"When I've finished looking at it." She got to her feet before Julia's expression of protest could be vocalized. She wasn't certain yet if the diary would be appropriate viewing for a child, no matter how precocious. She crossed her arms, still somewhat groggy. "What I want to know is, just what are you doing up so late, young lady?"

"I couldn't sleep. I keep thinking about that school."

"Oh?" Karissa draped a comforting arm around the shoulders of her daughter. "There's nothing to worry about."

"But you have always been my teacher, Mother."

"Yes, but I think it's time for you to be exposed to other teachers, to other ways of thinking, and to make friends with children your own age."

"But I don't like children."

Karissa squeezed Julia's shoulders and tried to hide her smile of amusement. "You might change your mind. You really haven't been around that many young people."

"Most of the ones I've met are silly."

"Still, I think you'll like the school, and I want you to make an honest effort at getting along with everyone."

Oh." Julia sighed and pulled away. "All right."

"As for now, help me put away the obelisks, would you?"

"Sure." Julia bent over the sandalwood box and quickly arranged the rods so that she could place the lid on top. Karissa watched while she rubbed the backs of her stiff upper arms. Then Julia turned her bright face to her mother, which caught the last gleam of light before the moon disappeared behind a bank of clouds.

"Could I listen to the music in my room, Mother? It will help me go to sleep more quickly."

"If you promise to go right to sleep."

"I promise."

"All right then. Come along, *azeez*. It's late."

10

The next morning, just before Karissa was about to break for lunch, she heard Eisha's step in the doorway and looked up from her sculpture. In the seven years she had known the housekeeper, the woman hadn't changed. Her black hair, slightly shot with gray, still hung in a braid down her back, and her round florid face didn't betray Eisha's advancing age of sixty-two. Karissa had liked the woman from the very first, and Eisha had always acted in a kindly manner to Julia, as if she were more grandmother than housekeeper.

"Yes, Eisha?" Karissa said, setting her knife on the table.

"There's someone to see you, a Mr. Walter Duncan."

"Dr. Walter Duncan?" she repeated in surprise. She remembered well the young red-haired doctor from Baltimore who had known her father's work. What was he doing in Egypt?

"He says he is from the United States. Will you see him?"

"Yes. Ask him if he'd like to join me for lunch in the garden, Eisha, will you? I'll be out as soon as I clean up."

Eisha nodded and quietly slipped out of the studio.

Karissa washed the clay from her hands and took a quick look at her face in the mirror. In the throes of her work, she sometimes got clay smudges on her cheeks and forehead, and she wanted to make sure her skin was clean. She thought of changing from her khaki shorts and light cotton shirt, her usual work clothes, but decided against it. She had lost valuable working hours lately, what with entering Julia into school, reading her father's journals, and listening to Tasharyana's tale, and wasn't about to waste time needlessly changing clothes.

Wally Duncan stood up and grinned when he spotted her coming through the garden. "Ms. Spencer!" he greeted, holding out his hand. He had a terrible sunburn on his face, which must have made it painful to smile.

She shook his hand. "Dr. Duncan, what a surprise to see you!"

"Should I have called first?"

"Not at all." She motioned to the chair. "Sit down, won't you?"

"Thanks." He sank to the chair, still grinning.

Karissa settled back in her chair. "Will you join me for lunch? I was just about ready to take a break when you arrived."

"That would be great." He glanced around. "How is Julia?"

"She's fine. She's at school today. In fact, it's her first day."

"What a great little kid she was. I got a kick out of her."

"She's still an unusual little girl."

"I imagine she always will be. As I recall, her IQ scores were off the chart."

Karissa smiled stiffly, deciding to turn the conversation away from Julia. She didn't like to focus on the peculiarities of her daughter, and would have been content to have a normal well-adjusted child, not the brilliant beauty who would always find it difficult to fit into the world.

"It looks as if you've become acquainted with our powerful Egyptian sun," she ventured.

"Yeah. No wonder the sun was a god here." Gingerly, he touched his forehead. "I used a sun block, though."

"You should get a hat as well."

"Good idea."

"And if you like, I'll have Eisha give you some of her aloe cream. She makes it herself, and it's highly effective on burns."

"Thanks. I'd appreciate it, Ms. Spencer."

At that moment Eisha appeared at the table, carrying a tray laden with their lunch. Karissa sat back as Eisha placed lamb kebobs and tahini in front of them, along with a plate of fruit.

Wally eyed the skewered meat. "That looks great!" he commented.

"Eisha is an excellent cook." Karissa looked up at the housekeeper and smiled. "Thank you, Eisha."

Pleased at the compliment, Eisha blushed.

"I was telling Dr. Duncan about your aloe cream. Do you have any we could give him for his burn?"

Eisha glanced at Wally's red face and forearms. "Yes. I just made a fresh batch the other day. I'll bring it out in a few minutes."

"Thanks," Wally replied. "I'd appreciate it."

Eisha nodded to him and then quickly left them to their meal. For a few minutes they served themselves and the conversation dropped off. Karissa smiled to herself, realizing that her American compatriot had a definite character trait, one more evident to her with each year she spent away from the United States. Americans were enthusiastic and eager, not nearly as reserved as most of the other people she met during her travels in Europe and the Mediterranean region. Sometimes she missed the spontaneity and spunk of Americans, and Wally Duncan possessed more eagerness than most.

"So what brings you to Luxor, Dr. Duncan?"

"Call me Wally, would you? I really hate formal titles."

"All right."

"I've come with a group of scientists to study the Sphinx at Giza."

"The Sphinx? Why?"

"Well, there's been some controversy going on about it lately, you know."

"You mean about it being much older than historians thought?"

"Exactly. A bunch of us scientists—geologists mostly—plan to do some experiments, to see if the erosion factor is advanced enough to convince archaeologists and other scholars to rethink their theories."

"What erosion factor?"

"There's a wall around the Sphinx, Ms. Spencer, carved out of the bedrock of the Giza Plateau. The wall shows classic erosion lines usually made by years and years of rainfall." He stabbed a chunk of lamb with his fork. "Now, how do you suppose water erosion could have occurred in a country that gets about an inch of rainfall a year? An inch a year would hardly erode a bar of soap, much less solid rock."

"I don't know. I haven't heard about this before."

"Some of us think the Sphinx was built when the North African climate was much wetter, before the Sahara became a giant sandbox. That would account for the erosion. And that would make the Sphinx not forty-five hundred years old, but eight thousand years or more."

"Double its presumed age."

"Yes, and that has the archaeologists throwing academic cold water on our theory."

"Why?"

"They say there isn't a shred of evidence of an earlier society—no buildings, no bones, no pottery shards. They think our theory is preposterous. We think they just haven't dug deep enough."

"But you aren't a geologist or an archaeologist, Wally. Why are you here?"

"I'm responsible for exploring the ground around the Sphinx using sound waves. The authorities won't let people dig anymore, you know."

"If they allowed everyone to excavate, the Giza Plateau would be destroyed."

"Exactly." He ate a piece of watermelon. "So I am hoping my high-tech sound equipment will come up with something to support our theory. I'm hoping to find evidence in the earth, far beneath the sand, where no man has been for centuries, evidence of an earlier civilization."

"The Sphinx is in Cairo, though. Why did you come to Luxor?"

"To see you and to check in on Julia. I mean, I was so close, I couldn't pass up the opportunity. I hope you don't mind."

"Not at all. In fact, it's the strangest thing." She sipped her water. "I was going to write to you."

"You were?" he asked eagerly. "Why?"

"I was just sent a crate of my father's things a few days ago. And when I looked through them, I found some of the lab tests he saved, the ones you thought he might have made."

"Really?" Wally's eyes lit up, glowing as green as the tips of young papyrus. "What did they entail?"

"I haven't the faintest idea, Wally. I flipped through them, but it was like a foreign language to me."

"Oh, this is wonderful!" he beamed. "This works out great, as if it were meant to be."

"Yes," Karissa replied. "I think it was fated that you see them."

"Can we look at them now?"

"Right this minute?" She laughed softly at his eagerness.

"Yeah!" He scrambled to his feet.

"What about lunch?"

"Who could eat knowing Julian Spencer's notebooks are waiting?" He stared at her. "I mean, if you don't mind."

"All right." Smiling, she rose and guided him to the chest, which had been taken into the library for safekeeping.

Wally spent the entire afternoon in the library, drinking cup after cup of tea while he read Julian Spencer's documents. Karissa left him shortly after three to drive to the school to pick up Julia. When Karissa returned to the house, she was surprised to see Asheris standing in the living room, the first room off the main entryway. He usually left for the university shortly after noon and rarely returned until midnight or beyond. Why had he come back early—to hear about Julia's first day at school or to insist that she not attend another day? Karissa steeled herself for a confrontation.

Asheris turned when he heard them come in. He was dressed in tan slacks and a striped shirt with the sleeves folded up on his forearms, the very image of the day she had made love with him on a ship traveling up the Nile seven years ago. How well she could still recall that day and the way his lips and hands and body had driven her to the heights of ecstasy. Even yet, when she thought of his mouth on her, a flush blossomed across her skin. She pushed the vision out of her mind, for she knew she must concentrate on the future of her daughter, not on the ashes of her own romantic past.

Setting her mouth in a grim line, she turned and closed the door. Julia rushed across the floor and threw her arms around Asheris's waist, free in her innocent child's way to embrace him as Karissa longed to hold him.

"Hello, Father!" Julia cried, happy to find him at home.

"Hello, Bean," he replied, hugging her back and avoiding eye contact with Karissa. "How was your first day at school?"

"It was interesting. Most of the day they just gave me placement examinations, though."

"And did you do well?"

"I'm fairly certain." She turned and smiled. "They have a great many books and musical instruments of all kinds. Could I learn to play the bassoon, Father?"

He chuckled at her enthusiasm. "Perhaps."

"And they have a huge swimming pool with a high dive. I can't wait to jump off that board!"

"What about the other girls, Julia," Karissa put in. "Did you meet any one you liked?"

"I ate lunch with a girl from Syria. Her father's an engineer at the Aswan Dam. She wasn't half as silly as the others I met."

"That's encouraging."

Julia stepped back from Asheris. "Could we have tea together, Mother, seeing that Father is home today? Wouldn't it be fun to take tea together? We haven't done that in such a long time!"

Karissa met Asheris's brief but cool glance. Obviously he was still upset with her about the school. Asheris straightened. "I'm sorry, *azeez,* but I should go back to my office."

"Why?"

"I have much to do."

"But don't you want to hear about my new teachers and the school?"

"Of course I do."

"But when will you be back—when I'm asleep?" She stepped away from the link of his arm. "Now that I am in school I won't ever get to see you!"

Asheris regarded Julia silently, his eyes dark.

Karissa flowed from the door. "Perhaps your father will join us for the evening meal, tonight, Julia, as a special treat to you, and to honor our guest."

Asheris's head came up in surprise. "Guest?"

"Yes. Dr. Duncan stopped in for a visit. You remember him, don't you?"

"He is here? Now?"

"Yes. In the library, looking over my father's lab notes."

"Dr. Wally is here?" Julia exclaimed in delight.

"Yes, in the library. But you don't remember him do you, Julia?"

"Of course I do! I liked him very much."

Karissa was surprised that Julia could recall a man she had seen only once when she was two years old. Her daughter's mind never ceased to amaze her.

"I'm going to tell him about the science lab at my school!" Julia dropped her schoolbag and rushed down the hall toward the east wing where the library opened onto the atrium at the center of the house. Asheris stood where he was, and Karissa could feel the force of his gaze on her. Unsure of Asheris's reaction to the news of a guest, Karissa reached down for Julia's bag, preparing herself to meet his wrath.

"Did you send for Dr. Duncan?" he asked, his voice chilly.

Karissa straightened and kept her gaze level. "No. He's in Egypt as part of a team of scientists who are studying the Sphinx."

"Why did he come here?"

"Why?" Karissa wished Asheris wouldn't be so distrustful of people. "To pay a friendly visit. Nothing more."

"I suspect he has a motive other than friendship."

"I don't. Besides, I want him to look over my father's papers to see if there is anything of merit in them."

"First the school and now this Dr. Duncan." Asheris glared at her, his nostrils flaring slightly. "Do you seek to rule this household, Karissa?"

"No. I seek a normal life for our daughter." She clutched the schoolbag closer. "And I seek to welcome guests into my home, not as potential enemies, but as friends."

"And in so doing, endanger Julia."

"Wally is no threat to Julia!" Exasperated, Karissa

shook her head and walked past her rigid husband. "You've become so paranoid, Asheris, I hardly know you!"

"For good reason."

She whirled to face him. "Such as?"

He glared at her, made a movement as if he was about to reply, and then pressed his lips together. The muscle of his jaw flinched back and forth as he stared at her, looking for all the world like a caged, tormented panther.

"Asheris, tell me!"

He looked into her eyes, the first real glance he had bestowed upon her in weeks. For a moment she saw the depth of his love and the extent of his sincerity in his golden-brown eyes, just as she had seen in them years ago. For a moment she was certain he was on the verge of telling her what was distressing him. Then without a word, he turned on his heel, strode to the door, and closed it gently behind him.

That night when Karissa went into Julia's room to kiss her good night, she nearly bumped into Wally, who was hurrying down the hall carrying the serving dish Karissa recognized from her father's crate.

"There you are!" Wally exclaimed. "Eisha said you might be here."

"I'm on my way to say good night to Julia."

Wally glanced at the nearby doorway out of which came the beautiful sound of Julia humming to herself, and then back to Karissa. With fumbling hands he tucked the dish under his arm.

"What are you doing with that dish?" she asked.

"It isn't a dish. It's a ceremonial disk."

"But why are you carrying it around?"

"I want to use it in an experiment." He shifted his weight, as if unsure of his position with her. "I know this is going to sound like a strange request, Ms. Spencer, but would you allow me to try something with Julia before I go?"

"What do you mean?" Karissa glanced from his face to the metal disk and then back again, wondering if Asheris was correct about Wally being a danger to their daughter.

"It won't take long. I just want her to sing for a few minutes."

"Sing?"

"Yes. I came across the most fascinating theory in your father's notes. It has to do with this disk."

"I thought that was a bowl of some kind."

Wally grinned. "Actually, I think it's a solar disk of Aten, symbol of the sun god. And something I'm not sure your father wanted people to know about. It probably belongs in a museum."

"You mean it's a stolen artifact?"

"It might be. Regardless, it's very valuable, even if you forget its historical value and just consider the amount of gold it's made of."

Karissa raised her eyebrows in surprise. "I didn't even pick it up. I thought it was made of brass."

"Well, your father knew it was important. He thought these disks might have been used to build monuments."

"You mean as decoration on statues?"

"No, as levitation devices."

"What?" Karissa glanced at the plain golden disk, which had no visible power source or moving parts. The idea seemed preposterous.

"Even yet no one is certain how the pyramids were built, how those big blocks were moved such great distances by people who had neither the wheel nor the horse."

"And my father came up with a new theory on that?"

"Yes!" Wally stepped closer, his face appearing almost feverish with his enthusiasm and sunburn. "Your father believed that disks such as this one might have been used as amplifiers. Some sort of concentrated sound was directed at them. The curvature of the disk focused and reflected the sound much like a glass lens focuses and reflects light."

"But what does that have to do with building pyramids?"

"Well, that's the interesting part. Your father proposed that sounds of particular frequencies could be amplified to excite the molecules of large objects. Only the surface molecules of the objects would jiggle, though, which would create a kind of liquid layer between the ground and the object. Everyone knows that friction and gravity are the biggest problems in moving a large object. So if the friction was minimized by liquefying the underside layer of an object, it would be very easy to just push a two-thousand pound block of granite along a prepared surface. It would be like floating a large ship in a body of water."

Karissa stared at him. Although he had translated her father's theory into layman's terms that could be easily understood, she still found the idea difficult to swallow.

"So what does my daughter have to do with it?"

"Well, your father tried all kinds of sounds with this disk and nothing worked. Not even a bit." He ran a hand over his shock of red hair. "Then I remembered how you said Julia's voice could move objects, and I have documented proof that her voice is highly unusual in its frequency. She just might be capable of producing the right type of sound to prove your father's theory."

Karissa crossed her arms. The theory sounded highly questionable, but what could it hurt to allow Julia to sing for a few minutes? What could happen? She knew her father hadn't been a lunatic or a man given over to wild schemes. What if he had been close to discovering the real construction technique of the ancient Egyptians? A thrill of excitement passed through her at the thought of proving her father's theories and vindicating him in the eyes of the world.

"All right, Wally. I'm game."

"Great!" He motioned toward the door. "Lead the way."

Julia looked up in surprise to see Wally come in with her mother. They briefly explained that they wanted to carry out a scientific experiment, using her voice, and Julia eagerly agreed to participate. Karissa closed the door and joined her daughter to watch the American scientist set up for his test.

Wally placed the disk on her small writing desk and then piled a few small objects on a table halfway between Julia and the disk, explaining his hopes that the sound waves would move or jiggle the objects enough to prove his point.

Julia stood near her bed in her long cotton nightgown, intently watching the proceedings, and appearing strikingly similar to the statues of women from the days of the pharaohs. Karissa stared at her daughter, a miniature likeness of Senefret, a priestess of the temple of Sekhmet the lion goddess—the woman Asheris had lost his heart and his mortal life to thousands of years ago. Because he had unknowingly deflowered a priestess of the temple who had been groomed to become the Great Wife of the pharaoh of Egypt, Asheris had been cursed to spend his nights as a panther and his days in silent suspended animation for countless centuries.

Yet Senefret's blood somehow flowed through Karissa's veins, which was why she had been able to lift the curse seven years ago. The same blood must have been given to Julia, branding her with the beautiful dark features and delicate bone structure of Senefret. Why hadn't she seen the similarities before? Was it the white nightgown so like the linen sheaths worn by the ancient ones? Was it the way Julia stood so quietly with her arms at her sides, just like a statue? Had Julia's childlike face been changing subtly over the years, so subtly that Karissa hadn't noticed the transformation to this image of the past?

Finished with his preparations, Wally brushed his hands together and looked over at Julia, snapping Karissa out of her thoughts. "Well, let's give it a try, shall we?"

At that moment, the bedroom door opened and Asheris stepped into the room. Karissa's heart rose into her throat at the stormy look on his face.

"What is going on here?" Asheris boomed.

"An experiment, Father!" Julia piped up. "Come and see."

Asheris ignored Julia and glared from Wally to Karissa, and then his stare swept across the table in the center of the room. "There will be no experimentation involving my daughter," he stated, his voice tight and clipped. "Not now, not ever. Is that clear?"

"But Asheris," Karissa put in, "There's nothing—"

Asheris turned to her, his eyes flashing with anger. "You assured me that Dr. Duncan was here to read the papers of your father, nothing else. Is that not true?"

"Yes, but—"

"If he cannot contain himself to reading, then he must leave."

"Father, no!" Julia cried. "Dr. Wally is nice!"

"I'll go anyway," Wally replied, all the Yankee enthusiasm dashed from his voice. "I never intended to cause any trouble, Mr. Asher, please believe me."

"I told you before that Julia was not to be used as a

laboratory animal and that requirement still stands, Doctor."

"I will respect your wishes, sir." Wally grabbed the heavy disk and shot a quick glance at Karissa.

"You don't have to go, Wally," Karissa said, stepping toward him. "If you'd like to spend the night with us, you are more than welcome."

"Thanks, but I've already got a hotel room in town." He stumbled for the door. "Thanks anyway, Ms. Spencer."

"Let me have someone drive you back to town then." She ushered him into the hall, hoping she could convince him to come back the next day when Asheris wasn't around. At the very least, she wanted to hear what other information Wally had gleaned from her father's papers.

Asheris scowled as he walked to Julia's bedside. He had made a special effort to come back to the house in time to say good night to his sweet daughter and listen to her tales of her first day at school, and what should he find upon his return but a scientific investigation going on under his very roof, an investigation that involved Julia.

Worse yet, Julia was staring at him as if he had just killed her favorite puppy.

"I do not want Dr. Duncan testing you," Asheris blurted out, as if to explain himself.

"But why did you have to treat him so cruelly?"

"I wasn't cruel. I was simply firm."

"You shouted at him. And at Mother."

"They should not have been keeping you from your sleep." He lifted her off the ground. "Now up with you, Bean, and into bed."

He set her upon the downturned bed and she slipped her slender legs between the sheets. Asheris hoped she would forget the incident quickly, as he intended to do, but Julia turned a troubled face up to him.

"Why are you and Mother angry at each other all the time?"

Her blunt question took him by surprise. Searching for the right words to explain the situation, he sat down beside her and reached for her hand.

"We are not angry at each other, sweet Bean."

"You never kiss her. You never hug her. Does that mean you are not in love anymore? Does that mean you will be getting a divorce?"

"No, not at all." Asheris squeezed her hand in reassurance. "I love your mother very much. Do not doubt that for a moment."

"Then she doesn't love you?"

Asheris looked at the sisal mat on the tile floor, uncertain of the answer to her question. He sighed. "Your mother and I are not seeing the world with one heart these days, *azeez*. That is all. It will pass. Do not worry."

"Sometimes I think if I weren't here, you would still be nice to each other."

Asheris stared at her. "Why would you ever think that?"

"Because you are always arguing over me. I can hear you sometimes. Perhaps if I hadn't been born, you would still like each other."

"Oh no, Bean." Shocked by her flawed line of reasoning, Asheris pressed her hand to his lips and tenderly kissed her small palm. She might have adultlike learning abilities, but her reasoning was still that of a child, and it broke his heart to hear words of self-recrimination spilling from her mouth. Gently he folded her graceful fingers over the kiss he had left on her palm. "Never think that, Julia. Never. Never! You are the best thing that ever happened to your mother and me."

Tears pooled in her eyes. "Really?"

"Really." He pulled her into a strong embrace, and his heart twisted as her small arms wrapped tightly around his neck.

"Oh, Father!" she cried, her warm voice near the base of his neck. "Sometimes I worry."

"I know, Bean. But worrying is for parents, not for sweet little girls like you."

He held her and stroked her shoulders until he felt her grip ease on his neck. Then he gently urged her to lie back on the pillow. He smoothed away the ebony strands of hair tangled by tears on the sides of her face and gazed at her, his heart overflowing with love.

"Do not give a second thought to your mother and me." He passed his thumb across the slight curve of her forehead. "There is nothing to worry about. Absolutely nothing. All right?"

She took a deep shuddering breath. "All right."

"Good." Lightly, he tapped the end of her nose, hoping to snap her out of her troubled mood. "So tell me, then, how did you like your school?"

"It wasn't as bad as I had thought it would be."

"Everyone treated you with kindness, with respect?"

"Yes. But there was one lady, whom I was told was a nurse—"

"Yes?"

"Well, I didn't like her much. She was really old and fat. And she wore a bunch of rings and she inspected me."

Asheris stopped stroking her hair. "Inspected you? In what way?"

"She looked at my hair. She said I might have lice

and they had to make certain I did not." Julia opened her eyes. "Can you imagine that?"

"No. But I think perhaps school officials check on such things."

"Well, I didn't like it."

Asheris studied her face carefully while a cold feeling crept through him. "Is that the only place she looked—in your hair?"

Julia nodded. "I didn't like her. Not a bit. She reminded me of one of those old fortunetellers at the bazaar. She didn't look like a nurse."

"But she did not harm you in any way?"

"No."

"The rings she wore—did you notice any of them in particular?"

"Only that they were large and ugly, and her hands were puffy and fat." Julia paused, as her brows drew together. "Well, now that you mention it, I did notice one ring because it was so different."

"In what way?"

"It was shaped like the head of a lion. Not the kind with the big mane. A female lion. A lioness."

Asheris felt the blood grow cold in his veins, and he had to struggle to keep his voice even so as not to alarm his daughter. "You are certain, Julia?"

"Yes. There was no mistaking it, the head was so large. It was a lion."

Asheris rose, feeling as if the room were shrinking around him. A ring in the shape of a lion meant only one thing: the priestesses of Sekhmet still roamed the earth, just as he had suspected. Over the last six years he had gathered small clues that they still existed, but nothing as blatant as the information just delivered by his daughter.

"Father, what's wrong?"

He caught himself and forced a calm smile to

appear on his lips. "Nothing, *azeez.* I will see you tomorrow. Sleep well."

He bent and kissed her forehead, while his thoughts were already far away, preparing for the discussion he would have with Karissa about Julia's soon-to-be aborted educational career.

Asheris located Karissa closing the front door, on her way in from saying good-bye to Dr. Duncan. He found it ironic that his wife should show more interest and care for the American stranger than she did for her husband of seven years. Was it because she was lonesome for people of her own culture? Did his Egyptian outlook and habits displease her? Did she miss America and long to return to the country of her birth? He couldn't believe these things to be true, not the Karissa who had claimed to love the Valley of the Nile as no other place. Yet perhaps her love of place had been linked to her love of a man, and if that love were fading, her interest in Egypt would wane as well.

Karissa turned and caught sight of him, and her eyes glinted with angry lights. "How could you be so horrible!" she cried. "Treating Wally Duncan that way!"

Asheris bristled at her words of reproach. Not many people in this life had spoken to him in such a fashion, and never a woman. He crossed his arms over his chest. "He violated his promise."

"Violated, hell! Wally is a well-intentioned, good-natured man who didn't deserve to be driven from our home like that."

"I warned him about Julia."

"All he wanted her to do was sing, and I told him it was perfectly all right! Don't I have a say in this house?"

"I thought you were the only person in this house to *have* a say," Asheris countered heatedly. As soon as the words left his lips, he realized how petty he sounded. Karissa stormed past him, but he reached out to keep her from leaving.

"Karissa!" he exclaimed.

She shot him a glare of such outrage that he immediately released her.

"Karissa." He forced his voice lower and tried to control his anger. Otherwise she would only fly from his rage or strike back at him, and neither reaction would help them solve their problems. "I am sorry. I have reacted too strongly."

She rubbed her arms and surveyed him from the side as if surprised to hear an apology. He longed to reach out for her but knew she would shrink from his hands.

"You do things without thought to Julia's safety, and when I think of Julia in danger, I react strongly."

"You can't isolate her forever. What will you do when she gets older, when she wants more freedom?"

"I will deal with that when the time comes."

"But Asheris, the time *has* come. Don't you see?"

"Still, she must not attend the Luxor Language School."

Shocked, Karissa dropped her arms to her sides. "Why?"

"Because it is not in her best interests to do so." He turned and stepped away, intent upon leaving before she asked more questions than he was willing to answer.

"Asheris!" This time Karissa grabbed the sleeve of his left arm. "Come back here! Talk to me!"

He stopped but did not look back at her. It frightened him to think they had come to the point of yelling and clutching each other in anger. Perhaps Julia was more perceptive than he was and could foresee a separation before he could.

"Just because I let Wally begin an experiment isn't cause for you to punish me by taking Julia out of school."

"I am punishing no one. I am protecting."

"Why are you insisting she be taken out of the school?"

"Because I believe the past is coming back to haunt us." He turned and glared at her. For a moment their eyes held as fire flared between them.

"What past?" Karissa asked in a quiet, extremely controlled voice.

"Mine. And when I know for certain what must be done, I will tell you." He pulled his arm from her grasp and walked away. She made no further protest, but her silence was louder than anything she could have shouted at him.

Shaken, Karissa hurried to her room. What had come out of the past to haunt Asheris? His long-lost love, Senefret? The priestesses of Sekhmet? She didn't like either possibility. Could Asheris be in danger of suffering a curse again? Would he lose his ability to remain a mortal man? She couldn't fathom returning to the life they had once known, when every night Asheris transformed into a black panther.

She was equally appalled that she had lost her temper enough to grab his sleeve in anger. What was happening to them? Even worse, Asheris was issuing demands without justification, a sure sign that their ability to communicate was in tatters and that he felt his control slipping. What could she do? How could she convince him to let Julia continue her education at the language school? Perhaps for the time being it would be best to concede to Asheris's demands that she withdraw Julia from the school.

Full of despair, she took a long bath, lying back in the tub and weeping out of sheer loneliness and disappointment. Asheris was quickly pulling away from her and she didn't know what to do to bring him back. Her husband had been her closest friend, her soul mate, and she couldn't believe they had so completely lost touch.

After the bath, she dressed in a light cotton galabia and slipped her feet into a pair of soft leather sandals. She checked on Julia, who slept peacefully, obviously unaware of the trouble between her parents, and then walked slowly to her room, wishing somehow that Asheris had read her mind—picking up her secret thoughts that she loved him and missed him— and would be waiting in her room to ease her down onto the bed and tenderly make love to her. If they could quit arguing and just touch each other the way they once did, she was certain their wounds would start to heal.

But as she opened her door and turned on the light, she saw only her vacant room, the white cotton fabrics and mahogany furnishings, the white plaster walls and tan tile floor. Asheris was nowhere in sight, as always. But there on her bureau sat the cat music box, like an old friend, beckoning to her. She crossed the floor and picked it up. Absently she wound the music box and listened to the melody as she stared out the window, oddly comforted by the haunting song.

The moon shone down, full and bright, shedding a silver sheen on the palm fronds outside her window. She thought of Tasharyana and her father, and wondered what would happen between the two. She wondered if Tasharyana would ever get away from Madame Hepera. Perhaps another installment of the visions would answer her questions. She knew she couldn't sleep anyway, not in her current state of mind. Why not spend an hour scrying and learn more about the mysterious opera singer and her father? She carried the box to the garden.

* * *

Tasharyana's Tale—Philadelphia, 1966

Tasharyana stepped out of the cab she'd taken from the train station and paid the driver, and in dismay discovered the combination of cab fares, tips, and train ticket had sorely depleted her funds. If she didn't sell the diamonds soon, she would have no resources. As it was, she barely had enough money for a night in a hotel, and a cheap one at that.

The taxi pulled away from the curb while Tasharyana looked up at the apartment house, a modern construction of concrete and metal columns with large blue metal diamonds serving as decoration on the side of the building—the complete opposite of her idea of what an opera singer would choose as her place of residence. If she should ever purchase a house in America, it would be an older one, with nooks and crannies mellowed by time, not a modern, unimaginative box like this. She shivered, half from standing in the chill of the early morning without a coat and half from facing the unknown. What if her friend weren't home? What would she do? Where would she go? She should have asked the taxi driver to wait.

Clutching her arms to her chest, she hurried up the walkway. She should have called ahead but had been too worried about being followed to waste any time at the train station. It would have been better had she called so that she could have taken the cab to a hotel in the event her friend was not at home. Unfortunately, she was not accustomed to planning ahead or arranging schedules, since Madame Hepera had seen to her every need for years.

Vowing to plan her moves more thoroughly from now on, Tasharyana pulled at the handle of the front door and was surprised to find the small lobby was open. Quietly she slipped in, glad to be out of the cold predawn wind blowing off the Schuylkill River and away from the chilly April air, which was hung with unfamiliar dampness and strange earthy smells that set her senses on edge. Nights in America were nothing like the arid evenings of Egypt. She scanned the rows of mailboxes and located the name of her friend, Dorothy Marchant. The number 312 was typed next to her name. Tasharyana took the elevator up to the third floor and got off. Arrows on the wall indicated the direction of the odd and even numbers. She turned right and stole softly down the hall, not anxious to awaken anyone unnecessarily at such an early hour.

Her heart pounded in her chest by the time she found the correct apartment. For a moment she paused, hoping she wouldn't be considered the rudest person in the world for rousing her friend at four o'clock in the morning. But it was either ring the bell or try to find a cab in what she assumed was a questionable American neighborhood, even in her limited experience with such things. Taking a deep breath, Tasharyana pushed the lighted button to the right of the door and heard chimes sound deep in the room beyond. She waited, preparing words of apology.

After a few moments she realized there was no movement inside the apartment. Tasharyana pressed the button again. She waited longer this time, while worry spread through her. No one came to the door. Tasharyana tried the bell one more time and folded her arms over her chest, still cold from her taxi ride.

"Please be there," she muttered under her breath, even though she knew the possibility became more doubtful with each passing minute.

The apartment behind the door remained mute and unyielding. With a sigh, Tasharyana turned. Now what? Go out in the cold and find a taxi? She hated the thought. But she had no alternative. Slowly she returned to the elevator, trudged through the lobby, and pushed open the heavy metal and glass door. In the east, the sky was showing the first glow of pink, far down at the horizon. Heartened a bit by the fact that the sun was coming up, Tasharyana hurried down the sidewalk, searching for a phone booth. The neighborhood was still and quiet, except for a couple of dogs behind a high wooden fence, who barked at the unfamiliar cadence of her walk.

Four blocks later she came to a corner market that hadn't yet opened for the day, and hanging on a wall near the door was a blue-and-silver pay phone. Though Tasharyana had never used a pay phone before, she was certain she could figure it out. She picked up the receiver. The instructions said to put in the money and then dial the number. She dug in her pocket for some change, and then hung up the receiver, realizing she didn't know what number she was calling. Flustered by the task of doing something unfamiliar, she fumbled for the phone book chained below the booth. After a few moments she located the number for a cab company and slipped the money into a little hole at the top of the phone. The coin clanked into place, then she dialed the number and waited for the connection.

She gave the dispatcher the names of the cross streets where she stood and was assured she would be picked up in fifteen minutes. Tasharyana hugged her arms and waited near the side of the building, hoping the cab would be prompt. Her teeth were already chattering, and she didn't like the idea of standing alone on the street, nor did she like the way a few of the cars slowed down when they drove past.

Twenty minutes later a yellow cab pulled up, its exhaust white and billowy in the crisp morning air. Tasharyana hurried to the vehicle before the driver could get out and help her. She slid into the car, grateful for the blanket of warm air that met her as she closed the door.

"Where to?" the driver asked.

Tasharyana fumbled for the business card in her pocket and drew it out. "Twenty-five and a half Elfreth's Alley," she read from J. B.'s card.

She sat back and ran the nail of her index finger around the edge of the card. She hadn't wanted to take advantage of J. B.'s offer, but if she didn't stay in his home, she would be forced by her depleted finances to spend the night in a cheap hotel, which certainly would be dangerous for a young single female. Besides, J. B. had explained he could use a guest in his deserted town house. And it wasn't as if she were throwing herself at him for support. She could pay him later, and pay him well, once she sold the diamonds.

Tasharyana slipped her hand in her jacket pocket and felt the small velvet pouch. Yes, the diamonds were still there. She looked out the window at the run-down houses of this section of Germantown, made shabbier by the dull light of morning, and wondered what kind of place J. B. owned. Seeing how his address was located in an alley, she expected the worst.

Tasharyana was pleasantly surprised when the cab sped out of the shabby neighborhood, into the historic section of Philadelphia, and up a one-way street made of brick. The lane was lined with quaint red brick town houses, each of which was quite narrow but which climbed three or four stories high and boasted small balconies and shutters. Most were decorated with planters of daffodils and pansies and looked cheerful in the first real sunlight of the day.

"Elfreth's Alley," the taxi driver announced.

"Are you certain?" she replied, glancing up and down the old-fashioned street. "It doesn't look like an alley to me. It looks like a regular street."

"Naw, it's Elfreth's Alley all right, the oldest continuously occupied street in the U.S.A."

"Really? When did people first live here?"

"I don't know, lady. Probably the sixteen hundreds or so."

Tasharyana wasn't impressed by the American

definition of age. In Egypt, things weren't considered out of the ordinary if they were built even sixteen hundred years before Christ. But at least J. B. had found one of the oldest places to live in the United States, which led her to believe that he retained some of his appreciation for the value of antiquity.

Heartened, Tasharyana paid the driver and climbed out of the cab. J. B.'s town house was a neat three-story place with black shutters and white window trim. A brass eagle with wings spread outward hung over his door, and a large clay pot near the entry brimmed with ivy and a shrub of some sort that had been pruned in the shape of two orbs. She remembered him telling her the hiding place for his extra key was in the clay pot. Before she looked for the key, she made certain no other people were on the street and no suspicious figures lurked in the shadows. Then she quickly ducked down and poked her finger in the dirt. On her third try she located the key in a small plastic bag buried just an inch below the surface of the potting soil.

She slipped the key in the lock and squeezed the old latch. The door swung open and she stepped into J. B.'s home.

Immediately, her day improved as she was surrounded by J. B.'s world, full of his possessions, his scent, and the spirit of her long-time friend. She closed the door and felt the ever-present worry she had suffered for the last few days falling from her shoulders as she looked around. The ground floor consisted primarily of a laundry room, a powder room, and a storeroom full of scientific equipment and crates with foreign stamps on them. Looking for the main living area, she slowly climbed the stairs, gazing at the photographs clustered in the stairwell.

Most of them were pictures of Egypt and many were familiar landmarks and buildings. Others were pictures of cathedrals and castles, probably taken in England and Europe.

At the top of the stairs was his living room, done in sand and cream with brass accents and a thick Persian carpet of muted red and gold. Though he lived in an area best known for being the birthplace of the American Revolution, J. B. still clung to his Egyptian roots and had decorated his house in kind. Tasharyana was grateful, for his home provided a small oasis of familiarity in what had been a sea of strangers and even stranger surroundings. She had to smile at his curious sense of housekeeping, however. The room wasn't dirty but appeared somewhat untidy, for there were books stacked on every surface and piles of journals and papers held down by unlikely paperweights such as balls of compressed aluminum foil, large wooden models of molecules, and big horseshoe magnets. A glance at the titles of the volumes showed his interest in physics, sound, and Egyptian history, a far cry from the law books she had expected to see.

She passed through the living room to the dining room and peeked in to view a small spotless kitchen at the back of the house. Another set of stairs led to the third floor, where she found the master bedroom and a study crammed with more scientific equipment wired together and an unlikely brass disk hanging from the light fixture in the center of the room. This must be where he conducted his experiments when not at his law practice.

At the front of the house she discovered a charming sitting area comprised of two chairs and a chaise arranged before of a set of French doors that opened onto a small balcony. J. B. had surrounded the furniture with palms and ferns and had chosen upholstery in a subdued print of green and maroon that reminded her of the Moorish floral patterns seen throughout Egypt. She fell in love with the sitting area at first sight, and stood with her hand resting on the back of the chaise as she gazed out the windows. From the ivy-covered balcony was a marvelous view of the Delaware River, the Ben Franklin Bridge, and Front Street down below, all bathed in the April morning sun. A few people on their way to work walked by, and cars rolled slowly down the narrow bumpy street as the day began. Tasharyana was certain she could see them, but she herself could not be seen due to the green curtain of ivy spilling from numerous boxes on the balcony railing, which gave her a welcome sensation of safety.

For a moment she gazed at the scene outside the French doors, her first real chance to catch her breath after an entire night of traveling, trying to outdistance and outwit Madame Hepera and her henchman. But with her newfound feeling of safety came the realization that she was exhausted. She hadn't so much as closed her eyes on the train or in the taxi. Yawning, she turned and retraced her steps to the bedroom.

Kicking off her shoes, she sank upon the fluffy beige comforter, intending to rest for a few minutes before she took a shower. Next to the phone on the night table was an old framed photograph of the two of them as children, with J. B. proudly displaying his new bicycle on the event of his ninth birthday and Tasharyana grinning near his elbow, both her top teeth missing. As tired as she was, the photograph brought a smile to her lips. She had been seven then, without a care in the world. But just after the photograph was taken, her mother—one of the maids of the Spencer household—had taken ill with a mysterious ailment, never to rise from her bed again. She closed her eyes on the faded vision of her mother's faint memory and fell asleep.

Tasharyana woke up hours later, to a room full of afternoon shadows and the smell of something delicious cooking in the kitchen. She sat bolt upright and threw off the blanket now covering her. Something plopped onto the floor. What was cooking? And where had the blanket come from? Who was in the house with her? And why hadn't she heard anyone come in? She looked down, wondering what had fallen to the floor, and saw a red rose on the carpet. One look at the flower and she knew who was in the house with her, who had covered her, and who was cooking dinner down below.

Tasharyana raised the flower to her nose and took a sniff while a smile curved upon her lips. It was just like J. B. to leave such a romantic calling card. She padded across the floor and found another rose in the doorway. Picking it up, she advanced to the hall. Another rose. And three more on the staircase. She followed the trail of posies to the kitchen, and by the time she got there, she had a dozen perfect red roses in her hand.

Before she got to the doorway, she paused, listening for sounds in the kitchen. She could hear J. B. chopping vegetables and the familiar rhythm of coffee percolating. Her stomach growled fiercely. Then he started singing the popular Nat King Cole song, "Unforgettable," which she had been hearing on every radio station during her trip. With love bursting in her heart, she leaned against the wall in the hallway and listened to him sing. She sank her face into the cool rose petals and wondered if the song meant anything to him regarding the way he felt about her, or whether he sang it simply because he enjoyed the melody and the words. She longed to be unforgettable to J. B., just as he was unforgettable to her and held a permanent and indestructible place in her heart.

Wishing she had thought to freshen up before coming downstairs, Tasharyana flowed forward as the song ended. She stopped in the doorway, unwilling to be the first to break the delicate silence following his song, and waited only a fraction of a second before he sensed her presence and turned around.

"Tasha!" For a moment their eyes locked and held as if they were seeing each other for the first time in years. Then he smiled. "I see you found your way down."

"The roses, J. B.," she said. "They're beautiful! Thank you."

He smiled and turned for a vase he already had sitting on the counter. "Here, let's put them in water."

She walked forward and he took the bouquet from her, arranging the roses in the crystal vase with deft and capable hands. Then he turned to her and put his hand on her arm. "Are you all right?"

"Yes," she blurted, "but I never heard you come in."

"You were sleeping very deeply."

"You came up to the bedroom?"

"Yes, to see if you were here. You didn't even know I put a blanket on you, did you?"

"No, and that's frightening."

"Don't be frightened. I took care not to wake you." He gazed at her, lapsing into silence. And then he made a slight turn from the counter and before she knew it, she was in his arms. He wrapped himself around her and pulled her close. She shut her eyes and savored the pressure of his arms. To have her old friend with her during this time of personal upheaval was a blessing and a much needed comfort.

"Oh, J. B.!" she cried, hugging him.

He held her tightly. "Where did you go last night?"

"I ran, J. B., trying to get away from Madame Hepera. I took a train here."

"And no one followed you?"

"I don't think so."

He squeezed her tightly. "Rivers, the doorman, informed me that you left early in the morning in some distress."

"I did because that man in the tweed coat was after me. Madame Hepera came to my room with him after I went to bed, and she threatened to hurt you if I didn't cooperate."

"Hurt me?"

"Yes! But I got away." She snuggled into him, pressing her cheek against the warm skin above the opening in his shirt. "I tried my opera friend's apartment first. But she wasn't home. I didn't know what else to do but come here."

"I'm glad you did." He pulled back to look at her and tenderly touched the side of her face. "You should have called me, though. I was worried sick about you."

"I didn't want to put you in any more danger than I already had."

"Forget about that, Tasha. I want to be involved. From now on, I want you to call me and confide in me, no matter if it's dangerous or not. I don't want those people threatening you. If I had been with you, none of that would have happened."

"You can't be with me all the time," she countered.

"Why can't I?" He raised his chin and looked

down his nose at her without breaking eye contact, as if daring her to give reasons why he should stay away.

"You have your other life, your job, your clients—"

"All that can be put on hold until we are certain you are safe."

"But what about Christine and her mother? What will they think if they find out I am staying in your house?"

His dark eyes glinted with anger. "They can think whatever they like."

"It doesn't look good to have a woman here, especially if she stays all night. Won't they assume—"

"That we care for each other as we will always care for each other?"

She gazed at him, knowing she should back away but unable to muster the will to break out of his embrace.

"Don't you worry that they might think—" She broke off as J. B. increased the pressure of his arms.

"That we are doing what we should have been doing for the last six years?"

"And that is?"

"Showing how we feel about each other. What could be so wrong in that?"

"Because of the way it will look to the others."

"I don't care how it will look. I'm not concerned with the others. This is about you and me, Tasha."

"J. B.—" she whispered in protest, unsure of what she should do or how to interpret his statement. Did he love her as he had claimed to love her so long ago? Or did he only want to experience the pleasure of her body? Madame Hepera had warned her about men who took women to bed, one after the other, seeking variety instead of love. Handsome men like J. B. Spencer could easily attract droves of willing females, should it be his desire to have many women. She spread her hands on his chest, ready to push him away, but the firmness of his body beneath his shirt made her pause. "It's not the time to—"

"Forget the time, forget the Petries. Listen to your heart, Tasha, and tell me what it's telling you."

"I can't forget them!" She pushed away. "Christine is part of your life, a part I can't overlook."

"Does Christine affect your feelings for me?"

"No. But she affects what I should do." Tasharyana backed away.

"She shouldn't."

"Well, she should affect your behavior."

A shadow passed through J. B.'s eyes. He frowned and sighed. "You don't know everything about Christine and me."

"Maybe you should enlighten me then."

"Perhaps I will. But I assure you that it will have little bearing on my feelings for you. Or yours for me." He advanced a step toward her, as if to take her in his arms once more. At the thought of being embraced by J. B. again, Tasharyana felt a twisting ache of love and need deep inside her. The sensation was not a safe reaction for someone who had been cruelly operated on and who should never get physically involved with a man. She reached for the woodwork of the doorway, using it as a protective barrier between J. B. and herself.

"I think I should go, J. B."

"Why? Because I asked you to admit the truth?"

"I don't think it's wise for us to be here together like this."

"What if I promise to keep my distance?"

She hesitated, wondering if he actually would stay away, and if she could stay away from him.

"Tasha, you need to be here for your own safety. And I want you here, where I can be certain you are safe. Please, don't run off."

"I'm not sure I should stay."

"I'm sorry if I came on too strong," he put in. "I thought you were ready to take up where we left off. I was wrong?"

She ached to tell him she was more than ready to take up where they had left off at the banks of the Nile, ready to learn what it was like to make love with him, finally to know his body as well as she knew her own. But she could never experience such ecstasy with Julian. Madame Emide and Dr. Shirazzi had seen to that. She didn't know how he truly felt about Christine, either, or what plans he had in mind for the blond woman. And as long as J. B. thought she held back because of Christine, he would never have to find out about her "evening surgery."

"Tasha?"

She hadn't realized she was standing there, staring at him without speaking.

"All right. I'll stay. But you must promise to be a gentleman."

"Sounds like a prison sentence," he retorted. Then he smiled sadly. "But all right, I'll be good if that's what it will take to keep you here." He turned and picked up the knife. "If you'd like to take a shower, I'll finish up dinner."

Relieved that he hadn't pressed the personal issue, she smiled back. "I would. Which bathroom should I use?"

"The one off the bedroom. And if you'd like a change of clothes, you may help yourself to anything in the closet that will work."

"Thank you."

"I hope you realize that nothing in there has sequins." He winked and she grinned, glad to be back to their familiar humorous bantering.

"I only wear sequins after eight o'clock," she replied. "And only to very important functions."

"You don't call a Chez Spencer seafood linguini dinner important?"

"I don't know. I've never attended one."

"Well, be in the dining room in twenty minutes, my pet, and you will experience the finest cuisine to be had in Elfreth's Alley."

"I assume the rest of the chefs are out of town?" she remarked, teasing him.

"Hah." His eyes sparkled. "Don't think I can sauté an onion, do you?"

"The last I knew of you, J. B., you never even buttered a piece of your own bread. Your mother spoiled you rotten."

"Well, they say you can't teach an old dog new tricks, my dear, but it's amazing what a young buck can do when he sets his mind to it."

She gazed at him, caught up by his sense of humor and positive outlook.

"Now off with you," he said, wagging the knife at her. "Chef Spencer must work his magic unhindered by the stares of beautiful opera singers."

She chuckled and turned to go back up the stairs.

Much to her surprise, the seafood linguini was succulent, the accompanying salad colorful and delicious, and the pinot grigio he had urged her to taste was pleasantly light and satisfying. She found herself sipping an entire glass as they sat and talked. The roses, fragrant and romantic, cast a heady spell on both of them. Before she knew it, two hours had slipped by and the dining room was bathed in darkness. Commenting on how time had flown, J. B. lit the candle on the center of the table and then got up to clear the dishes.

She rose to help.

"No, sit," he said.

"But I wish to help you. After all, you went to the trouble to make dinner for me."

"It was my pleasure." He swept their plates off the table. "Besides, if I see you traipsing around in that shirt of mine, I can't guarantee the promised gentlemanly behavior."

She blushed.

"Pour us another glass and we can go upstairs to the sitting area. The view should be great tonight, it's so clear outside." He picked up the unused silverware. "I'll come up when I'm finished, all right?"

"All right." She reached for the tall slender bottle of wine but then paused and looked at him as he passed by her shoulder. "Thank you, J. B. Dinner was wonderful."

"You're welcome." Then, as if it were the most natural thing to do, he gave her a quick peck on the mouth and continued to the kitchen. She fumbled with the wine bottle, trying not to think of the kiss as anything but the most casual of gestures.

She found a tray on the sideboard on which she placed the bottle and two glasses. Then she walked upstairs to the sitting room to wait for J. B. In only moments, she heard his tread on the stairs.

Tasharyana handed a goblet of wine to J. B. and picked up hers when he crossed the floor to the chaise. But instead of sitting down, he ambled to the French doors and opened one of them. A breeze sighed through the palms near the chaise, rustling the branches, but it was warm enough to be comfortable. The weather had changed considerably from the chilliness of yesterday. Tasharyana stood up, curious to discover what the night was like on J. B.'s private balcony. She joined him outside and drifted to the railing, sipping her wine as the breeze ruffled the tails of his long shirt.

Ahead of her stretched the eastern landscape, a sea of lights twinkling on a field of black. The bridge with its illuminated span was far more striking in the dark, as was the river, an ebony expanse bobbing with lighted ships. A few pedestrians, enjoying the unseasonably warm evening, strolled along the river walk, and snatches of their laughter drifted upward.

J. B. came up behind her, close enough so she felt his warm breath on her neck but not so close as to trap her against the railing.

"Beautiful, isn't it?" he commented.

"Very. I can't imagine you wanting to sell this place."

"I don't really want to. But it's a waste of money to pay rent in Baltimore and a mortgage here. I don't have that kind of cash to throw around."

"Have you let your Philadelphia clients go?"

"No, but I haven't taken on any new ones. I expect I'll end up living permanently in Baltimore."

"But this house is so charming and the area so picturesque."

"I know. But do you want to hear something curious?"

She glanced back at him. "What?"

"This place never felt like home to me, not once, not until tonight when you sat in the dining room in my shirt talking with me in the dark."

She flushed with pleasure. "You're not serious."

"I am. I've lived in this house for over two years and I've never felt connected to it. But having you here—using my things, wearing my clothes, eating what I made for you in the kitchen—well, for the first time I felt a sensation of home here."

Tasharyana quickly turned away and sipped her drink, unsure how to take his remark.

"I've had parties certainly, friends who stayed over, and that sort of thing. But none of those occasions had the easy feeling of just sitting there with you while time flew by unnoticed."

She laughed softly. "We did manage to talk quite a while."

"I think that's a big clue in knowing you're spending time with the right kind of person."

"I've always enjoyed my time with you," she admitted, realizing that even J. B.'s close proximity behind her didn't make her nervous, not when they chatted easily like this, alone in the calm night air.

"With other people I find myself working at being witty and interesting and hope I come across as someone who is halfway intelligent." Out of the corner of her eye she saw J. B. take a drink of wine as she fingered the stem of her glass. Then he continued. "But with you, I don't have to work at it at all, because there's something about you that engenders those qualities in me naturally. Do you know what I'm saying?"

"Yes." She lowered her head, too overcome to say anything more, for J. B. had articulated her thoughts far more eloquently than she could have. She heard the soft clink of his wineglass as he set it on the small patio table. When he straightened, he closed his hands on her shoulders.

"I don't believe the easiness comes from knowing each other as children either," J. B. continued, still holding her. "That was just a fluke, growing up together."

"You think we would be here like this had we not grown up together?" she asked.

"Yes," he replied near her ear. His warm breath sent delicious tingles down her neck. "There's something about your spirit that I would recognize anywhere, anytime."

"The feeling of belonging."

"Yes. Had we met only yesterday, we would still be here, talking just like this, and connecting just like this." As if prompted by his words, he stepped closer and slid his arms around her torso. "Ah," he murmured, "just like this." Then he lowered his mouth to the small of her shoulder and pressed a long heartfelt kiss upon her skin.

She drew in a deep breath at his touch and let out

a ragged sigh. Slowly, tenderly, he pressed a trail of kisses up her neck to her jaw line as she tilted her head and allowed him passage, enraptured by the chills of delight brought on by his kisses.

His words and embrace intoxicated her far more quickly than the pinot grigio, and she closed her eyes, aching to succumb to everything J. B. might request. She let her head ease back to his shoulder and held her breath as his hands moved up to cup her breasts. A shaft of arousal spiked through her when he gently caressed her breasts and then sighed, as if the touch of her overwhelmed his senses.

"I have so longed to hold you," he said hoarsely. "Just like this."

She clutched her wineglass with one hand and wondered what to do with the other. Not to be facing J. B. put her at a distinct disadvantage for returning his caress. And at this point, returning his caress was the only thing on her mind.

When his hands slid down to stroke her bare thighs and push up the shirt tail, she suddenly froze, remembering that she wore no underwear, because she had rinsed out her panties and left them to dry in the bathroom. She couldn't allow him to go any farther, and yet she didn't want him to stop holding her and speaking such exquisite words. So, to gain more time to decide, she turned in his embrace and backed against the railing.

Without questioning her, he reached for her goblet, and without protesting she allowed him to lift the glass to her lips. He watched her drink and took a sip himself where her own lips had smudged the glass. Then J. B. set the glass aside and turned back to her, his eyes smoldering and serious. He took her elbows in his hands and gazed at her with a direct searching expression.

She gazed back, staring into the depths of eyes as dark and intense as her own, and knew they needed no words to accompany the communication that flowed between their hearts and minds. He bent down to her and she raised her chin toward him, drawn to the kiss that each of them had known was inevitable from the moment they recognized each other in the opera house.

The tip of his nose brushed hers and he tilted his head slightly to close his lips upon her mouth, tenderly at first. Then his grip tightened on her elbows and his jaw slanted across hers as the kiss deepened. She felt herself opening to him, her soul swelling upward to meet his, and without thinking, she raised her arms and wrapped them around his neck, sinking one hand into the glossy locks of his black hair. Gently she pressed the back of his head to keep his mouth joined to hers as he was meant to be joined, and then she kissed him with a fire born of unquestioning, unwavering love.

Tasharyana had never kissed any man but J. B., that day on the bank of the Nile. And though she had brought out the vision from her youth and reviewed it a thousand times, her memory kiss was nothing like the one here and now, with his arms crushing her close and his breath fanning her face. This J. B. was older, stronger, more assured. His kiss had mellowed from the desperate youth-driven passion she remembered to an appreciative adoration of her mouth and neck that melted her resolve to remain separate from him. Even though he had told her that he cared for her, that his house became a home when she was in it, and that they knew each other on the deepest levels, such words were totally unnecessary, for his kisses clearly spoke of the devotion and reverence he felt for her. Tasharyana's defenses to his lips and hands toppled like dominoes.

The night air enfolded them in a private cloud of discovery as they explored each other. She could have stayed in his arms forever, just kissing him and stroking his face and hair. But after a while, J. B. reached for the buttons of her shirt. Flustered, she kept kissing him, trying to decide how she would tell him to stop, and knowing in her heart she really didn't want him to back away. Soon he had undone every button. Tasharyana closed her eyes and tried to wrap her arms around him to deter him from his present course, but his calm, insistent hands slowly pulled the shirt open. Then he raised up, breaking from her kiss, and she was forced to stand apart from him.

The breeze fluttered around them, playing with the tails of the shirt as J. B. held the front edges away from her body and gazed at her nakedness. Tasharyana glanced down at herself, aware that her face was flushed, but knowing the sight of her was a gift that she wanted to offer without hesitation. Her scar could not be seen from this angle, especially in the dim light, and she was fairly certain the rest of her slender figure would please him. Slowly, she raised her glance to his face and saw the heated gratification in his eyes. She felt no shame as he gazed at her breasts and belly and thighs. In fact, a wave of primal satisfaction washed over her while she stood before him out in the open with the night wind sweeping by, naked to the sky and to him but shielded from anyone down below. She found it highly erotic to share this delicious secret with him, which the others could never know.

Then J. B. bent down and tasted her nipples, one at

a time, as if they were the sweetest fruit he had ever eaten. She thought she would explode right there on the balcony, that she would burst into a million glittering shards and scatter upon the night sky like the stars above.

"Julian!" she cried in a constricted voice. She wasn't prepared for the way his warm tongue titillated her breasts, the way his teeth pulled at them until she gasped and nearly collapsed backward, overwhelmed by the newfound desire that streaked through her. He clutched her tightly to keep her from falling, and she could feel the smile on his lips as he kissed her between her breasts.

"Didn't you know what your breasts were for?" he murmured softly.

"I never dreamed they could feel like this!" She gasped as she felt his lips trailing back to one of her aching peaks.

She watched the top of his head as he licked her nipple with the flat surface of his tongue, laving the sensitive nub until she cried out again. The sensation shot like lightning down to a place deep inside her, forcing her breath to grow harsh, her heart to pound, and the womanly place between her legs to throb and ache for him.

"Oh, Julian," she whispered. "Oh!" She closed her eyes and let her head loll back. "You are driving me so—" she gasped again as he took her other breast in his mouth, "—so crazy!"

"That's my intention, miss."

She smiled through the flood of desire coursing down her body, unconcerned with the rest of the universe while she hung in his arms. But soon she wondered what it would be like to see J. B.'s body as naked as her own, and how it would feel to touch the solid planes of his chest. Nearly blinded by passion, she raised her head and reached for the buttons of his shirt. He let her unfasten them as he nuzzled her ear and the ticklish area along her hairline. When his shirt fell open, he slipped out of it and tossed it on the table next to their wine goblets. As if he anticipated the coming together of their bare flesh as much as she did, he slowly drew her against him, savoring the moment until the tips of her breasts met his lean muscled chest. Then he slipped his arms around her and closed the small distance between them. His naked flesh came in heated contact with hers and she soared to a whole new level of ecstasy. J. B. sighed and hugged her fiercely.

For a moment she clung to him, galvanized. He was firmer, warmer, and his hard male body more powerfully arousing than she had ever imagined. She held him tightly and pressed her cheek against the smooth skin of his shoulder, reveling in the rise and fall of his breathing, the thudding of his heart, the glowing scent of him, and the thought that she was as close to the essence of his living being as anyone could ever get.

Then J. B. began to stroke her, cherishing the curves of her soft yielding body, and exploring the slope and lines of her feminine form. To be caressed by his smooth bare hands on her naked skin was the most wonderful sensation she had ever known. In response, she ran her hands over the muscles of his shoulders and his arms and gloried in the wide powerful wedge of his back, wondering what it would be like to have that back hovering above her as they made love.

Tasharyana flushed at the notion and her heart twisted in her chest. She wanted him to make love to her. Though she wasn't quite sure how it would feel or how they would fit together exactly, she wanted him inside her. Could she hide the truth from him? In the dark, would it be possible for him not to see the effects of her "evening surgery"? There was just a small scar, a line of discolored flesh and a patch where her soft brown hair didn't grow. Even though she had been told all pleasure would be missing for her during lovemaking, she still yearned to join with him, if only on an emotional plane. Could she take the chance that he might see her mutilation? And what if he did? What would he think? She would rather die than have J. B. turn away from her now, or worse yet hide his pity and disgust and carry on as if nothing was wrong. Should he not notice her mutilation, she wondered if he could tell if she was not experiencing all she should be during lovemaking.

While her thoughts churned, she felt a few light drops of rain on her cheek as the capricious April weather turned. But the rain was warm and she saw no reason to seek shelter, no reason to move from the balcony and the haven of J. B.'s embrace. As long as they stood together like this, clinging to each other, she didn't have to make a decision about what to do next.

Then J. B. slipped his hands over her rump. He let out a long sigh. "You're driving me absolutely stark raving mad."

"That's my intention, sir."

He chuckled as his palms moved over her. Her behind fit easily into his hands and she couldn't resist arching into him. His shaft angled to one side, hard as stone beside the zipper of his slacks, and the feeling of him against her made any thoughts of resisting vanish instantly. The rain came harder, in big warm plops, as they moved against each other, too engrossed in each other to care if they got wet. Without releasing her hips, J. B. nudged her against the balcony railing and stepped between her legs, until she was pressed between him and the rail. She heard the clink of his belt buckle as he unfastened it, and his knuckles brushed her belly as he undid his pants. Her mouth went dry. What should she do?

She heard the rough grate of his zipper as he leaned forward to kiss her, his breath coming in strident puffs above the patter of the rain. The sound of his breathing set her on fire and she raised one leg along the outside of his hard thigh. For one heart-stopping moment he paused and his body tensed beneath her hands. And then he carefully came up against her hot moist flesh with the tip of his straining manhood.

Tasharyana went completely rigid.

"Tasha!" he gasped. "Ah, God!" He dropped his face to her shoulder.

"J. B., we mustn't—"

"How can we not?" he whispered.

"Julian—"

Her faint words of protest washed away in the rain as she closed her eyes and embraced him, realizing she was on the brink of becoming his and soon could not turn back—didn't want to turn back. She kissed him passionately, knowing she was blissfully lost. Her plan to refuse him, to ask him to stop before he discovered too much, to remind him of his loyalty to Christine—all of it faded in the face of her need of him, the most primal need between a man and a woman made infinitely more urgent by her intense love for him. As she kissed J. B., she eased her tongue into his mouth and moved her hips so that his shaft passed over her achingly sensitive skin. He groaned and lifted her off the ground.

"We've got to go in," he said near her ear.

"To where?" she asked.

"Anywhere! The chaise." He swept her off her feet in a quick fluid movement, urging her to straddle his midsection.

Her heart beat wildly as he carried her across the balcony and through the French doors, holding her as if she were weightless while pressing fervent kisses on her mouth and neck.

Instead of stopping at the chaise, J. B. carried her down the hall and carefully set her on his bed. Then he slipped out of his pants and underwear and straightened. In the darkness she could discern his arousal in silhouette, and the sight of him made her ache for him more.

The mattress gave under his weight as he knelt on the bed and gently helped her out of her damp shirt. Without breaking eye contact, he tossed it on a nearby chair. She sank against the pillows, acutely aware that they were both stark naked. Her heart banged against her chest, nearly as loud as the rain on the roof.

J. B. seemed to sense her apprehension. He took her left hand and slowly brought it to his mouth, all the while gazing at her. He kissed the back of it, the palm, and then her wrist.

"I've wanted you here with me like this since I was sixteen," he said.

"That's a long time."

He caressed the side of her face. "But I want you to be sure that—"

"I want it. I want you. I always have." She stared at his dark eyes and knew he was as lost as she was to the flames of heat flaring between them. "It's just that I . . ."

"Go on."

"I've never done this before."

"I didn't think so." He smiled and the warmth in his eyes burrowed directly into her heart. He kissed her with infinite care and swept his hand from her breasts to the nest of hair between her legs. She trembled, never having been touched in such a way before. Then to her consternation, his hand slipped between her thighs and he touched her in the most intimate spot. She nearly jumped up from the bed at the flash of electricity that passed through her.

"Ah, there," he said and smiled slowly. She could hardly meet his gaze. What was he doing to her? Why could she feel what he was doing to her? Hadn't such a sensation been forever denied her?

He continued to touch her, caress her, and kiss her until she was writhing beneath his hand and moaning his name. What part wasn't she going to feel? The part when he came into her? She hoped she would be able to sense at least a fraction of it, for she could only imagine that this lovemaking with Julian was just going to get better and better.

Then she felt him move in between her legs and he put his hands on either side of her shoulders.

"Shall I use some protection?" he asked. "Or—"

"It will be all right, Julian. I want to feel you, all of you."

"Tell me to stop and I will," he rasped.

"I don't want you to stop."

"If you get frightened or feel anything painful—"

"I won't, J. B., I won't!" She reached up and wrapped her arms around his torso to assure him of her willingness to go on.

He nudged into her. His firm bluntness surprised her. Tasharyana sucked in a breath of astonishment as he sighed with rapture. Then he pulled away and she held her breath until he came back into her, more deeply this time. She moaned and the tenseness drained out of her shoulders as she relaxed. Whatever she had been robbed of by Madame Emide and Dr. Shirazzi, she had yet to discover it, for so far she could feel every pleasurable inch of J. B. Spencer.

"Okay?" he said.

"Yes!" she replied, hugging him. "Oh, yes!"

He pushed into her again and bent down to kiss her. Their lips met and clung together as their bodies joined to become one glorious undulating entity. She closed her eyes and abandoned herself to his irresistible rhythm and the sound of his heavy breathing, the unmistakable proof of his passion. There with J. B., Tasharyana forgot about everything—Madame Hepera, Mr. Gregg, her plans, her fears—as she fused with the man who had always been a part of her heart. Taking J. B. into her, she had never felt more connected to the true meaning of being a woman and yet so disengaged from the rest of the world. Locked together, she and J. B. were as close as any two human beings could be as their love for each other created a totally new and totally absorbing universe to which she gladly surrendered.

Sometime during the night, Tasharyana awoke to find herself nestled in J. B.'s arms, her cheek in the soft space between his shoulder and chest and his arms wrapped protectively around her. Their legs lay tangled together, with his left thigh casually angled between hers. All night they had made love, time after time, as if to compensate for the years they had lost, and now their bodies truly felt as if they were one. Tasharyana stretched her fingers across his right breast and looked at her hand. This was where she belonged, so closely entwined with J. B. that it was hard to tell where his hard masculine body stopped and her soft feminine shape began. How wonderful it would be if she could always share such closeness with him. But she knew better than to entertain a hopeless dream for the future. She should be glad just to have one night together with him, for she knew he was meant for another.

Tasharyana rose, contentedly exhausted, and padded to the bathroom. As she relieved herself, she thought about her chances of becoming pregnant, considering the number of times she had made love with J. B. She had read snippets of information in women's magazines about birth control and ovulation, but she had never had a reason to use the knowledge, sketchy as it was. Surely she wouldn't get pregnant from her very first time with a man. And if she did, would a child of J. B.'s be unwanted? She knew the answer to that question before the thought had completely formed. A child of J. B.'s would be a gift to her, not a burden.

She also wondered just what Dr. Shirazzi had done to her. Or *hadn't* done. She vaguely recalled him gloating about tricking Madame Emide. Could he have only *pretended* to circumcise her? She had felt every glorious moment of lovemaking with J. B., scars and all, and had begun to doubt the extent of her circumcision.

After washing her hands, she turned to open the door, just as she heard an unfamiliar metallic *clink* nearby. Tasharyana froze, her hand on the doorknob.

"J. B.?" she called softly.

She waited for an answer, listening intently, but

heard nothing. Perhaps she had imagined the sound. After all, the house was unfamiliar to her, and old houses emitted many peculiar noises, especially during the night.

Cautiously she opened the door and peered around the woodwork. She could see J. B. in bed, half-covered, his chest rising and falling in sleep. All was calm and peaceful. She took a step into the bedroom. The next instant she saw a flash of movement on the left.

"J.—!" she screamed, and then something hit her over the head, cutting off her cry for help. Everything went black.

Luxor, Present Day

"Ms. Spencer!" a gruff voice called, drawing Karissa out of the captivating world of Tasharyana's diary. She resisted, wanting to know what had happened to Tasharyana and longing to remain in the sweet memory of the lovemaking between the two people in the Philadelphia town house. She had known such lovemaking with Asheris and was loath to give up the wonderful vision for bleak reality. Karissa sighed and remained lying on the warm sand near the pond.

Had Tasharyana not shown up just before the engagement party, J. B. and Christine's marriage might have got off to a better start, which certainly would have affected the rest of their years together. Now Karissa could see why her mother had suspected J. B. of being in love with another woman. After Tasharyana's entrance into her life, Christine must never have fully trusted J. B. again, which was not a healthy foundation for any relationship.

Knowing how J. B. had adored Tasharyana, Karissa

was surprised that he would have gone on to marry Christine. Surely after the night in Philadelphia, J. B. must have felt more uncertain than ever about his upcoming commitment to Christine, for he obviously loved Tasharyana far more deeply than he did his fiancée. Karissa should have been resentful, perhaps even hurt, that the Egyptian woman had come between the happiness of her parents. But seeing the vignettes of Tasharyana's life during the scrying sessions, Karissa felt as if she knew Tasharyana and understood her more than Karissa had ever understood her own mother.

Consumed by an overwhelming sadness that as an adult she would never really know Tasharyana or her father, she slowly opened her eyes.

"Ms. Spencer!"

Hamid bent over her, his contorted old man's body twisted even more to one side so he could see her face.

"Ms. Spencer, are you ill?"

"No, I'm all right." Hoping to allay his fears, she struggled to get up as quickly as possible. But the scrying session had taken an even greater toll this time. Karissa was so weary, she could barely force herself to stand. She gave Hamid a shaky smile. "I just fell asleep, that's all."

Hamid glanced at the music box and then back to her, his bearded face wrinkling in concern. "You'd best be careful, Ms. Spencer."

His words puzzled her. Did Hamid know something about the box?

"Careful about what?" she asked.

"All things." He turned to go and then looked back over his humped shoulder. "Especially Julia."

"Julia?" she repeated.

He didn't respond and shuffled into the shadows of the acacia grove. Karissa didn't follow him to demand what he meant. She was too tired, and he was just an old man who spent all his time puttering around the grounds. What could he possibly know about Julia? He must have heard the arguments between Asheris and herself and had chosen to take sides with her husband.

She fought off the uncommon fatigue, put the obelisks away in the box, and trudged back to the house. On her way to bed, she slipped into the library to look through her father's journals. Burning questions remained from the scrying. What had happened to Tasharyana? And why would J. B. have proceeded with a marriage doomed to fail when he knew his heart lay elsewhere? He must have written about that turbulent time in his life, and she was determined to find the entry. She selected journals spanning the corresponding months and carried them to her bedroom.

14

Karissa woke up to find herself in bed surrounded by her father's journals. She must have fallen asleep still holding one of them, for it had slipped from her grip and slid to the floor, spilling loose papers and postcards on the tile. Hurriedly, she gathered up the papers and stuffed them in the journal, promising herself to come back later and arrange them in proper chronological order, the way her father would have left them.

Then, glancing at her watch, she was shocked to find it was already eight o'clock in the morning—only a few minutes before Julia was to leave for school, should she be going to school. Karissa hadn't set her alarm because she decided to honor Asheris's demand of the previous evening that Julia not attend. Unfortunately, she had forgotten to inform Julia and hadn't had a chance to notify the school yet either. And she suddenly remembered that the school van was scheduled to pick up Julia in front of the house.

What if Julia had got herself ready and went off to school on her own? Asheris would be infuriated.

Chiding herself for not thinking ahead, Karissa jumped out of bed and pulled on her robe. She hurried down the hall to the front of the house, calling for Eisha and Julia. To her dismay, she heard the distant rumble of an engine outside the house. Had the van just arrived? If so, she just might be able to stop it in time.

Karissa yanked open the front door and almost ran into Eisha, who stood on the front porch waving to the back of the van as it rolled down the street.

"Wait!" Karissa cried, but her voice was drowned out by the hum of the engine.

"What's the matter, Ms. Spencer?" Eisha asked, turning to her mistress.

"Julia wasn't supposed to go to school today."

"She wasn't?"

"No. Why didn't someone wake me up?"

"I tried to, Ms. Spencer. But you seemed so tired."

Karissa sighed in exasperation. "Of all the days to sleep in."

"She'll be all right, Ms. Spencer. I packed her an extra special lunch."

"It isn't that, Eisha. Her father decided the school wasn't right for her. I'll have to drive out there and get her. If Asheris should happen to get up before I get back, please tell him where I went, would you?"

"Of course. I'm sorry, Ms. Spencer, but I didn't know, and Julia was so excited."

"It's all right, Eisha. You did what seemed best." Karissa retraced her steps to her room. She dressed, frowning the whole time, knowing how disappointed Julia would be when she learned she wouldn't be going to the school after all. Karissa would have to make up some excuse that Julia wouldn't see through, because she didn't want to tell her the real reason for the suspension of her studies, that Asheris thought the school was a dangerous place.

Before Karissa left, she called the school to have Julia detained in the office so it would be less of a disruption when Karissa arrived to take her home. The secretary in the office was surprised to hear that Julia was to go home and tried to discover the reason, but Karissa didn't care to discuss the matter with anyone but the headmistress.

Karissa drove through the morning sunshine, but the storm inside her doused all the cheer from the bright April day. Surely the officials at the conservatory would be anxious to hear why a student would drop out after a single day of school, but she had no desire to confront them with her weak excuses. Moreover, she didn't want Julia to feel any guilt or embarrassment because of the change in plans.

Distracted and more than a little angry with Asheris for making such an imperious demand, then leaving her to deal with the consequences, Karissa pulled into the parking lot on the side of the school. She grabbed her purse and walked briskly to the front entrance.

The secretary showed her to the headmistress's office, a small oppressive room with heavy dark woodwork from the turn of the century, made even more oppressive by shelves and shelves of books. Everything in the room, from furniture to decorative motifs appeared to have gone unchanged for a hundred years or more. At Karissa's entrance, the headmistress rose from her chair and motioned for Karissa to take a seat.

Stiffly, Karissa sat on the edge of the hard wooden chair, too nervous to relax. She briefly surveyed the head of the school, a middle-aged woman with shrunken breasts and thin, birdlike bones in her hands and wrists, as she resumed her position behind the desk.

"I'm Mrs. Farag," she began. "The headmistress here at the Luxor Language School. What can I do for you, Mrs. Asher?" She tilted her head and smiled in a calm manner that Karissa guessed she had practiced for years in order to assuage the concerns of worried parents and frightened children.

Karissa ignored the smile and the incomplete last name. "I've come to take my daughter home," Karissa replied. "Her father and I have decided to postpone her studies for a while."

"I am sorry to hear that, Mrs. Asher. Julia is quite bright, you know." She folded her hands primly. "Was there a particular reason for your decision?"

"Well, actually, we've just learned we have to go out of the country for a while."

"We do have a boarding option, if you recall."

"My husband and I prefer to have Julia accompany us abroad." Karissa kept her gaze steady in hopes that the headmistress wouldn't see through her lies.

"Travel is an education in itself," Mrs. Farag commented. "But I do hope you will reenroll Julia upon your return."

"We will certainly consider it." Karissa clutched her bag with both hands. "I'd like to leave as soon as possible, Mrs. Farag. If you would call for Julia?"

"Certainly." Mrs. Farag pushed a button on an intercom and asked that Julia be shown in. She was answered by static and then the secretary opened the door. The headmistress stood up. "Miss Ibrahms, I just buzzed you to see if Julia Spencer-Asher has come to the office yet."

"No," the secretary exclaimed, throwing a worried

glance at Karissa and then back again to the headmistress. "No one has seen her this morning, ma'am."

"What?" Karissa jumped to her feet.

"She didn't show up for her first class. No one has seen her."

"How can this be?" Karissa glanced wildly at Mrs. Farag. "She rode in the van from the school this morning. It came to the house to pick her up! How can she not be here!"

"Please, Ms. Spencer, please calm down." The headmistress bestowed another charming smile upon her. "There must be some explanation. Miss Ibrahms, would you find the driver and send him in?"

"Yes, ma'am."

Karissa watched the secretary leave the room and then she turned back to the headmistress. "I saw Julia. She was in the van—the van from this school!"

"You saw her get into the van?"

"Well," Karissa paused, not anxious to admit she had slept in. "Not exactly. But I saw the van leaving."

"Could Julia possibly be playing the truant?"

"No!" Karissa shook her head vehemently. "She's not like that. In fact, she was anxious to go to school today. She wanted to come here."

They discussed other possibilities for a few moments until the driver appeared in the doorway. He was a young man, close to Karissa's age, dressed in modern western clothes. Mrs. Farag introduced him and then asked him questions about his route that morning.

He fingered his cap and looked at the floor. "I didn't pick up any new girls this morning. Nobody told me there was a new girl."

"That's impossible!" Karissa cried. "The van came to the house this morning."

The driver looked up, squinted his eyes, and hung his head again. "It wasn't my van. I just did my usual route."

So that was it! His route hadn't included the Asher home. Karissa turned to the headmistress. "Where are your other drivers?"

"We don't have any other drivers. Only this one."

Her confusion quickly transformed into panic as she faced the driver again. "Then you must be thinking of another day. I saw the van. My child got in the van. And the van drove away."

"Not my van, ma'am." He shrugged. "Sorry."

"You don't remember a tall slender girl with black hair? Six years old? Wearing a light blue dress and white socks and black shoes?"

The driver shook his head. "No. I didn't see a girl like that. I am sure of it."

"I'll have the grounds searched, Mrs. Asher," the headmistress put in. "And in the meantime, I think we should call the police."

The search of the school produced nothing, not even a clue that Julia had been there earlier. The police promised to come at once and check the school more thoroughly, while an inspector agreed to bring his officers to the Asher estate and search for the girl there. Karissa was to meet them outside the house as soon as possible.

Sick with worry, Karissa returned home, praying she would find Julia reading in her room or playing with George out in the garden. The police were waiting for her when she drove up, as was Asheris whose face was an impassive, grim-lipped mask with haunted, burning eyes. Karissa could hardly bear to look at him. The police made an exhaustive search of the entire house as well as the grounds and the nearby homes. But Julia was nowhere to be found.

The inspector wrote notes in a little tablet and barely said a word as they stood in the atrium, not knowing what to do next, not knowing where else they could possibly look for a six-year-old girl.

"Poor, poor Julia!" Eisha wailed. "May Allah protect her!"

The inspector frowned at the housekeeper's outburst and then flipped his tablet shut. "We'll continue the investigation in town. Will someone be here to answer the phone?"

"Yes," Asheris replied, his voice clipped and cold.

"We'll do all we can to find your daughter, Mr. Asher." He held out his hand and the men shook. "We will call you the moment we find anything."

"Thank you."

Asheris showed the police to the front door and then turned. His expression was so controlled Karissa had no idea what he was feeling or thinking. She stared at him, engulfed by a maelstrom of emotions: panic, worry, fear, exasperation, and guilt. Her ears hummed loudly, and for an instant she thought she might faint. She was vaguely aware of Eisha's quick retreat from the atrium, as if the housekeeper sensed the impending blowup between Asheris and Karissa and was anxious to be clear of the scene.

"Asheris—" she gasped, not knowing how to begin. Her stomach churned with panic and self-recrimination. What had she done? In what danger had she put her dear little child? And what was Asheris thinking? He would probably never speak to her again and never forgive her. She would never forgive herself.

"Asheris!" Her voice cracked. Karissa could feel herself breaking apart, from her heart outward, and didn't know how much longer she could stand up.

She forgot her dread of being chastised by Asheris and remembered only the ways in which he had come to her assistance in the years long since past, how he had given her comfort and understanding, and had helped her overcome her deepest troubles. She longed to collapse against him and feel his arms around her, but instead she stood before him, ramrod straight with self-reproach and worry.

"Karissa," he replied. "Tell me now, in your own words again, what happened."

"Eisha saw Julia to the van this morning—the school van, you know—quite by accident because neither one of them knew that Julia was not to go to school, since I hadn't—"

"Wait!" he exclaimed, striding toward her. "Slow down." He reached for her wrist. "I cannot understand when you go so quickly. You say that Julia got in the school van?"

"Yes. She didn't know you had forbidden her to go to school. I slept in, you see, and Eisha thought she was doing me a favor by letting me sleep. So she got Julia ready for school."

"And a vehicle from the school arrived to collect her?"

"Yes. Eisha saw her get on. That's when I woke up to see the van leaving."

"And then what did you do?"

"I drove out to the school, but when I got there, the headmistress claimed that Julia had never shown up at school."

"Never arrived?"

"No. And when I talked to the van driver, he said that no one fitting Julia's description ever got in his van."

"Osiris!" Asheris whispered, his troubled gaze focusing on the far wall. "My Julia!"

"That's when I called the police. Then I came back here to see if Julia had somehow got off the van without our knowledge, if she had somehow come back home." She stared at him, her heart cracking into jagged shards. "What have I done, Asheris? What have I *done*?"

She felt Asheris's fingers tighten around her wrist, which had the strange effect of squeezing tears out of her eyes. Much to her dismay, she started to cry, crumbling under the pressure of learning her child was missing, all because of her negligence. With her free hand she concealed her eyes from him, ashamed of her tears, but she couldn't keep her shoulders from shaking. Karissa dreaded what Asheris would say, sure that his heart was already turning to stone. She was surprised, then, when he drew her against his chest and wrapped his arms around her. His arms were strong and his embrace full of support.

"You have done nothing wrong, my sweet," he murmured, holding her head to the small of his shoulder, his hand in her hair. "This is the work of the priestesses of Sekhmet."

"Who?"

"The lion worshippers. The strongest priesthood in ancient Egypt."

Karissa recalled the priestesses of Sekhmet were the same women who had cursed her husband centuries ago, and had put him under a spell. "But what have they to do with Julia?"

"They want our daughter. Why, I do not know. But I suspect the school or someone at the school is directly related to the temple of Sekhmet."

She raised her head to glare at him through her tears. "Why didn't you tell me?"

"I have harbored suspicions for some time, but I

could not confirm them until last night, when Julia told me of a ring one of the women wore, and that they inspected her hair."

"They inspected her hair?"

"I fear they were searching for the birthmark like the one which you bear and Julia also, as well as the ancient priestess Senefret."

"To prove she is of the special lineage?"

"Yes," Asheris replied, his voice husky. "So she can serve the temple."

"No! Julia is our daughter! They can't have her!"

But even as she cried out the words, she knew Julia had never quite belonged to her. Julia had always been different, special, more like a gift for her to cherish than a human child to raise. Had the priestesses of Sekhmet been waiting all along for Julia to reach a certain age, allowing her to remain in the hands of her ordinary parents until the time came for her to enter this priesthood? Yet *were* both her parents ordinary? Karissa glanced at Asheris's proud handsome face, still in awe of his appearance. His seed had produced Julia, and his seed sprang from a well thousands of years old. Who could tell what genetic information had been passed along to their child—and what ancient attributes Julia might possess?

"Oh, Julia," she cried again, consumed with anguish. "Oh, God!"

Asheris caressed the side of her face and looked deep into her eyes. "That is why I wanted so much to protect Julia. I have sensed danger all around us. For years I have sensed it, ever since Julia's birth."

"But why didn't you tell me?"

"I had no proof. I could not support my fears. I felt like a worried old woman who must look over her shoulder and flinch at shadows."

"Asheris, I am the person with whom you should share everything. The good and the bad. This silence between us has torn us apart!"

"Yes. And I regret not telling you." He squeezed her and then held her away from him, as if to check to make sure she could stand on her own. "But now we must work together and find our child."

"How?"

"I will go to the school and confront the woman with the lioness ring. You will stay here and wait for news."

"I'll go crazy just waiting!"

"We cannot both go to the school. If something should befall one of us, Julia will still have the other. Besides, there may be some contact made regarding Julia while I am gone, either from the priestesses or the police. Someone must be here to receive it."

"All right." She breathed in, feeling somewhat better now that Asheris had formed a tentative plan.

Asheris continued. "You might tell Hamid to ask if anyone has heard or seen anything. He knows many people in the neighborhood and is a good resource."

"All right. I'll talk to him."

Asheris squeezed her shoulders. "We will find her, Karissa. We will."

Karissa nodded mutely, too shattered to speak.

He took a step toward her and drew her into his arms again. For a long moment he held her and stroked her. "Do not blame yourself, sweet," he said softly. "I know that you are and it should not be so."

"I should have listened to you, Asheris. I should have heard what you were trying to tell me."

"And I should have *told* you." With a hand under her chin, he tipped her head back to look in her eyes. "I should have trusted your faith in me."

She flung her arms around his neck as new tears came. Then their mouths joined in a desperate kiss, each of them plunged into their own private agony over Julia.

Asheris sighed and pulled away. “I must go, before the trail gets cold.”

“Call me if you find out anything!”

“I will.”

He touched her cheek and hurried out of the house.

15

Karissa spent the entire day pacing, first in the atrium near the telephone, and then in the garden—too agitated to sit still and too preoccupied with worry for Julia to keep her mind on even a small task. Asheris had returned from the school empty-handed but had decided to make another trip that night when he could inspect the files and search the grounds on his own. Hamid had fared no better. None of his acquaintances had seen six-year-old Julia Spencer-Asher, and surely they would have noticed, for everyone thought the child was one of the loveliest little girls they had ever seen. In fact, Karissa was surprised at the number of people who knew her daughter and what she looked like. Apparently Asheris's attempts at keeping Julia's existence a secret had failed.

Neither of them ate the entire day, and when night fell, Asheris strode out to the Land Rover to return to the school. Karissa walked out with him.

"Try to sleep," he said, looking at her over the car door.

"I won't be able to. Not with Julia gone."

"You won't be doing her any good if you lose sleep, Karissa. You need to keep up your strength. Tomorrow we'll go to the police, and it will be a trying day."

Karissa swallowed and wrapped her arms around her midriff. She felt haggard, drained, and hollow. With Julia missing, she felt as if half of her heart were missing as well.

"I can't imagine what it must be like for her, what she must be thinking, what's happening to her—"

"Do not imagine, Karissa. You will drive yourself crazy."

He got in the vehicle and closed the door. For a moment he gazed at her, his arm resting on the open window frame. Then he started the engine.

"I'll be back as soon as I can," he promised.

She nodded and gave a small wave as the car pulled away from the curb.

She walked back into the house, going over the things she knew about the school and the priestesses again and again, hoping a stray fact might pop out to help them find Julia. Lion-headed rings. Red birthmarks at the hairline. Priestesses and the lost sphinx. Old ladies with rings. As she opened the front door, she recalled a fragment from Tasharyana's tale. *Old ladies with rings!*

In her visions, Tasharyana had mentioned rings. Madame Hepera had worn many rings. And she had mentioned the lions, too. Madame Hepera had performed rites in the basement of her Cairo home involving braziers and statues of lions. Karissa's pace quickened, as did her heartbeat. What did Madame

Hepera have to do with the temple of Sekhmet? Could Karissa possibly learn something to help find Julia by viewing the rest of the diary? What might be gained by scrying again while she waited for Asheris to return?

Spurred on by new resolve, she found Eisha and gave her instructions to come out to the pond and rouse her if anyone should call regarding Julia. When Asheris returned, she was to send him out to the garden immediately. Eisha nodded gravely, as upset as Karissa and Asheris over Julia's disappearance.

Karissa hurried to her room to get the sandalwood box, which she carried to the garden. Then, humming in a quavering voice, she put in the fourth obelisk and sat down upon the warm sand by the pond, hoping the moonlight was strong enough to activate the magic.

As in all the other times, Tasharyana gradually appeared in her shimmering galabia on the surface of the water.

Tasharyana's Tale—Baltimore, 1966

Groggy and half-nauseous, Tasharyana raised her head, only to find herself subjected to a stabbing pain behind her eyes.

"Tasha," a familiar voice exclaimed. "How are you feeling?"

She rolled her head to look at J. B. and experienced another wave of nausea. She suddenly realized they were in a car and she sat slumped in the front seat next to Julian who was at the wheel. He glanced at her, his eyes full of concern.

"Are you okay?" he asked.

"I think so." She licked her dry lips and closed her eyes against the pain in her head. "What happened?"

"That guy in the tweed coat—what was his name again?"

"Mr. Gregg?"

"Yes, Mr. Gregg." He turned the wheel to maneuver a corner, "The bastard broke into my house early this morning and attacked you. He hit you over the head with his gun, probably to knock you out so he could abduct you."

"So what happened?"

"You screamed and woke me up. I managed to fight him off and knock his gun away, but the bastard got loose and ran off."

"I must have been followed after all."

"Yes. And I thought it best that we leave before Mr. Gregg came back for more."

"I've been unconscious?"

"Not for long."

Tasharyana looked down at the cotton shift and jacket she wore. Instinctively, she checked for the diamonds hidden in the pocket. The gems were there. "How did I get dressed?"

"I dressed you."

"You did?" She blushed.

"Yes." J. B. cocked an eyebrow at her. "And I don't know what I liked best—dressing or undressing you."

She smiled in spite of her throbbing headache. "Perhaps you'll have another chance to find out someday."

"Soon I hope." His gaze leveled upon hers and he reached out with his right hand to stroke her leg. "I've never had a night like last night. Never."

"Yes, it was wonderful."

"Wonderful? It was incredible! Do you know how incredible such a night like that is? How rare it is that two people like us find each other?"

"I haven't much experience in such things, J. B."

"My pet," he lifted her hand to his lips. "Our love-making was exquisite. You were exquisite. And quite uninhibited, I might add."

"You make me feel free and well loved," she replied, as a warm wave of love rushed over her. "It is a most wonderful feeling."

"Yes, it is."

She watched him as he kissed her hand again and gradually lowered their hands to his thigh. His actions were full of tenderness and care, but he hadn't once told her he loved her. Tasharyana glanced at the side of his face, longing to hear some kind of affirmation from him.

After a moment he looked over at her again. "How are you feeling now, though? Gregg gave you a nasty bump on your right temple."

"I feel rather ill, actually. Are we going to stop soon?"

"Are you going to be sick?"

"Not immediately. But I don't know how much more driving I can take, J. B. My stomach is upset and my head is throbbing."

"We're almost there."

"Where are you taking me?"

"To the Petrie's house. Your Madame Hepera will never think to look for you there—I hope."

Tasharyana fell silent and slipped her hand out of J. B.'s tender grasp. The last place she wanted to spend any time was in a house belonging to Frances Petrie.

"What's the matter, Tasha?"

"I don't think the Petries will appreciate my presence, J. B., especially when they're planning that big party."

"Don't worry about it. Besides, they have all kinds of household help. Frances and Christine rarely lift a finger when they give a party. The most they do is plan the menu and draw up a guest list. They just like to make a big deal of all the trouble they go to."

"I'm not speaking of the work involved, J. B. I'm talking about the way it will look to Christine and her friends and family—you bringing me to her home two days before a party where her engagement to you will be announced."

"That's not written in stone, Tasha, the engagement announcement."

"Are you sure? It seems that Christine is convinced it will happen."

J. B. sighed. "I promised to tell you about the Petries, didn't I?"

"Yes."

"Would you like to hear? Do you feel well enough?"

"Yes. Go on, J. B."

J. B. waited for a light to turn green and then accelerated through the intersection before he spoke. He gripped the wheel with both hands. "I met Christine through her twin brother, Charlie, who was my roommate at Eton. I told you that, didn't I?"

"Yes."

"Well, Charlie and I were good pals. He'd often invite me to go home with him on holidays or travel in Europe. The Petries were rich as sin and he had money to burn. I'd go with him, which was fine with Frances, because I apparently kept Charlie out of trouble. He didn't have much sense in those days, you see. He didn't improve with age, either. He usually lost more on the stock exchange than I made in a year. And it didn't faze him in the least."

Tasharyana raised her brows, surprised.

"Well, over the years I got to know the Petries intimately. Christine hung on my every word and wrote to me often. She used to send me poems. They were nothing out of the ordinary, but the thought was nice. Having Frances for a mother must have put a damper on her character, though, because she would never loosen up, never really talk to me as you and I talk."

"You mean from the heart?"

"Yes. In many ways, she's still a stranger to me. I really don't know who she is."

"Then why in the world would you ask her to marry you?"

"Purely out of guilt." He sighed and shot her a dark look of repressed anger. The look stunned her. What had he done that forced him to ask a woman to marry him? Then the answer struck her, nearly as hard as the bump on her head, but with infinitely more pain. Christine was pregnant.

"What do you mean, guilt?" Her voice wavered at the thought of J. B. fathering a child by Christine. Yet what else could induce him to marry her? And if J. B. was to have a child with Christine, he was as good as married to her as far as Tasharyana was concerned. She would never put herself between a father and his child.

"I'm not proud of what I have to tell you, Tasha. And maybe after you hear what I've done, you might not think I'm such a great guy. I wouldn't blame you either."

She watched the muscle of his jaw work back and forth as he clenched his teeth. Dread poured over her. Yet she had to know the truth. She had to hear him say it. *Christine's pregnant and I've got to stand by her.*

"So what did you do that was so awful?"

"Because of me, Tasha, because of my self-indulgence, Charles Petrie was killed."

"What?" Tasharyana gaped at him, completely flabbergasted.

"Because of me, the Petries lost their only male

heir. Christine lost her twin brother and only sibling, with whom she was inordinately close. Frances lost her son, and the Petrie law firm lost its junior partner." He sighed heavily. "After causing such grief, I couldn't pursue my own happiness. It would have been far too selfish, dishonorable."

"I don't believe it!" In her shock, Tasharyana entirely forgot about the pregnancy possibility. She reached for J. B.'s hand. "Julian, what happened? How did he die?"

"It was after we graduated. It started out just like any normal Saturday here in Baltimore." His knuckles turned white as he gripped the steering wheel. "Charlie played polo all afternoon while I grabbed the chance to do a bit of sonic research. I never had the time to do any experiments during the week, since my client load was fairly heavy, so I always saved my weekends for my real work."

Tasharyana nodded, urging him to continue.

"Well, Charlie was the kind of fellow who played hard and drank hard. He and his buddies would start drinking late in the afternoon, after the match. Christine would often go out to the club and meet Charlie and his friends. They'd have dinner and chum around all night and do the town, dancing and the like, you know."

"Didn't Christine drag you out as her escort?"

J. B. gave a short dry laugh. "Oh, she knew better than to ask. I never liked spending my time that way. Still don't. I suppose I lived too many years in a society that didn't countenance alcohol to ever get accustomed to the drinking and dancing routine."

"And yet Christine thinks you'd make a compatible mate?"

J. B. shrugged. "I'm not certain Christine thinks in

those terms, Tasha. Or she probably thinks I'll change eventually, once we're married."

Tasharyana knew J. B. well enough to predict that he would never give up his varied interests for something as frivolous as drinking and dancing.

"So, what happened that night?"

"Christine was ill. She called me to say she didn't feel up to going out with Charlie and the gang. Of the two twins, she was the responsible one. She didn't ever drink too much and always made sure Charlie got home in one piece—which had been my job at Eton, you know."

Tasharyana nodded, fairly certain now how the story would end, but wondering why J. B. would blame himself. "And?"

"Well, she asked me to go round to such and such a club at closing time to make sure Charlie was in a condition to drive. She worried about such things, for good reason. Charlie never knew his limits. He always went one step beyond, no matter what he did, be it women, playing the market, drinking, or what have you. He always went over the line. And he always relied on somebody else to be responsible for him."

J. B. sighed again and stared straight ahead, as if trying to control himself enough to continue speaking. She saw his Adam's apple bob in his throat. Tasharyana squeezed his fingers and stroked the back of his hand, longing to give him support, but knowing he had to forgive himself before he could accept support from anyone else.

"So I said, sure, I'd track Charlie down and make certain he got home safely. Christine never thought twice about asking. I was always available and dependable, too. But that night—" he shook his head slowly and pressed his lips together. Tasharyana squeezed his hand again. "That night I was on to something in my research. Something really big. Something that might entirely change our theories on sound and movement." He pulled his hand away and clutched both fists around the wheel. "I'd like to say I forgot. I'd like to say that Charlie just slipped my mind. But to tell you the truth, I didn't want to stop. I didn't want to rescue that drunken sot for the thousandth time and tuck him into bed. Just once, I decided to let the bastard take care of himself."

Tasharyana stared at J. B.'s grim profile, knowing exactly what he was going to say. "So he drove home drunk," she put in.

"Not quite home, my pet." His voice had a hard bitter edge. "On the way back to the house, Charlie made a little detour—into the Patapsco River."

"Oh, Julian!"

"He had a woman with him, too."

J. B. rolled his tongue around in his mouth, as if it had suddenly grown too dry to speak. Tasharyana stared through the windshield, lost for words. For a long moment the roar of the wheels on the highway seemed unbearably loud.

After an extensive pause, Julian spoke, his voice quiet and strained. "When the bodies were found, Old Man Petrie—Charles Senior—who'd had a stroke a few months earlier, suffered a relapse and died three days after the accident. I forgot to tell you that."

"Oh, J. B.!" She ached to hold him, to wrap her arms around him. But she could tell by his rigid posture that gestures of support and comfort would not be accepted.

"Of course I handled all the funeral arrangements. And then what with Charles Senior's passing I took over the estate settlement, too. I've been some type of custodian or executor for the Petries' lives for quite a while now. And I'm sure they expect me to always be around." He sighed again. "So you see, Tasha, why I feel as if I owe them all something?" He gave her another hard look, as if daring her to refute him.

She gazed at him, struggling to find the right words. What would it take to convince J. B. of the error in his logic? Through the fog in her aching head, she fought for reason, realizing the importance of coming up with pointed questions to reveal the gaps in his thinking. Hoping the pain wouldn't muddle her thoughts, she pressed on.

"Julian, don't you see? You will never be Charlie. You can't replace him. You'll never be like him."

"But I can manage the family business. I can take Frances to the opera. I can become a lifetime companion to Christine."

"Will doing those things bring Charlie back?"

J. B. started to say something, fell silent, and then let out a long exasperated breath. He whipped around the steering wheel to make a sharp turn, his abrupt driving style reflecting his mood. Then he scowled.

Tasharyana reached out to stroke him, from the crown of his head to the collar of his shirt. She gazed at him, trying to send him a silent message from her heart, a message that might get past his sense of honor and his stubborn attachment to guilt. For a few minutes she simply stroked him, until she saw his eyelids flutter as if he were succumbing to her touch. Then she felt his tenseness ebb and she knew it was time to speak.

"J. B., listen to me. You can't give up your life for Charlie like this. If you do, it will be as if you'd died in the car, too. A life with Christine will kill you. You'll die slowly and gradually, little by little, until one day you'll look at yourself and know you've wasted your entire life *and* hers."

"Hers?"

"Do you think a soulless man is going to make her happy? Because that's what you'll be. You'll be unavailable in all the ways that matter to a woman."

"What do you mean?"

"Your marriage will be loveless, passionless."

"I don't think that would matter to Christine." J. B. let up on the gas and drifted toward a stop light. "Love and passion are unknown concepts to her. Of all the things people like you and me crave—connecting, passion, intimacy—Christine comprehends nothing. It's not as if she's failed a test of any kind. She hasn't. She's simply different from you and me. Her main goal in life is to find the best of all possible escorts."

"But in time you won't even care to escort her to her social events, will you?"

"Probably not. I don't much now."

"And she doesn't care a fig about physics or history, does she?"

"Hardly."

"Is she desirable to you on a purely physical level?"

"Actually, I've always thought of Christine as a sister more than anything else."

"So what will you share with her?" Tasharyana sat back, knowing she had forced him into a corner. She tried to ignore her pounding head.

J. B. glanced at her and then away, his expression dark and stormy as he struggled to find an answer using his logic and reason. After a moment he glanced at her again, and this time she could see his eyebrows had raised just a little, enough to betray the dawning of understanding.

"Damn," he whispered, shaking his head. He sped through the yellow light.

"I don't think Frances particularly likes you, either, J. B., certainly not enough to take the place of her son."

"What are you trying to say—that I not only failed to keep Charlie alive, I'm failing utterly at being his substitute as well?"

"What I'm trying to say, J. B., is that being Charlie is not the answer. You're not going to please anyone trying to make up for his absence."

"But if I'd just gone to the club that night—"

"Well, you didn't. Of all the hundreds of times you were there for him, this was just one instance you decided to let him take care of himself. It was just one time, Julian."

"But that one time caused his death."

"Charlie caused his death. Not you. He decided to get drunk. He decided to drive home. It was his choice."

"But I could have prevented his death."

"Can't you put that single night behind you? Can't you just tell yourself that you made the wrong decision that night?"

"And forget it, just like that? What kind of man does that make me?"

"Human."

"No, sir. That's too easy, Tasha."

"So you'll beat yourself up for the rest of your life? And drag Christine along with you? What kind of man does *that* make you, J. B.?"

For a long moment he didn't say anything. Then he looked at her, silent and grim. "Touché," he said softly.

Tasharyana took a deep breath against the pain in her head and regarded him. She felt as if she had spent an entire night watching over a sick person whose fever had just broken. And now she knew she had finally brought him to where true healing could begin.

"So are you going to tell Christine the marriage is off?"

J. B. clenched the wheel. "It isn't that easy. Christine has told all of her friends. If I tell her I want to break it off, she'll be devastated, not because her heart will be broken, but because she will look like a fool to the rest of the world."

"And this makes you reluctant to tell her?"

"Yes. For Christine, the social humiliation would be devastating. I can't do that to her."

Tasharyana stared out the window as the warmth between them dissipated. Though he was having second thoughts about his upcoming engagement to Christine, he had never once made any reference to a future with her or mentioned that she might be the reason for his change of heart. In fact he hadn't said one way or the other whether or not he planned to call the engagement off. She chided herself for wanting to have some effect on him. It wouldn't be fair to anyone concerned if she distracted him from his path with an unspoken promise that she would be there for him. Her life wasn't meant to intersect with his. That should have been obvious eight years ago.

"I hope you don't think I'm trying to talk you out of marriage to Christine because of an ulterior motive of mine." She said at last. "I said all those things as your friend."

"I know," he patted her hand. "And I can't tell you how much your friendship means to me."

Friendship? Wasn't there more between them than friendship? His reply did nothing to ease the ache in her heart.

"Still, it isn't fair to Christine that you should take me to her house."

"I hope she'll understand. And it's only temporary.

I've got a friend in San Francisco who can hide you until Madame Hepera gives up." He turned up a narrow drive. "And speaking of the Petries, here we are."

A few minutes later Tasharyana stood supported by the strong link of J. B.'s right arm in the main hall of the Petrie house as the butler carefully shut the door behind them. Though her head pounded and her stomach churned, Tasharyana savored the feeling of standing close to J. B. She had spent so much of her life alone, without meaning anything to anyone or having anyone mean anything to her. Such a lack in her life made her treasure his nearness and support even though she knew it wouldn't last. A movement caught her attention, however, and she looked up to see Christine on the stairs.

"Julian!" Christine exclaimed, pausing on the landing. "What a surprise to see you! You, too, Miss Higazi." Hiding her confusion, she smoothly remembered her manners and swept a hand out toward them. "Won't you come in?"

"Thanks, Christine," J. B. replied. "I need to ask you a favor."

"Certainly. Why don't you come into the parlor where we can talk?"

"I'm afraid Miss Higazi isn't feeling well. Can she rest somewhere?"

"Oh, dear." Christine glanced again at Tasharyana with true concern in her eyes. "Of course. Come this way."

She turned back up the stairs and ascended to the second floor with J. B. following close behind. Tasharyana thought her temples would burst before she ever made it to the top of the stairs. If it hadn't been for J. B., she would have crumpled to the ground.

Christine showed her into a beautiful bedchamber decorated in blue-and-ivory striped wallpaper and quickly turned down a bed covered with a fluffy chintz comforter and mounds of pillows and shams. J. B. helped toss the pillows aside to make room for Tasharyana. She slipped out of her flats and gratefully sank onto the cool sheets.

"What's wrong with her?" Christine asked. "Does she need a doctor?"

"She suffered a nasty blow to the head. But I think she'll be all right. Could you have Johnson get her things out of the car and bring them up?"

"Yes." Christine glanced at Tasharyana. "Do you want anything, Miss Higazi? A drink of some kind? Something to eat?"

"Nothing, thank you."

"Can she stay here for a day or two, Christine?" J. B. asked, gently drawing the covers over Tasharyana. "Until I make arrangements for her to go to California?"

"Of course. But why here in particular?"

"She's in danger. Someone's trying to harm her."

"Oh, dear!"

"I don't think anyone would look for her here."

Suddenly the door opened wide and Frances Petrie loomed on the threshold, the angles of her spare body accentuated in silhouette.

"What's going on here?" she snapped.

Christine straightened her shoulders as if called to attention by a commanding officer. "Miss Higazi is in danger, Mother. She needs to stay with us for a few days."

"Danger?" Frances swept forward, her jersey dress swishing around her calves. "What type of danger?"

"Attempted kidnapping, Frances," said J. B.

"Why would anyone want to kidnap her?" Frances asked, obviously incredulous that Tasharyana might have some value.

"We're not sure. But I don't want to take the chance of finding out."

"If it's inconvenient, Mrs. Petrie," Tasharyana put in, struggling to rise up on her elbow and nearly blacking out from the throbbing in her head. "I would be happy to go somewhere else."

Frances glared at her and then turned her attention to J. B. "You realize of course that we're having a large party here on Friday."

"She'll be fine by then."

"But what about the criminal element? Who is trying to kidnap her and why? I don't want hoodlums lurking around my home."

"There won't be any, Frances. No one knows she's here."

"Mother, it's just for a few days," Christine put in. "I'm sure it will be fine."

"Just one more thing to worry about!" Frances pursed her lips. "As if I didn't have enough on my mind, what with the engagement party just about upon us. This is a very important event for both of you, I hope you realize!"

"Believe me," J. B. replied. "I know."

"And if some inept kidnapper ruins everything, why, I don't know what I'll do!"

"I should leave." Tasharyana sat up. "I don't want to cause any problems."

"No." J. B. turned to her. "You're going to stay right there. I'll make arrangements for your departure as soon as possible."

"You're as white as a sheet, Miss Higazi. Please lie down." Christine stepped toward the door. "And we'll leave you alone so you can rest."

"Thank you," Tasharyana replied.

Frances huffed out of the room behind her daughter

while J. B. lingered by the side of the bed. Tasharyana sank upon the pillow and looked at him, trying to give him a smile of encouragement. He reached for her hand.

"I can see why you don't want to hurt her," Tasharyana remarked. "She's kind."

"Yes, she is." J. B. kissed her fingers and gazed at her, his eyes dark with troubled lights. "I don't know how, but this has to be worked out, and carefully." He slowly lowered her hand. "Now get some rest, my pet, and I'll call my firm's San Francisco office. I have a friend there who will be happy to take you in for a few weeks. You'll love his wife. She's a cellist for the San Francisco Symphony."

"Thanks, J. B."

He walked to the door and turned. "But be forewarned, Tasharyana Higazi. I know your style. Don't try to run off. I'm going to alert all the servants to watch the doors and the windows."

"I promise not to leave this room."

"Good. See you in a while."

When Tasharyana awoke, it was evening. She sat up and looked around the room, which was bathed in shadows, and wondered at first where she was. Then she remembered. She was sleeping in a guest room in the Petrie house. Had she slept all afternoon? She stretched, feeling much better. Her headache was gone and her stomach growled with hunger.

She used the bathroom, and was grateful for the toothbrush J. B. had packed in a small bag for her. After splashing water on her face and running a brush across her tender scalp, she felt ready to face the Petries, and hoped she hadn't missed dinner.

Stretching, she walked across the room and drew

back the chintz curtain. In the dusk a beautiful garden of azaleas, tulips, and daffodils still showed shades of red and yellow, and a thick carpet of lawn stretched out toward a gazebo. Tasharyana wasn't accustomed to such lush landscaping and thought it was the most gorgeous yard she'd ever seen at a private residence. Car lights poured through the shrubbery as a vehicle turned down the drive, shooting strange patterns across the grass. Tasharyana thought of the possibility that someone might be hiding in the shadows of the gazebo and the yard took on an entirely different atmosphere. She shivered, never quite certain she hadn't been followed.

A soft knock interrupted her thoughts. She turned at the window.

"Yes?"

The door opened a crack. "Are you decent?" J. B. asked.

"Yes. Come in."

He slipped into the room without turning on the light. Tasharyana smiled and let the curtain fall into place behind her, forgetting about the experiences with Mr. Gregg and Madame Hepera, while she watched J. B. walk across the floor. Without speaking further he surrounded her in his arms and gave her a long, passionate kiss. Tasharyana returned the kiss, and in moments was on fire for him.

"How are you feeling?" he murmured.

"Much better." She put her hands on either side of his face and gazed at his handsome features. Even in the dim light the sharp planes of his face were easily discernible, and the shadow beneath his lower lip looked very enticing. A feeling of exquisite tenderness washed over her as she gazed at him, and her heart swelled with love as he gazed back with soft glinting lights shining in his eyes.

He smiled. "I couldn't wait until you got up."

"Why?"

"To hold you like this. And make sure you're safe."

"You take such good care of me," she answered softly. She hugged him tightly, aware of the tenderness of her breasts from the previous evening's love-making. Even so, she wished they could fall into bed right now and share each other's bodies again.

J. B. kissed her throat and caressed her breasts, and soon their breathing became ragged with desire. While they kissed, she slid her hands over his shoulders, his back, and then cradled his jaw and slowly pushed her fingers into his hair, loving every sleek inch of him. He could have asked her to make love right where they stood and she would have gladly complied. Everywhere he kissed her, everywhere he touched her, her body reacted with delicious bursts of desire.

"Ah," she moaned. "J. B., you're torturing me."

"You're torturing me."

"We shouldn't—"

"It's hard to stay away from you."

The thought of keeping him at a distance made her ache even more for his intimate touch. She leaned into his hips and cupped his rear with her hands to bring him closer. He groaned.

"Keep doing that, miss, and you won't get any dinner."

"I don't care about dinner," she replied against his mouth.

"Aren't you hungry?"

"Not for food."

She felt his smile on her lips just before he kissed her, and his tongue swept into her mouth as he pinned her to his loins. She moved against him in a sinuous dance as his tongue repeated the rhythm between her lips, each of them well aware of what their bodies yearned to do. Tasharyana felt herself going wet with wanting him, and a throbbing ache pulsed between her legs.

"Tasha," J. B. whispered, pulling back slightly, "let's not do that here. It's not good enough for us."

She wasn't sure what he meant. She only knew she loved him at that moment more than she had ever loved anyone. Fervently she kissed the lean indentation below his cheekbone and then sighed as the tips of their noses brushed together.

"You make me feel so wonderful," she whispered. "So alive."

He opened his eyes and gazed at her intently, as if he had never heard such words before and had to make certain what she was saying.

"I forget the world when I am with you like this," she continued, stirred by his serious expression.

"So do I." He dropped a kiss on her mouth. "And I want to stay in this world with you more than anything. But we really should go down. They'll be wondering where we are and what's going on up here."

Slightly deflated by his quick transition from their bubble of lovemaking to reality, Tasharyana tried to mask her disappointment with humor. She forced a smile.

"Mrs. Petrie would have a fit if she knew."

"Fit, nothing." J. B. chuckled dryly, playing along with her change in mood, as he readjusted his clothing. "She'd have us shot if she found out what we were doing!"

"You don't think she'll be able to tell when she sees our faces?"

"She might." J. B. smoothed back her hair. "Your face is literally glowing."

"I can't hide how I feel about you."

"And I never want you to. You're beautiful when you shine like that for me." He squeezed her and then released her. "Now off with you to the bathroom. I'll wait for you."

"All right." She walked to the bathroom to freshen up and didn't look back, not wanting to know if he had completely stepped out of their bubble.

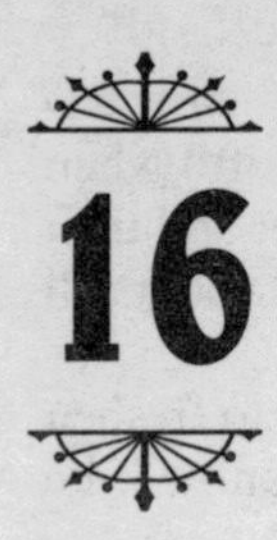

Late the next morning Tasharyana sat in the sun room drinking coffee and wearing a dress Christine had lent her, while she scanned a magazine. J. B. had gone into town to pick up airline tickets for her trip to San Francisco. She hoped he would be getting two tickets so he could accompany her to California, but hadn't wanted to ask about his plans in front of the Petries during breakfast.

Just as she set her coffee cup down on the delicate saucer, she heard a step in the doorway and turned to see Frances Petrie, a newspaper in one hand and the velvet bag containing Tasharyana's diamonds in the other. Tasharyana stood up, alarmed that Frances had violated the privacy of her room and searched her belongings.

"I knew there was more to this whole affair than J. B. let on," Frances declared, marching forward. She was dressed in a severe navy suit that perfectly complemented the unyielding harshness of her personality.

Did Frances know that she and J. B. were lovers,

that he wasn't sure if he should marry Christine? What did she know? And what did the diamonds have to do with it?

"What are you doing with my bag?" she countered, hoping to lead the subject away from J. B.

"Your bag? You'd like to think it was yours!"

"It is!"

Frances sniffed, obviously immune to Tasharyana's sincere indignation. "No wonder you're being chased up and down the east coast. You're a common thief."

"I am not!"

"And a liar, too, I see."

"If you are referring to the diamonds, Mrs. Petrie. They are mine. I purchased them."

"Where did a girl like you get money enough to buy diamonds?"

"I've saved my earnings for years, Mrs. Petrie."

"A likely story!"

"It's true!"

"Hmph." Frances unfolded the newspaper to reveal the bottom of the front page. "Then explain this, Miss Higazi."

Tasharyana lowered her glance and took in the small headline. OPERA STAR HEISTS GEMS AND FLEES. A sickening dread grew in her stomach. Frances held the paper closer.

"Read the article, Miss Higazi. Go ahead."

The words swam before Tasharyana's disbelieving eyes as she read a completely false account of her flight from the theater. She was made to look like a felon who had duped everyone and had run off into the night with stolen diamonds belonging to her benefactor, Iniman el Hepera. How had anyone known about the diamonds? She had shown them to no one except J. B. Tasharyana paled, wondering if Mr. Gregg had watched her dump the diamonds in J. B.'s palm at the hotel. Then Mr. Gregg must have relayed the information to Madame Hepera. How could she have been so naïve?

"This isn't true," she said in a choked voice. "These are all lies about me."

"That's what you'd like everyone to believe."

"Whoever wrote this obviously made it up!"

Frances snatched away the paper and threw it on the table. "The fact is, you have stolen these diamonds." She held up the bag.

"No, I haven't," Tasharyana retorted. "And how dare you go through my clothing?"

"I was getting it ready to be laundered."

"My jacket didn't need cleaning."

"In my opinion it did. And I'm glad I searched the pockets because I found proof as to your real character."

"You're mistaken. Just ask J. B."

Frances gave a short scornful laugh. "Julian's so smitten by you that he couldn't see the truth if it reared up and bit him."

"That's not—"

"You've got him fooled just like the rest of them, don't you?" Frances interrupted. "Well, you don't fool me. I had a feeling about you from the moment I laid eyes on you." She crossed her arms. "And I'm not about to let a tramp like you ruin my daughter's future."

Tasharyana felt her blood grow cold. "What are you planning to do?"

"I'm turning you over to the police, Miss Higazi. In fact, they're already here, waiting for you."

Frantic, Tasharyana glanced at the doorway behind Frances Petrie and then wildly looked around for another route of escape. But though the sun room was built almost entirely of glass, it had no door to the outside. She was trapped.

Frances smiled coldly. "Don't think you can escape. The officers are in the hall standing by. If you try to run, it will only be worse for you."

"Really? Everyone thinks I'm guilty anyway. What good would it do to surrender peacefully?"

"Your sentence might be milder if you cooperate. Besides, just how far do you think you can run before they catch you? Use your head, girl."

Frightened and desperate, Tasharyana knew she had no recourse but to surrender to the officers of the law and hope that J. B. would come to her assistance when he found out what had happened. She sighed in exasperation.

"I see you're being sensible," Frances remarked. She turned to the doorway. "Officers?" She motioned for the policemen to enter the sun room. Tasharyana watched the two men file in, their billy clubs brushing their thighs as they sauntered toward her.

"Miss Higazi?" one of them asked.

"Yes?"

"You're under arrest for grand larceny." He handcuffed her wrists together behind her back as the other officer advised her of her rights. Tasharyana stood proudly through the humiliating treatment, her shoulders thrown back, and her eyes blazing at Frances Petrie. The older woman returned her stare, with a smug expression on her face and her cold, spiteful gaze never wavering.

Luxor, Present Day

The vision on the water faded for a few moments as Karissa sat on the sand, stunned by the cruelty and viciousness of her grandmother. How could Frances have been so awful to Tasharyana? And yet she shouldn't have been surprised. Frances Petrie had never been a kind person. Karissa had known only coldness and criticism from her grandmother, and it overshadowed what little kindness Christine managed to bestow. Between her mother's frequent bouts of illness and her father's increasing absences, growing up in the Petrie household had been a chilly, alienating experience for a child—one Karissa had vowed never to repeat with her own children.

Before Karissa rose out of her childhood memories, she noticed a new vision appearing on the surface of the pond and turned her attention to the shimmering scene. In the vision Tasharyana was being helped into an ornate medieval costume. A female attendant carefully arranged the folds of the long claret velvet gown heavy with jewels and gold trim over the shining satin bliaut beneath. The tight gathered sleeves of the moss green bliaut, embroidered with flowers and seed pearls, hugged Tasharyana's delicate wrists and accentuated her fine bone structure. The dress was gorgeous but Karissa could tell by the dark expression on Tasharyana's face that she cared nothing for the costume and was not happy to be preparing for a performance.

Tasharyana's Tale—Ahmed Abyad Bey's Home, Cairo

"Almost ready?" Madame Hepera asked, coming into the vaulted chamber, one of the many richly appointed rooms in the luxurious home of the minister of antiquities.

Tasharyana didn't so much as glance at her voice teacher. She was still too angry to be civil. Madame Hepera had posted bail for her, swept her away from

Baltimore before J. B. had a chance to see her, and then dropped the charges. She had even admitted to feeding the story of lies to the newspapers for their articles. The moment Tasharyana stepped out of the police station, she had been under constant guard. And if that wasn't enough, Madame Hepera had administered sedatives to her against her will, making it possible to fly Tasharyana back to Cairo, a docile prisoner.

A month had passed since her return to Egypt, and she had not had a single moment to herself, no access to a phone, and no chance of escape. She wondered what J. B. must have thought when he discovered she had been arrested. And what had he gone through, trying to find her? Yet why hadn't she heard from him? Surely in a month's time he could have tracked her down. And was he now engaged to Christine? Her heart ached at the thought.

"Your silence will get you nowhere, my dear," Madame Hepera added, adjusting the train of the dress.

Tasharyana stepped away, loathing the woman's slightest touch.

"No one can make me sing," Tasharyana retorted, her voice icy. "No matter how closely you guard me, you will never make me sing."

"Oh, you'll sing. Please Ahmed Abyod Bey and you will be set for life."

"I have no desire to please him."

"Your career is at stake."

"I don't care about my career."

Madame Hepera raised her triangular eyebrows, doubtful. Both of them knew her career meant much to Tasharyana, as much as J.B meant to her.

The thought of J. B. plunged another shaft of loneliness and despair through her. Would she ever see him again? She missed him, unbearably so. His silence made her wonder if J. B. had decided to limit the complications in his life by not pursuing her. And if he was not meant to be part of her life, she knew she might as well begin the difficult task of relegating him to the realm of her memories instead of her dreams. Tasharyana flowed to the mirror and fussed with her hair while her hands shook at the prospect of once again pushing J. B. Spencer from her thoughts.

Madame Hepera came up behind her, her wide figure dwarfing Tasharyana's slim torso. "So this Julian Spencer is the only thing you care about in the entire world, is he?"

"I love him," she retorted proudly, glad to admit it, if only to Madame Hepera. "I always have."

"You would throw away everything for him—your training, your career?"

"If I had to."

"Then I will strike a bargain with you."

Surprised, Tasharyana glanced at the reflection of Madame Hepera's face.

Madame Hepera passed the tip of her tongue over her brightly colored lips. "Ahmed Bey has promised to get governmental approval for me to excavate an old temple in the desert, a sphinx long covered by sand." She frowned, as if unwilling to tell more.

"Yes?"

"This approval to excavate means as much to me as your British lover means to you. There are things I need inside the sphinx, things I must have."

"What kind of things?"

"Nothing that concerns you."

"And the bargain?"

"If you please the minister and gain his support, then I will release you—with no further obligation to me whatsoever."

Tasharyana regarded her, shocked.

"Did you hear what I said, my dear?"

"Yes, but I don't believe it."

"The minister must be pleased, however. I cannot stress it enough, Tasharyana."

"And you will let me go, just like that."

"Yes."

"I want it written down and signed. I want you to swear that you will honor the bargain."

Madame Hepera tilted her head and regarded Tasharyana. "You have learned much from this attorney lover of yours."

"This is my own idea, Madame Hepera. Because, frankly, I don't trust you."

A dark cloud of displeasure passed quickly across the fat woman's face, but she instantly covered it up with a smile and a short laugh. "So be it, my dear. I will get a paper and pen. Then will you sing?"

"When I have the contract in my hand."

She finished fixing her hair while Madame Hepera drew up a short document, dated it, and signed it. Tasharyana signed it as well, folded it, and then slipped it into the bodice of her gown.

"Are you satisfied?" Madame Hepera asked haughtily.

"*Appeased* might be a better word."

"Well, then, let's go perform for the minister." Madame Hepera picked up the piano score for *Tristan und Isolde* and led Tasharyana out to the hall.

"Ah, Miss Higazi!" Ahmed Abyad Bey rose from a low bench decorated with brocade cushions, and quickly adjusted the front of his cream-colored double-breasted suit. The room was apparently a casual meeting area, with a small reflecting pool in the center surrounded by low benches and tables and piles of cushions.

Tasharyana glanced around and could see no evidence of a piano. A feeling of unease filtered down upon her.

Undaunted by her lack of enthusiasm, the minister of antiquities strode forward, the tassel of his fez swinging against the side of the felt hat, and his hands outstretched to greet her. "A pleasure to meet you at last."

Her immediate reaction was to hide her hands behind her back so that she wouldn't have to touch him. His gaunt looks lent him a hungry appearance like a vulture or a hyena, an association that repulsed her. He was a tall man with a bony face and prominent teeth that showed long and white beneath his black mustache. His nose was sharply hawked, and his black eyes deep set beneath heavy black brows. She had the distinct impression that as he looked at her—completely ignoring Madame Hepera—he was visualizing Tasharyana naked.

She raised one hand and allowed him to squeeze her fingers in a light handshake meant for women. He had long bony hands and clammy skin.

"You are even lovelier in person than onstage."

"Thank you." His compliment meant nothing to her, not when he devoured her appearance as a jackal devours a kill.

"Please, make yourself comfortable." He indicated a bench near the pool as he hovered too close. "May I get you some refreshment?"

"Not until after I sing, thank you."

He smiled and finally glanced at Madame Hepera. "Madame, you may leave us now, if you would be so kind."

"But I am to provide piano accompaniment," Madame Hepera protested, holding up the musical score.

"I prefer to hear Miss Higazi's voice a cappella," the minister replied. "In that way I may judge her talent without the distraction of another instrument."

Madame Hepera was uncharacteristically lost for words at his brusque dismissal. She glanced at Tasharyana and then back to the government official as he continued to speak.

"You may have your driver take you back immediately, or you may stay for a refreshment if you like. My servants will attend you."

"But what about Miss Higazi?"

"I would be honored if she would stay and dine with me this evening." He turned and looked expectantly at Tasharyana.

Behind him, Madame Hepera gave a curt nod of approval. Tasharyana felt her unease deepen. For her freedom, however, she could endure an afternoon with the gaunt minister. She forced a small smile, hating every minute of the charade of politeness. "Of course."

"When shall I send someone to get her this evening?" Madame Hepera asked.

"Oh, you needn't trouble yourself, madame. I will make the necessary arrangements for Miss Higazi's safe return."

"Very good." Madame Hepera glanced at Tasharyana and smiled, but her eyes remained full of concern. Was she reluctant to leave her protégée, afraid that Tasharyana might try to escape? Tasharyana hoped Madame Hepera would spend the entire afternoon in a cold sweat, worrying. It would serve her right. "I will see you tonight, Tasharyana."

"Yes," she replied.

A servant opened the door for Madame Hepera, discreetly followed her out of the room, and shut the door behind him.

The minister cleared his throat. "Tasharyana. That's a beautiful name." He sidled closer to her. His cloying cologne enveloped her in an unwelcome cloud. "A very old name, isn't it?"

"So I've been told." She eyed him warily.

"I have been an admirer of yours since I first heard you sing *Aïda.* You have an exquisite voice."

"Thank you."

"With the right connections, dear Miss Higazi, you could go far." He leaned forward, assuming a familiarity he had not earned, and would never achieve as far as she was concerned. "I, for one, would be honored to do all that I can for you and Madame Hepera."

"That is generous of you, sir."

"I would also be most gratified if you would call me Ahmed."

She inclined her head. "Ahmed."

His eyes glittered and focused on her mouth when she repeated the word, as if he was greedy to hear the sound of his name on her lips. She took the opportunity to step away from him.

"And I would be honored to sing the part of Isolde for you."

"Excellent. A most excellent character. And a ravishing gown, Tasharyana. I grow speechless from your beauty."

She hadn't noticed a lack of words on his part but didn't remark on it. She bowed by dipping her head slightly, anxious for the hours to pass. Perhaps after she sang she could feign illness and leave early. But would her quick retreat offend Ahmed Abyad Bey? If her behavior displeased him, she would remain Madame Hepera's prisoner indefinitely. Better to indulge the man now than suffer later.

Ahmed took a seat on a bench and watched her prepare for the musical performance. She explained the scene briefly so that he would be aware of the course of the story, and then she took a deep breath and sang out the first note.

He asked her to continue singing twice, and by the time she finished, nearly an hour had elapsed. Tasharyana let the final sad note hang on the air as she felt her energy drain out as well. She wasn't accustomed to singing nonstop with such intensity, and she was exhausted.

When the note died out, the minister rose to his feet and clapped enthusiastically. "Excellent!" he exclaimed. "Most excellent! You are the perfect diva for my production!"

She smiled tiredly, wishing she could go home that moment, but Ahmed rang for a servant. He ordered tea and pastries and urged Tasharyana to sit on a pile of cushions near the pool.

"Sit down. Relax," he said. "You deserve it."

The velvet gown was heavy and hot, and she wanted more than anything to be rid of it. But she sat on the pillows without remarking how stifling her costume was, because she didn't wish to plant any seeds in the man's mind about removing articles of clothing. She suspected he would offer to help her undress without a moment's hesitation.

The servant soon returned with the refreshments, along with a hookah for Ahmed's use. He smoked thoughtfully while the servant poured tea and offered a cup to Tasharyana. Then just as quickly, the servant left her alone with the government official.

He drew on the mouthpiece of the hookah and openly surveyed her until she dropped her glance, put off by his insolent stare. Only one man had the right to look at her in that way, and even he would never stare at her with such blatant lust.

"When I say that I can help you, Tasharyana," the minister said at last, "I mean every word."

"I am sure you do."

"I ask only one thing of you."

She looked up. "And what is that?"

"That you become—how do the Americans say it?—my mistress."

Her heart skipped a beat out of dread, not surprise. She had suspected from the beginning that the minister was interested in more than her voice. "You wish to exchange your favors for mine?"

"I can be very generous. Very generous." He stood up. "In fact, you will want for nothing."

"What about your wife? Aren't you married?"

"Of course. But that has nothing to do with anything."

His matter-of-fact answer didn't surprise Tasharyana. She was well aware that many Egyptian men kept women on the side. She had no desire to be of their number, yet she had no wish to be Madame Hepera's prisoner either. How could she please Ahmed, and thereby meet Madame Hepera's conditions, without consenting to sleep with the man? Could she promise herself to him but put him off until she decided what to do?

"You are silent, my beautiful songbird." He came up behind her and curved his long hands over the tops of her shoulders. The strong smell of tobacco wafted from his clothes. She fought down a shudder. "How can you hesitate when I have offered to lay the riches of the world at your feet?"

Instead of shaking off his caress, she mustered all the acting ability she possessed and turned to him with a smile. "I am merely speechless at my good fortune, Ahmed. You are so cultured, so accomplished, while I am but a—"

"You are the most beautiful woman I have ever seen, Tasharyana. The good fortune is mine, believe me." He slipped his right hand over the bodice of her dress where the scooped neckline revealed the swell of her breasts. The touch of his clammy fingers made her shiver. "I am gratified you have agreed to an arrangement with me."

"How could I not?" she replied, her words true even though she had no intention of actually becoming his mistress.

"You tremble for me, little bird," he crooned. "My touch gives you pleasure."

She bit back the protest that sprang to her lips and let him jump to his mistaken conclusions. His fingers explored further, slipping beneath the gold trimmed neckline as his breathing grew more rapid. Would he find the contract she had hidden there? What would he do when he saw the terms? She couldn't take the chance that he might discover the folded paper.

"My costume is much too constricting," she wheezed and struggled to get up in the weighty velvet dress. He held out a hand to assist her, which she accepted but released as soon as she rose to her feet. Then she took a step away from him and glanced up to see his face flushed with desire. His feverish gaze darted over her body. "If you will excuse me," she continued. "I would like to change into something more comfortable."

"Something more comfortable?" he asked, his mustache turning up with his hopeful grin.

"I brought more suitable clothing with me. It is in the room where I dressed in this costume. Would you mind if I changed?"

"Not at all." He led the way toward the door and opened it for her. "Would you like a female servant to attend you? I can summon Fatima, if you wish."

"No, thank you." She smiled and forced herself to

raise her hand and touch his cheek. "I will be right back, Ahmed."

"I will accompany you, to show you the way."

"No." A rush of panic washed over her. If Ahmed went with her, there would be no chance of escape. "I mean to say, it isn't necessary. I am sure I can find my way back."

"Are you certain?" he grinned again, showing nearly all of his teeth. "I wouldn't mind playing the maid for you. It might prove very exciting."

"We have all the time in the world for games, Ahmed," she replied. "Let us not rush into things and ruin the surprise, hmm?"

His eyes lit up at her seductive tone. Ahmed Abyad Bey, minister of antiquities, was proving to be easy to manipulate, and for that she was grateful. He leaned forward. "I will be waiting, little bird." Then he ran a palm down the front of his suit, as a man strokes his stomach in anticipation of a good meal. "Don't be long."

"I won't. I promise."

Tasharyana walked down the hall, making certain she didn't hurry. She could feel his regard on her back the entire time it took for her to reach the corridor that led to the chamber where she had left her street clothes. The stench of his tobacco and the oppressive smell of his cologne lingered on her shoulders and in her hair, and she knew that no matter how quickly she walked, she would never escape the memory of his unwelcome caress.

Once in the room, she closed and locked the door. Then, unmindful of the fragility of the expensive costume, she pulled it off, tossing aside first the velvet and then the satin. As quickly as she could she reached for her slip and dress, pulling them on with shaking hands. The sooner she got out of the room, the more time she would have before Ahmed came looking for her.

Tasharyana struggled with the long zipper in the back of her dress as she pushed her feet into her black pumps. Then she grabbed her bag, though it was empty of money since Madame Hepera had given her no funds at all after her escape attempt in the United States. However, she had packed some essential items such as a toothbrush and extra underclothes, in case she ever had a chance to flee. But most important of all, she carried the music box J. B. had given her years ago. Never again would she make an escape as unprepared as she had been the last time.

Dashing into the hall, she took the opposite direction from the room in which Ahmed waited for her and avoided the path to the front door, hoping the back entrance would be in a logical place. The house was huge, however, and she wondered if she would be able to find her way out.

Quietly she hurried along the tile floor, carefully approaching doorways and listening intently to make certain the path ahead was clear. Her shoes were too noisy on the ceramic tile, so she slipped them off and carried them.

Suddenly, she heard two women chatting and coming her way. She glanced around, saw a door on her left and opened it. Before her yawned a stairway to the cellar. Though it was dark and perhaps had no outlet, she had no choice but to go in that direction. Carefully, she closed the door so it wouldn't make any noise, and waited behind it in case the women should be headed for the lower level as well. As she pressed against the wall, she heard the voice of the minister of antiquities.

"Have you seen Miss Higazi?" he asked. "I think she must be lost."

"No, sir," the women replied at the same time.

Tasharyana frowned, damning the man's eagerness. He hadn't waited for her more than five minutes.

"You saw no one come this way?" he continued.

Again they denied having seen anyone.

Tasharyana realized she couldn't waste time mincing around the minister's house. She had to get out as soon as possible, before the entire staff was sent to search for her. With her heart pounding, she tiptoed down the cool stairs, letting her eyes grow accustomed to the darkness. Off in another area of the basement, she could hear a machine running and men talking to one another over the hum. She crept closer, hoping to find a door to the outside, and discovered the laundry, with clothes hanging waiting to be pressed, stacks of folded garments, and bins containing dirty items. Near the bins was a woman loading a washing machine. Behind her two men smoked and talked in the open bay of a loading dock where a delivery truck had been pulled up and partially unloaded.

Tasharyana crouched in the shadows, knowing she could get out of the house if she could just get to the bay. When the men left in their truck, she would run for the bay, jump down, and break for freedom. How she would get back to town and what she would do once she got there, were problems she'd address later. For now, she had to escape Ahmed Abyad Bey.

The minutes ticked by as she watched the men toss aside their cigarettes and reach for cardboard cartons in the back of the truck. Slowly they carried the boxes into another room in the basement, one after another, while the laundress folded clothes near the dryer. Then suddenly, Tasharyana heard someone clumping down the stairs behind her.

17

Tasharyana crept around one of the large canvas bins, keeping her head low and making sure she would be out of the sight of whoever approached.

"Nawal!" a short pudgy man barked to the laundress.

She continued to work, obviously unable to hear him above the din.

"Nawal!" the man repeated, huffing past the bin where Tasharyana crouched on hands and knees.

The laundress looked up. The men loading the truck ambled forward, curious, as the pudgy man explained that the master's friend, a Miss Higazi, had disappeared from a room upstairs. The master suspected foul play and was desperate to find Miss Higazi and make sure she was safe. The pudgy man asked if any of them had seen anything out of the ordinary.

The others talked earnestly, forming a tight ring in front of the noisy dryer. None of them were paying attention to the loading dock. Perhaps now was her time to run. She crept forward, scurrying behind other bins, boxes, and large metal drums, thankful for the loud laundry equipment that covered up most sounds in the cellar. Just as she reached the bay, however, she saw two men trotting down the drive toward the back of the house. If she jumped down to the ground, they would surely see her. Yet if she went back into the house, she would surely be found.

Tasharyana made a snap decision, based on desperation instead of planning. Tightly grabbing the straps of her purse in one hand and her shoes in the other, she leapt into the back of the truck and skittered all the way to the front, where boxes were piled nearly to the top of the roof. She scooted a few cartons aside to allow room for her to squeeze into a space against the wall, where she would be surrounded by boxes and hidden from view. There she waited, perspiration running down her face and body from standing in close quarters in the sweltering heat, and her heart pounding with the fear of being discovered.

Outside she could hear men shouting to each other and hurrying past the truck. As she suspected, the entire staff at the home of the minister of antiquities had been roused to search for her. She closed her eyes, trying to regulate the hammering of her heart while she hoped and prayed the delivery men wouldn't unload the entire truck.

Much to her good fortune, they didn't remove all the cartons. And after ten minutes or so, they closed up the back with a loud clang of the metal door. Then they hopped in the cab and the truck pulled away from the house, gradually picking up speed as it rolled out of the gates of the estate. Tasharyana collapsed against the wall behind her and let her muscles relax, as she felt a wave of light-headedness pass over her. She didn't care where the truck was headed. All she knew was that she had got away from Ahmed Bey and Madame Hepera. And she would do everything in her power to remain free of anyone who would make her a prisoner.

Luxor, Present Day

Karissa was roused out of the deep lethargy produced by the scrying session by someone insistently shaking her shoulder. She raised her head, the thought of her missing daughter never fully out of her consciousness, which gave her the ability to wake quickly and with most of her faculties alert.

"George?"

"*Sayyidah!*" The houseboy bent over her, his young face pinched with worry. "Come quickly. The master has returned wounded."

"Wounded?"

"Yes. It seems he was in a fight, *sayyidah*."

"Is he seriously wounded?"

"Beaten, *sayyidah*. He came back of his own accord, but he doesn't look good, I tell you."

Karissa scrambled to her feet, her senses swimming and her knees wobbling as if they would give out any moment. Frantically she snatched up the box and the obelisks and stuffed them under her arm. Then she hurriedly followed George back to the house, stumbling on footprints in the sand and joints in the tiled path of the garden, unusually clumsy and jittery. But her concern for Asheris forced new life into her trembling legs.

"Where is he?" she asked upon entering the house.

"In his chambers, *sayyidah*. Eisha has drawn him a bath."

"Thanks." She dropped the box on a table in the hall and rushed to Asheris's bedchamber.

She opened the door and found him just stepping into the bath. He turned at the sound of her entrance, and at the sight of him she sucked in a breath of alarm. Red blotches covered his abdomen, and his right cheek was bleeding beneath a swelled eyelid. His lip was split as well.

"Asheris, what happened?" she gasped, shocked at seeing his beautiful body marred and battered.

Wincing, he lowered himself into the tub. "I ran into the night watchmen at the school."

"They did this to you?"

"They and about five of their cohorts."

"Why so many watchmen?" She knelt at his side and surveyed his discolored stomach, wondering how many times he had been pummeled.

"There must be something very important which they are protecting—Julia." Asheris lay against the back of the tub and sighed. "Unfortunately, I did not find her."

"No trace of her? No clues as to where she might be?"

"Nothing."

She stroked his hair and then rose. "I'll be right back. I'm going to get a piece of meat for that eye of yours."

"A piece of meat?"

"It will take down the swelling."

She left his bathroom and hurried to the kitchen, feeling her strength returning little by little. On the way back with the piece of steak, she stopped in the library where she poured Asheris a generous glass of brandy, hoping to soothe his other pains. With each step back to the bath, however, she saw Julia's face looming before her, and her burning anguish flared up. How could they go on, not knowing what was happening to their little girl?

Karissa handed the brandy to her husband, waited for him take a drink, and then carefully positioned the thick slice of meat over his eye. She heard Asheris sigh as the cool meat soothed his throbbing skin. Then he held out the brandy snifter.

"Thank you, Karissa," he said softly. For a moment they sat in silence, he in the tub and she kneeling at his side. Then he opened his good eye and inspected her face. Her pain must have been obvious because he slipped his warm wet hand around her dry one. "I regret I have returned to you with bruises instead of information."

She nodded, her mouth trembling against a flood of tears.

Asheris reached out and stroked her cheek. "Do not worry so. Julia will be all right. In the old days the priestesses did not harm the young acolytes. I do not expect that to change."

"Provided she *has* been kidnapped by the priestesses of Sekhmet."

"Who else would have taken her?"

"Any number of people." Karissa clutched the glass of brandy tightly. "Common thugs, white slavers, you name it, Asheris."

"I believe the priestesses are responsible. Why else would she have been inspected for the birthmark?"

"Perhaps you're right," Karissa conceded. "And all we have to do is discover where they are hiding her."

"Yes. Since there were many guards at the school, I would guess Julia may have been hidden there. But the priestesses have probably moved her by now, in the event I should come back with officers of the law."

"So now we just wait until morning, to see if the police have found any leads?"

"Yes." He squeezed her hand. "There is nothing more I can think to do, Karissa."

Long past midnight, Karissa lay awake in bed listening to Asheris sleep. He had asked her to stay with him, and she should have been thrilled to spend the night with him. But his body was too battered to allow an embrace, and both of them were far too preoccupied to talk. She couldn't even kiss him because of the cut on his lip. So she just lay there, aching for him, aching for Julia, and blaming herself once again for bringing tragedy to those she loved.

After hours of tossing and turning, she decided to give up all thoughts of sleep and quit disturbing her husband. She'd retire to her own room, perhaps look at her father's journals, the only comfort she had during this troubled time. So she put on her light robe and slippers and quietly left the bedroom. Then she suddenly recalled the mess she had made of her father's journal, which she had dropped on the floor. She might as well attack the task of reordering the loose pages, just to keep her hands busy.

She slipped into her bedroom and walked to the side of her bed near the nightstand where she had stacked the journals. On the way, she kicked something that had been partially concealed by the corner of her bedspread, and sent it sailing across the floor. Karissa reached for the yellowed envelope and turned it over in her hands. The paper was brittle with age, addressed to Tasharyana Higazi in care of Madame Hepera and sent to Cairo. But the letter had been returned, stamped ADDRESSEE UNKNOWN. The faded cancellation mark showed a date close to the time Tasharyana would have been in the United States. Why had her father written to her? Had he never found Tasharyana after her return to Egypt? What had happened to Tasharyana? Carefully, Karissa slipped the letter out of the envelope and opened it to reveal her father's tiny handwriting.

J. B. Spencer's Letter—April 26, 1966

My Sweet Tasha,

I have pen in hand and at least a million thoughts in my head. I'm on an airplane headed for Rome, and then to Cairo. The plane is somewhere over the Atlantic now, and all there is to see are some clouds and miles of blue ocean. It's not hard for me to stare into the distance and see you though, because I see your face everywhere I go, and I cannot accept the fact you are gone.

Tasha, I swear I will not rest until I find you, and I pray that somehow this letter will find you, too. It's so difficult to believe you've decided to return to Egypt and leave behind all the things we'd just begun. We are meant to be together. With all my heart, I know this more certainly than anything I've ever known before. And I vow that we will be together soon, and together always.

Last Friday morning, Frances explained you'd left her house in a hurry, saying your opera career was just too important to ignore, and that we both had separate lives to live. She gave me the note you'd left, and it seemed it was written by someone I hardly knew. I guess I didn't accept what you'd written because I simply didn't want to believe it. We are of like minds, you and I, meant to be together, and you must explain why you've suddenly decided differently.

You had no way of knowing this, but I bought two tickets to San Francisco Friday morning, and was hoping to ask you to marry me there. I arrived at the Petrie house, bursting with plans for our future, only to find you gone. Then I saw a newspaper article which implicated you in a jewel theft. What was that all about? Was it Madame Hepera's way of tracking you down? Are you with her now, back in Cairo?

If only I could turn the clock back a few years, back to the day along the Nile when you and I were in each others' arms. Had I known of love then what I've learned as a man now, I never would have left your side. It seems we are destined to be torn apart. I look back to when we were separated in Egypt, and how our letters failed to reach their marks. Isn't it sad how quickly we decided the other person just didn't care? Isn't it profoundly sad to know how untrue it was at the time? Yet here I am once again, wondering if this letter I'm writing will ever find you—and wondering even more what I must do to convince you of my deep feelings for you.

The night we spent in Philadelphia was the most exquisite experience I'm sure I'll ever have. When I find you, won't you tell me the same memory endures for you ? Don't you realize this type of love shared between two people is a fuel to burn brightly forever? The hours we spent intimately entwined was but a taste of a lifetime of happiness that lies before us. I close my eyes and see your beautiful face before me on my balcony. With the rain softly falling and the sweet evening air all around, I see your eyes looking into mine.

Tasha, I love you. I want nothing more than to have you near me. How I wish I had told you! Perhaps you would still be with me if I had spoken the words of my heart.

The so-called engagement party occurred as scheduled on Friday night, and I've never felt so empty and so false. You must have laughed at the farce of a relationship I have with Christine. I know now I cannot let the charade continue, and I shouldn't have allowed it to get this far in the first place. Even though my intentions were to protect her feelings and reputation, I realize now that putting off the inevitable has benefited no one, especially you.

Subconsciously, I've always known Christine and her family weren't right for me, but as I told you, I felt a deep responsibility for the tragedy that happened three years ago. What else could I do but make reparation by stepping in for the Petrie's lost son? Remorse and guilt were the direction markers in my life until you showed me a new way of looking at the world. You don't know how much you taught me, showed me, and helped me during our talk about Charlie. How do you know me so well? Could it be because you love me? I think so.

Remember the music box I gave you so long ago? And the verse about roses? I'm reminded of another poet I studied while in school in England. The poet's name was O'Reilly, and he wrote about roses, too. White roses for love, red roses for passion. Having come to know you and truly love you, I can see how I was compromising myself to a life with Christine. That kind of partnership would have been a life of neither white nor red roses, but a bouquet of pink ones, looking pretty from a distance but carrying no true emotion or feeling in reality.

Tasha, with you I've glimpsed how fulfilling life can be. I'm willing to throw away a predictable future because I've discovered what it's like to be truly loved by another. How could I have been blind to what was so obvious to you—that life should be both red and white roses together! It should be both torrid passions and tender love at the same time, and it is *when I have you near me.*

Red and white roses—this is what I want to give to you. I want to shower these gifts on you because I know I have them within me to give, because you deserve to have them, and because there is no higher reason in this world for a person to exist. Tasha, I'm a much better man because of you. I have a clarity of vision and a new purpose because of you. I hope you have discovered new heights within yourself through your love for me. That's what true lovers do for each other, you know—allow each other to soar to new and better places. I've known this higher plane with no other woman but you. That's why I must find you and convince you that my heart lives inside of yours.

I wonder what would have happened if I had said all these things to you in Philadelphia. I wanted to—God, how I wanted to tell you that I loved you. But I thought I had no right to speak of love until I broke cleanly with Christine. Had I told you of my feelings that night, would you still be in the States with me? Would you be helping me with the task of truthfully explaining all to Christine without devastating her feelings? Would we be announcing our own engagement and planning our own life together?

I sincerely regret not telling you what was on my mind and in my heart until now. I am responsible for the consequences of your departure back to Egypt, and I'm traveling toward you now so we can begin anew.

Until I find you, Tasha, until I see your beautiful face, remember that I love you. Never lose faith in me, my darling, my dearest love. We will be together soon, and we will be together always.

Yours forever,
J. B.

Karissa sat back, stunned. How could fate rip the two lovers apart again? Something wet plopped on the yellowed paper of the letter, and she realized with a jolt that she'd been crying. How could a love letter written by her father to a woman who was not her mother make her cry? It seemed impossible. She should have despised the woman who stole her father's heart. And yet, she didn't despise Tasharyana. She felt sorry for her, worried about her, and ached for her. She almost felt as if she knew her.

Sniffing, Karissa read the letter again, lingering over the heartfelt words of her father, amazed that the man she had known was capable of such sentimentality. He had never shown a hint of this romantic streak during the years he was married to her mother. More than ever she wondered why her father had married Christine instead of Tasharyana.

After she had read the letter a third time and set the journal to rights, she was still unable to sleep. So she decided to make herself a cup of chamomile tea. Karissa walked down the shadowed hall toward the kitchen without turning on any lights. As she passed through the central atrium, however, she heard a soft thump in the library. Curious as to what had made the noise, she tiptoed down the connecting hall and soundlessly moved to the open door of the library.

Cautiously she peeked around the doorway and was shocked to see a woman dressed in a black milayah with the hood concealing her hair, standing in front of her father's crate. The woman held up the lid with a hand covered by silver and gold rings, and bent over the box as if inspecting the contents.

Karissa rushed into the room. "What do you think you're doing!" she cried, unafraid of the older, heavier female.

The woman's head whipped up, showing the sweep of steel gray hair and a wide forehead. Then her big body rotated as she turned to face Karissa, her hand still on the lid. She had a round face with prominent eyebrows and black eyes that were dark and unafraid. She stood there, undeniably regal, without a hint of chagrin for having been caught in someone else's home. In fact, she surveyed Karissa as if the younger woman were the intruder, not her.

"Who are you?" Karissa demanded. "What are you doing in my house?"

"I have come to claim what is mine, Karissa Spencer." The woman was nonplussed, her eyes cold, her voice deep and resonant.

How did the stranger know her name? And what could Karissa possibly have that belonged to her? "And what might I have of yours?"

"A golden disk, the lunar disk of Sekhmet, Mother of All Things, the Great One of Magic."

Karissa forced herself not to look at the crate, well aware that the solar disk Wally Duncan had found was hidden there, and she didn't want to give away its location with the direction of her glance. "Why do you look here for it?"

"Because it was stolen from us by your father, Julian Bedrani Spencer, and I have learned that it is here."

"Stolen?"

"Yes!" Her red mouth twisted with the effort to suppress her anger. "He pilfered the contents of a sacred temple. And for such a transgression, he forfeited his life."

"My father died in a freak accident."

"Accident? Bah!" The woman let the lid ease down on top of the crate. "The granite block that killed Julian Spencer and his assistant was no accident."

"I was told it was a booby trap, just like the ones in the pyramids."

"That is what everyone believes. But the Watchful Ones triggered the release of the block that killed Julian before he could—in his revenge—discover too much about the sphinx and steal things that did not belong to him or his world. He had to be stopped."

"But I thought my voice activated the booby trap, which made the block fall."

"Then you were mistaken."

Karissa stared at the large woman. For years she had blamed herself for the death of her own father. Asheris had tried to make her see otherwise, and now this stranger was telling her for a fact that her scream had had nothing to do with the granite block that had crushed her father in the sphinx. But the woman had mentioned her father's revenge. What was that all about? As far as she knew, her father had been an Egyptologist because of his love of history, not because he had a desire to seek revenge on someone or something. She crossed her arms.

"You speak of my father's revenge. What do you mean by that?"

"Your father thought to find the center of power of the temple of Sekhmet and crush it." She laughed sharply. "Foolish man!"

"My father was not foolish!"

"Oh, he was not. He was a formidable opponent, I must admit. But he knew nothing of the powers he sought to defeat."

"Why would he want to so such a thing?"

"In his ignorance he believed the temple was an evil society that had taken away the woman he loved."

"You mean Tasharyana?"

The woman's eyes narrowed, increasing their cold glittering quality. "And what do you know of Tasharyana?"

"Nothing more than the name," Karissa hastened to put in, damning her own loose tongue. She paused as a heavy sense of dread descended upon her. Why had she mentioned the name? Why had she admitted any knowledge to this stranger, who had been the enemy of her father? Why hadn't she had the sense to feign ignorance? She stared at the woman and for the first time saw the bright red lipstick, the triangular brows. Could this woman be Madame Hepera, of Tasharyana's visions? She was much older now, her hair grayer, blending in with the white streak in the center. The lines on her face cut much deeper, but there was something about her haughty expression that seemed familiar. She couldn't believe that

Madame Hepera might be standing before her, right that minute, and that she was talking to the hateful woman. She swallowed, knowing the power and cruelty behind the woman's smile, and decided she must be extremely careful in what she said.

"Actually, Tasharyana was just a strange name I came across in my father's journals. He seemed fairly attracted to the woman, but I think it was a fleeting romance."

"Your father's relationship to Tasharyana Higazi should have been fleeting. They were never meant to be together. Fate ordained that Tasharyana be a member of the priesthood. But neither she nor your father heeded the higher wisdom of the gods. Their love obsessed them. They desperately clung to each other, believing they might have a life together one day, when all along the goddess meant to tear them apart." The woman shook her head. "Foolish, foolish people—to think they could take what belonged to the goddess and not pay a price."

"Goddess?" Karissa repeated. "What are you talking about? The gods of ancient Egypt are long gone."

"In that, Ms. Spencer, you are gravely mistaken. When the Nile River is reborn, so shall the goddess Sekhmet begin a new life. She will rise from her sleep and bring Het-ka-ptah to its rightful glory."

"Het-ka-ptah?"

"Yes. The Black Land. It is the name for this country in the tongue of its people. Not English, Ms. Spencer, not Arabic, not Greek. But the tongue of Sekhmet, the Lady of the Way of the Five Bodies. Het-ka-ptah has bowed too long to undeserving foreigners. All that shall be swept away by the goddess."

"How?"

The woman smirked. "You will soon see, Ms. Spencer. All in Egypt will know the wrath of Sekhmet,

Lady of the Place of the Beginning of Time, Mother of All the Gods. She will wash away all unbelievers to the sea and make the land pure again for her followers. Then, one by one she will awaken the others: Ptah—her brother and husband, and Nefer-Tem, her son, and all the lesser gods and goddesses. And they shall rule once more."

Karissa doubted the woman's sanity after such a burst of religious fervor, but she never once doubted her power or her anger. She stepped forward. "I will gladly give you the lunar disk, since I am convinced it belongs to you. But in return I want something you have that belongs to me—my daughter."

"The one you call Julia."

Karissa's heart skipped a beat. So the priestesses did have Julia. "Yes!"

"She does not belong to you. She is the Goddess Incarnate, born of mortals but not of this world."

Not of this world? Karissa had carried the child inside her for nine months, had given her the milk of her body and the security of her arms, and had cherished her above all else. How could anyone say Julia did not belong to her? They were connected as only mothers and daughters could be joined. "She is just a little girl—a six-year-old child!"

"You know yourself the child is special. She has the voice, the mark, and the heritage for which we have been waiting thousands of years. None of the others had the true power, for they did not have the correct paternal lineage."

"You're spouting nonsense!"

"Deep down you know I am not, Ms. Spencer."

"She is my baby!"

"Born of your body, but that is all."

"No!"

The woman laughed again. "Do you not find it

ironic that Julian Spencer, dabbler in history and thief of antiquities, should have sired the woman who has given back to the temple its lost goddess?"

"She is not a goddess. She is just a child. And she needs her mother."

"Nonsense. She has outgrown you, Ms. Spencer."

"No, I don't believe you!"

"Do not trouble yourself about her. The child is well taken care of and is happy with us. In fact, it was she who told me about the disk in your possession."

Karissa gaped at her, grief-stricken. Julia was happy to be in the company of the priestesses? Didn't she miss her mother and father? Or was the old woman feeding her lies and concealing the fact that Julia was imprisoned somewhere, just as Tasharyana had been imprisoned most of her life. Could they have tortured her to get her to tell them about the contents of the crate?

"I must see Julia," Karissa exclaimed. "I must hear her own voice telling me she is happy."

"I am afraid that is not possible, Ms. Spencer."

"Then you won't get the lunar disk."

"I won't?" The woman laughed again, heartier this time. "Do you think you can stop me?"

"Yes. I want you to leave. This instant."

"Leave?" The woman threw back her shoulders and laughed, and her breasts thrust forward beneath the milayah.

"Yes. Leave. Or I will call for my husband and he'll make you leave."

"Your husband, if I am not mistaken, is in no condition to make me do anything."

Outraged by the woman's smugness, her own distress for Julia, and her lack of power, Karissa lost control and rushed at the woman, intending to knock her to the floor and away from the crate. But before she had gone more than two steps, the intruder threw a handful of powder in her face. Instantly, Karissa's eyes and nose started to water. She stopped in her tracks, sneezing uncontrollably, unable to open her eyes long enough to see what the woman was doing. It grew difficult to take a breath, for her lungs were full of harsh burning air. Darkness encroached on her blurred vision, as if she were in a tunnel with narrowing walls. Soon all went black and Karissa fell to the floor.

When Karissa woke up, she found herself on the floor of the library with a pillow from the couch cushioning her head and shoulders from the hard tile floor. Hamid bent over her, a drink of water in his hand.

"Are you all right, Ms. Spencer?" he asked.

Karissa blinked and glanced around the room, half-expecting to see the large woman still rifling through her father's crate. But the woman was gone, and so, too, most likely, was the golden disk, the only bargaining power she might have possessed.

"Ms. Spencer?"

She wiped her nose with a handkerchief he offered. Both her nose and eyes were still watering from the effects of the powder the stranger had thrown.

"I'm—" she broke off as the words stuck in her congested throat. She coughed, choking and sputtering, until Hamid tipped the glass of water to her lips and urged her to take a drink. The water settled her somewhat, and she dabbed at her eyes. "Thank you, Hamid."

"Did she hurt you?" The old man inspected her carefully, his thick gray brows lowering over his bleary eyes.

Karissa glanced at him, wondering when he had seen the intruder. "No."

"You are fortunate. Madame Hepera could just as easily have killed you."

So the intruder *had* been Madame Hepera! Karissa turned and looked at him closely. "Do you know about her?"

"It was she who sent me here long ago."

As if touched by a hot poker, Karissa scooted away from him. Hamid had been sent by Madame Hepera? Had he been spying on them all these years, reporting to the priestesses of Sekhmet about the progress of their little goddess-in-training?

"Do not fear, *sayyidah*. Madame Hepera sent me, believing me to be a servant of the temple of Sekhmet. But in truth I am a servant of another."

"Who?"

"Tasharyana Higazi."

A chill zipped down Karissa's back. More and more it seemed as if Tasharyana's life was enmeshed with more than just her father's.

"You were her servant?"

"Not in the way you think. But I was devoted to her. She had the voice of an angel. I knew her as a girl and watched her grow into a beautiful young woman. She was kind, always kind to me. There was something very special about her."

Karissa felt a second chill. "Wait a minute." She cocked her head, trying to see through the man's advanced age and his gray beard and mustache to the younger man he once had been. "You are Jabar, the caretaker of the school that Tasharyana once attended, aren't you?"

It was Hamid's turn to be surprised. He stepped back. "How do you know of this?"

"I was told about you, only I didn't make the connection. You were the one who fixed the music box for Tasharyana, aren't you? You were the one who glued it together!"

"Yes. You speak the truth," he answered simply.

"I should have noticed the resemblance. But your name is different."

"To conceal my identity."

"All these years you've been secretly watching over Julia?" Karissa asked. "Why?"

"I would have done anything for Tasharyana. I would have died for her. And when the priestesses sent me here to watch over the baby Julia, I came gladly."

"But why? What connection does my daughter have with Tasharyana?"

"They are of the same line. They were both marked to be the high priestess of the temple, the Chosen One. But it was discovered later that Tasharyana did not have the purity of blood to become the true goddess."

"If you knew they were waiting to snatch Julia away, why didn't you tell us?"

"I was hoping she would fail the test, as Tasharyana failed it. Then Julia would have been returned to you unharmed. No one would have been hurt, and nothing would have changed. I might have even been allowed to remain here to watch over beautiful little Julia and tend your gardens. But—" he shrugged eloquently "—she did not fail the test."

"What kind of test are you talking about?"

"I am not certain, *sayyidah*. It is some ancient method of proving kinship and ancestry, which is secret to the priestesses and is done during certain planetary movements."

"So they think she is the goddess."

"Yes. And that is why I am here, Ms. Spencer. We must find Julia before she is killed."

"What do you mean, killed?"

"She will be killed when the goddess is reborn."

"How?" Karissa scrambled to her feet. "When?"

"She will be a sacrifice to the Nile, *sayyidah.* Then her spirit will rise into the heavens, to become Sekhmet, the Vengeful One, who the priestesses believe will—"

"Enough of this Sekhmet deity! What about Julia? When is this going to happen?"

"I am not certain. It has to do with the planets and stars again."

"Do you know where she is?" Karissa screeched, unable to control the panic in her voice. "Do you know where they're hiding her?"

"I believe she has been taken to the sphinx."

"The lost sphinx?" Karissa's palms began to sweat. "Where my father was killed?"

"The very same, I am sorry to say."

"But it's buried under the sand. I saw the sphinx sinking beneath the sand with my own eyes seven years ago!"

"There must be a way in, *sayyidah.* I followed Madame Hepera out to her car when she left here a few minutes ago. And I heard her tell her driver to take her to the temple. When the priestesses speak of the temple, they are talking about the sphinx."

"Then we must go there."

Hamid nodded.

"I'm going to get some tools," Karissa declared, wiping her nose again. "Meet me in the garage."

"Yes, *sayyidah.* And what about Mr. Asher?"

"I'll let him sleep. He is in no condition to help us."

Karissa scrawled a quick note to Asheris, telling him where she was going. Then, with two flashlights, some rope, a shovel, and a very old man, Karissa set off for the Eastern Desert.

Dawn colored the sky by the time they arrived at the huge rock formation that marked the site of the sphinx. Pinks and lavenders and the palest of yellows streaked the heavens as the powerful Egyptian sun pushed its way up from the sand. In a few hours, the sun would climb to its glory and turn the desert into a blazing inferno. Karissa worried that old Hamid wouldn't be able to stand the heat.

She parked the Land Rover behind a pile of rocks, hoping to conceal it from view. Then she jumped out of the vehicle and plopped on her hat, barely feeling the effects of her sleepless night. During the drive into the desert, her panic and fear had settled into grim determination. She would find the opening to the sphinx and she would find Julia, even if it meant her own death.

Across the sand they walked as Karissa remembered the last time she had been here. Seven years ago she had fled the scene with Asheris during a cataclysmic storm and an earthquake, which had buried the sphinx and their pursuers under tons of red granite and sand. How would she ever be able to find the sphinx again, let alone a door in which to enter? Karissa looked down at the sand. If the priestesses had come before them, all traces of their footprints had been blown away by the evening wind.

"Well, Hamid," Karissa stated, stopping to let him rest, and lowering the end of the spade to the ground, "do you have any notion where we might try looking?"

"No, *sayyidah.* I see no sign of the sphinx."

"You're sure it was here where they have their temple."

"Yes. I know that to be true."

Karissa squinted, wishing she had remembered her sunglasses, and stared out at the unchanging expanse of sand. Not a ripple, not a lump betrayed the presence of the huge stone monument. Digging for it would be like looking for a needle in an incredibly huge haystack. She was willing to try but worried that too much precious time would be wasted in arbitrary excavation.

"If the priestesses had been going in and out, there would have to be some sign," she mused. "Some mound of sand, some marker."

"One would think so, yes," Hamid put in. He wiped his perspiring forehead with the back of his sleeve. "Perhaps there is a trap door covered with sand."

"Quite possibly there is. We just have to locate it." She glanced behind her at the rock formation, trying to remember where she'd stood seven years ago in relation to the sandstone outcropping behind her, but nothing helped.

As a last resort, she told Hamid to sit and wait while she made a wide circle, poking at the sand with the tip of the spade, hoping to hit something hard and unyielding. She made another circle and then another, desperately hoping to hear the chink of metal striking granite, yet all the while fearing she might sink into a thinly covered jumble of blocks and fall into the collapsed monument. Since her father's death in the sphinx, the place had forever frightened her.

After a couple of hours Karissa gave up. She could see Hamid suffering in the heat and knew she should return him to the compound. She suffered as well: her arms were weary of wielding the shovel, and her body ached with fatigue, and drooped from lack of rest. She hoped she could make the drive home without falling asleep at the wheel.

"Perhaps Mr. Asher can help," Hamid said, trying to cheer her up as they climbed into the Land Rover. "Perhaps he can remember."

"Maybe." Karissa felt cranky, tired, and discouraged. Sick with worry about Julia spending another night with the priestesses, she started the engine, while Hamid opened a canteen. "We'd do better with somebody who could see through sand."

"No one can do that, *sayyidah*."

Karissa had said the words sarcastically. But she suddenly realized that seeing through sand might not be as preposterous as it sounded.

"Wally can!" she declared, backing out from between the rocks.

"Wally? Who is Wally?"

"An American scientist. He has special equipment that can see through sand, dirt, water—you name it."

"This I do not believe." Hamid capped his canteen. "How can this be done?"

"You'll see. I'll give him a call as soon as we get back. I know he'll want to help us."

* * *

Trying to reach Wally Duncan proved more difficult than Karissa had thought. For most of the day he worked at remote sites and could not be contacted. In early evening, however, her call was returned and Wally said he would take the first plane he could find out of Cairo. Unfortunately he had just missed the final flight of the day and would have to wait until morning. Asheris assured him that they would meet him at the airport at nine o'clock in the morning, and if it were agreeable, would drive directly to the site of the lost sphinx. Wally told them he'd be ready to go the instant he claimed his equipment from the baggage carousel.

Asheris hung up the phone and turned to Karissa. "And now, Karissa, you must rest. You will be useless to Julia if you do not sleep."

She nodded, her body weary to the bone, but her mind still humming at a high speed. She had been glad to hear Asheris talking to Wally and finally accepting him as an ally instead of an adversary. It would be good for Asheris to learn he could depend on the help of a stranger, and a man of modern science at that. Karissa prayed they *could* depend upon Wally and his equipment, as he was their last hope. If he couldn't find the entrance to the lost sphinx, they wouldn't know where else to turn in their quest to find Julia.

"Must I throw you over my shoulder and carry you to bed?" Asheris added, his hands on his hips.

"No," she replied. In the old days, his question would surely have been provocative. But under the circumstances, she heard his words simply for what they were, a demand that she get some sleep as soon as possible. "I'm going right now."

"Shall I ask Eisha to draw a bath for you?"

"That would be nice." She took a few steps toward her room and turned. "What are you going to do?"

"Call the inspector again and see if they've found anything."

"Good."

She headed toward the bathroom.

Hours later Karissa woke up to a bright light streaming through her open bedroom window. She squinted, thinking someone had turned on the light in her room, but then she realized the nearly full moon was riding high in the sky and pouring its cool luminance into the house. Karissa sat up and was surprised to see Asheris dozing in a chair near the door on the other side of the bed. A warm feeling swept over her at his gesture of protection. She recalled the night she had spent trapped in the sphinx with his dark panther body stretched out beside her, guarding her, keeping her safe until the light of morning.

Karissa slipped out of bed. She had dozed long enough to feel refreshed. In fact, she felt unusually alert as she padded across the floor and paused to gaze at her husband's dark handsome face. She loved his sharp nose and his wide lower lip, and the way his ebony hair swept back at his temples. Even in sleep he appeared aware and present, as a cat sleeps with one ear tracking sound and movement. She expected to see his eyes open any moment now to find her standing there, gawking at him.

Soundlessly she tiptoed away, not wanting to wake him, for she had decided to view the information stored in the fifth and final obelisk and didn't want to be kept from her purpose. She had yet to tell Asheris about any of the scrying, and had revealed nothing of what she had discovered of her father's life as a young man. Until she learned the outcome of Tasharyana's tale—should she ever find out what happened to the opera singer and her father—she didn't want to share the story with anyone.

Reaching in the closet, Karissa pulled a light robe off a hanger and drew it on as she left the room. She picked up the music box in the hall where it had been left on a table the previous evening, and walked out to the shadowed garden. A ring had formed around the full moon and Karissa watched the halo increase as she headed for the pond. The ring might be a harbinger of the approach of the khamsin, the intense desert wind that swept across Egypt in late April and early May, bringing with it soaring temperatures and clouds of sand that could block out the sun for days on end. Karissa hoped the khamsin would wait a bit longer, until she and Asheris could search for the sphinx. If the winds came, Wally wouldn't be able to use his equipment. They wouldn't be able to drive through the desert, for the road would be impassable and the sandstorm far too dangerous. If the khamsin came, Julia might be lost to them forever.

As if to confirm her fears, an unseasonably warm breeze wafted across the pond, lifting the tendrils of her hair and fluttering the sleeves of her gossamer robe. Far off in the papyrus reeds a night bird cried out. Then just as quickly the wind dropped, leaving the garden in a state of eerie stillness.

Shuddering, Karissa wound up the music box and set it on the sand while she hummed along with the now familiar melody. Her voice quavered as she fought down the possibility of never seeing her little daughter again, but then she took a deep breath and made herself think only positive thoughts. She forced herself to concentrate on the scrying session, hoping that some clue to Julia's future would be found in the story of Tasharyana.

Seconds later Tasharyana appeared on the surface of the pond. She slowly tilted her head, in a gesture of resignation and fatigue. She sighed and clasped her hands together in front of her and then began to speak.

This is the fifth installment of my story. I don't know how many more memories I will be able to document, for my strength is waning. To muster the concentration it takes to record my life becomes more difficult with each session. I will continue as long as I can, for I am convinced that someday this record will be valuable—perhaps to those who live on after me and are interested in my story. At the very least, these memories will serve to warn the world about the temple of Sekhmet and its priestesses. They do exist and they *are* dangerous. It is a pleasing irony to me to know that I am tapping their arcane knowledge to inscribe my thoughts on these obelisks, and that these very same obelisks may someday be used against them.

"This memory rod contains images from the winter of 1966. I am now back in Luxor. For many months I have been running from Madame Hepera. All over Egypt I tried to find work in the large towns and tiny villages. But each time I began to establish myself, Madame Hepera would find me and I would have to flee again. Soon, I could no longer hide my condition. And very few employers would hire an unmarried woman carrying a child. By autumn I had no money left, nowhere to go, and I was constantly sick—whether from the pregnancy or exhaustion, I wasn't certain. I had lost all hope that J. B. would find me since my travels were very erratic. And I tried not to dwell on the possibility that he had never even looked for me. After a few months I was convinced he had chosen to continue his life with the Petries and marry Christine. Since that was probably the case, I thought it best not to contact him. If he learned I carried his child, he would come to me out of duty—something I could never accept. I wanted J. B. to come to me out of love.

"My only joy, my only reason to keep struggling for freedom, was the baby growing inside me. Though I had never looked into her eyes or heard her voice, and had only felt her strong little kicks and rolls, I loved my baby more than I had loved anything in my entire life, even J. B. Spencer. During my treks when I was all alone, sleeping in the desert off the road or beneath a mimosa tree along the river, I would wrap my arms around my swelled abdomen and embrace the child within, sustained by the knowledge that my baby would soon be born and I would have someone to love for the rest of my life.

"Alone and ill, I trudged to the south, toward the only home I had ever known: Luxor. It was in Luxor that I dropped my guard, too tired to take every precaution to hide my face and conceal my identity. I had walked all day and night to get to the city, and I had spent my last coins on a drink of cold tea and a piece of flat bread at a street vendor cart.

"Like vultures, Madame Hepera's servants swept down on me. I struggled, but I hadn't the strength to resist any longer. I was starving, dehydrated, and suffering from exposure, and I just couldn't fight anymore. They took me to a large house at the edge of town on the eastern bank of the Nile.

* * *

Tasharyana's Tale—Luxor, 1966

"So!" Madame Hepera gloated, walking around the bed where Tasharyana lay. She nodded toward Tasharyana's taut swollen belly. "Your little adventure in the United States left you with quite a souvenir, I see."

Tasharyana didn't answer. She had been bathed, fed, and put to bed, and could hardly keep her eyes open, but her distrust of Madame Hepera gave her the strength to remain awake and wary.

"Or do you carry the child of the minister of antiquities?"

The thought of spawning that man's child filled Tasharyana with disgust. Had the minister told Madame Hepera he took Tasharyana to his bed? She fought down a wave of nausea and closed her eyes.

"The child is J. B. Spencer's," she replied, her voice strained.

"I thought so." Madame Hepera gave a snort of derision. "You didn't listen to me when I told you about men, did you? You thought you knew better, didn't you?"

Tasharyana couldn't let J. B. take all the blame for her condition. "It was my choice, Madame Hepera."

"To have his child?"

"To open myself to the possibility."

"You are a fool!" Madame Hepera exclaimed. "A little fool!"

Tasharyana slowly opened her eyes and leveled them on the woman. "If I am such a fool, madame, why have you gone to so much trouble and expense to track me down?"

"Because I have spent years training your voice. And the time has come to put the training to use."

"I am no longer interested in opera," Tasharyana lied.

"Opera has nothing to do with it. I am speaking of your true destiny."

"And what might that be?"

"To serve the temple of Sekhmet. To become the servant of the goddess herself."

Tasharyana pulled herself up on her elbows. "What are you talking about, madame?"

"I am talking about using the voice you have been given by the goddess to serve her and to save Egypt."

"Save Egypt? How? In what way?"

"A dam which spans the Nile is destroying the ancient patterns of flood and drought. It must be brought down."

"Do you mean the Aswan Dam?"

"Yes. For thousands of years our people have lived along the banks of the Nile, taking fish for their plates and silt to enrich the soil. But the Aswan Dam is an abomination to the Nile and is altering our way of life. It will destroy Egypt."

"No, it won't. The fellahin can harvest crops almost year round now instead of waiting for the floods."

Madame Hepera shook her head. "But to feed their crops, the fellahin scatter chemicals upon the earth instead of using the silt that piles up behind the dam. These poisons are becoming part of our land. We are eating them, drinking them."

Tasharyana fell silent, uncertain how she could argue with the woman.

Madame Hepera continued, "And the snails are everywhere. They do not die off because there is no dry season. This sounds like a little thing, does it not? But the fellahin are suffering greatly because of the worms that come from the snails."

"The farmers can get medical attention for parasites."

"There is not enough money. The fellahin work hard, but there is never enough money. You know that. And the snail worms sap their strength, making their lives harder, poorer, and desperate. All this angers the Goddess Sekhmet, Mother of All. She can see that the Aswan High Dam must be destroyed."

Tasharyana sank back on the pillow, hardly believing what Madame Hepera was saying. During the eight years she had lived with the woman, Tasharyana never suspected her to be so deeply devoted to the cause of an antiquated deity. Certainly she knew of Madame Hepera's secret rites, and she had witnessed some strange facets of the woman's character, but she had never suspected this kind of fanaticism.

Madame Hepera thought the Aswan High Dam should be destroyed? The dam was just being completed. Behind it grew a huge lake, more than three hundred miles long. If Madame Hepera carried out her plan, millions of people would perish in the ensuing flood, cities would be destroyed, farmlands wiped out, and irreplaceable temples swept to the sea.

"So you plan to destroy the dam somehow," Tasharyana ventured, angling for more information in the hopes that she could thwart her plans.

"With your help."

"Mine?" Tasharyana sat up. "How?"

"Your voice is the key to the destruction of this modern travesty, my dear. You have been trained to sing far beyond *Carmen*."

"What can my voice do to the Aswan Dam?"

"You would be surprised, my dear." Madame Hepera gave her a knowing smile and clasped her hands below her large bosom. "Amplified by the lunar disks of Sekhmet, your voice will be able to shake mountains."

"No!" Tasharyana shook her head. "I won't have anything to do with such a thing! People will die if the dam breaks, lots of people!"

"You will have no choice. When the goddess speaks, you will obey her."

"No, I won't!"

Madame Hepera chuckled derisively. "You cannot conceive of the strength of the goddess. But first, we must perform certain tests to make certain you are worthy of being the Chosen One."

She turned to a tray by the bedside and poured a cup of tea which she held out for Tasharyana. "Here, my dear, drink this. I'm afraid I've upset you."

"Why shouldn't I be upset?" Tasharyana cried, struggling to her feet. "And I don't want any of your damned tea!" She flung out her arm, knocking the cup from the saucer, spilling its contents over the front of Madame Hepera's dress and sending the china shattering to the floor.

"Thoughtless child!" Madame Hepera shrieked, stumbling backward and brushing at her dress as if to wipe away the tea. "Ali!" she screamed for one of her servants. "Ali!"

"You drugged me for years with that stuff, didn't you?" Tasharyana demanded, edging toward the door, even though she knew Ali would soon arrive and manhandle her into submission, just as he had done in the marketplace that morning. "You always kept me half-numb with your tea!"

"You were a nervous girl!"

"I was not!"

"Hard to manage. A histrionic young lady!"

"I wasn't!"

She reached for the doorknob just as the door burst open. Ali, a muscular man with huge shoulders and short legs, stepped into the room, glowering at Tasharyana as if to stare her into compliance.

"Ali!" Madame Hepera ordered. "Grab her and hold her until I come back!"

"Yes, *as-sayyidah!*"

Ali pulled her roughly against him. Knowing her failing strength was useless against him, Tasharyana didn't struggle. But she never once let her body relax against his, and was well aware of his grin as he looked down at her from behind. His stare made her skin crawl.

Madame Hepera returned a few minutes later, armed with a hypodermic needle, which she plunged into Tasharyana's shoulder.

"Count to ten, Miss Higazi," Ali chided, snickering. "One, two—"

The sound of his mocking voice drifted to a faint drone as the vision faded to darkness.

When Tasharyana awoke, she found herself lying on an elevated stone slab in a shadowed, windowless room. The colors of the murals on the wall swirled and merged as Tasharyana felt the aftereffects of the drug she had been given. Desperate to get away, she tried to sit up, but she could not move her limbs, even though she wasn't bound to the stone in any way. Had the drug administered by Madame Hepera paralyzed her? Would she forever be a prisoner of Madame Hepera's potions and magic? A sharp pain cut through her at the base of her belly, just above her left hip. For an instant the intensity of the pain brought tears to eyes and she had to concentrate on her breathing to get through her physical distress. Then the pain subsided to a dull ache.

What effect would the drugs have on her unborn child? She didn't like to think of the possibility that her baby lay in her womb unconscious or disoriented, or perhaps in pain.

Where was she? In the basement of Madame Hepera's Luxor house? Blinking the tears from her eyes, she glanced around the room and saw clusters of candles in brass stands near her feet and head. Over her pregnant body was draped a covering of the finest linen bordered in gold trim, and on her hand, which she was unable to raise, was a ring shaped in the head of a lioness with eyes fashioned of rubies. From all appearances, she was laid out upon an altar in preparation for a rite of some kind. What did Madame Hepera have in mind? Whatever it was, Tasharyana decided to spend her time thinking about ways to escape instead of lying there dreading the future for herself and her baby.

All she could move were her eyes. She used them to take in as much as she could of the room, searching for a way out. But she could see neither door nor window. Colorful murals surrounded her on every wall, depicting the goddess Sekhmet in her various forms—a beautiful female with the head of a lioness, a seductress dressed in red and dancing with a sistrum before her brother/husband, and an avenging fury bearing down upon her enemies in the form of a powerful black panther. The murals seemed more fitting to a tomb or temple than a private sanctuary.

Another pain stabbed her abdomen and Tasharyana squinted, enduring it as best she could. The baby rolled inside her, and its movements sent her into a paroxysm of agony. If she could only command her limbs and change position, she might be able to alleviate her discomfort. But Madame Hepera's drugs had made movement impossible. Panting, she gave herself over to riding out the pain, and forgot all about escape.

She didn't know how much time had passed when a group of people filed into the room. She could hear the scuffling sound of many sandals echoing in the bare chamber. Slowly Tasharyana opened her eyes, her senses dulled by pain, and discovered a part of the mural had cleverly disguised a doorway, which was now opened. Five women, dressed in white linen and heavily braided black hair and draped in gold and jewels, made a ring around the altar while they swung smoking incense burners and played the sistrum and bone clappers. One woman, who took a stand at the middle of the altar, wore the skin of a black panther over her shoulders and a huge collar made of gold, lapis lazuli, and carnelian. Tasharyana looked at her face and wasn't surprised to see Madame Hepera in full temple-of-Sekhmet regalia.

Madame Hepera looked down upon her and passed her hand through the air over Tasharyana. "We have numbed your body, Tasharyana, so that we may perform our rites upon it. But your spirit remains awake, so that it may contribute to the completion of the ceremony."

Majestically, Madame Hepera turned to an attendant who held a tray full of metal and wood implements. The woman selected one and held it up. Tasharyana stared at it in horror. The instrument looked like a giant needle, ten inches long, with a very sharp point. What were they going to do with it?

Tasharyana tried to speak, to tell Madame Hepera that her body wasn't numb at all. She was immobilized but still able to feel pain. She suddenly remembered how she had been conscious throughout her supposed circumcision, too. Perhaps her body had an abnormally high tolerance level for narcotics. Dr. Shirazzi had given her too low a dosage of anesthetic years ago in Luxor, and now Madame Hepera had also assumed she was numbed, when in fact she was very much sentient. But there was no way of apprising Madame Hepera of the fact.

Terrified, she watched as Madame Hepera chanted while raising the large needle above her head.

19

Madame Hepera sank the needle into the bottom of Tasharyana's foot. Searing pain shot through her and a silent scream rose in her throat. But the priestesses heard nothing and saw no clue to Tasharyana's reaction, other than a widening of her eyes as the needle sank farther. The baby inside her kicked furiously and an intense cramp wracked her body. Madame Hepera straightened and reached for another needle. She raised it above her head and continued their chant. Unable to bear the onslaught of agony, Tasharyana fainted.

Much later, Tasharyana was awakened by more cramping, which destroyed her blessed state of unconsciousness. Bathed in sweat and nearly crippled by a band of fire in her abdomen, Tasharyana opened her eyes and rolled to her side. At least she could move now. She was grateful for that. She lay for a minute on the hard stone slab, her hip and shoulder pressed against the granite, panting, while she glanced around.

The priestesses were gone and only a single candle remained burning. The door to the room had been left open and off in the distance in some other chamber, she could hear the rattle of the sistrum and the singsong voices of the priestesses as they continued their rite. They must be using her blood in their ceremony. Would the rite tie her to the goddess Sekhmet against her will? She had to get out. No matter if she died trying, she would use her final breath, her last heartbeat, to get her child away from the priestesses.

Tasharyana slid to the floor, gasping as her left foot hit the ground. The needle wound was deep, and sent a shaft of pain up her leg. She could feel a tenderness in her thigh, abdomen, chest, and throat. Her lower back felt as if it had an iron spike sticking in it. Had they plunged needles in those places, too? She ignored the pain and gathered the linen wrap around her. Then, cradling her belly with her right arm, she limped out of the room, stopping every few steps to lean against the dusty limestone wall and gather her strength. Going in the opposite direction of the chanting, she hobbled down a dark hallway, and soon felt an unusual heavy pressure between her legs. Could her baby be coming? She prayed it wasn't so—she wasn't due for another month.

Her legs wobbled as she continued down the corridor. After a few minutes the hall widened to a gallery of huge statues of Sekhmet, at least six meters tall, carved in red granite and polished to shining perfection. Obviously she wasn't in the cellar of any house. She must be in a temple of some kind. But where?

Tasharyana stumbled through the gallery, staring up at the monstrous lioness faces, certain that the eyes of the goddess followed her and that the massive stone hand resting so motionless on the granite knee would suddenly reach out with the deadly swiftness of a cat and grab her. Fighting down her childish terror, Tasharyana pressed onward, headed for the inky blackness of the doorway beyond the statues. She had no idea whether she ran toward the outside world or plunged deeper into the tomblike bowels of the temple.

Just as she was about to clear the final statue, someone reached out and grabbed her wrist. Tasharyana screamed. The sound echoed through the hypostyle hall, bouncing off the looming shapes of Sekhmet and careering through the labyrinth of corridors beyond.

"Quiet!" a male voice whispered harshly.

The voice sounded vaguely familiar. Tasharyana peered into the darkness, trying to focus on the face in the shadows while her heart pounded savagely. "Who's there?" she called.

"It is Jabar, Miss Higazi."

"Jabar!"

"Come with me. There is no time to waste!" He urged her to join him behind the statue. She hung back, not fully trusting him.

"The priestesses will have heard your cry," he put in, tugging at her wrist. "They will be coming."

"Where are you taking me?"

"I know of a secret passage." He pulled her to the wall. "It will get us from here to the outside and quickly."

He pushed a hieroglyph in the wall and a small hole appeared, large enough to duck through. Jabar led the way and then turned to press another glyph that closed the passage. Tasharyana leaned against the side of the tunnel and tried to catch her breath.

"Do not tarry!" Jabar warned. "They will have time to cut us off before we can get out."

"I'm ill, Jabar. I have to sit down for a minute." Her vision clouded as another cramp clutched her abdomen. She started to slide down the wall. "Just for a minute—"

"No! They will catch us and kill us both."

She closed her eyes. Sweat trickled down her temples and between her breasts. The pain was like a fire now, twisting inside her and dominating her thoughts. The threat of the priestesses seemed insignificant compared to the battle she waged with her own body.

"Please, Miss Higazi! It is not far. Then you can rest."

He fumbled for her hand. His fingers were rough and callused, but his strong grip gave her enough reassurance to pull her back to reality. She pushed away from the wall and stumbled after him.

They hurried through the darkness, the passage slanting ever upward. Time swirled before her and her vision dipped and spun, as she reeled through a world of throbbing agony. All she wanted to do was collapse on the floor and curl around her misery. But the threat of danger to her child and to Jabar induced her to keeping dragging one foot in front of the other, and her pride made her clench her teeth against the screams that boiled inside.

After an eternity, Jabar pushed another mark on the tunnel wall and a doorway opened. Beyond it lay the desert, bathed in a strange glow, which Tasharyana soon realized was moonlight. Jabar ducked through the doorway, looked right and left, and then reached back for her.

"Come. They are not out here."

She held out her hand and he pulled her out to the desert. She could hardly stand, but she could receive no support from Jabar, crippled as he was by polio. He had trouble enough shuffling with his withered and twisted left side. She paused to rub the ache in the small of her back. It was then she felt something warm trickling down her leg.

"I can't go much farther," Tasharyana gasped. "I think my baby's coming!"

Jabar stared at her face and then at her belly, as if to see the proof of her statement. He glanced over his shoulder, into the darkness of the desert night.

"There is a rock formation over there," he pointed east. "Can you make it that far?"

She squinted and, in the darkness, could barely make out a large shape not more than a hundred meters away.

"My truck is hidden in the rocks. If you can just get to it, we will be able to drive away."

She nodded, nearly overcome by another contraction. Trembling, she stepped out to the avenue leading to the temple behind her while Jabar limped ahead of her in a gamboling run that was surprisingly swift. The wind off the desert whipped her light wrap, and she caught up the edges of the linen as she looked back over her shoulder to where she had been imprisoned.

Behind her crouched a huge sphinx, at least three stories tall from head to paw and twice as long. The face of the sphinx was half-eroded, with most of the nose and one cheek missing. But the face was definitely that of a woman. Tasharyana stumbled backward, awed by the eerily majestic view of the temple bathed in moonlight. She had never seen a female likeness on a sphinx before and was struck by the sight.

Jabar reached for her elbow. "Hurry, Miss Higazi. They will find us!"

"I'll try." Tasharyana focused her attention on moving again, each footstep a battle to be won or lost against exhaustion and pain. Jabar did his best, encouraging her and praising her, until his voice became a song in her head, like a lullaby or nursery rhyme. Soon she lost sense of the words and heard only the drone of his voice as she plummeted to a primal level where the only thing keeping her going was the will to endure.

Just as they reached the rock formation, Jabar whispered, "Down!" and shoved her to the ground. She fell headlong into the sand, jarring her abdomen. She muffled her cry of distress, knowing he wouldn't have manhandled her without a reason.

"The priestesses have come from the temple!" he whispered. "They must not see your white robe."

Tasharyana panted, too exhausted to form words with her parched lips. "Take my shirt," Jabar said, offering his dark garment. "And give me the white linen." She slipped on his worn cotton shirt and pulled off the linen wrap. His shirt barely covered her nakedness, but she was too tired to care. He balled up the linen and stuffed it under his dark undershirt. "Can you crawl?" he asked, and she noticed he didn't look at her when he spoke, even though he couldn't have seen much of her in the darkness.

"Yes."

"Good. Follow me." He set off on hands and knees. She trailed behind, thankful to be off her feet.

"Jabar, I can't go on much longer. I must . . . stop."

"There is a spring nearby. A pool. Rocks to hide behind."

She swallowed and kept crawling. The thought of immersing her burning body in a pool of water was enough to sustain her for a few more meters.

Hand, knee, hand, knee. She chanted the movements

to herself so she could get her mind on something other than the agony inside her. And just when she thought she couldn't crawl a centimeter more, she saw Jabar stop behind a huge boulder and stand up.

"My truck isn't far from here."

"I can't," Tasharyana grunted. A sudden urge deep inside her forced her to press down. "I must stop. Oh, Jabar—"

She broke off as the pressure between her legs intensified.

"Miss Higazi, we must get to the truck!"

"I can't! My baby is coming. Now!"

He yanked the linen out of his shirt and threw it upon the ground, smoothing out the wrinkles with short strokes. "Here then. Lie down!"

"It's coming!" she gasped. Another wave of pressure seized her. "Jabar!" She collapsed onto the linen and gave up to the heavy feeling between her legs, panting, gasping for breath as the cramps came ever faster.

He hovered beside her, trying to comfort her. But all he could do was wipe the sweat away from her brow with his handkerchief and croon gruff male words of encouragement. His hands were shaking even more than hers. Then, she felt something shift inside her.

"The baby!" She clutched his thick dry hand as her body seemed to rip apart.

"What, Miss Higazi?" Jabar whispered. "What should I do?"

"I don't know. Try to guide it out!"

He moved in between her legs. "I see a head!" he cried. "I see its head! There is a head, Miss Higazi!"

Even through her pain she had to smile at his gleeful outburst. She pushed down again, forcing the baby out with all her strength.

"A shoulder now, Miss Higazi. There's the shoulder!"

Tasharyana raised up on an elbow and tried to look between her legs. But all she could see was the top of Jabar's head. She grinned as tears and sweat mingled together and coursed down her cheeks. She couldn't believe she was having J. B.'s baby out in the desert like this, naked under the stars, with a crippled man for a midwife. Yet, what more fitting place to give birth to her precious child than in the stark beauty of the Eastern Desert?

"Keep going, Miss Higazi!" Jabar exclaimed. "You are almost done!"

She mustered all of her strength, all of her will, reaching into the very depths of her heart, and gave a final push. With a great rush, the baby slid all the way out, into the waiting hands of Jabar. Tasharyana sagged with relief as the fire in her body went out, just like that.

"It is a girl!" Jabar crowed. "A little girl child!"

"Oh, let me see!"

Tasharyana watched as Jabar held up a small wrinkled creature with black hair and tiny jerking limbs. When she saw her baby, she thought she would die of happiness. In that moment, everything she had done, everything she had ever thought important, was as nothing compared to the love she felt for the helpless little child cradled in Jabar's two palms.

He beamed and stared at the baby as if he had never seen anything more precious. But soon, however, the baby arched and let out a wail that pierced the night. Tasharyana was too exhausted to worry that the sound would carry to the priestesses who were searching for them.

"Give her to me," Tasharyana whispered. "Oh, give her to me!"

"She is wet. She is covered with much—"

"I don't care. She is my baby!" Tasharyana reached out, and the miracle that had come of her joining with J. B. was placed in her hands. Immediately the baby's cries ceased. Tasharyana thought her heart would break with pure joy as she lowered her tiny daughter to her body. The infant knew her, knew the sound of her and the feel of her, and she snuggled contentedly against Tasharyana's chest. Without being shown, the baby nuzzled her breast, found the nipple, and began to nurse.

"If only J. B. could see her." Tasharyana sighed and relaxed upon the linen. She had never felt such an all-encompassing reason for being than when suckling this child of her heart. The only possible addition to her happiness would be the company of the father of her child, and the opportunity to see the look on J. B.'s face when he beheld their daughter.

Jabar jerked to attention.

"What is it?" Tasharyana murmured, still half-drugged with love and relief, and so weak she could barely lift her head.

"They are coming. The priestesses are coming! What are we to do?"

"I don't know. I can't go yet. I was told there would be more after the baby."

"We can't wait here. I have no gun, Miss Higazi! What will I do?"

"Run, Jabar. You've done all you can for me. Run!"

"No, I will not leave you."

"Get the truck, then. Drive as close as you can. Maybe you can get here before they do."

"It is worth a try." He scrambled to his feet. "I will be back!"

He turned and hurried into the gloom.

A faint cramp washed over Tasharyana as she glanced around, wondering if she could hide behind the rocks. She would do anything to keep her baby out of the hands of the priestesses. And yet, she knew that she hadn't the strength left to walk, let alone pick her way through the rubble.

Would they recapture her so easily? What would become of her? What would become of her baby?

Moments later, she saw the flash of white robes in the darkness and the dull gleam of gold in the moonlight as the priestesses marched around the rock promontory.

"Ah, Miss Higazi!" Madame Hepera exclaimed, tipping back her head in a triumphant smile. "There you are! And with your new baby!"

Tasharyana clutched the child to her breasts, ready to fight to the death to protect her newborn daughter.

"And what have you produced for the illustrious J. B. Spencer?" Madame Hepera continued. "A boy or a girl?"

Tasharyana paused. She didn't know why, but she felt the need to conceal the gender of her baby. "A boy," she answered.

"A boy! Won't the father be proud!" The woman chuckled. "That is, if he ever bothers to look into the matter."

"Leave us be," Tasharyana put in. "For the love of Allah, leave us be!"

"Allah? Allah has nothing to do with this!" Madame Hepera snapped, stepping closer. "You are to serve Sekhmet. And the child will be taken to the temple to be purified for the goddess."

"No!"

"Yes, Miss Higazi!" Madame Hepera stepped forward to snatch the child away from her.

Just then a blood-curdling snarl echoed in the rocks. Everyone looked up, shocked by the sound. In a graceful arc, an inky black shape leaped off the limestone outcropping and landed with a light thud between Tasharyana and Madame Hepera. Tasharyana gasped in fright as a huge black panther laid back the ears of his massive head and roared at the high priestess.

Madame Hepera screamed and stumbled backward. The panther hissed and snarled, taking a menacing step toward her. The priestesses recoiled, terrified.

"Oh, Great Sekhmet, Mother of All," Madame Hepera began in a tremulous voice, raising her palms in supplication.

Tasharyana could see the back end of the panther and knew that the animal was certainly not the embodiment of a female deity. This creature was a male, undeniably so.

"It is I, your humble servant," Madame Hepera continued, genuflecting. "I, who—"

The panther growled sharply, cutting her off, and lashed out with a huge paw. His voice reverberated like thunder, as if to shake the sand beneath her. Madame Hepera and her priestesses fell back even farther.

"Lord Azhur?" she stuttered, her voice trailing off in fright.

Tasharyana glanced down at her baby, hoping the sound of the big cat wouldn't frighten her, and was shocked to find the tiny girl child calmly regarding the enormous panther as though she could see the animal clearly and knew the creature posed no threat. She didn't think babies were supposed to be able to see well at birth, but it was obvious her child was an exception.

The panther growled again. Behind her, Tasharyana heard the approach of a vehicle. She glanced to the right and saw a battered old truck rolling toward her. With any luck Jabar's identity would not be discernible in the darkness. She didn't want to be responsible for exposing Jabar's role in her escape attempt. But protecting Jabar's identity meant getting herself into the truck without any help.

She would have to do it.

The truck idled to a stop and Tasharyana forced herself to her knees. She swayed with the effort but remained upright. The panther growled deep in his throat as if to warn the priestesses not to approach. Then, keeping himself between Tasharyana and the others, he sidled close to her as Tasharyana picked up the linen covering. Though it was soiled, she wrapped it around her and the baby as she limped toward the truck. She couldn't believe a wild creature had chosen to protect her and her baby, but now was not the time to question Providence. Determined to save her child, she doggedly dragged herself to the waiting truck. Jabar flung open the door for her and she half fell, half pulled herself into the cab.

Jabar reached across her and grabbed the door, shutting it as he pushed down on the accelerator. The truck lurched to a start, fishtailing in the sand. Tasharyana moaned and braced herself with a hand on the dashboard as Jabar got control of the vehicle and sped off toward the main road.

"Did you see it?" Tasharyana gasped. "The panther?"

"Yes, Miss Higazi!"

"He saved our lives. A wild animal saved our lives!"

"Oh, the panther is not a wild animal, miss. He is Lord Azhur, who haunts the sphinx."

"Lord Azhur?"

"Yes. Our stories tell of Lord Azhur, how once he was the son of a pharaoh but was cursed by the priestesses of Sekhmet and thereby forced to spend eternity as a panther."

"Son of a pharaoh? That would make him awfully old, wouldn't it?"

"No, for Lord Azhur is immortal, cursed forever."

The truck bounced as Jabar drove from the dirt lane onto the shoulder of the main highway. The asphalt road was smoother, much easier for Tasharyana to endure. She leaned back against the seat.

Jabar turned to look at her, his face shadowed. "But you, Miss Higazi. You have seen Lord Azhur. He protected you and your child. This is great good luck for you to be under his protection."

"I can't understand why he did it."

"He would do anything to thwart the priestesses."

"I see." She closed her eyes as a dull cramp swirled in her flaccid abdomen. The afterbirth was about to be delivered and there was nothing she could do to stop it. For a moment she worried that someone should cut the baby's cord soon, but suddenly nothing seemed to matter other than her need for rest. Tasharyana tried to open her eyes, tried to focus on what Jabar was saying. But she had suffered too much in the last few hours. She could hold on no longer. She let herself fall into blessed blackness.

The next thing she knew, she and her baby were being handed down to someone. She heard a female voice exclaim, "Ah, poor girl! So much blood! So much blood!"

Tasharyana hadn't the strength to open her eyes, but never once did she allow her grip to loosen on her daughter. No one was going take her baby from her. No one.

20

Luxor, Present Day

Something tickled Karissa awake, and she looked down to see a small dung beetle crawling over the back of her hand.

"Acch!" she gasped and shook it off. She scrambled to a sitting position and saw that dawn streaked the sky above the eastern wall of the garden. Stiff and sore from sleeping on the ground again, she pushed back her disheveled hair. Odd, but she distinctly remembered Tasharyana mentioning two visions in the obelisk and yet she recalled seeing only one; the memory of the woman giving birth in the desert. She thought she remembered an interval of static after the first vision and could recall nothing afterward. Had there truly been two visions and she had slept through the second one? Or had Tasharyana succumbed to whatever illness had robbed her of vitality and flesh, and failed to record the final entry to her visual diary? There was no way of knowing for sure until Karissa did another scrying session, and that would have to wait until the moon was bright.

What Karissa had learned from the scrying session, however, was the connection of the priestesses of Sekhmet to the lost sphinx in the desert. She was certain now that Julia was somewhere deep in the temple, laid upon an altar just as Tasharyana had been in the vision. Had the priestesses already performed their rituals on Julia, drugging her and piercing her body with the awful needles? She flushed with dread at the thought and snatched up the music box with trembling hands. They had to find Julia today. They had to rescue her before she was subjected to the terrors that Tasharyana had suffered. She would never be able to live with the knowledge that Julia had been terrified and hurt and all alone in the darkness of the sphinx.

Karissa hurried to the house to wake Asheris. On the way, she glanced at the sky, hoping the day would be bright and clear. "Please, God," she murmured under her breath, "let the khamsin wait for just one day. One day is all I ask."

Wally Duncan's plane was an hour late, and Asheris and Karissa waited in the airport terminal while the minutes ticked by. Like a trapped cat, Asheris paced the width of the gate, striding from one end of the bank of windows to the other, his eyes trained on the sky, searching for any sign of the jet. Karissa watched him, remembering how he had looked as a panther, how he had paced and turned, paced and turned, just as he was doing now—patient but unable to wait without constantly moving. He still possessed the sinuous moves of a big cat, the result of having spent hundreds of thousands of nights in the form of a panther, haunting the Eastern Desert, padding through the dark streets of Luxor, or guiding her to safety—always guiding her, always protecting her. The vision of the big cat had been with her ever since she could remember, as if it was the first visual impression to have been burned into her child's mind and would remain flaring brightly there until the day she died.

Asheris was a man now. But to Karissa, he would always be part panther, and forever part of her soul.

After Wally finally arrived and they packed his equipment into the back of the Land Rover, Asheris jumped behind the wheel and they took off for the Eastern Desert. Karissa filled Wally in on what had happened, and he listened in disbelief and outrage as the story unfolded. Then Karissa explained in detail why they needed him.

"I know approximately where the lost sphinx is located," she said. "But seven years ago, there was an earthquake. The sphinx collapsed and sank into the sand. Now it is so covered by sand that there is no discernible trace of it whatsoever."

Asheris nodded. "And we are concerned that the entrance we knew of before may be blocked by rubble."

Wally leaned forward. "There's probably a few escape routes built in to the temple that we could use for access."

"Yes, but we do not know where they are or if they are passable."

"That's why we thought you could help." Karissa raised her eyebrows.

"Depending upon the depth of the sand and the extent of damage to the temple, I might be able to locate some openings. But it could take hours."

"Time is precious, Wally," Karissa said. "Julia could be in danger."

He held up a hand. "I'll work as fast as possible. You and Mr. Asher can help me set up and move my gear. Can we drive off the road, Mr. Asher, so we don't have to lug the equipment back and forth?"

"It is dangerous to drive on the dunes. The Land Rover may get stuck."

"We're going to have to try. Otherwise we'll waste valuable time carrying my stuff and setting it up."

"So be it." Asheris set his jaw and sped up the canyon road that wound to the desert above. Sunlight glinted on his dark glasses. Karissa reached out and slipped her fingers over the hand he had clenched around the gearshift. At her touch, she could feel him relax. He glanced at her. Though the sunglasses concealed his eyes and his grim expression hid his emotional reaction to her touch, she knew he was grateful for their connection. She squeezed his hand, stroked his forearm, and sat back with a sigh, worrying about the hours to come. Asheris touched her knee reassuringly and then returned his attention to the road ahead.

They labored for hours, setting up Wally's machines, drawing diagrams of what they had found, and coming up with impassable dead ends time after time. Asheris worked like a fiend alongside Wally and racked his brain for a single speck of memory that would give them a clue to a usable passage. He had roamed for thousands of years as a panther in this part of the desert, haunting the site of his immortal imprisonment. But then as now, he had no memory of the nights he spent as a cat. He had no idea what he had seen, what he had done—nothing other than the stories in the newspapers about criminals being killed by a big cat, or the accounts Karissa had relayed to him when she had seen him as a panther. If he could recall a single memory of one of those nights, he might be able to recall the sphinx as it looked when it was newly constructed, how the terrain might have given clues to the secret entrances, the hidden passageways. But he could remember nothing.

Desperate to rescue his daughter, he grew impatient with Wally and the temperamental machines. How could he have thought graphs and charts would point the way to Julia? The sun was already sinking on the horizon and they were no closer to finding her than when they first arrived.

"Hold on," Wally said, leaning forward for a better view of his sonar equipment. "What's this?"

Karissa hurried to his side, seemingly indefatigable when it came to Julia. Asheris watched her adjust her hat. The back of her shirt was drenched with sweat, and her hair blew behind her like a tattered flag. She was dusty and hot and must be ravenous. But she didn't seem to be aware of her physical discomfort. Something big and bittersweet swelled in Asheris's heart at the sight of her. How could he have spent all these months holding her at arm's length, trying to protect her from harm, but in doing so discounting the very strength in her which he admired.

"This could be it!" Wally exclaimed. "Let's move over to the right."

Ignoring the soreness of his battered abdomen, Asheris picked up the machine, cart and all, and hauled it ten paces in Wally's direction.

The American sent more sound waves into the ground. The resulting bleeps on the screen showed a difference of density, indicating a hollow area, in a straight line leading to the west. "Again, Mr. Asher."

They repeated the action, with Asheris moving the equipment and Wally pacing the desert floor until he found the location of the tunnel beneath their feet. Karissa sketched a diagram of the tunnel onto a map that showed the others they had found, but which had all resulted in obstructed dead ends.

"Dig here," Wally cried, pointing near his feet.

Glad to be useful, Asheris loped to the Land Rover and got two shovels. He gave one to Wally and the two men quickly scooped sand away, while Karissa watched anxiously. The task was daunting at first, because nearly as much sand poured into the hole as they could throw over their shoulders. But eventually they hit compressed sand that was easier to excavate. And before long, Wally's shovel struck something hard, sending a metallic ping through the evening air.

"That must be it!" Asheris cried, leaning over to get a better look. "The entrance to a passageway."

"Let's hope it isn't blocked. I didn't check it all the way."

"We're running out of time," Karissa said. "It's already seven o'clock."

"Okay. Let's keep digging." Wally threw himself into his work. Asheris joined in, energized by the determination of the American scientist. Wally had nothing to gain in helping them find Julia. There was no other reason for his dogged determination but a good heart and a love for the little girl. Wally's unselfish love for Julia gave Asheris newfound strength. He flung sand to the side with more vigor than before. Shoulder to shoulder they labored, muscles bunching, chests heaving, until a clump of sand gave way and Karissa cried out in excitement.

"There's a door!" she exclaimed.

The men dug more furiously until they could pull open the ancient wooden door, still bearing traces of gilt and colorful hieroglyphics. Asheris put aside his shovel as Karissa handed the flashlight to her husband.

Asheris trained the beam into the gloom of the corridor. He glanced over his shoulder. "Follow me, but tread carefully. There could be traps waiting for us. There could also be scorpions and cobras. Be watchful."

"Great," Wally commented, glancing around his feet. "I've never seen a cobra up close and personal."

"You don't want to, either," Karissa put in, stepping behind Asheris. "They're deadly."

"Come." Asheris leaned over, too tall to walk upright in the tunnel. "We must not waste any time. And speak only in whispers. Our voices will carry surprisingly well in the temple."

Karissa kept close behind Asheris as they paced through the corridor. The tunnel sloped downward without twisting or turning, for no obstacles naturally found aboveground blocked its course. After twenty minutes or so, they came upon the end of the tunnel, a flat stone wall.

"Great," Wally whispered. "Caught, like rats in a maze. Now what?"

"Feel around the blocks for a release stone," Karissa put in.

"How do you know of release stones?" Asheris asked. She never ceased to surprise him.

"Oh, it's something I learned over the years—from my father, you know." She ran her hands over the right side of the wall while Asheris searched the left.

Something gave under Asheris's fingertips, and with a loud scraping sound the block swung open, sending a cascade of sand from overhead pouring onto the stone floor.

"Is it safe?" Wally asked, peering through the last trails of sand.

"Trust in Osiris for guidance," Asheris answered.

"Right. Osiris. And who's he?"

"God of the Underworld," Asheris replied with a grim smile. "The Dead."

"No offense, Mr. Asher, but I'd rather stick with my lucky rabbit's foot."

Asheris didn't understand the reference to a lucky rabbit, but now was not the time to discuss religious differences. They had to press on and explore the inside of the lost sphinx. A feeling of doom pressed in on him. This temple had been his prison, his own living hell. If not for Julia, he would never have returned. But there was no avoiding it now.

Asheris ducked through the opening and reached back for his wife's hand to guide her through. He also helped Wally, and then ran the beam of light around the large hallway before them. The walls were covered with murals and a latticework of grape leaves and vines covered the ceiling. Though he had spent three thousand years inside this temple, he had never seen it with the eyes of a man, only with the unrecording eyes of a feral cat, or with the unseeing eyes of a mummy, destined by day to lie motionless, helpless, but entirely and agonizingly sentient for all eternity. He had heard every footstep in the temple, had devoured every spoken word to feed his starving intellect, had fed his psyche on every scrap of human drama he had witnessed over the years, including the friendship between Karissa's father and his archaeological assistant. But for three thousand years he hadn't seen a single ray of light until Karissa freed him with the special quality of her voice and years later had lifted the panther curse with the depth of her love.

Karissa took a step forward.

"Wait," Asheris whispered, cocking his head. "I hear something." He paused, listening intently, calling upon his preternatural hearing, the only vestige of his former animal abilities. "The priestesses begin their rites," he said and pointed toward a dim hallway. "In that direction."

"Their rites?" Karissa hissed. "We must stop them! They will hurt Julia! I know they will!" She pulled away from him, heading for the dim doorway. "They have drugs and needles and—"

"Wait, Karissa." Asheris wondered how his wife knew so much about the rites of the temple of Sekhmet. He himself wasn't quite certain what ceremonies the priestesses carried out, for in his day they had been the ultimate secret society. "We will search other chambers while they are occupied with their ceremony."

Karissa wilted.

"Come, Karissa." Asheris held out his hand. "Perhaps we will not have to confront the priestesses if we find Julia first. They can be very dangerous. And we have no weapons."

"Sounds sensible," Wally interjected. "I vote for Asher's plan."

They picked their way through rubble, fallen blocks of granite, and piles of sand that had leaked through cracks in the walls. Beetles and spiders skittered across the floor, frightened out of their hiding places. They saw no snakes, however, and for that Asheris was thankful. They discovered only two chambers, one full of urns, chalices, canopic jars, and clay vessels, filled with a variety of dried herbs, ground minerals, and oils. Asheris guessed the room served as a storage facility for the ingredients of the medicine and magic of the priestesses. The other room was full of cedar chests stuffed with garments, jewelry, and ceremonial objects belonging to the temple.

Julia was not to be found.

"She's in with the priestesses, I tell you," Karissa said. "I'm going back. I don't care if you come or not."

"All right," Asheris answered. "We will go with you."

They retraced their steps and were surprised to discover that even more sand had fallen, enough to cover their tracks from their previous trip.

"This place isn't safe," Wally commented, grimacing at a pile of sand. "The sooner we get out of here, the better."

"Agreed," Asheris answered. Each minute spent in the temple was a nightmare of worry that they might be trapped inside, just as he had been imprisoned years ago.

They returned to the hall decorated with the grapevine motif and headed toward the passageway directly opposite to the one they had initially chosen. It led to a hypostyle hall flanked by enormous statues of the lion goddess. Asheris ignored the majestic sculptures and forged ahead, intent on finding Julia. Just as they gained the other side of the hall, they were surprised to see four priestesses step out of the shadows of the connecting doorway. Each of them had a gun.

"That is far enough!" one of them exclaimed.

Behind them four more priestesses moved in, headed by a large woman draped in a black panther skin.

"It's Madame Hepera!" Karissa whispered to Asheris.

He inspected the woman in the panther skin. Karissa had told him how Madame Hepera had broken into their house and taken the golden disk. So this was the modern-day version of a high priestess of Sekhmet. Oddly enough, the character type hadn't changed much over the centuries. The priestess who had cursed him had been very similar to the one standing before him.

Madame Hepera smiled and put a hand on her hip in a gesture of bravado. "Welcome, Mr. Asher!" she crowed. "Or should I say Prince Asheris?"

Asheris gazed at her, unwilling to let her see his surprise at hearing his ancient name said by a modern woman.

"Are you not surprised I know who you are?"

"Not at all." Asheris's felt his heart sinking in his chest. He would rather die than spend a single night as a prisoner in this godforsaken temple. And now that Madame Hepera knew who he was, she would do her utmost to carry on the tradition of the temple of Sekhmet by putting another curse on him.

"Well, it was quite a surprise for us," Madame Hepera continued undaunted. "We didn't know who you were until we tested the blood of your daughter and found that she was a direct descendent of an ancient line—a line that ended with you, Prince Asheris, about three thousand years ago."

"What in the hell is this witch talking about?" Wally drawled in an aside to Karissa.

"What is that you say, American?" Madame Hepera demanded, stalking forward. "Speak up!"

"I said I think the place could use some light fixtures."

"Ah, a funny man—how do you say it?—a class clown!" But Madame Hepera was no longer smiling. She waved her gun at them. "All of you, go to the center of the room."

"Where is Julia?" Karissa interjected, refusing to budge. "Where is my baby?"

"She is being prepared for the ceremony."

"The one with the needles?"

Madame Hepera's eyes narrowed. "For an American, you know too much about our ways. Who has told you these things?"

"My father knew all about you!"

"Not enough to save his life. And you won't know enough to save yours either! You will learn a difficult lesson, all three of you, about interfering with the goddess."

"But why our daughter?" Asheris demanded.

"Because in her veins flows the blood of the royal house of Egypt and a Chosen One of the temple of Sekhmet. The combination produces the goddess Incarnate, a female of extraordinary powers and high intelligence. We have traced the bloodlines through the ages, from Senefret onward, waiting for a child to be born that could bring the goddess back to power. Only you, Asheris, remain of the royal house. And only Karissa Spencer remains of the lineage of Senefret."

"And will you use Julia to try to destroy the Aswan Dam?" Karissa asked.

Madame Hepera whirled to face her. "How do you know of these things! Only the priestesses can know of this!"

Karissa didn't answer. She returned the woman's stare, refusing to show a single blink of fear, remembering Tasharyana's courage in the face of adversity and promising herself to uphold the tradition of defying Madame Hepera.

"You plan to topple the Aswan Dam?" Wally blew out a breath of incredulity. "How?"

"With the voice of the goddess." Madame Hepera smiled again, obviously eager to share the culmination of years of preparation and centuries of waiting. "With the help of the lunar disks, Julia will be able to vibrate the dam, which will cause a crack at the base. The crack will weaken the structure until it can no longer hold the waters behind it."

Asheris stared at her. "You cannot mean it!"

"We're talking massive destruction here," Wally added.

"Oh, yes. Massive destruction. Needful destruction. And from the destruction, Egypt will be reborn!"

Wally turned to Asheris. "She's crazy."

Madame Hepera glowered at him. "You are the crazy ones, to think you can stand in the way of Sekhmet!"

With a sweep of her hand Madame Hepera motioned for her assistants to close the passageway behind them. "You shall be sealed in this hall while we perform tonight's sacred ceremony. Pray to the goddess for forgiveness. Perhaps when the flood comes, she will allow you to die without too much suffering."

At a heavy scraping sound, Asheris looked over his shoulder and saw a stone lower to block the door. Quickly, he turned back and saw Madame Hepera retreating through the other doorway.

"No!" he shouted, bolting toward her.

Madame Hepera raised her gun.

"Asheris!" Karissa screamed. She threw herself in his path, knocking him aside as Madame Hepera squeezed the trigger of the pistol. The shot whizzed by, ricocheting off the far wall.

Asheris scrambled to regain his footing and glared at his wife.

"She will kill you!" Karissa cried.

"As prisoners we will not be able to save our daughter!"

"We won't be able to save her if we're dead either!"

Madame Hepera laughed and backed through the doorway, motioning for the second door to be blocked. The stone slid in place as Asheris ran toward it, too late to stop its descent.

For a few moments they stood together in the room with the huge statues of Sekhmet holding up the roof, not quite believing they were trapped inside a temple, far below the sand, where no one would hear their cries for help. The priestesses were probably leaving for the Aswan High Dam, taking Julia with them. If their plot was carried out, the dam would crack and the Valley of the Nile would be swept by a wall of water. Who knew what devastation it would cause? If they were still trapped in the hypostyle hall when the waters tore through Luxor, they might escape because the location of the Eastern Desert was higher than that of the Nile River. But even so, they would die because no one would know where they were. Millions of people would be carried off by the flood. What would three missing people matter then? No one would look for them.

Trapped. Helplessly trapped. Asheris knew the feeling well, and he could not abide the thought it was happening all over again. And Julia? What would become of her? Asheris paced the floor, rubbing the back of his neck, nearly out of his mind with worry and dread.

"So how do we order room service in a place like this?" Wally asked, grinning.

Before Asheris could make a reply, he heard a wrenching metallic noise. High in the ceiling a block moved to reveal an iron grate, about the span of a man's hand.

"What's going on?" Wally asked, ambling close to the source of the sound. His curiosity was rewarded by a spray of sand. He staggered backward, brushing off his hair and clothes while a stream of sand poured into the hall. Another grate opened, letting more sand pour down around them. Before too long, there were five grates open and sand was quickly piling up around their ankles.

Wally looked at the ceiling and then at Asheris. All traces of his irreverent humor had vanished. "We're going to be buried alive!" he exclaimed.

"Not necessarily," Karissa replied. This hypostyle hall appeared to be the same one where Jabar had found Tasharyana and led her to safety. And if that were the case, Karissa knew she should be able to locate the secret passage and they could make their escape—that is, if the tunnel hadn't been blocked in the collapse of the sphinx years ago, when Karissa had been a teenager.

Once again the scrying sessions had provided knowledge useful to her. Perhaps Tasharyana's efforts to record her life would pay off after all by bringing down the priestesses, or at least by keeping them from using Julia in their ceremonies. Silently Karissa thanked the beautiful opera singer who had suffered so much in her life, for having had the foresight to record the images in the obelisks, and for giving her the inspiration to continue the fight with Madame Hepera and her assistants.

"What do you mean, not necessarily?" Asheris asked, stepping closer to her.

"There's a door here somewhere," she explained, wading through the sand and avoiding the cascades of sand falling down from the ceiling grates. Since the hall was symmetrical in every way, she had no idea in which corner to search for the secret door. "But I'm not exactly sure where."

"You mean a secret panel type of situation?" Wally put in. "Where spies looked through peepholes at the goings on in here?"

"Something like that," Karissa replied. "Remember how we used a release stone to get in the sphinx?"

"Yes." Wally ran his hand through his red hair, made even more dull and wispy by the sand that had showered down on his head.

Asheris stood silent, listening to her.

"Well, the door I'm talking about is probably activated by a certain hieroglyph, one that's part of the mural painted along the border of the wall."

"You mean we'll have to try each symbol of the mural? That could take hours! We'll be buried by that time!"

"We don't have to try all of them, only some. The door is near the corner of the room, the left corner. And the glyph is on the left side of the door at shoulder level." She hurried to the nearest corner to demonstrate. "Somewhere in this location. So if we each take a corner, we can cut the time considerably."

"How do you know of this?" Asheris asked, his golden eyes regarding her, his expression serious.

"I was here once or twice with my father," Karissa explained. "But I will explain it all later."

"I thought as much," Asheris replied. "You have learned of this from his journals?"

"Some."

"And from that strange music box—"

"Come on," Wally urged, interrupting Asheris. "Enough chit chat, you two. Let's look for the door!"

Karissa turned to her corner and carefully pressed each symbol. The massive statues bathed the wall in shadow, which made it difficult to see the designs beneath her fingertips. Asheris still had the flashlight, which eased his task, allowing him to finish first. He loped diagonally across the room to the final corner. By now the floor was knee deep in sand and filling quickly. Karissa was sure the door was here somewhere, but what if the sand buried the release stone before they could locate it?

"No luck!" Wally called, tramping around the gigantic legs of the goddess. Karissa frantically pressed her portion of the wall, praying that she or Asheris would be successful.

Suddenly they were rewarded by the familiar scraping sound of moving limestone blocks. Asheris straightened. "Here it is!" he shouted. "Hurry!"

Coughing, Karissa scrambled around the nearest statue and slipped and slid through the piles of sand. The air in the room hung with dust from the falling sand, and all of them were coughing and sneezing by the time they ducked through yet another secret passage.

"Remind me to take you with me on my next visit to the pyramids," Wally commented to Karissa. "This secret-passageway stuff could come in handy."

"I only know about this one," Karissa answered. "And I hope it's unobstructed up ahead."

Asheris said nothing. He pointed the flashlight to the corridor in front of them and reached for Karissa's hand. She linked her fingers in his, glad to be connected to Asheris and glad to be responsible in some small way for getting him out of the temple.

Surely he must detest and fear the sphinx even more than she, for though she had lost her father here, Asheris had been imprisoned inside these walls for what must have seemed an eternity. That he could even step foot inside the place was a tribute to his courage and his love for Julia.

Unfortunately, their progress was agonizingly slow. Many blocks had fallen into the tunnel, followed by mounds of sand that had to be cleared in order to get by. At one point, the corridor was completely sealed off by a meter of debris, which they cleared by digging at the sand and rocks with their shoes. After an hour, the flashlight gradually dimmed, and Karissa worried that they would be plunged into darkness before they ever found the exit door.

The air was hot in the corridor and their exertions made them even hotter. The walkway was at a continual uphill slant, which sapped her energy. Karissa trudged behind Asheris, drenched in sweat, and too tired to reach for his dusty hand. Her shirt sleeves were shredded, her knee was bleeding, and her boots and socks were filled with gritty sand. Each step she took rubbed more skin away from her ankles and heels. But she walked on doggedly.

Two hours after they first entered the tunnel, they came upon a door. Asheris handed the light to Karissa and reached out to search for the release stone.

"What if the doorway outside is filled with sand?" Wally asked near her shoulder.

"It may very well be," Asheris replied. "But what choice do we have other than to go forward?"

"Let's move back a bit then," Karissa said, shuffling in reverse. "We don't want to get buried."

"I think I've found the release," Asheris called over his shoulder. "Are you ready?"

"Yes." Karissa trained the faint light on the stone door as Asheris pushed part of the border surrounding it. The stone swung in a partial arc, allowing sand to pour in through a crack of about ten inches, and then stopped with a loud grating sound.

"It's jammed!" Wally exclaimed.

"Oh, no!" Karissa sighed, her shoulders drooping.

Asheris lowered to one knee at the opening and craned his neck to look upward. "I cannot tell how far beneath the ground we are, either. It could be centimeters. It could be far more than that."

Wally sagged against the tunnel and wiped his sleeve across his perspiring forehead. "Now what?" he asked, his voice muffled by his arm.

Asheris straightened as much as he could in the cramped tunnel. He planted his hands on his knees and leaned forward slightly. "I propose we clear the sand from the edge of the block. Then I will try to wedge in beside it and push it open with my feet."

Wally lowered his arm and surveyed the opening as he considered Asheris's plan. "I don't know," he ventured. "That stone looks awfully heavy."

"These doors were expertly balanced at one time, Dr. Duncan. If I can push against the wall behind me," Asheris tilted his head, "I might be able to move it."

"I say we try it." Karissa frowned. "What other alternative is there?"

"If I manage to move the stone, I shall be engulfed by sand. You must be prepared to dig me out and quickly."

"Right." Wally moved closer, ready to act.

Then Asheris positioned himself between the wall and the stone, tucking his knees close to his chest. Karissa watched him, wincing in sympathy, because she was sure the position must be very painful for him, due to the blows he had taken to his abdomen. Asheris, however, didn't make the slightest indication that he was suffering.

"Ready?" he asked, cocking one black eyebrow.

Karissa nodded.

Asheris strained, pushing against the stone. Karissa could see the veins bulging in his neck. He grimaced, pushing even harder. The stone budged less than an inch. Sand trickled down on his right arm and shoulder.

"You moved it!" Wally cried. "Try again."

Asheris's chest rose and fell as his breathing increased from the effort. He wiped his left cheekbone with the back of his hand and then repositioned himself for another try.

"Try to put your feet closer together," Wally observed. "You'll get more p.s.i. that way."

"P-S-I?" Asheris questioned.

"Pounds per square inch. Pressure. We're talking physics here, Mr. Asher. I didn't go to ten years of college for nothing, you know!"

Asheris made no comment. But he took the scientist's advice and moved his feet.

Once again he pushed, straining. The block moved another inch. Then Karissa heard a clinking noise inside the wall beside the door, and the portal swung open on its own. Asheris had the presence of mind to roll to the left, just as the outside sand flooded through the opening.

He scrambled to his hands and knees, stamping to rid himself of the sand while Wally and Karissa bent to the task of clearing the doorway.

At last their luck changed for the better. The exit door was not as deeply buried as the door they had entered to get to the sphinx. After pushing the sand out of the opening, Karissa spotted the twinkling stars above.

"We made it!" she exclaimed. "I see the sky!"

Wally whooped for joy and slapped Asheris on the back. "Come on!" he exclaimed. "We're outta here!"

No one questioned Asheris's decision to drive upriver to the Aswan Dam. Though they were hungry, tired, and battered, not one of them even considered sparing the time to stop for food or rest. The full moon already hung high in the sky, glowing like a huge eye watching over the land. Karissa wondered whom the moon watched over—the priestesses of Sekhmet who seemed to worship it in some fashion, or her little girl, who was innocent and trusting in all people.

Karissa glanced at her watch. It was a few minutes to midnight. At such a late hour the highway was nearly deserted. Only a few big trucks passed them, hauling goods to Luxor and cities to the north. The bright moon lit up the valley, gleaming off the water and the green bands of vegetation on the banks of the Nile. Beyond the trees, however, the rocky cliffs rose in stark contrast to the lushness below.

No one talked in the Land Rover. Wally spent most of his time cleaning his shoes and shaking his socks out the window. Karissa did the same. Asheris, silent and deadly serious, didn't make a move, other than shift gears once in a while. She recognized the present mode of her husband. At this point he was running on a primal level, much like the panther that was still very much a part of him. Asheris had a goal in mind and absolutely no remorse for anyone who might stand in his way.

Soon they saw the old Aswan Dam, built by the British at the turn of the century but now dwarfed by the newer Aswan High Dam five miles farther upstream. Karissa saw the logic in Madame Hepera's plan. She could have destroyed the older dam and caused some damage. But the destruction of the Aswan High Dam, backed by Lake Nasser, a three-hundred-mile-long reservoir, would obliterate the smaller dam below it in a matter of seconds.

Asheris pulled off the highway and sped up a gravel road to the right.

"Where are we going?" Wally asked.

"This road will take us to the cliffs above the dam," Asheris explained. "From there we must locate Madame Hepera and formulate our strategy."

"Good plan," Wally answered. "I wish we had a gun, though. How are we going to round up those priestesses and turn them over to the police?"

"All we must do is rescue Julia. I am not concerned about capturing the priestesses. They will manage to slip away from the authorities anyway, you can be sure of that."

Another few minutes passed as they crawled up the side of the cliff on a narrow road. Then it leveled out on the bluff. Asheris drove a kilometer or so and pulled off to the side.

"We will walk from here. The priestesses may recognize the vehicle, and then we would lose our advantage of surprise."

Karissa hopped out, knowing her husband was in his element now. Long ago he had commanded the armies of the pharaoh and was known as a brilliant strategist and fearless warrior. She was glad to be on his side. Though they were crippled by the lack of weapons, they had his experience and cunning to draw upon.

He took them to the side of the cliff, telling them to duck as they approached the edge. Then they flopped down on the rocks and surveyed the land and water below.

"What's that in the water?" Wally said, pointing to a platform in the reservoir dangerously close to the spillway.

"A boat?" Karissa asked, trying to focus in the dim light.

Asheris shook his head. "A barge. And there are people on it. One of them is Julia."

"Julia?" Karissa gasped. "Oh, my God, Asheris. What if she falls in? She'll be swept over the dam!" She felt Asheris's warm hand slide over hers.

"Julia will be careful. She is a careful child."

"You've got great night vision," Wally remarked. "I can't see who's what. Who is with Julia?"

"Madame Hepera and two others." Asheris pointed behind her. "And look. Do you see the metal disks set up on either side of Julia?"

"Yes, I can see that much." Wally squinted. "Aren't those like that solar disk you had in your father's crate, Ms. Spencer?"

"I suspect one of them is my father's disk. Although I've been told it isn't a solar disk, but a lunar disk."

"Told by whom?" Asheris questioned.

"Madame Hepera, when she broke into the house the other night."

"Look at the way the disks are angled," Wally went on.

"Explain the significance," Asheris said.

"Well, they're angled to catch the sound of Julia's voice, amplify it, and then redirect the sound waves to converge at a single point—directly at the center of the dam."

"Which will cause the vibration needed to crack the dam." Karissa shook her head in dread.

"Exactly. Just as your father theorized." Wally

pursed his lips. "The thing is, how can they force someone to sing?"

"They have ways," Karissa answered bitterly, "from hypnotism to secret potions. Julia is certainly under their influence right now."

"So they drug her, make her sing, and she breaks the dam."

Karissa nodded grimly, trying not to imagine the worst. "Yes."

"And when the dam breaks," Asheris added in a hoarse voice, "Julia will perish."

"Maybe not," Wally put in. "I mean, after all, Madame Hepera is out there. Do you think she'd put herself in danger?"

"Most likely she and her attendants will leave in a timely manner." Asheris sighed. "Long ago it was a yearly rite to sacrifice a young maiden to the Nile. But never would I have dreamed that my own daughter would be the sacrifice one day."

"Dear God," Karissa whispered, "what are we going to do!"

"We will do something." Asheris squeezed her hand. "I must think."

Wally inched forward, closer to the edge of the cliff. "Look down there," he whispered, pointing almost directly below them. "There's some of the priestesses."

Karissa strained to see over the cliff to the boat launch below. Sure enough, three priestesses stood near a truck with a boat trailer hitched to it.

"They must have a small motorboat out there, too," Wally commented.

Silently, Asheris surveyed the scene below him. Then he turned to Karissa. "Here is my plan. You and Wally will stay here while I climb down to the edge of the lake. If the priestesses take notice of me, pelt them with rocks to keep them distracted. You will be fairly safe, for this cliff is high enough to be out of range of their guns. If they set out to come up here, take the Land Rover and drive north." He reached in his pocket and gave her the keys.

She curled her sore fingers around them. "What will you do, Asheris?"

"I will swim out to the barge and get Julia."

"No!" Karissa grabbed his wrist. "What if there are currents near the dam? You could be swept away!"

"I am a strong swimmer, Karissa, with an even stronger determination. Do not fear for me." He moved away from the edge and stood up. Karissa followed him, sick with worry. In the last few days Asheris had been beaten severely and had just spent a day and most of the night without much water and no food. In his condition, what kind of strength could he possibly possess?

"Asheris!"

"Do not worry." He hugged her fiercely. "There will be no sacrifice to the river tonight, not from the Spencer-Asher family. This I promise you!"

He bent down and kissed her as fiercely as he had held her. For a moment they stared deep into each other's eyes, knowing it might be the last time they saw one another. Then Asheris stepped away from her arms and she let him go.

Asheris estimated it took him a quarter of an hour to pick his way down the rock face. The trip had been easier than he thought, for he had found a gully full of gravel and simply slid most of the way to the bottom, hoping all the while that he wouldn't slide into a snake or scorpion. The priestesses in the parking lot hadn't even taken notice of him on his way down the cliff or when he stole across the highway to the edge of the lake, since their attention was focused on the ritual being performed on the water. He paused on the bank to slip off his shoes and glanced at the barge. Smoke from a brazier drifted upward, and every once in a while he heard the faint rattle of the sistrum above the roar of water cascading over the dam. He waded into the water, which wasn't much cooler than the air. The bottom of the lake sloped precipitously, and in seconds he eased into the water with long powerful strokes. Karissa was correct about the current. He could feel the pull of the forces below. As he swam, he mentally calculated how far the current would pull him from his desired course. And then instead of swimming directly toward the barge, he set off for a point south of it, so that he could take advantage of the current instead of fighting it near the barge, where he would need time and strength to overcome the three priestesses. If he were battling the water near the barge, he would be fighting for his own life, not just Julia's.

Desperately, Asheris swam across the reservoir, his muscles aching, his throat parched, his chest heaving as he struggled for breath. But still he pressed on. He hadn't the faintest idea how he would save Julia. Certainly they couldn't swim back to shore. They would be much too close to the dam at that point. And Julia was not nearly a strong enough swimmer to buck the current. Somehow he would either have to commandeer the smaller boat he could see tied to the barge, or to try and tow the barge to shore. But he doubted he'd have the strength to pull the barge away from the dam, let alone pull it across the lake.

Asheris swam, realizing this was the ultimate test for him. As a panther, he had always been able to protect Karissa, or so she had told him. And from what he'd read in the papers about the big cat, the panther's size alone had been enough to paralyze most men with fright, and his reputation as being the legendary Lord Azhur had intimidated most all others. As a man, however, he had never been tested, and he had to admit that he was afraid of failing. He had no superhuman strength and few animal instincts to rely upon. All he had was himself and the empowering love of his daughter and wife. Yet this was a test he could not fail and survive; if he could not protect them as a man, he would die trying.

As he drew closer to the barge, he allowed the current to pull him silently toward the craft. The smaller boat motored in place before him, its speed set to keep the barge in a constant position. A priestess sat at the wheel but was turned in her seat to watch the proceedings behind her. Like a deadly water snake, Asheris floated to the opposite side of the boat, close to the hull where he would not be seen. He rapped on the hull and waited. The craft tipped slightly as the priestess rose and came to his side to investigate.

He rapped again. Then Asheris waited in silence, hoping her curiosity would impel her to come closer.

The priestess leaned over the side of the boat, just as he hoped she would. In one fluid movement, he vaulted upward, using the boat to pull him out of the water. The vessel tipped, knocking the priestess forward. He grabbed her hair and yanked her straight down. With a splash, she fell into the water, disappeared, and then bobbed to the surface, splashing and flailing, as she was pulled past the barge by the strong current. Asheris was fairly certain she would go over the dam but he didn't watch her progress. He pulled his aching body over the side of the boat and slid in, scraping his chest and groin in the process. He scrambled to his feet and looked back at the barge.

Pandemonium had broken out. The other priestesses had seen their companion going over the dam and were screaming and crying her name, and causing the barge to tip. Only his daughter hung back, standing between the large golden disks, clinging to the brass stands that held them up. She looked more fragile and bewildered than he had ever seen her.

"Julia!" Asheris cried, wiping the water away that streamed down his face.

At her name she turned. Her eyes lit up at the sight of him. Apparently she wasn't drugged enough not to recognize him.

"Father!"

"Jump to me!" he cried frantically, holding out his arms as he spied the large form of Madame Hepera turning around.

Julia moved to the back edge of the barge, which was tipped out of the water by at least a meter, due to the weight of the priestesses on the other side.

"Jump!" Asheris commanded, stretching out his hands toward her. He tried to dash the desperation out of his voice. The leap was more than a meter wide. If she didn't make a successful jump, she would be lost to him. In her favor was the fact that she'd be leaping downward. But it was quite a span and between the two vessels flowed a stretch of dangerous water.

Julia, however, was the daughter of the sun, a member of an ancient and royal house. The blood of kings and queens flowed through her veins. It was in her heritage to possess the courage to try. But even more so, the spirit of her indomitable mother, Karissa Spencer, was an integral part of her. Julia could do it. She could make the jump.

"Jump! You can do it!" Asheris shouted. Madame Hepera thundered across the barge, her face full of outrage and disbelief, her ceremonial panther skin flapping around her shoulders.

Julia flung back her arms and leaped forward, easily vaulting the distance and landing in the arms of her father. Quickly he set her aside as Madame Hepera reached down for something. A gun? Would the woman shoot them and take the chance of harming the child she believed was the lost goddess? Wildly, Asheris glanced around. He had to do something—find a weapon, something to throw, anything! He caught sight of the metal gas can in the stern of the boat. He flung it at her, hitting her just as she straightened with a gun in her hand. She fell backward with a thump, causing one of the disks to clang to the wooden deck and bounce perilously close to the edge of the barge. The other priestesses scattered, trying to help their mistress and save the precious lunar disks. Madame Hepera sat up, struggling against her bulk to get to her knees and take aim.

What could he do? There was nothing left to throw at her. Frantic, he felt Julia slip past him, between his body and the stern, in clear view of the priestesses.

"Get back, Julia!" he cried. She didn't answer. Just like her mother, she was full of blind determination after having made a decision. He saw her lunge toward the rope that connected the barge to the boat. And then in amazement he saw her yank the end of the rope, which was fastened in a strange knot.

"No!" Madame Hepera screamed.

The knot unraveled and the force of the current snagged the barge away from the motorboat. The rope slipped away from the metal cleat it had been tied around, allowing the barge to drift in the current as it was pulled toward the edge of the dam. Free of the barge, the launch surged forward.

Amazed by the quick thinking of his daughter, Asheris turned to the controls of the boat. "Hang on, Julia!" he yelled over his shoulder.

Deftly he turned the wheel to the right, ignoring the terrified screams of the priestesses behind him as he sent the little boat bouncing over the surface of the lake, far from the edge of the dam. After a few seconds, he managed to look back and saw the barge sweeping into the main spillway. No one would be able to survive the 1000-meter drop to the churning whirlpools and granite boulders below.

Julia made her way to the bow, keeping one hand tightly wrapped around the rail. When she got to Asheris she flung her arms around him from the back.

"Oh, Daddy!" she cried. "You saved me! I knew you'd save me!"

His heart burst with joy as he felt her little arms around his neck. She was nearly squeezing the breath from his throat, but he hardly noticed. Julia was safe. He had gotten to her in time. But it wasn't all his doing, he knew that well enough. They had all worked together—Wally, Karissa, himself, and Julia. Together they had been strong enough, smart enough, and lucky enough to outwit the priestesses of Sekhmet. Never again would he stubbornly stand alone against the world, not when he had family and friends to help him through.

He reached behind Julia, slipped his right arm around her slender torso, and held her close. She leaned her head on his shoulder and stood there with him.

"Of course we saved you," he said, his eyes full of tears. "I love you, Bean."

"I love you, too, Daddy!"

He could feel her smile pressing into his upper arm.

Asheris beamed through his tears and looked toward the shore. The remaining priestesses had jumped into their truck and were driving down the highway, either to check for unlikely survivors or simply to flee the scene of the accident. He raised his glance to the cliff, hoping to catch sight of Karissa and Wally. Instead, he spotted the Land Rover speeding down the cliff road toward the reservoir.

"I told your mother to stay on the cliff," he exclaimed. "What does she think she is doing?"

"She's coming to get us, silly," Julia replied, as if it were obvious.

It *was* obvious—to anyone who was not a slave to outdated rules for the behavior of men and women. As usual, Karissa had seen what had to be done and decided to do it, no matter what initial plan had been agreed upon. Asheris had to shake his head at his own intractability and his wife's usual good sense. He glanced over to Julia and cocked his eyebrow. "So, you think I am silly, do you?"

"Sometimes."

He was surprised and slightly dismayed at her quick answer. "You do?"

"But most of the time I think you're the best father in the whole wide world! Like right now!"

He hugged her tightly. "I will gladly settle for that."

The sky was still black when they returned to the house, the moon having set hours ago, as if in observance of the deaths of the priestesses of Sekhmet. Bedraggled and exhausted, Asheris, Karissa, and Wally trudged into the house with Julia and were met by the household servants who had kept a worried vigil until their return.

"Julia!" Eisha exclaimed with joy, seeing the child safe and sound. She opened her arms for a warm hug, which Julia gladly accepted and returned. Hamid stood by, beaming, his chipped, discolored tooth showing prominently beneath his scraggly gray mustache.

"Praise Allah!" he declared.

Julia pulled herself away from Eisha and looked at him. "You should have seen where we were, Hamid! The Aswan Dam! Practically going over the top!"

His eyebrows raised in surprise. Karissa stepped closer to him and lightly touched his shoulder.

"If not for your help, Hamid, we never would have found her."

"What help?" he countered, shrugging. "I am but a gardener."

For a moment, Karissa stared at him, surprised by his simple reply. If not for Hamid's loyalty to Tasharyana, and Tasharyana's visual diary, Julia would still be lost to them. Yet, Hamid must feel the need to conceal his real reason for being at the Spencer-Asher house. She would honor that wish.

She smiled. "You are much too humble, Hamid."

"Allah teaches us to be humble," he replied. But his bleary eyes met hers as if he was well aware of what she was thinking. "However, I am glad to have been a part of Miss Julia's safe return, in some small way."

Asheris strode forward, his clothes still damp from his swim. "Show Wally to the guest room, if you please, Eisha, and prepare a bath for him." He glanced at the others. "And then, if I am not mistaken, we would all like a light meal. Wally?"

"Sounds great!" he replied, rubbing his stomach. "I'm starved."

"I'll see to Julia," Karissa put in, ushering her daughter toward the hall.

"I will call the police and let them know you are safe." Asheris stroked the top of Julia's head. "And ask them to send out a guard to make sure no one bothers you during the night."

George, the houseboy, stepped forward. "Until the police come, Hamid and I thought we would stand guard. One outside Julia's window and one at her door."

Asheris glanced at the boy in surprise, as if he never considered George capable of a man's job. Then he looked over at Hamid. The old man nodded sagely as if to reassure Asheris of George's ability.

"Thank you, George. An excellent suggestion."

The boy grinned and hurried to his post, eager to prove himself. Hamid followed Karissa and Julia to her room and remained outside the door, his arms crossed.

Asheris and Karissa were the last ones at the table. Julia had fallen asleep an hour ago, claiming she wasn't hungry. Wally had wolfed down enough food to feed three people and then practically fell asleep at his plate before excusing himself for bed. Eisha bustled in and out, clearing the table and throwing happy sidelong glances at her employers, because it was obvious to anyone that the difficulties between them were swiftly dissipating. Karissa could feel it. At first she thought she was completely exhausted and the last of her energy was draining out of her in relief, and she thought she might fall asleep in her chair, too. But the languid feeling was replaced by a wonderful glow of burgeoning contentment, especially when she looked up to see Asheris gazing at her, his golden eyes glinting with affection. Yet, it had been so long since they had shared anything more than a hurried kiss, and she felt uncharacteristically nervous being alone with him.

She rose, pushing back her chair. "I guess I'll turn in," she announced, unable to break eye contact with her husband.

"And where will you turn in?" he asked, holding out his hand.

Without thinking, she put her left hand in his. "Pardon me?" she answered softly as her voice gave out.

"I said, where will you turn in?" Slowly he drew her to him, until she came to rest in his lap. She sank down upon him, unable to resist. He was warm, fragrant with his peculiar scent of coriander, and firm, as only a male can feel to a woman.

"Asheris, your stomach—"

"Do not worry about my stomach." He reached for the side of her face and turned her head toward him, stroking her cheek and jaw as he gazed at her. "I have something to say to you, Karissa."

"Yes?"

"I have been a fool."

She couldn't believe her ears. Asheris admitting he was a fool? Impossible! She had never thought to hear such words come from the mouth of her proud, obstinate husband.

"Asheris—"

He silenced her protest with a finger upon her lips. "No," he said softly, "let me finish."

She gazed at him, listening as she had never listened before, certain that his next words were words hammered out of the pain of their crumbling marriage, annealed over the past few days, and tempered with a new and greater appreciation for each other.

"I have been a fool to stand alone all this time when I had you to stand with me." He smiled sadly and ran his thumb across her lower lip. "Not to stand behind me or beside me. But with me. Do you know what I am telling you?"

"Yes." The word tumbled out of her like a giant wave.

"I come from an ancient time, *azeez*, with ancient ideas. But I am not too old to learn new ways."

"You already have learned so much."

"But not enough. Because I was a man I thought I knew what was best for everyone—for you, Julia, and even myself. But I have come to realize that our wisdom and ideas put together are better than mine alone."

Karissa caressed his cheek, marveling at his words and letting him speak uninterrupted.

"Only a fool would have turned a deaf ear to the counsel of an intelligent and courageous woman," Asheris continued. "You are such a woman, *azeez*."

"I have only tried to do what was best for Julia," she replied softly. "I wanted her to be strong and good and self-confident."

"Which she could never have become growing up in the protected environment I wanted to provide for her. I see that now."

"I'm glad you do, Asheris." She gazed intensely at him. "For so long I was afraid we would never see eye to eye when it came to Julia."

"My fear as well. And there are still many things that I will not understand without your insight." He looked directly into her eyes. "Will you have the patience to help me learn to accept these things?"

"Oh, Asheris!" she cried, her heart breaking with happiness. "Of course I will."

"Good." He pushed his fingers into the hair at her temple and drew her mouth down to his.

"Wait, your cut lip—" she murmured against his mouth.

"It is but a scratch," he replied, surrounding her with his strong arms. "I feel none of my pain when you are here with me."

She flung her arms around him and kissed him, turning in his embrace to press her chest against his. The kiss broke the remaining wall between them, and their love for each other poured out in a torrent. Karissa couldn't get enough of his warm skin, his strong hands, his insistent mouth. She had been in the desert far too long, and coming back to the haven of Asheris's love and understanding was like finding a cool, lush oasis of indescribable pleasures.

"I love you," she said close to his ear. "And I was so proud of you tonight."

"And I of you, my beloved." He held her close. "We are a good team."

"Yes, we are. And I'm glad we're working together again at last." She smiled. "But I hope that's the end of the lost sphinx for us."

"You must not forget the good that came of the sphinx."

"What good?"

"The sphinx brought us together many times—when you were a teenager, when you helped me find it seven years ago, and these past few days when it made us realize how deeply we love each other."

"Yes, that's true."

He kissed her again. "If it had not been the sphinx, you would not be sitting here with me."

She stroked his cheek, a gesture once so familiar but now even more precious to her. "Let's never be silent again, Asheris," she said softly. "No more unhappiness."

"None." Asheris gazed at her. "From this day forward, I know we will be happy together. We will make it so. Because we know our worth and our value to each other."

Karissa nodded, her tongue mute, but her eyes brimming with love.

The next evening, Karissa walked out of Julia's room with the sandalwood box under her arm, happier than she had been in years. She had just tucked her daughter into bed, and they had listened to the haunting melody of the music box together. Asheris had sat beside her, his arm around her shoulders, just like the old days. He seemed to have mellowed even more since the night at the Aswan Dam, especially after seeing on the evening news that Iniman el Hepera, longtime Cairo resident, had been found drowned south of Luxor. Karissa knew he felt a sense of relief that Madame Hepera was no longer a threat, but she was sure the change in Asheris went deeper than that. He had turned over a new leaf since that night, and had made a promise to accept and understand the ways of modern women. He had taken a leave of absence from the university and was making plans to take them on a long trip, away from Egypt, even though they were both convinced the danger from the priestesses was over, now that Madame Hepera was dead. Wally Duncan had just left to return to Cairo and to his research, with a promise to come back in a week for a longer stay. Everything was turning out just fine. But one small detail bothered her, that of the unseen vision of the fifth obelisk. Was the second vision missing or had she dozed through it? She wouldn't sleep that night until she knew for sure what had happened to Tasharyana.

Asheris caught up with her near the atrium at the center of the house. "Would you like to share a glass of wine with me?" he asked.

Karissa knew she should say yes, to keep their relationship on the new and wonderful course it had suddenly taken. But if she did share a glass of wine, they'd end up talking half the night and spending the other half making glorious, passionate love, just as they had last night.

"You pause," Asheris put in, tilting his head. "Why?"

"I would love to share a glass with you, Asheris," she said, "but how about a little later?"

"Is there something you must do?" He glanced at the sandalwood box.

"Yes. It's very important. Something I have to find out."

She expected him to back away, to succumb to his old silent habits. She expected his eyes to grow cold and distant, as only his golden eyes could grow. She was surprised when he touched her elbow and smiled.

"Then I will wait for you." He bent down and kissed her, slipping his hand around the back of her neck. Tingles of delight danced through her at his touch. She felt her breasts responding to his nearness, felt her heart swelling with love for this new yet familiar version of her husband. He drew back and eased his fingers through the tendrils of her hair. "But I want to know all when you are done. I am curious to learn what you see in the box shaped like a cat."

"It's the last portion of Tasharyana's diary," she blurted, knowing she didn't make sense. "I have to know what happens. I have to find out! Then I'll tell you."

He chuckled. "I see that it is important to you, my sweet. So be off with you. I will come for you later."

She stared at him, amazed at the return of his understanding. "I won't be long."

"I hope not." He brushed back the hair at her left temple and his eyes smoldered at her. "I am dying to make love to you. Last night was but an appetizer for the feast that is to come."

Her body responded with an intense throbbing sensation. She longed to be in his arms as well. But not until she was done with the scrying sessions. Not until her mind was clear of all questions, her suspicions confirmed.

"I'll be in the garden."

"I know. I will come out and get you, by and by." He kissed the tip of her nose and left her.

In a pleasant daze, Karissa sat near the pond and arranged the sandalwood box, putting in the fifth obelisk as she hummed the melody, her voice much stronger and purer than the last time she had activated a scry. The last time she had done this, her child was missing and her husband lay wounded in his bed.

Patiently Karissa sat through the first portion, the part portraying Tasharyana's escape from the sphinx, the knowledge of which had helped Karissa so much during her own escape. She gave a silent prayer of thanks to the woman for having left such a useful legacy. At the end of the first portion came a stretch of static and then darkness, just as she had remembered from the previous scrying session. At the point where the darkness appeared, she must have fallen asleep, exhausted by worry and lack of rest. This time, Karissa waited for the darkness to pass, certain that Tasharyana wouldn't have spoken in error about having put down two visions. After a few minutes the darkness diffused and Tasharyana's faint shape gradually materialized. Karissa watched in fascination as a new and different Tasharyana appeared on the surface of the pond.

This Tasharyana was still thin, still dressed in the ornate galabia, but the outline of her body shimmered more than usual, as though her body had lost distinct form. Even her skin appeared different, almost translucent. Usually Karissa had glimpsed a background in the other scrying sessions—a room, painted in pale peach. But this time Tasharyana's figure floated against a blue color, appearing to stand on a hilltop with only the sky behind her. Why had her appearance changed? Did she run out of energy as she had mentioned in the earlier session? Did a lack of energy affect the way her form was transmitted by the obelisk?

Karissa put aside her questions as Tasharyana clasped her hands together and began to speak.

"This is the last entry of my diary," she said, her voice soft and whispery. "It takes all of my concentration to finish my task, but I have to continue. I have to put this down in the event that my child carries the blood of the Chosen One and will need knowledge of the temple. I long to know my child, long to see her grow into a woman. But if it does not come to pass, at least she will have a glimpse of my life. So this is my loving legacy to her, the last chapter of my struggle with the priestesses of Sekhmet."

Tasharyana's Tale—1966

So hot she was, so terribly hot.

Tasharyana floated in a world full of memories. J. B. occupied much of that world and Madame Hepera made dramatic entrances every so often to chase her down—always chasing her down. And Tasharyana would run and run and run, desperate and terrified. Every once in a while she would hear a faint but vaguely welcome and familiar female voice speaking softly to her in Arabic. Was it the voice of Menmet Bedrani—J. B.'s Egyptian-born mother—or some benevolent stranger? She couldn't remember. Her thoughts kept getting muddled. Sometimes the woman would hold her hand. Sometimes she would put cool cloths on her forehead. The coolness felt good and would bring on pleasant dreams of J. B. talking to her, laughing at something she said, making love to her, or appearing to her on the banks of the Nile as he had done nearly nine years ago.

She had no concept of the passage of time. She knew she had spent the first day in this safe house with Jabar, laboring to record information on the obelisks for her daughter, who slept in a cradle near her bed. Unbeknownst to the high priestess, he had brought the music box from Madame Hepera's house and then had stayed to teach her the necessary magic used by the priestesses to set down their memories into the electrum rods.

Jabar explained to her that he had given his life to the service of the temple, a choice made for him in childhood, and a career he could not leave except through death. Most thought him dull-witted, but he had only taken on the mask of a dullard to disguise a mind that missed nothing, especially the magic of the priestesses. He had spied on them for years and had learned their ways, which he gladly employed to help Tasharyana. Even though Jabar was forced to swear loyalty to the temple, he did so without conviction, always sensing a great emptiness in his life. Then coming to know Tasharyana as a girl and watching as she brought a new life into the world had made him aware of his true loyalty. He would risk his life to help her.

Together they spent hours documenting the days between her first kiss with J. B. on the bank of the Nile and the night in the desert when she had given birth to her baby. But the day had been her undoing. The mental concentration it took to infuse her memories into the rods sapped what little strength remained in her. That evening she had suffered chills and a throbbing headache. Soon she slipped into a dreamworld where nothing remained as it should be. Her dreamworld interval could have been a minute or a year. Sometimes she worried about her baby and longed to ask where the child was, but she couldn't get her mouth to form words and couldn't seem to emerge all the way from the depths of her dreams.

So hot she was, so terribly hot.

Then after a particularly horrifying dream about Madame Hepera coming after her with needles, Tasharyana heard someone enter the room.

"Here she is," the familiar female voice said softly, as if afraid to wake her.

Tasharyana was aware of steps approaching and caught a slight whiff of a familiar smell, a clean smell of soap and after-shave. The fragrance brought with it the vision of J. B. when she had collided with him at the opera house. Then that scene whirled and merged into the memory of him putting the earrings on her at the hotel boutique. The next thing she knew he was standing behind her on the balcony of the Philadelphia house, embracing her and whispering in her ear about connecting. *Connecting, connecting, connecting.*

The thought of him went straight to her heart, like a burning ball of fire. He would burn in her soul forever, as the sun burned over the Sahara desert. If she could only see him once again, touch him once again, and kiss him once again! Everything would be all right if J. B. was with her.

Then she became aware of another smell—the powdery scent of roses. Roses in Egypt? Something inside her told her to wake up. Roses had always held a special meaning for her and J. B., ever since he gave her the music box in the shape of the cat and the red rose with the Robert Burns poem. She had kept the rose. In fact, the petals of the flower were pressed inside his farewell note, a token of love with which she would never part.

Julian. She mouthed his name, aching to know what had happened to him and why he had never searched for her. Even if he had abandoned her, she still loved him with all her heart. She would always love him.

Julian. Scalding hot tears slid out of the corners of her eyes. She felt so weak, so tired, nearly too tired to go on—especially if going on meant a life without J. B.

"Tasha!"

It was almost as if she heard him calling to her. She wept, crushed by the cruel trick her ears were playing on her.

"Tasha." The voice softened and broke.

So hot she was. So terribly hot.

A cool hand cupped her face. Gentle fingertips wiped away her tears. No one had gentler hands than J. B. Tasharyana tried to blink away the illusion. To believe the voice and hands were real was to torture herself heartlessly . She couldn't allow herself to succumb to the vision, no matter how comforting. Her dreams were becoming so lifelike, she could barely tell fantasy from reality. Was this how it felt to die—lost in a jumbled world of memories and sensations? Was she going to die?

"She's awfully hot, Mother."

"Her fever will not abate," the female voice replied. "She's been delirious for two days now."

"And what does the doctor say?"

"He's done all he could. She hemorrhaged badly after the birth, and the doctor hasn't been able to stop it completely. She also contracted an infection in the desert that she hasn't the strength to fight. Poor thing."

"She looks terrible," the male voice added.

"She was skin and bones when she arrived here, just skin and bones. And she was always such a beautiful little girl. To see her like this breaks my heart."

"Ah, God!" The hand tenderly swept over her cheek again. "Tasha!"

"There's nothing you can do for her," the female voice put in sadly. "We can only pray that she finds the strength to hang on until the antibiotics have a chance to work."

"What happened to her? Where has she been all these months?"

"The man Jabar might be able to answer those questions. It was he who brought her here three days ago."

"Jabar? Who is he?"

"He claims to be her friend. He knew her when she was a girl at that school she was taken to."

So hot she was. So terribly hot.

"The Luxor Conservatory for Young Women?"

"Yes. That's the one."

The gentle hand lightly touched her forehead and swept over her hair. She reveled in the sensation, loving the memory of J. B.'s special tenderness. He had touched her this way, just this way. It made her heart break all over again, just thinking about the ways he had touched her.

"She must be dying of the heat," the man commented.

"I've been putting compresses on her head."

"What about a bath? I've heard a cool bath can lower a fever."

"I don't know. Would you like to give it a try?"

"Yes. Anything to relieve her distress. Look how the nightgown sticks to her skin. And look at her lips—they're like sandpaper."

"I'll draw a bath, then. It's worth a try."

Footsteps padded away but the gentle hand continued to stroke her. She could almost will herself to open her eyes. But then her senses swirled and she lost the thread of her intent. Madame Hepera's face loomed before her like a distorted caricature on a gigantic balloon, frightening her. She began to run. But her steps were too heavy, her feet dragged too much, and Madame Hepera was gaining on her, throwing teacups and panther skins at her.

"Tasha!" The gentle hands tried to hold her down, but she thrashed her arms and legs, desperate to get away from the high priestess. The thrashing broke something deep inside her, something sharp and painful, but she was too scared to concentrate on anything but getting away.

Then she felt herself gathered up and lifted into the air. Madame Hepera changed into a line of musical notes and faded away, obliterated by a loud rushing noise, like the sound of a waterfall.

So hot she was. So terribly hot.

She was vaguely aware of someone unbuttoning her nightgown, of drawing it up her body and over her head, shifting her until she was undressed. A slight feeling of relief washed over her as the sodden garment was discarded. Then she was gently, carefully lowered into a pool of cool water. She had yearned to submerge herself in such coolness, ever since she crawled on hands and knees through the desert. And now she was there, floating in heavenly soothing water. She felt the heat of her body draining away, running out of her, as a long sigh drifted from her lips. For a long while she was deafened by the roar of water crashing somewhere near her feet, but then the noise abruptly stopped. Gradually the coolness of the water cleared her head and she became aware of a man speaking to her.

"Tasha, wake up," he said. "Tasha!"

Only one person in the world called her Tasha.

Slowly, deliberately, she opened her eyes. For a moment the light stung them and she was blinded by the glare and the tears that sprang up. But the blurriness slowly gained color and definition—black hair, golden face, wide shoulders, sinewy forearms, slender torso. She blinked, not fully believing who knelt at the side of the tub, holding her.

"J.—" she croaked, her dry throat and lips cutting off the name.

"Tasha! Oh, God, you're awake!"

"J. B.!" she managed to utter before her voice gave out entirely. She stared at him and began to cry inconsolable tears of joy. They poured out of her as if she were made of water. She longed to touch him and yet she hadn't the strength to raise her hand.

Apparently he sensed her thoughts, for J. B. leaned forward and gathered her against him, pressing his smooth cheek to hers. She closed her eyes and sighed in rapture, even though she was like a cloth doll in his arms, languid and loose jointed, and unable to return his caress. She had thought she would never be this close to him again.

"Tasha," he whispered in her ear. "I've seen our little baby. She's beautiful!"

"Is she all right?"

"She's doing fine. My mother's taking care of her."

"Menmet is here?"

"Yes. That's whose house you are in."

"Good. I've been worrying so much about the baby."

"Don't. Save your strength." He pulled back to survey her. "God, Tasha, what happened to you?"

"The priestesses," she replied, licking her parched lips. "I had to run from them."

"Where did you go?" He caressed the side of her

face. "I searched everywhere!" he declared, his voice cracking. "For months!"

"I had to keep moving. Kept moving."

"But why did you leave Baltimore without telling me yourself?"

"I never had the chance. Frances turned me over to the police." She opened her eyes, too weak to conceal the resentment that flared in them at the memory of Frances Petrie.

"Frances did?"

"And Madame Hepera took me from jail to Egypt. I was her prisoner for weeks after that."

"Frances betrayed you to the police?"

"Yes," she rasped.

"Then she must have written the note, the note ostensibly from you, that said you were going back to Cairo, that your career was too important to abandon."

"I wrote no note, J. B."

"I knew it! I knew you wouldn't have turned your back on what we had together."

"No." Tasharyana tried to smile. "I would never do that, J. B."

"But you were pregnant. Why didn't you call me, write to me?"

"I couldn't. It would have been like trapping you."

"Trapping me! Tasha, I would have come in a minute. Don't you know how much I love you?"

"You never said it." She gazed into his handsome face and his serious brown eyes darkly intent with what? Grief? Why was he so sad? "How was I to know how you felt about me?"

"But couldn't you tell? My God—"

"I couldn't be sure. And there were so many others to consider."

"Tasha!" He slowly shook his head as he gazed at her. She could see sorrow and disbelief in his eyes and tears in his lashes. "I have always loved you. I always will. Never doubt it for an instant. Never!"

"Oh, Julian!" She stared at him, memorizing his tender expression to take back with her to dreamland, for she felt the enervating cloud descending upon her again.

"Forgive me," he exclaimed, burying his face in her hair. "Forgive me, my darling, darling Tasha."

"There is nothing to forgive." She swallowed, fighting the heavy drowsiness. With every ounce of willpower she possessed, she commanded her arms to rise, to encircle J. B.'s strong wide back. She hugged him, granting him forgiveness with the last shreds of her strength. She sank her head upon his shoulder and pushed her shaking hand into his coal black hair, cool and glossy and luxurious, just as she remembered. And then she turned her head slightly to press her lips to his neck.

"Name our daughter Karissa," she began, rallying the power to speak. "For she is the child of our hearts."

"I will," he answered. His voice was gruff, choked with emotion.

"Take her far away—far away from Egypt."

"I will. I promise."

"Keep her safe from the priestesses, J. B."

"I will. And I'm going to make that Madame Hepera pay for what she's done to you!"

"Never mind about me. Just worry—just worry about our baby. And when she is a young woman, give the box to her, the music box."

"I will. Tasha—" he broke off. "I've got to get you out of the water. You're hemorrhaging again."

"No, wait." She sighed, too tired to continue speaking. She could hear him weeping, could feel the shudders inside him as he tried to suppress his tears. Why must he weep when she was so happy—so happy she was about to float away in joy? They were here together, in each other's arms, speaking words of love at last. Their daughter was somewhere close by, being looked after with love and care by her Egyptian grandmother. What more could she possibly want in the world? What greater happiness than the bliss she possessed right then at this moment?

"Julian." Tasharyana caressed the back of his head, knowing it was her final gesture to the man she loved with every part of her being. "You are everything to me," she whispered, each word growing more faint. "Everything. And I love you so."

Epilogue

Luxor, Present Day

"This is the place?" Asheris asked, glancing out the window of the Land Rover at a crumbling wall and a rusty iron gate.

Karissa looked down at her notes. She had copied the address from her father's journal and was certain she hadn't made a mistake. She looked up at the wall, once painted a brilliant white but now a dull ivory with bricks showing through the plaster and weeds growing up at the base. Through the crooked gate she could see a house in equally bad shape, with most of the windows broken or boarded over.

"According to my father's notes, this was where he grew up."

"This was Menmet Bedrani's house?" Julia put in, staring out the window in disbelief.

"Yes. But she's been dead for many years."

"It appears no one has lived here since then,"

Asheris commented, setting the brake. "Shall we have a look?"

"Yes, let's!" Karissa smiled, anxious to see what lay behind the wall.

Asheris opened the car door for her and then slipped his arm around her, walking very close and offering the support and companionship she had so long desired. Julia took her other hand and quietly surveyed the overgrown gardens as they walked toward the house.

Looking at the modest but elegantly designed home, Karissa was seized by a sudden feeling of possessiveness. Though she disdained any inheritance from Grandmother Petrie—and now knew why she had never felt any connection to the Petrie family—she would cherish anything Grandmother Menmet might have left to her, especially this house.

Apparently Asheris read her mind, for he glanced at her and said, "This property might belong to you, Karissa."

"I wonder."

"I would wager you'd find the deed in your father's crate. Have you looked through all of his things?"

"I've barely scratched the surface. I wonder if the deed is there. Wouldn't it be great if this house did belong to us?"

"It's in rather poor condition," Julia commented, studying the front porch, as if she knew the finer points of real estate.

"Nothing a bit of paint and glass wouldn't fix." Asheris countered. "The foundation looks sound."

Karissa could only stare at the house, awash in the memories of her father and Tasharyana. This was where they had spent their last moments together, somewhere in this house. She closed her eyes for a minute, savoring the joy that welled up at the oddest times—joy that came from knowing her parents had truly loved each other, and that she had been the beloved child of a strong and courageous woman. All along her heart had known the truth, that Christine Petrie could not be her real mother, but no one had ever told her differently, and she had suffered years of loneliness and alienation. But now, after having learned of Tasharyana, those years of loneliness were turning to bits of sand and were drifting out of her memory. Slowly she opened her eyes.

"You know," she began at last, "when my father sent for me—when I was twelve—well, in his letter he mentioned a rose garden he wanted to show me. Do you suppose the garden was here, and that he wanted to show me this house and tell me about my real mother?"

"Most likely. A rose garden would be unusual in Luxor," Asheris replied. "But not so unusual at the home of an Englishman."

"Let's look for one," Julia exclaimed. "I would imagine a rose garden might be at the rear of the house, wouldn't it?"

"Good idea, Bean," Asheris replied. "Lead on."

They followed their daughter along the narrow cement walk that curved around the side of the house to the backyard. When they rounded the corner of the house Karissa gasped at the sight. Before her grew a veritable jungle of climbing roses, red and white entwined, stretching along the back wall near a stream, their blooms filling the air with a seductive perfume.

"Red and white," Karissa murmured, remembering the poignant letter her father had written to Tasharyana. "Passion and love."

"What is that you are saying?" Asheris asked.

But Karissa couldn't answer. Although over the course of the last two days she had told Asheris and Julia of the things she had learned in the scrying sessions, she couldn't share this acutely personal moment with him. She slipped away from his arm and stumbled along the path bordered by roses, swept away by visions from the scrying sessions. Had her father planted these roses? He must have! She was aware that Julia had come up behind her and was poking the brambles with a stick she had found.

"There are all kinds of bird nests in these briars, Mother. Look!"

"Oh?" Karissa glanced her way but couldn't concentrate on the present, lost as she was to the past.

"And look, Mother!"

The excitement in Julia's voice induced her to pay more attention. She sidled closer to her daughter and looked down.

"What is that, Mother?"

Julia lifted the rose brambles with her stick to allow Karissa a better view. Karissa bent over, hardly believing her eyes.

"It's a gravestone," she whispered, leaning closer to read the chiseled letters.

"Whose gravestone? Menmet Bedrani's?"

"No," Karissa replied, her eyes filling with tears. "It is my mother's, Tasharyana Higazi."

"What does it say below her name?" Julia asked. "That smaller writing?"

"It says, 'Together soon, beloved, and together always.'"

Karissa knelt beside the roses, unable to move or speak, as tears dropped out of her eyes. With the tears came a new awareness, a sensation of peace and completion, of coming around full circle. She had begun this journey to her mother with five dried rose petals falling out of a tattered note. And now she had ended the journey surrounded by hundreds of red and white roses, a tribute to the enduring love of J. B. and Tasha. Why was she crying? There was nothing sad here, only the wonderful revelation that she was the child of two people who had loved each other, and that she was a member of a long line of powerful, talented women—from Senefret to Tasharyana. She was proud to be the daughter of a woman who had given her life for freedom, who had triumphed over tremendous odds to break the chain of servitude to a heartless goddess and an even more heartless high priestess. Tasharyana had never once surrendered to her fears or given up her love for J. B. Spencer.

Such commitment and courage were values Karissa held close to her own heart. She would continue the tradition. It was her privilege and her obligation to pass Tasharyana's strength and her capacity to love on to her own daughter, Julia.

The priestesses of Sekhmet had thought Julia was the lost goddess. But to Karissa, the lost goddess had been her own mother, Tasharyana Higazi, lying practically unknown for all these years in an overgrown garden. But now Tasha was found. Now her story had been told and she could take her rightful place in the hearts of those to whom she truly mattered.

Karissa rose, wiping the tears from her cheeks as a huge grin blossomed on her face.

"Mother, what's wrong with you?" Julia inquired, letting the stick droop. "You're not yourself lately."

"On the contrary," Karissa replied, giving her daughter a hug. "I've never felt more myself. Never!" She looked up to see Asheris running toward them.

Asheris pointed to the sky behind her. "Karissa, Julia, hurry!" he shouted.

"What's the matter?" Alarmed by the worried expression on her husband's face, Karissa glanced over her shoulder to the west. Not far from town rose a wall of roiling dark clouds, boiling up sand in their path, and blotting out the daylight.

"The khamsin!" Asheris exclaimed, grabbing Julia's hand. "Come, we do not have much time!"

Karissa ran to the Land Rover, following Asheris and Julia. She got into the car and slammed the door, watching as the windstorm quickly overtook the valley. She sat back as Asheris drove away, thankful that the khamsin had waited this long to arrive, and was not at all worried that the onslaught of driving sand might ruin the flowers surrounding her mother's grave. Somehow she knew the roses would survive.

AVAILABLE NOW

Evensong by Candace Camp

A tale of love and deception in medieval England from the incomparable Candace Camp. When Aline was offered a fortune to impersonate a noble lady, the beautiful dancing girl thought it worth the risk. Then, in the arms of the handsome knight she was to deceive, she realized she chanced not just her life, but her heart.

Once Upon a Pirate by Nancy Block

When Zoe Dunham inadvertently plunged into the past, landing on the deck of a pirate ship, she thought her ex-husband had finally gone insane and kidnapped her under the persona of his infamous pirate ancestor, to whom he bore a strong resemblance. But sexy Black Jack Alexander was all too real, and Zoe would have to come to terms with the heartbreak of her divorce *and* her curious romp through time.

Angel's Aura by Brenda Jernigan

In the sleepy town of Martinsboro, North Carolina, local health club hunk Manly Richards turns up dead, and all fingers point to Angel Larue, the married muscleman's latest love-on-the-side. Of course, housewife and part-time reporter Barbara Upchurch knows her sister is no killer, but she must convince the police of Angel's innocence while the real culprit is out there making sure Barbara's snooping days are numbered!

The Lost Goddess by Patricia Simpson

Cursed by an ancient Egyptian cult, Asheris was doomed to immortal torment until Karissa's fiery desire freed him. Now they must put their love to the ultimate test and challenge dark forces to save the life of their young daughter Julia. A spellbinding novel from "one of the premier writers of supernatural romance." —*Romantic Times*

Fire and Water by Mary Spencer

On the run in the Sierra Nevadas, Mariette Call tried to figure out why her murdered husband's journals were so important to a politician back East. Along the way she and dashing Federal Marshal Matthew Kagan, sent to protect her, managed to elude their pursuers and also discovered a deep passion for each other.

Hearts of the Storm by Pamela Willis

Josie Campbell could put a bullet through a man's hat at a hundred yards with as much skill as she could nurse a fugitive slave baby back to health. She vowed never to belong to any man—until magnetic Clint McCarter rode into town. But the black clouds of the Civil War were gathering, and there was little time for love unless Clint and Josie could find happiness at the heart of the storm.